HUMAN BEING

BEING

A Story by

CHRISTOPHER

MORLEY

With a new Introduction by

THE AUTHOR

MODERN LIBRARY · NEW YORK

Random House IS THE PUBLISHER OF

THE MODERN LIBRARY

BENNETT A. CERF · DONALD S. KLOPFER · ROBERT K. HAAS

Manufactured in the United States of America

Printed by Parkway Printing Company   Paper by Richard Bauer & Co.

Bound by H. Wolff

AFFECTIONATELY DEDICATED TO
Felix Riesenberg, who insisted; to
Oliver Perry, who said "Bon Courage!"
and to George Seiffert
who took it on faith.

These, knowing the queer ways in
which fiction is born and nourished,
will understand that any identification,
either of person or incident,
would be quite false.

"Who will write me the book I crave —that vulgar, jocund, carnal, beautiful, rueful book?"—A Call for the Author.

"To catch a human being in the very act of being human, and to set it down without chemical preservatives."

A NOTE ON THE AUTHOR OF

Human Being

CHRISTOPHER MORLEY

(1890-   )

THE formidable list of novels, essays, short stories, children's books, poems and plays written by Christopher Morley gives testimony to the energy, enthusiasm and gifts of the most prolific writer and active bibliophile in America. For almost a quarter of a century, he has maintained without interruption a famous column, *The Bowling Green*, and also has found time for a wide variety of editorial services.

Morley was born in Haverford, Pennsylvania. His father was a professor of mathematics and his mother a musician and poet. When the elder Morley accepted a post at Johns Hopkins University, the family moved to Baltimore. Young Morley was graduated from Haverford College with highest honors and won a Rhodes Scholarship at Oxford. In 1912, his first book of poems appeared, and, like many young poets, he soon found himself working in a publishing house at $15 per week. With the success of *Where the Blue Begins* in 1921, Morley's reputation was established, and it was made firmer by *Thunder on the Left* in 1925. An old enthusiasm for the theatre led him into the adventure of undertaking revivals of such melodramas as *After Dark* and *The Black Crook* in Hoboken, New Jersey. *Human Being*, considered his best novel, appeared in 1932, in the midst of an avalanche of other writings from his pen. And in the season of 1939-1940, just to prove that the fertility of his imagination and the resourcefulness of his many skills remain inexhaustible, he has achieved another national best seller, *Kitty Foyle*.

Introduction

Soon after *Human Being* was first published a friend in London sent me a clipping from the Obituary column of *The Times*. It recorded the death of Richard Rowe, "only son of the late Richard Rowe, author of *Episodes in an Obscure Life.*" I have always wanted to look up that book in honor of my own Richard.

To christen a character with a symbolic name is an artistic weakness, but in this case justifiable, I think. I wanted the reader to realize as quickly as possible that Richard Roe must serve as the spearhead, or pinhead, for the innumerable congregation of the obscure. This book was writing itself about the time the phrase "the forgotten man" was revived (April 7, 1932, I believe is the historians' date), and the thought in my mind was that he is most likely to be forgotten because we see him everywhere. I hope I did not, either by Richard's name or by his association with the Pekinese dog, prejudice the reader toward any kind of condescension. He seemed to me, the more I studied him, a rather important person.

INTRODUCTION

It struck me from childhood that in all the traditional documents Richard Roe was always the one who started at a little disadvantage in his dealings with John Doe. During the period of this book's early life the United States was making its first serious attempt to contradict the cruel and damnable fantasy that all men are created equal. We only need to look around to see how pitiably ill-equipped many of us are to face the strains of civilization. I was the more amused to find myself writing in this vein because I had just been disposed of by an attractive young philosopher who said that I had no "sociological contemporaneity." He is still living under his low ceiling of economic catchwords, through which, however, in the past ten years he has valiantly pickaxed some breathing holes.

What I was most afraid of for this book did not entirely happen. I was afraid it might be esteemed by literary people as an interesting *tour de force* or experiment in backward narration. And indeed many reviewers, tipped off by the publisher, remarked upon that and said it was difficult. But the casual reader, when the book reached him, did not seem to be annoyed by it. Certainly the mind works mostly by retrospect. A more serious handicap, maybe, is the intrusion of the biographer Hubbard. I am not quite sure whether Hubbard is sufficiently differentiated from Richard Roe. As I look at Hubbard from now he is a little too much like John Doe.

From the point of view of popular appeal the story suffers by its resolute understatement. It would have been easy, and it would have been fun, to caricature Richard; but it would have been quite out of character both for him and for his biographer (Hubbard, not me). If the reader needs help—and readers always need help—he can amuse himself by studying the diagram on page 189. Put a marker in at that spot and see how methodically Hubbard—who began life as an accountant—followed his analytic scheme.

One of my pleasantest adventures in writing the book was going down to the Flatiron Building and interviewing the renting agent under the humble pretext that I wished to lease an office. He showed me the vacant suite which I have described as that of Richard Roe, Inc., and gave me a floor plan on which I carefully marked the details of layout. I often wonder who occupies those rooms now, and nothing pleases me more than comments, which I sometimes receive, from those who have worked in small business offices, saying that the picture is sociologically contemporaneous. I have often imagined that a motion-picture director who understands the esthetic excitement of great buildings in echelon and great masses of population in flow and the fiery patterns of Manhattan at night could have extraordinary fun in relieving the minute activity of Richard and his crew against that colossal background. New York City itself is probably the only hero of the story and Hubbard is at his best (as the author somewhere says) when he develops a sense of triviality. For instance, the vision of the Diana figure, the trail of the Sixth Avenue L, and the sound of the life-insurance chimes which assumed a powerful subconsciousness in Richard's adventures. There are, incidentally, some very acute sound effects in this book. I was going to tell you where you could find them, but you're reading this, not I.

I could talk for a long time about *Human Being,* but to conclude: I suggest to the reader his great blessing— he is not a reviewer. The unavoidable conditions of book review are strongly adverse to a novel of this sort which involved a year's hard labor in writing and cannot be digested in haste. Only a selfish writer would pack the container so tight. If one had to unravel the compressed baggage of the story, I think the gist of it is that Life has miraculous powers of healing and recuperation—or forgetfulness, if you will. Tragedy and comedy and heartbreak do at last comfortably turn into "recollection in tranquillity." I have been amused by some of the indignations caused by *Kitty Foyle* which disturbed many readers because they said it was so different from the author's previous doings. No one could have thought so who had read *Human Being.*

But how rarely it happens that any reader reads the book the author writes. My own private motto in the business of reading is "Dogs don't bark at the milkman." At least let the well-trained mastiff find out what the messenger is bringing before he begins to growl.

CHRISTOPHER MORLEY

April 8, 1940

Contents

ix

Human Being

I

The Time Is Now . . .

Hubbard speaks of this story as a biography, but perhaps it is more in the nature of an encyclopædia, or encyclical. It is the Round Robin of Richard Roe. The way it began was peculiar.

Hubbard drove into town to do an errand. Approaching the building where he had business he was surprised to see that since his last visit a block of old houses across the street had been demolished. In their place was a large vacant lot smoothed with cinders, and a sign PARK HERE, 1 HOUR 35¢, 4 HOURS 50¢. Accepting this as one of the convenient miracles that sometimes happen, he left the roadster there and went to his appointment.

The affair didn't last long, and when he returned to the parking space the hour was not quite up. At first he congratulated himself on being able to escape with the minimum fee. Then he reflected how much he would save by leaving the car there a while longer. If he took the full four hours, the rate would be only 12½ cents. It was a brilliant autumn noon and he was tempted by the idea of rambling about the streets in

leisurely haphazard. Most of his visits to the city were
so compactly timetabled that there was little room for
the zigzags of chance. His foot was already on the
running board of the car when this happy impulse
seized him.

He strolled off at random, luxuriating in a sense of
ease. It was one of those rare moods when one feels
suddenly abreast of life. For the moment he had
Caught Up. There were no letters that should have
been answered, no appointments at the dentist, no Unfinished Business. There were toothpaste and shaving
cream and mouthwash in his medicine cabinet at home.
Of course there were a few tentative commitments for
the future, what the lawyers call pollicitations; nothing irrevocable. The horizon was wide open. What delight that is.

Idling along the pavement he enjoyed the colorful
shop windows. He had the immensely superior feeling
with which one who does not need to buy anything con-
templates the anxious ingenuity of merchants eager to
reduce inventory. He talked to himself in that tone of
affectionate approval which does us so much good
when self-administered. Good old boy, he said to himself. A breathing space! He checked over his methodical pocket-system. Money, yes; keys and penknife, yes;
pipe, matches, tobacco, yes; wallet, yes; driving license,
yes; memorandum book and spare handkerchief, yes,
yes. For a few minutes he was his own reassuring yes-
man. His clothes felt elderly and familiar; the whole
physiological mass of his body was orderly and comforting. Self-approval, as usual, led to a larger benevo-
lence. Drifting up the sunny street he relished the rich
variation of human types. How agile, kindly, and
enigmatic they were. With what physical dexterity they

moved, weaving in and out, avoiding collisions. Good old boy, he repeated, and found himself walking fast just by habit. "Godlike, godlike! I can think of a thousand shames and errors, yet here we are, Riding on the Moment. (Sometimes I prefer to think of myself as *we* rather than *I;* it is less embarrassing.)" Even catching sight of his reflection in the windows did not grieve him for more than an instant. There are always compensations, old son, he persuaded himself.

You see, Hubbard said, I tell you my absurdities frankly, at the very outset. An inexperienced narrator probably reveals more than is mannerly. But I can't expect you to believe that I have been honest with Richard Roe unless I can be equally honest with myself. By the irony of chance, as I moved blithely along Madison Avenue like a convention of unanimously instructed delegates, I approached the most doubtful and arduous task of a lifetime.

He paused at a corner, partly to knock out his pipe on a lamp-post and partly to undergo the agreeable pains of indecision. Which way should he turn? Any of these four streets might reach to the ends of the earth. An idiotic phrase, he then reflected, because all four, accurately and inexorably prolonged, would come directly back to the same spot. Provided, of course, that the earth is a perfect sphere.

"But it isn't!" he exclaimed to himself joyfully.

"What isn't?" said a voice, and George Work greeted him in his usual quizzical humor. How is it that we so often meet just the people we need? With so enormously many chances of not meeting, how does it happen? Or is it that when we encounter someone, we instantly (with a dangerously subtle convulsion of

soul) revise our whole existence into the appropriate
phase of *us* that exists for him? Pitiable chameleons
that we are! Oh, by taking different turnings or step-
ping briefly into cigar-stores and soda-fountains have
we missed the very meetings we most required?

"It *isn't* a perfect sphere, that's the grand thing
about it," Hubbard explained.

"What are you doing in town on Saturday?" George
asked. "Come and have some lunch."

Hubbard had no particular desire for lunch, but he
had committed himself to chance and it would have
been dishonest to demur. George led him a couple of
blocks eastward and rang at an iron-grilled door
beneath the stairs of a dingy brownstone front. It was
a surreptitious Mediterranean hideaway where the
regular customers eat not in the dining room but in
the kitchen itself, with the family. Madame, in an
ample white apron, presides at the stove. The *patron*,
in waistcoat and shirtsleeves, slices lengths of crisp loaf
and shakes cocktails at a sideboard. There is no menu,
you eat whatever happens to be on the fire, and it's
delicious. There is a Provençal aroma of roast lamb
just faintly rubbed with herbs, and tall greenish bottles
of *ordinaire* on the table. Jules makes it himself in the
cellar. All this George explained as they neared the
place. He was one of a mixed little group that usually
lunched there on Saturdays. He was eloquent on the
subject. Cold winter afternoons when the dusk comes
early; the sense of snugness and a bolted door. The
glowing stove and the white steam of soup mixed with
the gray smoke of cigarettes. The crackle of bread-
sticks. Madame's little girl studying her lessons (in
"Americanism") in a rocking chair in the corner. Fruit
and cheese and hams on a shelf over the washtubs. On

the walls the rainbow calendars of Italian grocery jobbers. These appealed to George, who is a salesman for a big lithographing house, and thereby regarded by the others as the artistic member of their cenacle.

Six or seven gentlemen were already at table, and George introduced Hubbard. Some of the names he did not catch, but those he heard he tried to fix in mind by simple association-pictures. Mr. Vogelsang was easy, for behind him hung the canary cage. For Mr. Schaefer he conjured up a flock of sheep. Mr. Furness he symbolized as heating apparatus, and Mr. Von Ulm as a tall elm tree. His experience at one time as a collection manager taught him how important this mental habit is. Often a customer who comes in to ask for an extension can be persuaded to pay something if his name is tactfully remembered.

As he was greeting the men at the far end of the table, Madame leaned over them with a tureen of soup. A glass of wine was upset by accident, and in the general halloo he missed their names. One was a man of perhaps fifty, medium sized and slightly gray; his face though heavily lined had a fresh color and clear hazel eyes that were unusually friendly. While everyone else was shouting this gentleman had already mopped up the puddle. But Hubbard didn't pay special attention to him, for he was busy focussing his pictures of birds, sheep, furnaces and elm trees. Also there was nothing in his manner that an expert in overdue accounts would be likely to recognize. He looked thirty-day pay, unquestionably reliable. "As I recall the scene now," Hubbard says, "I realize that he had a talent for not being noticeable—except perhaps that he kept the ash on his cigar longer than anyone else in that group would have been likely to. Yet he was not conspicuously silent. He made one remark I still remember. 'Not long ago,' he said, 'I went up Riverside Drive at night on a bus. Suddenly an electric sign across the river flashed on in the dark, caught me right on the eyeball. It said THE TIME IS NOW 7:59. You know, the damn thing frightened me.' "

Because several of the group worked for a publisher it was George's idea of tact to turn the conversation on books. He did so by remarking that he himself never read them; every book that he had been told was really worthwhile he had found unbearably dull, except a few detective stories. What with the lithographing business, the movies, bridge, and radio, he did not find books necessary. His idea of chivalry was to leave them for women and children. One of the others suggested that biographies are a good kind of reading. George said he tried a biography once but found nothing in it he could apply to his own perplexities. The trouble is, he said, the kind of people they write biographies about are too darned different. Now a biography of Bill Schaefer, he added, that would be something like. I could get that.

"You'd be surprised," retorted Schaefer, "how different it might be from what you expected."

"Biographies are quite useless," someone else said, "unless they're written about people you know a lot about already."

"Another trouble with them," said George, "you know it's all over anyhow; it worked itself out some way or another." He looked unusually serious for a moment. "Poor devils," he added.

Mr. Vogelsang said that on a long business trip he had read Papini's *Life of Christ* with great profit; it had done more for his selling morale than any amount

of letters from the home office. Mr. Von Ulm objected to this point of view, which he called sacrilege.
The argument became vigorous, and as honorably absurd as most disputes of its kind. It might have gone
on endlessly but eventually Schaefer said, "Well, you
gentlemen can fight it out. I've got to go; I'm getting
behind with my home work." When he had gone Hubbard noticed that the gray man at the end of the
table had gone too.

"Who was that?" he asked.

"Bill Schaefer? You know the Schaefer Windshield
Wiper, don't you? You've seen their ads in the *Satur
day Evening Post*."

"No, no, I mean the other. The quiet fellow who
smoked a cigar."

"Oh, has Dick gone too? So he has. His name's
Roe. The Roe Pen; desk-furnishings, stationery and so
on."

"Richard Roe? The name's familiar anyhow."

"Sure," said George. "Dick says he's the fellow
who always gets just a little the worst of it in the contracts with John Doe."

That was the only time Hubbard ever saw Richard
Roe. Certainly he cannot be accused of being prejudiced by intimate personal relations. That evening,
as he drove back to the country (the man at the parking space insisted that after four hours the time began
again, and he had to pay 35 cents for the fifth hour)
the thought of Richard Roe was least in his mind.

The difficulties involved in collecting material for
such a biography may fairly be mentioned; even sometimes the patience required in listening to the biographer. The footprints of one who trod so lightly

and with such complete ignorance of his own possible importance are soon obliterated. He had made no provision for being remembered: it was one of the many things that never occurred to him. His family, his friends, and his business associates were not only surprised and shocked at Hubbard's project, but for a while placed considerable obstacles in the way. It is generally agreed, apparently, that the lives of such men are better left unrecorded. Also in conscientiously assembling testimony from many different sources Hubbard found contradictions and inconsistencies that would have horrified a more experienced editor. In spite of these discouragements he persevered, but the reader must watch him compile the memoir in his own way; casually and in fragments, as it came to him. And I myself, now that I see the story in better perspective, understand that many grotesque or trivial episodes were in legitimate continuity, and logical preparation for Roe's final achievement.

"I look back with a miserable sense of frustration," Hubbard said, "when I realize that I once sat at table with Richard Roe himself and guessed so little. If I had known then a fraction of what I do now, how I should have longed to tell him that I also understood. But to know what we need to know, at the moment when we need to know it, is few men's privilege. He was gone almost before I knew he was there. There are many like that. To all such I would like to dedicate my record. Like Richard I am frightened when I see electric letters flash out THE TIME IS NOW 7:59. Therefore, though the data are imperfect, I delay no longer."

II

The Pekinese

Richard Roe of 50 West 81st Street, manufacturer of stationery novelties with an office in the Flatiron Building, was taken ill on a Lackawanna Railroad ferryboat last night and died before the boat reached Hoboken. A heart attack was said to be the cause.— *News item.*

LUCILLE ROE and her sister Hazel (Mrs. Herman Schmaltz) were agreed that it was inconsiderate of Richard to die on a ferryboat; and going toward Hoboken, too, from which she and Hazel had escaped many years ago. It would take some explaining. Hazel tried to console Mrs. Roe. A great many very nice people pass through Hoboken, she said; they go under cover from the ferry into the Lackawanna train and are quietly on their way to Montclair and the Oranges. All very well, thought Lucille, but the notice in the paper only mentioned Hoboken. Besides what for was he on a ferryboat at all? To this question nothing on Richard's person gave any clue, and we shall have to wait long for the answer. In the inside pocket of his overcoat was a small packet of cinnamon gum, such as he always chewed vigorously on the way home when he had had a cocktail. But it had not been opened and there was no flavor of liquor on his cold lips. Curiously enough it was this that burst Lucille into tears. Poor darling, I wish he'd had a drink to die with.

The gloomy dimness of the Lackawanna terminal at night, when she finally got over there, and the appalling rigidity of Richard Roe (usually so flexible) on the stationmaster's couch, were a displeasing memory. It was not put into words (that is the task of this narrative) but the feeling was that a man of any decency takes care to die in bed at home. If one insisted on dying, surely the apartment was a pleasant place for it? Doctors, nurses, and telling the switchboard not to put through any calls, give death a certain dignity. For one awful moment the poor soul wondered if there weren't any way by which they could pretend Richard was alive, just prop him up somehow, until they got him back to 81st Street, into the elevator and past the hall-boys? Suddenly Lucille was almost aware of the hellish exposure of life in New York where you can't even be born or die without elevator boys knowing about it.

However, that was all over now. Richard had seemed to find it dignified enough. It wasn't as bad as it might have been (they took him up in the baggage elevator) and the details were smoothly accomplished. When Richard's eyes were closed it was better: he seemed to go to sleep then and lose that disquieting look of surprise—not an unpleasant surprise, really; more as though he had suddenly learned that it's all much simpler than we suppose. A pity we have to die to realize that life is really quite simple. And the increased sympathetic deference of the elevator boys during succeeding days was rather flattering. It didn't take long to purge the apartment of Richard. Clothes to the unemployed. Never until then did it occur to Lucille that those fellows who hang about uptown subway exits carrying men's suits on their arms are perhaps buying clothes of people who have died. But really you can't get very sentimental about men's garments; and Gladys had long been complaining she didn't have enough closet space for her dresses.

Herman had been very kind, and during the first few evenings came round at ten o'clock to take the Pekinese for his comfort stroll. It did not look well, Mr. Schmaltz thought, for the widow or the daughter to take the dog out during the first days of bereavement. Lucille would have welcomed a little fresh air, but remembered the elevator boys. It's because they're so black, thought Herman, they have such a respect for death. Herman had not entirely abandoned his sense of humor; indeed he and Hazel were often both amused by the same thing simultaneously, which is one of life's triumphs. The period of mourning would have been easier for Peke if Herman had known exactly the route Peke and Richard took together so many evenings. The railing round the Museum of Natural History is traditional in all that neighborhood, but Herman, more selfish, liked to look at the show windows on Columbus Avenue, where Peke was agitated by the sudden thunders of the L.

New York is the most anonymous of cities. Is that the word we want? I mean it shows no traces; like Peke it doesn't retain well. Even the very great leave few marks on it, personal marks. Apartment houses show no sign of who may have lived there. As soon as any building begins to accumulate rich human flavor they tear it down, or sterilize it into offices. Perhaps it is superb to have a city in which the mood is all brittle Now, unmitigated by disturbing suggestions of the past. The L is one of New York's few genuine antiquities: those grim old trestles, the Swiss chalets of stations, the Gothic rolling stock. Yet even in New York, city of no memories, it was extraordinary that Richard Roe could have left so little physical spoor. He was so elusive that no God or Recording Angel could ever have tracked him; only people as humble and absurd as himself. If it hadn't been for Peke there might hardly have been any trace at all. Some scratches against a certain lamp-post where he always knocked out his pipe when he and Peke walked together, and a few patches of oxidized iron railing, are all Hubbard could be sure of as memorial of the pair. It was only on those evening walks that Richard smoked a pipe. He broke himself of the habit long ago: Gladys couldn't endure the smell of it, and believed it kept her young men from calling. Thousands of times he walked round outside the Museum of Natural History, filled with sincere respect for the marvels it contains. How little he guessed that he himself was more interesting and more enigmatic than its rarest specimen. He carried no identifying baggage through life. Furniture, books, bric-à-brac? These were Lucille's province. They bought nothing that might not be duplicated at the nearest department store. I hope a few merchandising managers offer up grateful orisons for the Roes and Schmaltzes when they say their evening prayers. When telephones began to be dressed in petticoats, Lucille and Hazel were delighted. Richard, though, was always a little shocked; he was relieved when the phone went biped years later. But he never offered any resistance to the heavy battalions of Mode. Like the Chinese, he did not even know he was invaded and conquered. For him the great wheels of commerce revolved, statesmen and parsons flung their arms, artisans reeked in excavations. Uniform soaps, tires, maga-

zines, music, bedsteads, cellophane, came trundling
forth. Satirists smile at his simplicity. Perhaps after
all he was wise in his generation. He had the naïve eye
of the instinctive artist who does not even see the irrelevant, reserving his strength for the crisis. Great
commanders do not engage their troops on a side
issue. The tricks of Taste can be taught to almost any
clever rascal. He did not even know they existed. He
accepted what came.

Once he heard a speech in Congress, from the Visitors' Gallery—some deplorable rhodomontade with a
ludicrous Star-Spangled peroration. He was moved;
he tingled and applauded. But what else would you
have him do? In France he would have been a good
Frenchman, in Turkey a good Turk, in an anthill a
good ant.

Exceptions will be taken and admitted, as they appear.

So there he is, going past the Museum with Peke,
who imagined himself shrewder than he really was and
had a notion that his host was not of much conse-
quence; chiefly because when they halted Richard
sometimes fell into a muse and had to be tugged on.
God would have been uncertain which of them was
really on the leash. A Pekinese is only a very small
micturating mandarin on four legs, subject to numer-
ous snobbish fallacies. But they did not usually stay
out very long, for sometimes Lucille thought that the
leash (which hung in the hall cupboard, with Peke's
winter waistcoat) was merely an excuse for Richard to
go out and walk. She and Gladys would have been
horrified if they had known that on that last night,
when Richard really felt a necessity of furious walk-

ing, faster than Peke could manage, he picked up the
small creature and strode all the way down to the end
of the pier at 79th Street and Riverside. It is a thrilling place at night. Behind is the great barrier reef of
apartment houses against which monthly rentals dash
themselves in vain. The river hisses under the piles, the
lights of the great Washington Bridge make their
exquisite curve. There was a bitter wind across the
Hudson that night, and even underneath Richard's
overcoat Peke caught cold. His big huckleberry eyes
watered for days, and they all thought it was so touching, he was weeping for his master.

Lucille did not like Richard to stay out alone very
long because in some obscure way she feared he might
be thinking. This was wise of her, for she observed as
he grew older that thinking was his chief danger.
There was the grotesque matter, for instance, that
came out later, of his leaving the control of the business to the employees. She counted on Peke, not without reason, to stand between Richard and evil spirits,
as medieval bishops put small gargoyles on their cathe-
drals. She was more at ease if she knew he had gone to
a modest clubhouse where Upper West Side husbands
grown too mature for discipline sped the hours with
billiards and bridge. There they had lockers, and heads
of moose, the symbolic emblems of American man-
hood, and Lucille innocently supposed that these were
complete consolation. It is true that Richard kept a
bottle of Scotch in his locker, but he rarely uncorked
it: after his death it was found almost full, and according to club custom the House Committee drank it to
his memory.

You will be patient with this narrative, I hope, because your collaboration is necessary in this intricate

affair. Do you remember Walt Whitman crying out one time:

> *When I read the book, the biography famous,*
> *And is this then (said I) what the author*
> *calls a man's life?*

Walt was disgusted with the illicit sentimentalism, the false magnanimity, of historians. Clumsy and faltering as this must be, it is not written for anyone except Richard Roe himself. Exempt now from his besetting unselfishness, he must be able to recognize it. Hubbard began with the fact of Roe's death and proceeded backward because it was in that sequence that we first learned about him. We move from necessarily false impressions to those at least less false, for he must grow in your mind as he did in mine. He will seem at first merely like a sculptor's armature on which the clay is to be kneaded. There is plenty of clay.

It was an easy matter to clean up after Richard's death. Nothing had ever improved his standing like being dead: both Lucille and Gladys, and even Hazel by sympathetic proximity, wept luxuriously. At any rate Hazel was moist with tears, though some of them were Lucille's.

It was only by chance that Hubbard happened to see the note in the newspaper. He had arrived at that time of life when a man often looks over the obits because almost anyone he knows is likely to be dead at any moment. He waited for a discreet interval and then managed a letter of introduction from George Work to Mrs. Roe. This was a mistake. The widow considered that Richard's cronies, Mr. Work, Mr.

Vogelsang, Mr. Von Ulm and the others, had been a
bad influence on Richard. Consequently she was doubtful from the start. "I can't imagine," she said bitterly,
"why you should be so prejudiced against my husband
that you want to write a book about him." Is base sub-
terfuge permissible in the honorable pursuit of truth?
It was only by getting George Work to convey to Mrs.
Roe—through Herman Schmaltz and without dangerously explicit statement—the idea that the biographer
had long cherished a secret admiration for her,
which now at last he felt free to admit, that her hos-
tility was appeased. I hope that publishers in arranging terms for a book make some allowance for the cost-
accounting of the author? It was a boon to several uptown florists when Hubbard began calling on Mrs.
Roe. Eventually he was allowed to take Peke for an
occasional evening stroll and do errands to the delicatessen. His desire to see the room which had been
Richard's was thought a trifle morbid; but by that time
Gladys had moved into it. It had already a strong bou-
quet of Lebanon cedar, the favored aroma of American virginity. Except for a photograph, firmly en-
caged in silver on Mrs. Roe's dressing table, and a few
forgotten cigar ashes now covered by cigarette stubs
in the shank of an untippable scarlet smoking-stand,
there were no evidences in that apartment of Richard
Roe. Yet the biographer never rose past the figure 9
in the elevator shaft without a twinge of recognition
that that number had meant home. What had Richard
thought when he saw it?

Mrs. Roe was a very spirited woman, and the curiosity that began by policy became genuine enough.
There were even moments when the student feared
that for the full prosecution of his research he should

make the supreme sacrifice and marry her. But a biographer may be pardoned for feeling the importance of life, even of his own life, and he was always prudent. The idea of serving indeterminate sentence as father-in-law of the kind of young men whom Gladys enjoyed was enough to restore caution.

III

The Biographer

THIS is not only the biography of Richard Roe but a biography of that biography.

What are the qualifications desirable in a man who dares to write another man's life? Lawrence Hubbard had several. He had been an accountant, and credit man for Erskine Brothers (the big publishing house), therefore he had a desirable tincture of pessimism, a respect for probity, and pencils always beautifully sharpened. He had been what is called disappointed in love, which operated, fifteen years later, as a good-humored tolerance of sentiment. He had inherited a little money and by some incredible chance had taken "a piece of the show" in a successful musical comedy. He was a great believer in the only law that is unerringly enforced, the law of averages.

He had reached that period—it usually comes somewhere in the fifth decade—when a man decides that if he is ever going to do anything worth while he had better get started. Worth whose while? he then asked himself, and decided that no one's while was as important as his own. Certainly his idea of writing a

book seemed preposterous. In the days when he worked
for Erskine he had accumulated quite a number of
books, but the idea of reading them scarcely occurred
to him. They still stood in a bookcase in their original
jackets. Now he got out several, especially the biographies, and looked at them. Extraordinary thought,
how does one write a book? He remembered the
authors, mostly a shambling and ill-favored crew,
whom he had seen passing in and out of the Erskine
office. He had subconsciously resented them, as a publisher's accountant does: he symbolized them graphi-
cally as a wedge-shaped gouge (like a large slab of
pie) excising something like 22% from that perfect
but imaginary circle called The Publisher's Dollar.
When independence came to him he did not jeopardize
it by uttering any Declaration. His first acquaintance
with disinterested thought, arriving in maturity, found
him shrewd in practice and naïve in spirit. He was unspoiled by education and sophistry. Now that he had
no job it was amazing how much pleasure there was
just feeling his mind in motion. He flirted with all sorts
of æsthetic notions, such as taking piano lessons, collecting china and glass, adopting a child, studying international economics. He thought of going to college,
preferably to a graduate school of Business Administration. The prophecies uttered by fiscal pundits during the notorious Depression of 1929–32 averted him
from that intention. Instead, he went to some lectures
on anatomy with a vague idea of painting nudes. How
marvellous, and how rare, is that new boyhood of middle life for those few souls who have opportunity to
cultivate it.

Into his unexpected scheme of writing the Life of
Roe he put both a serious and a mystical fervor. At

least he had the prime requisite of a biographer, conviction of his subject's importance. When he learned that Roe also had once worked for Erskine Brothers he felt a queer twinge of excitement.

Hubbard was methodical. He hired a room where he would be entirely undisturbed. He put in a large table, a pencil-sharpener, and a series of deep pigeon-holed shelves against the wall. Each compartment he labelled for the various people who had known Richard Roe, or the different phases of Roe's career as he learned about them. In their proper divisions he filed letters, memoranda, and the gradually accumulating testimony.

To begin with he had only a dozen such pigeonholes. They were allotted as follows:

Lucille Roe, *widow*
Gladys Roe, *daughter*
Peke, *the dog*
Hazel Schmaltz, *Lucille's sister*
Herman Schmaltz, *Hazel's husband*
George Work ⎫
William J. Schaefer ⎪
Vogelsang ⎬ *friends of R. R.*
Furness ⎪
Von Ulm ⎭
Morris ("Shad") Roe, *brother*
Erskine Bros., *former employers*

It was characteristic of the perplexities of biography that a pigeonhole just as important as any of these was not even included in his first layout.

Unaware how much work there was to be done, Hubbard stood off and contemplated the shelves thoughtfully. What strange wraiths of that obscure and vanished life would come drifting into the several compartments? It was a great thing to be the un-authorized biographer of an unknown human being. Perhaps all biographies should be unauthorized? In that way, unimpeded by influence or prejudice, the fatal germ of human identity might be isolated. He remembered something George Work said one day. George had visited a foundry where they showed him the actual mixing of type-metal. Behind every bit of printed matter, George said, is the basic alloy, the special formula for the mixture of tin, brass, lead, zinc (whatever it is) from which the types are cast. The phrase ran in Hubbard's mind—"Behind every book is the basic alloy." What was the basic alloy involved in being human?

In this biography, Hubbard suddenly thought, he might not only Make a Name for Richard Roe, but also for himself.

IV

Herman and Hazel

HERMAN SCHMALTZ, a loyal soul, used to say of the two sisters, "I took the pick of the pair. Lucille's got more bosom, but Hazel's got more bean. Just the same, marrying sisters is bound to give two fellows something in common. Like two salesmen shooting at the same prospect. Richard and me got along fine."

It was not easy to lure Herman into talk. Solid Germanic wariness lay deep in him; there was clam-juice in his blood. He rarely joined the boys at lunch in Jules's back-kitchen, preferring to have sandwiches of tuna fish and liverwurst and a bucket of coffee sent up to his office, where he munched solemnly, dripping a little mayonnaise on his blotter and studying graphs of the paper-box business. But Hazel Schmaltz was clever enough to know how to get conversation started. When Herman arrived home one afternoon and found her on the living room couch with the evening paper and a frosty cocktail shaker waiting on the card-table he was too surprised and pleased to suspect any manœuvre. By the time they sat down to dinner he was genially primed for examination.

Hazel was dangerously casual. She knew that the average husband is a more sensitive organism than generally supposed. A lowering brow sends the cautious creature into deep recesses, the gloomy sea caverns where the masculine mind lurks like the squid.

"How's business?" she asked.

"Rotten," he replied. "We got a little pick-up just after the first of the year, but I noticed in the diagrams we got the same in January '30 and January '31; it didn't mean nothing. People ain't selling goods, naturally they don't need cartoons to pack 'em in."

"Never mind, Herm; I expect you get your share."

"Maybe so. Anyhow I'm going to call in one of the men off the road. The way things are we can sell cheaper by phone."

"Don't let it get your goat. Have some of the boys up here for a party some night. They can play poker and I'll go and cheer up Lucille. Why don't you ask that Mr. Hubbard? What's the idea anyway, wanting to write a story about Dick? Is he a nut? Dick never did anything to make books about, did he?"

"I think it's some kind of a notion George Work put into his head," said Herman. "He got an idea that a plain everyday bird like Dick ought to get a break somehow. I don't exactly tumble to it myself, but I guess it's all right."

"But he's not in the writing business, is he? I thought you said he was a collection agent or something."

"Those collection men write some pretty smart letters; I've had 'em in the mail."

"There wasn't anything fishy in Dick's life, was there? I mean, you might think Hubbard was a detective, he wants to know the craziest things. The other

evening Lucille just happened to let out how Dick liked
to make himself a bowl of crackers and milk before he
went to bed; Hubbard wants to see the bowl. They
had a laugh out of that because she's using it for the
dog. I mean to say, what's Hubbard think he's doing,
writing a mystery story? Books are all right to read
once and a while, but you don't want 'em getting inside
the family."

"I wouldn't worry about Dick," said Herman. "He
was all right. Besides Hubbard couldn't possibly dig
up enough stuff to make more'n a magazine article
about him. He was one crackerjack salesman and
that's about all there was to it. He certainly made a
good thing out of those desk-sets. Remember when he
was on the road for Erskine Brothers; that's when he
got the idea. There was a party one night, somebody
stuck a cigar-holder in a baked potato—I don't know
why, just one of those crazy things—and Dick happened to be writing something. He sticks his pen in the
tube for a moment, and that gives him the idea for
those swivel pen holders. Minnie Hutzler was there—
she was stationery buyer for Jake and Ed Hack in
Detroit. She says, you put the idea on the market and
I can sell a raft of 'em. I guess if Hubbard wants dope
on Dick he could get a load of it from Minnie."

"She's one of the trustees, isn't she?"

"Good thing, too. She'll keep that business going
if anyone can. You know she was Dick's secretary
when he started his own outfit. She grew up to be a
member of the firm, but he never could give dictation
to nobody but her."

"I always wondered how much was there between
them two," suggested Hazel; too crafty to lift her
voice to a question-mark at the end of the sentence.

"It struck me funny to see Lucille highhat Minnie; as a matter of fact if it hadn't been for Minnie, Lucille would have had a lot less than she's got. Minnie Hutzler stood up to Dick and made him revise the papers. I know, because I was one of the executors. Minnie's a good sport."

"I guess maybe she can afford to be," was Hazel's only comment.

Herman had a feeling that his retreat was being cut off.

"Well, there ain't anything in all that stuff that would make a story," he observed cautiously. "By the way, you don't happen to know what Dick's birthday was, do you? Hubbard was asking. It seems Lucille and Gladys don't remember. I guess it don't matter."

"Miss Hutzler might know."

"Aw honey, let it lay," said Herman uneasily. "What say we go out and catch a picture?"

He surrendered himself comfortably to the movie. The brilliant front of the theatre, the tall doorman in a long maroon coat, the gilded lobby, the crowded house, visions of luxury on the screen, all these were what his mood required; the perfect drug. Not even yet had he outgrown those half shamefaced twinges of ambitious impulse caused by the heroes of the films: secret resolutions to be handsome and notable. How pleasantly positive are the sounds transmitted by the talking film. Footsteps, tappings, crumpled paper, rippling water, ringing telephones—all just delicately unlifelike, the subtle consolation of unreality. They pop, hiss, crackle and crepitate as though each sound were frying in just a little too much grease.

With faint sheepishness Herman submitted to the

more sentimental passages, those amorous bussings which directors prolong by ingenious calculus: almost long enough to satisfy the women in the audience, but not quite so long as to embarrass the men. There was a stenographer in the picture who reminded him of Minnie Hutzler. "I guess maybe there *is* something about some of those Jewish women," he brooded. "They seem to have a capacity for giving a man what he needs, love him for himself." . . . He might have been on the edge of some interesting racial speculations, but the blessed anodyne of the film swept thought away. He loosened the top trouser button, patted Hazel's knee, and sat back to enjoy. The audience squatted in twilight, just eyes bulged over a warm stupor, like a thousand frogs in a swamp.

V

AMbergris 2–5922

INFATUATED country-dwellers make fun of apartment houses. Why, an apartment is one of men's few victories. Victory over fear, loneliness, tempest, drudgery. Warm, secure and snug, hear the whisper of the steam-pipes. Far below, somewhere in the foundations of the great building, a red fire is blazing. Cunning meshwork of wires, tubes, conduits and dumb-waiters, stands between you and the terror of the world. Pause a moment and think about Terror. An apartment house is built like a battleship against that unseen enemy. Oh subtle intruder that can even slip by a doorman with braided coat and white neck-cloth. Did you think you were the only one whose address was known to that universal spectre? Even Richard Roe was not too humble for that visitor to call. But mostly those big dwellings seem solid as a squadron of ironclads in line of battle. Even their names are proud, and the doormen ornate as admirals.

Richard Roe loved rainy nights. In weather too wild for Peke he walked on pavements as on the deck of a strong vessel. The hiss of taxies on slick asphalt was like the sea against a hull. In gusts of wind and wet he could almost feel the whole block slant underfoot, lean like a stubborn ship, tough against the gale. From the corner of the street he could see the lights of his own apartment. If Lucille's windows went dark he hurried back to say goodnight. He could not sleep unless he felt she had gone to bed cheerful. Often he woke her several times to ask anxiously if she was all right.

The apartment showed few visible signs of Richard's memory, so Hubbard told us; yet that compact space must still hold some reality of life therein contained.

When the elevator reached 9, and the colored boy said watch your step, you turned left. It was a few yards along the corridor; the heavy door was painted mahogany color, with brass insignia, 9A. Richard liked that A: it was like first-class rating at Lloyd's. There had been a slit for mail, but they had it blocked up: Lucille believed it caused a draft along the floor which goosed her shins and made Peke sneeze. The door also was naval, sheathed in metal like a bulkhead. It closed with discreet decision. "Pop used to say the craziest things," Gladys told Mr. Hubbard. "When we asked him to oil the hinges, so's the door would open easier, he said he did it to make it close easier. As if it wasn't both the same."

"I guess it all depends which side of the door you are," said Hubbard.

"Well that was Pop all over; always trying to get some double meaning out of obvious things."

You were met at the door by yourself coming out; your reflection in a mirror on the opposite side of the little lobby. It was rather startling the first time. On

the right was the cupboard for coats and hats, Peke's
mud-specked waistcoat, the leash, and the silver-
handled cane which Richard Roe would have felt an
indecency in carrying except on Sundays.

On the left of the front door was a small catch-all
table, sacred to whatever novelty was fashionable at
the time along Central Park West. At the epoch of
Hubbard's first visit it was a red swan with some sort
of cactus growing out of a nest of colored pebbles between its raised wings. Mr. Roe had been with difficulty cured of depositing cigar ashes among the pebbles. Just beyond the table, still further to the left,
was the door into the kitchen. This was well thought
out: an active Swede could carry on, in one straight
line, from kitchen to front door. It is making sharp
turns that wears down Swedish feet towards evening.

The prime ingenuity of apartment architecture lies
in arranging vistas that suggest an illusion of space. A
little jog in the front lobby assured the privacy of the
entry and allowed the visitor a chance to examine himself in the mirror before being received. Then, turning
left to the swan table, a short passage opened, leading toward the living room. Approaching this, a small
alcove on the left harbored the telephone and its chair;
on the right another passage offered a new perspective,
somewhat more intimate, for if the bathroom door
was open you could see in the distance a lilac washcloth
and Lucille's shelf of bath salts. This bathroom lay
between Lucille's chamber and Richard's and was used
by them both. Gladys used the other bathroom. It was
necessary: no one but an only child could have enjoyed
such leisure in ablution. Gladys's bath, with a series of
linen closets, formed a kind of central pivot around
which the rest of the apartment was arranged. Per-

haps there was symbolism in this. Peke's bathing was done in a washtub in the kitchen, but he had his own bath salts.

Averting your eyes from Lucille's battery of utensils another turn to the right led to Richard's room. It was at the back and looked into a central crypt visited briefly by diagonals of sunlight. In that crepuscular shaft sudden spasms of alarm clocks trilled in early morning, the larks of Manhattan; and the heavy carillon of ash cans. When the wind blew strongly and westward it boomed and volleyed over that hollow space. Slack ends of radio wires flapped in the breeze, picking up the mysterious merriment surcharged on ether. Here Richard sometimes lay awake before rising. By unconscious habit he began every day with a few moments of pure passiveness, his mind pleasantly blank. It is a great gift, to let the mind trail at large, like radio antennæ, picking up whatever chance wavelengths may be moving. He lay on his back with his right elbow crooked protectively over his forehead. The skin inside the elbow is cool and soft, comforting to the brow. It is the forehead that seems to carry the full impact of existence.

But we were at the door of the living room. On the right, beyond Gladys's piano, was a capacious couch. Between the two front windows was a table with flowers. The biggest chair was near the right-hand window; between it and the couch were a tall reading lamp and the scarlet untippable smoking-stand. There is always one chair that has special meaning, and as you sit in it you try to divine what it meant to Richard. It had a curious oscillating seat that apparently moved on a differential; disconcerting at first but very comfortable when it settled in equilibrium. Lucille said that it had, in long practice, accommodated itself so to Richard's sedentary parts that it was not hospitable to anyone else. It was turned so as to look diagonally through the wide opening into the dining room—on the left of the living room as you enter. Its view ended in the far corner of the dining room, on what looked like a Jacobean desk, with pigeonholes, and a quill pen resting in a vase of small shot. This was misleading; it was the radio.

Peke's basket, trimmed with a blue satin bow for masculinity, was in the inward corner of the living room, in front of the electric hearth. A pulsating glow among glass nuggets was as pretty as the boreal aurora and equally cold. But it appealed to Peke and soothed his midget irritability. It cast a pleasant shimmer on the blue ribbon and perhaps consoled the futility of his useless maleness. That was his corner, and few of this world's harassed inhabitants have such undisputed tenure.

Off the dining room was a small rectangle known in the plans as a panelled breakfast room. It was never used for breakfast because it involved a sharp left-hand turn for the labor-saving Swede. Richard had established there what he regarded tentatively as a den. There was a rolltop desk, an old favorite of his, where he kept some papers; an etching of a Scottish terrier; a model of a sailing ship in a flask. This had been considered a genuine Nantucket antiquity until, in a moment of gloom, the bottle was discovered marked on the bottom with the name of a ginger-ale brewer in the Bronx. There was a framed autographed letter from a former governor to whom, on his inauguration, Richard had presented a desk-set. "My dear Mr. Roe," the statesman dictated, "I am very greatly obligated by your generous present, which I am bound to think of as a gift to the people of the State of New York. It is a great satisfaction to the executive office. When I see the name ROE on any stationery novelties I always know these are well-made goods and a credit to our Empire State. With best compliments, faithfully yours."

In this small room Richard held his occasional card parties. A door opened direct into the pantry, which was convenient. In the pantry was the electric ice-box which he always visited before retiring. It was probably a bad habit to drink a whole bottle of ice-cold milk, as he frequently did, taking down a tall glassful in two gulps. Lucille had often told him that milk taken like that turned into solid blocks in his stomach, and after drinking he sometimes worried about this, feeling a chill solemnity invade the intestine. Yet it would be just like life, he reflected, if some of the things we are always told are dangerous should really turn out to be very beneficial.

The convenience of the ice-box was marred by one circumstance. It was backed up against a thin partition on the other side of which was the telephone alcove. If the ice-box decided to resume freezing at the same time that anyone was phoning, it was difficult to hear. And, perhaps by some electro-magnetic contagion, the refrigerator usually did so: a soft purring murmur, the song of the perfect cubes, then crooned obbligato on the telephone wire. Richard had often promised to do something about this, but never did.

So they were in direct line: ice-box, telephone, bathroom, the three points which determine the home circle. But to determine a circle, geometry reminds us,

three points must not be in line. At any rate that little
passage, from telephone to lilac washcloth, had been
the scene of at least one important engagement. It was
due, I think, to the mental stimulus afforded by a hot
bath. That, and Lucille's natural quickness of ear,
which was extraordinary. She had once worked in a
theatre box-office, and perhaps hours of patient atten-
tiveness to telephone reservations had quickened her
hearing.

Richard was at home with a cold. It was late in the
afternoon, Lucille was quietly basking in the tub. Richard had remarked that he must call up the office. As
Lucille simmered, with just a faint granular sensation
where some of the lavender crystals had not completely melted, she heard him dial a number. But her
magnificent ear, indolently attentive, suddenly recognized that the rasping clicks of the instrument were
not those of his office call. No, this was in a different
rhythm altogether. Short, medium, short; then
medium, long, short, short. The least ripple died away
in the tub as she listened; a drop of cold water from
the shower fell disregarded on her steaming nape.

"That you, Minnie?" she heard him say.

So he was talking to Minnie Hutzler, not at the
office. Her home number!

Lucille was superb when in rage. The sudden riot
that filled every nerve and vein had nothing to do with
the immediate and trifling occasion. Even as she exploded she knew that. It was woman's heroic protest
against the unfairness of the world. If she could at
that moment have abolished telephones, electricity,
human speech itself, they would have been wiped out.
With a sudden riotous flowering of every faculty she
burst from the porcelain, crashed open the door, stood

there dripping, pink with heat. It was only a short tra-
jectory down the passage for a wet and soggy washcloth. It wrapped moistly round Richard's chin. He
gurgled, and Miss Hutzler must have supposed his
cold was even worse than they thought.

There was never any finer bit of detective work than
Lucille's subsequent and secret experiment with the
telephone dial. That particular succession of sounds
was engraved in her memory. Short, medium, short;
then medium, long, short, short. She fingered the dial
with accurate ear until she got it. AMbergris 2-5922.

"Hullo?" said a voice at the other end—an infuriat-
ingly clear, low, competent sort of voice.

"I just wanted to tell you, you're a Bitch," said
Lucille, and rang off.

VI

Celluloid Composition

Life is much more a matter of nervous agitation than historians admit. This Lawrence Hubbard realized sometimes when he tried to pull himself together to note down what he learned and divined about Richard Roe. He climbed the same stairs of the L-station, stood on the same high promenade-deck where Richard had taken the train every morning to go downtown. Sometimes Hubbard waited while several trains went by, to get the feeling of the situation. This was perhaps a mistake, for Richard always took the first train possible. Hubbard bought the same morning paper that Roe used to, and learned how to pleat it longways. (Minnie Hutzler told him about that.) But he did not read it carefully.

In fact Hubbard began to wonder if he was growing hysterical. He studied faces in those crowded cars. Help me, help me, cried eyes and hands. Sometimes he could feel his knees quiver with nervousness. Did Richard, neatly dressed in his good suit and inconspicuous hat, ever shake so? Hubbard decided he did. See how well I am hidden, said other faces; I defy you to guess anything about me. Remembering his one glimpse of the man, the biographer concluded that Richard also was a master of humanity's despairing secrecy. Innumerable virtuosos of reticence, how do we pursue you?

Hubbard found himself reading all sorts of books at random, trying to see how, if ever, writers manage to suggest the reality of human being. One day in the little kitchen at Jules's place one of the men read out a passage from a novel just published. Professional literary critics would be amazed if they knew what crisp and liberal judgments on books sometimes emerged in that humble place. The savor of roasting lamb and gravy filled the warm air with an actuality in which mere hokum perished. When Vogelsang produced a slip of paper on which he had copied out one sentence, the others listened attentively. The clippings and memorabilia which hardheaded citizens carry in their wallets are often important.

This was what Gene Vogelsang had found:

> *The contemplative desire is universal, being, in the spirit, what the sexual desire is in the flesh, the prime mover of mankind.*

I don't know that those fellows had thought much, consciously, about man's thwarted need of contemplation, but once put before them they understood it perfectly. About that time Jules was taken with a notion to play the accordion, which he sometimes does for his favorite patrons, and the mood changed; but I noticed Hubbard making a copy of the quotation. It fitted in with what he was thinking about Richard Roe. Of course I was anxious that he should stick to the actual

Richard Roe and not try to diffuse him into a vague symbolic phantom. "Remember," I said to him (as needs to be said to all biographers), "this isn't your own life you're writing. It's Richard Roe's."

"Gosh," he said, "I don't know. I don't know. How the devil——?"

I was always a home-office man, said Hubbard, and I never realized until I got talking to the boys at Jules's what going on the road means. Those travelling men are artists; temperamental as hell, each one of them, and what begins to come through to me is that you have to be an artist to handle them. I used to think that going on the road must be ghastly; long journeys, discomfort, bawdy stories, loneliness. Now I can see that in spite of its weary hardships they find in it the release, the escape from unbearable routine, that the artist must have or perish. They are carving the face of life. Yes, I've even gone so far as to take a trip over some of Roe's old territory that he covered for Erskine. I've got to step easy in telling about some of that. You know the trade's nickname for the four Erskine Brothers. Those sales boys are rough talkers, as rough as Shakespeare or James Joyce. There's a lot of things I've got to try to convey without saying them. But what I'm struggling to feel is that slow smooth pull when the train begins to slide out of the station. There he sits in his green Pullman chair, and the whole ragged landscape of life behind him—imperfect farewells and unfinished affairs, disputes pending and shipments delayed. He's got a folder of carbons and memoranda and advertisement-proofs and plans for Dealer-Coöperation and notes of bad credit. But for a while he hasn't the heart to open his brief-

case and look at them. He's still sweating a little from
that last telephone call and the run for the train. Now
comes that smooth gradual increment of speed. It
would never occur to him to think so, but now he is the
painter with the clean canvas, the sculptor with the
heap of moist clay. The long green vista of the car
sways and rumbles, measures time with undertone
click-click, swings with that sidling tilt round a curve.
He's drawn on, on, into unspoiled future; he feels the
flow of creation, Is and Was dividing in his brain. The
very name of the car he's in may be an omen of some
unexpected glamour. Now it is inevitable; something (I
don't know what) hangs ready to strike: he is let
loose in freedom of will to change the balance of
things. Perhaps he drifts for a flash—a minute or an
hour—into the luminous stupor of foreboding. No,
I'm not inventing: I know his mind. In that Pullman
trance he is a poet, rhyming the unlikely and the impossible. He rhymes the new window cut-out with Kitty
Chambers the buyer in Cleveland. He consoles fatigue
and disgust with some telephone number in his little
memo-book. Sparkle comes back into his nerves. He
has a word of comedy for the porter. He goes to the
stale smoking-washroom to deal wits against other
companions of chance. So he matches himself against
the impossible odds of life, and is Lord of his event.

Perhaps he's a frightened beginner, ambitious only
to sell goods. Has anyone ever told the hopeful anguish of a salesman on his maiden trip? What a story!
Or is he the seasoned performer who sells Himself
first of all and lets the merchandise follow in his
wake? Comedy and cajolery; persistence, tact, evasion;
knowing when to sidestep and when to strike. Oh mar-

velous tissue of contradictions! I see him looking forward to showing an obscene trick with matches to Kitty Chambers in Cleveland, and at the same time saying in humble sincerity as he turns in, "God bless and keep my Lucy and our baby." He wonders if prayers really work in a Pullman berth, because you have no chance to kneel.

It seems a little fanciful as a portrait of a travelling salesman, I demurred, to stimulate him.

Life's a mighty fanciful business and there's a lot of it that doesn't get into the balance-sheets, he replied. For a certified accountant Hubbard was maturing rapidly.

Richard Roe went through all that, and some of it we'll have to follow with him. I can't always be bothered to put in careful quotation-marks in the exact places. Quotation-marks try to imply that some definite person made some particular remark. But almost everybody says everything if you give them a chance.

Minnie Hutzler was not going to be drawn into candor too easily. Lawrence Hubbard looked to her like a bit of a simpleton; also he was over-eager, as we all are in the early stages of a project. It is going to take patience to get inside Minnie's protective defense. But what an enormous stride in human understandings it is when you realize that people have these outer shells of wariness. Old Mother Hubbard, as Minnie scornfully called him at first—judging too smartly by a certain finicky gentility in his demeanor— was beginning to learn this. But he made the mistake of thinking that because Minnie was an extremely competent business woman she would therefore be inter-

ested in a businesslike presentation of his plan. He
rashly showed her a diagram he had drawn up: it
looked rather like a target or a game of hopscotch.
The center represented Richard Roe, and around that
in concentric rings were arranged the people who had
known him. Mr. Hubbard naïvely explained that by
faithfully pursuing successive testimonies, moving
gradually inward, he hoped to draw near the bull's-
eye. The word was ill-chosen. Minnie kept her
paraphrase of it to herself, but she also kept to herself
many other thoughts that would have been valuable.
Dark, pale, controlled, she received the blundering
biographer with the watchful politeness she had
learned in difficult years. But she was capable of sudden
flushes of warmth which showed there was a circulation of blood not far below the surface. One lucky
chance gave Hubbard a better intuition. She had received him in her own private office, which opened off
the big room that had been Richard's. It was quite
evident she did not intend to admit him to any special
familiarity with the office routine. Hubbard, groping
about to put the conversation on happier terms, was
trying to visualize what view Richard Roe must have
looked out at in all those years. "It's ages since I've
been in the Flatiron Building," he said, gazing from
the window, and then noticed that Madison Square
looked different from old times. "Something's
changed," he remarked. "It didn't look like this—yes,
of course, Diana's gone." That tiny figure against the
sky (it lingers still in many memories) suddenly
silhouetted in his mind. That was what Richard must
have seen so many, many times.

Minnie was furious with him for having brought a
choking in her throat she had never had before. She

had been cold, efficient, almost frozen, ever since Roe's death; but the unexpected mention of Diana nearly broke her control. She was furious, but she saw that at any rate Hubbard was wise enough to understand the kind of thing that might have been important. After he had gone she shivered a little and escaped to the washroom downstairs, woman's only safe retreat in the stone world of business. What unguessed stories of tears and tantrums those bleak sanctuaries could tell.

In the early days of the desk-sets they were made out of a synthetic celluloid composition which was not really inflammable but if ignited would smoulder inextinguishably. One day in the office someone laid down a cigarette on a pen-stand; presently there was a curl of thick white smoke and a sizzling cancer began to crawl through the material. Richard tried to smother it with a handkerchief; Minnie poured ink on it; nothing could quell the progress of that sluggish combustion. The office filled with choking reek which poured out of the windows so thickly there was even danger of someone turning in an alarm. They brought a bucket filled with water from the hall and dropped the smouldering object into it. Still, under a foot of cold water, it kept fuming and hissing, jetting up creamy gurgles of smoke. It continued to burn and simmer until utterly consumed. Richard was shrewd enough to make use of this as a powerful sales-argument; thereafter all his own desk-sets were non-inflammable, and many an order was increased by the simple process of laying a lighted cigarette stub on a competitor's goods and illustrating the queer process, with a bucket of water handy. But Hubbard when he heard this anecdote from the young advertising man who wrote Roe's copy, always associated it with Minnie. Through the cool formality of her manner perhaps there were rising bubbles of memory, from some hidden joy or trouble that would burn to the end.

VII

The Flatiron Building

Hubbard wondered if Richard Roe ever speculated about the human variousness of the directory in the lobby of the Flatiron Building. Was it thrilling to him to feel himself immersed in a hive of such wildly mis-cellaneous affairs? No anthology of short stories was ever so dazzlingly surprising as that bulletin board of little white letters. The biographer studied it carefully while many others, all in a hurry, paused momentarily to glance for names and went on. There were several stocking and overgaiter enterprises (what is an over-gaiter?) which seemed appropriate to the old corner's ancient reputation for the exposure of shins. Hubbard noticed that the two long flanks of the building were not flat but gently rippled above with shallow bays. Was it the curvature in the walls that helped to create the upward eddies of draught on the pavement?

Presumably Richard had not given much regard to the rich mundane jumble of doing suggested by that directory. A man intent on his own affairs has little leisure to waste in considering his neighbors. Richard thought of them as just so many "concerns" (a lovely word in that usage), but Hubbard, the ripples of his attention now spreading wider and wider, was growing extravagantly curious. He found it a reasonable part of his picture that RICHARD ROE, INC., was listed among the Pegasus Publishing Company, the Prim Art Company, the Tydee Lady Company, We Moderns in Education, the Ice Cream Smack Corporation, the Copy Treating Service, the Bank Vault Inspection Company, the Bureau for Prevention of Business Fraud, the Metropolitan Ping-Pong Association, the Congo Temperature Control Corporation, the American Spaniel Club. The even hospitality of chance had catered with open hands both to serious and frolicsome phases: it was pleasing to know that Richard, sitting for a hygienic tissue-wrapped tunafish sandwich in the Walgreen pharmacy on the ground floor, might have been neighbored on one side by a scientist from a legal research bureau of Johns Hopkins University and on the other by an editor of *Broadway Brevities* or the Theme Song Publishing Company.

To Richard Roe the Flatiron Building was more than a tall wedge of masonry surrounded by lewd spirals of air. He was a young man when it was built and was the talk of the town. It symbolized the crossing of Fifth Avenue and Broadway: not a union but at least a liaison. Trade was momentarily spliced with Gentility or Swank. He never outgrew the delight of that steep rounded prow that seemed to shear the stream of traffic. No region of the city was more full of subtle appeal. The old Fifth Avenue Hotel bespoke luxurious breeding; Diana on the sky intimated the delicacies of art. Even when these perished there were still the Metropolitan Life Insurance chimes. Richard never became entirely deaf to them. He did not analyze precisely what they suggested—whether the fugitive melody of life or the recurring nature of premiums—but he liked their heavy floating toll. A great bubble of sound was struck off by the bronze concussion. It came leniently and sealed the mind inside a miraculously tiny instant of regret—a moment so precisely small that if he had ever mentioned it Richard would have called it "infetisimal." (Minnie would have corrected it in the transcript.) Horror so gentle is almost a luxury.

So when he set up in business for himself there was no location that would have meant so much to him. He said to himself proudly that it was "A National Address." He often remarked to callers that though his office was high up it was "not too high to be in touch with humanity." This was a phrase he had picked up from the renting agent. Richard himself would never have been too high for that.

We shall have to examine the dynamics of some of his working days. Gloriously ignorant, he went on; it never occurred to him that anyone can stop. Daily he plunged into that spinning wheel of being: the rising slope of morning, the meridian pause, the afternoon decline, the revival at dusk. Quickly, quickly, Time goes in an office. Blessed anæsthesia that takes away the sins of the world: the world's only sin, which is that life perishes in every instant. The ring of telephones—each, to the practised ear, a little different from the others. The comforting rattle of typewriters; opening and closing doors; voices recognized and strange; the rumble of filing-case drawers; the rasp of an adding machine. All are medicine for solitude, postponement of that single struggle with the regardless universe which every soul is aware of and prudently evades when it can.

You came along the hallway from the elevators; a glass-paned door was lettered in black and gold; RICHARD ROE, INC., STATIONERY SPECIAL-TIES. Inside, the corridor continued a few feet farther. A small sign projecting above a doorway on the right said INFORMATION. Just inside this door was a telephone switchboard on a typewriter desk. You looked down on the delightfully undulated blonde coiffure of Jenny Hoerl who was Richard's first line of defense. Jenny was wonderful at the telephone and could manage to do a good deal of typing at the same time. She had a black loose-leaf notebook in which she kept all the numbers called most often, but her native quickness was such that she hardly ever needed to refer to it. The phrase "According to Hoyle" was a byword in the office for accuracy; you might know her a long while before you learned that her name was really spelled Hoerl. Between the two windows (this is the Broadway side of the building) was another desk, where you saw Miss Whaley in profile. Miss Whaley was stenographer and file clerk. She took alternate dictation and chaff from all the salesmen; both in syntax and badinage she returned better than she received. She had fine cobalt eyes, relatively rare between Madison and Union Squares, and a way of murmuring a Wife of Bath repartee with the demure flush of the Prioress. This was irresistible. Miss Whaley's desk came out sideways from the wall; thus she and Jenny faced each other as they sat to their tasks, and managed a surprising amount of parenthetical con-

versation. Peggy Whaley's chair was on a swivel; by
one graceful fluttering swerve she could rotate to the
filing cases behind her. It was believed that she did this
more often when one of the salesmen happened to be
in the doorway.

This room had some pleasantly feminine touches. In
the corner behind Jenny was a stand on which you
would see hanging two fur-collared coats, two small
hats, two bright scarves. Frequently there were flowers
on the filing cabinet; perhaps a gardenia or a bunch of
violets keeping fresh in water for the evening. At this
end, above the little wash-basin and in a corner not
apparent to visitors, was a mysterious cupboard with a
mirror, a curling iron, a minute brazier for canned
heat, various small medicaments and antiseptics,
combs, nail polishes, cold cream, eyebrow tweezers,
brilliantine, cough-drops, and a wire brush that
squeaked in Jenny's hair. Feminine office life is far
more complicated than the average employer might
suspect. Jenny Hoerl and Peggy Whaley were specially
proud of the towels which by the ingenuity of some
supply company were stitched in red with the legend
RichardRoeInc. sewn in one word. They had ordered
these once as a Christmas present for Mr. Roe; to
have the name put on they had to order more towels
than so small a staff really needed. But young women's
capacity for using up towels is very great, and it was
an office vaunt that they were the best-washed bunch
in the building.

Jenny ascertained your business; you may have lingered a little in the doorway in the hope of a chat, for
the view from above of her neat parting and comely

neck was agreeable, and her gaze was innocently limpid, lifted politely upward from behind the switchboard. But she had her own skilful way of forwarding you across the corridor to the Reception Room. She called it that to impress visitors; its real name was the Sample Room. On each side of the entrance were settees. Under the windows (this was on the Fifth Avenue side of the wedge) were four desks set close in a row, for the use of the salesmen when they were in the office. On the right were shelves for the exhibition of the "line." For instance the Roe Centurion Calendar: it pleased Richard to think that this would give the correct day of the week until December 31, 1999, long after any of ourselves would be likely to need it. The Calculating Blotter, in which revolving disks inserted at the corners gave the answers for all sorts of emergencies in multiplication and percentage. The Diana Ash Tray was not only a sentimental reminder in replica of the Madison Square goddess, but also had a little moistened pad which extinguished cigarettes easily—"No Smell, No Smoulder." There was the Roe Revolving Inkwell (for draughtsmen) which carried four or six different colors of ink, and of course the onyx and agate pen-stands (non-inflammable) in many colors and prices. Not least was the Roe Double-Barrel Pen (for accountants), which would write black ink at one end and red at the other. Particularly useful, the salesmen said, in times of Depression.

The whole left side of the Sample Room was taken up with a big glass-fronted case which represented a retail show-window. It was illuminated with footlights and here Mr. Balaban, Roe's young advertising expert, tried out his ideas for new window display: the colored lithograph cut-outs showing a busy executive eased of computation by the mathematical Blotter, or the matron of fashion revelling in a jade writing-set. This show-window could be cunningly lit with variously colored bulbs, and was as much fun as a toy theatre. When Mr. Balaban had achieved the effect he liked, the set was photographed and prints sent round to the dealers. Mr. Roe, rather in awe of Mr. Balaban's talent, never dared tinker with the display himself, though he often wanted to. His own special pride was the huge flat mahogany desk in the middle of the room. This represented the nerve-center of an important "concern" and was equipped with the complete outfit known in the order-lists as Empire State Executive. This was a duplicate of the set—blotter, ink-well, pen-stand, calendar, ash-tray, combination paper-cutter and nail-file—given to the Governor's office at Albany. Strangers, not realizing the situation, sometimes inadvertently sat down at that desk; but the staff themselves regarded it as sacred. Horace, the office boy, was supposed to keep it dusted and in trim.

From the Sample Room a door, right, admitted to the Advertising and Accounting Department. The Advertising Department was Mr. Balaban, a tall very bass young man (growing bald), who had studied at a graduate school of Business Administration and used a difficult jargon to expound the simple cajoleries of publicity. This impressed Mr. Roe, who paid Mr. Balaban very nearly full-time salary for half-time work; he was in the office only from nine until twelve-thirty. His afternoons were spent in making other contacts; he hoped some day to start an advertising agency of his own. But he was worth what he was paid, for his ideas and copy were excellent. He was considered the artist of the office; he had a large table and drawing materials where he laid out sketches for advertising copy and window displays. On the other side of the room, his back resolutely turned upon Mr. Balaban's loud telephoning and whistling, sat Mr. Gall, the bookkeeper, who had once studied at Trinity College, Dublin. He was very bald with a fringe of bright pink floss encircling his head. He had cared for the accounts of the business since the beginning; he never wearied of Richard Roe's remark, "Charles, I wish you had more red hair and less red ink." There was something very reassuring in the solemnity with which he would cross the room, crouch down at the safe, skilfully click the dial, and take out a pile of ledgers. Round his pate mounted a steady fume of pipe-tobacco; inside it flickered a continual dance of figures, like the chorus of a revue, conducted by an imaginary leader called Cash Position. Occasionally Mr. Gall would have a sudden mechanical spasm with a pencil-grinder or an adding-engine; otherwise he was little heard from until five p. m., when he put his books away and became sociable. The world of business passes through a delicious transformation at that hour. Sometimes one of the salesmen would bring out a bottle of gin, as is permissible after office hours. Mr. Gall's pale blue eyes shone. He had been brought up on the genuine Hollands variety; gin still was to him a pure aromatic cordial which gentlemen drank neat. His austere and confiding mind had scarcely realized that the modern chemical was only a sort of household ammonia, fit for scrubbing tiles. Consequently one Lily cup of this caustic soda threw him into a fever of human-kindness. He would never take a drink until he was sure that both Richard Roe and the office boy had left. But as the boy left promptly at five he did not have to wait very long. He would tell anecdotes to Minnie and the two girls for as long as they would linger.

Minnie's room was on the Broadway side. It had one of those shallow bulges looking off over Madison Square. There were three doors, by which she commanded the whole suite. One, usually kept open, terminated the entrance corridor. Just outside this was a little alcove, where Horace had his table and chair with materials for parcels and shelves of office supplies. Another door connected with Mr. Gall and Mr. Balaban; and the third into Richard Roe's big room in the very nose of the building. In Minnie's room the little wash-stand was discreetly hidden behind a screen. Her desk was placed with strategic skill. It was against the partition between her room and that of Jenny and Peggy. Jenny's clear voice was audible: Minnie could often identify a telephone call before Jenny plugged it through and had a fraction of time to prepare for it, which is sometimes great advantage. She could keep an eye on the office boy, through the open doorway into the passage. She could hear, but not be seen by, any visitors who were shown into the Sample Room.

There was a buzzer from Richard Roe's desk to Minnie's. Sometimes, on days of high pressure, it was used very often. Then there would be long intervals when she would get anxious. She had a little trick of her own at such times. She would look over her left shoulder at the figure of Diana on the tower of Madison Square Garden. By concentrating her mind on

Diana and uttering some private runes of her own she could sometimes—or so it seemed—compel Richard to press the signal. She never told him that until after the statue had gone—"and left a lonesome place against the sky."

VIII

Show Business

At FIRST Hubbard supposed that Richard's brother, "Shad" Roe as they call him, was in some branch of the rubber-heel business. Lucille kept saying that he was with the Gilbert O'Sullivan Company. Then Hubbard chanced to pick up her weekly copy of *Variety,* encyclopædia of the theatre, and saw Shad's announcement that he was open for engagements. He had been trouping with *The Mikado.* When that came to an end, business was poor and the only job he could find was playing checkers against all comers in the basement of a so-called Flea Circus. Lucille imparted this information reluctantly: artists who have been in Legit regard the flea business as something of a come-down. But Shad, who was a quite remarkable performer at checkers, consoled himself by remarking that he was still "playing on the boards," and that business was lousy. This strong old epithet, unpardonable elsewhere, is justified in theatrical tradition, for Shakespeare used it.

Hubbard in his sheltered life as a Credit Man had not even known of the existence of such places. He went down there to try a game with Shad. Students of art's eccentric limboes know the general flavor of the Dime Museum. Side-shows of various monstrosities, Peeping Tom slot-machines, and a dreary posse of senescent females posturing briefly in a picture-frame as Art Models. The serfs and bumpkins gape sombrely and are lured on from one pruritus to another by the familiar suggestion that the next will be the Altogether—like philosophers pursuing the Absolute. But at one end of this dingy warehouse sit a row of men in derby hats, oblivious of the carnal show, brooding over checkers. It is a noble instance of intellect's triumph over flesh.

Hubbard recognized Shad at once by his likeness to Richard. There was the same softly frosting hair, the same square rather small head and sharp nose; the face was not so deeply seamed, for years of make-up keep an actor's skin lubricated. The stage wears its wrinkles inside. Hubbard loitered about, averting his eyes from the Dead Sea Aphrodites, until Shad's checker board was free. They played, and Shad soon disposed of Hubbard's innocent gambits. He didn't even look up at his opponent: he was artist enough to know by the way the other put the pieces on the board that as a checker-player he was negligible. Shad was the more surprised when Hubbard invited him to dinner. The biographer was beginning to realize that Shad and Gladys, the brother and the daughter, were the only available people who shared Richard Roe's actual blood or sperm. Perhaps from these agnates, if he was wary, he might learn more of the Roe character than from others.

An amusing fellow, Shad, was Hubbard's first impression. He must have absorbed a larger portion than

Richard of the volatile salts of temperament; or he had learned to utilize traits that in his brother were more deeply buried. When in New York he rarely left the Times Square region, the Main Stem as they call it. If he got a vaudeville job at an outlying theatre or on the Subway Circuit, he considered himself an adventurer into wild savannahs of the primitive and hurried back to his small bedroom in a hotel on the Forties. There, looking sideways from his window sill at night, he could get the impression (so comforting to the actor) that only a few yards away the whole town is burning up. He considered Richard a rustic for living as far uptown as the 80's. Old showmen smile when they read that the Social Centre of Manhattan is somewhere near Park Avenue and 71st. They know better: it is just about at Gray's Cut-Rate Drugstore, Broadway and 43rd. But in spite of Shad's conviction that Richard was a bit of a sap he was not above planning many ingenious raids on the treasury of the Flatiron office. These were mostly foiled by Minnie Hutzler.

When Shad learned that Hubbard had once had a remote but profitable connection with Show Business his cordiality improved. Though an excellent comedian, his heart was not in vaudeville: his ambition was to get back to producing, in which he had once taken a crash. In that levitating art, as in flying, it is not getting off the ground that is difficult, but returning safely to it. He at once began to wonder whether Hubbard would help to raise capital for a revue a friend of his was contemplating. Hubbard was naïve enough to ask whether it was written yet, thus showing his ignorance: revues are not written, they curdle together by a kind of insane ferment. *Oysters R in Season* was the title: the big idea seemed to be that the chorus, representing pearls, would be introduced in huge *papier-mâché* oyster-shells. Lots of shows, Shad insisted, have been put over with no more inspiration than that. We'd only need a shoestring; I can get one of the agencies to take a piece. He was engagingly candid in urging Hubbard not to be overpersuaded. I get lots of hunches, he said, but some of them are pretty rotten. I need someone to tick me off. It's a pity Dick got out of show business. He had no yen for the stage, but he was grand for the Front of the House. He had the makings of a swell Company Manager.

It was fascinating to see how well Shad understood the enigmatic region of Times Square. The elongated X from 42nd to 48th vibrated for him with instinctive meanings. Seventh Avenue was his seventh heaven. To all outsiders that area remains a grotesque paradox, from the squalor of its uncomfortable Comfort Station to the phœnix-fires of its topmost sky-sign. There is some mystery there that the layman cannot penetrate —mystery in its old sense of trade-secret. The visitor is acutely aware that here is a world of its own in which he is only a cash customer. It has its own language, its own humors, its own cruel despairs and its own warm hearts. In that world you are only one of the thousand midriffs needed to make up a belly-laugh. Once, morbidly inquisitive, I halted to discover what the barker was shouting in front of a burlesque theatre on 42nd Street. His melancholy and reiterated yell was this: "Feminine beauty predominates in the person of youth, beauty, and folly." I went in to catch the show and found very little of all three. Youth and beauty are all around us, in terrifying profusion, but how rare is really divine folly. "Through these portals," I said to myself (paraphrasing a line famous in that region) "pass the oldest jokes in the world." Which is not to condemn them: for as every showman knows, the oldest jokes are the most reliable. The main targets of human mirth were carefully bracketed long, long ago; Shad Roe and Aristophanes would have understood each other perfectly. The simplest comment on Greek drama is rarely made: the Athenian playwright, whether for tragedy or mirth, put on his show under open sky, in brilliant sunshine and fresh air. The audience could bear the impact of appalling horror or jest with less morbid convulsion. Perhaps it is chiefly a question of ventilation.

In every kind of commerce it is best that the customer should not know too much about the goods. In this realm Hubbard readily admitted his own ignorance. But even in walking through a few streets with Shad Roe, Hubbard could see that every glance of the eye brought to the actor highly specialized meanings and suggestions. His trained observation was automatically casting the people he saw for their appropriate parts. He saw them as Leading Men, Second Women, Ingénues or Comedy Relief. He knew his racket. Indeed the conventions of the old stock companies are the completest analogy for living.

The conflagration of evening was just brightening. The dying day, like a Hindoo widow, was on the funeral pyre, ready to expire among the electric holocaust. Rich oils and gums brightened her deathbed—motor oils and chewing gums. Mr. Hearst's newspapers for the following morning were almost out. On the crowded pavements Hubbard could feel the rising pressure of the universal need to be gulled, amused, consoled, horrified, outwitted. Here were a thousand traders ready to furnish the goods. Eyes were bright and faces handsome in strong saffron glare, and above that market-place of fiction disconcerting facts ran in letters of fire round and round the *Times* building. You would expect the burning legend to dart straight off into the air, but those words were well-trained, they turned the sharpest corners without missing a flicker.

"Did you ever see where the Tide Turned?" asked Shad. He pointed out a famous shoe-shop, much esteemed in the theatrical world. There, at the height of the now legendary Golden Age, the merchant had ornamented his luxurious new building with four graceful statues of beautiful actresses representing the varied arts of feminine impersonation. There were Ethel Barrymore as Ophelia, Marilyn Miller as Sunny (Hubbard tried to remember who Sunny was), Mary Pickford as Little Lord Fauntleroy, and Rosa Ponselle as Norma. Shad called his attention to the date on the tablet—October, 1929. "Just before business did a pratt-fall," he remarked. "The other side of the story's right across the street." Hubbard followed his gesture and saw a pawnbroker's office, with one ball missing from the symbolic three.

They had some very recent whiskey at what Shad called a whisper-low. But as Hubbard gently evaded Shad's efforts to lure him into various forms of partnership his central thought was of the invisible brother. Did Richard have that same quick faculty, in his own world, of knowing what was going on? Through the shifting fog of human observation he suddenly seemed to see Richard loom a little closer; more definite, more tragically human. But it was not going to be easy to pump Shad by overt suction. Living from day to day by rapid impromptu, opening cold every morning, the comedian was in no mood for leisurely reminiscence. There was even an air of caution in his talk about Richard. Whatever he knew must be siphoned off unsuspected.

IX

Somewhat Impassive

O N SUNDAYS a faint sound of rustling rises to the all-attentive ear, not unlike the rotation of a large dog curling for siesta among dry winter leaves. It is the American Middle Class settling down to its newspapers. Into that sea of print they subside in placid swoon. Like two goldfish in a crystal bowl, Lucille and Gladys floated softly inside the clear and tepid globe of the Sunday press. Outside that microcosmic round, the vast universe was vague and strange shadows moved; within the glassy circle of Now, life was definite and sharp. With an automatic pulsation of the gills they absorbed the oxygen fit for them. From whatever seemed likely to require thought they turned instinctively away. Poised in fascinated attention, they considered the pronouncements of wealthy ladies about Vanishing Creams or were tempted by the mage in Brooklyn who offers two mystic magnetic lodestones for $1.97—one to attract good fortune, the other to repel evil. Even minerals, cried this advertiser, are susceptible to sex. Yield Lucille and Gladys this tribute:

they never succumbed to the lodestone merchant.

Usually they became gently stupefied by the suggestions of the rotogravure sections. The distant orbits known as "smart circles" (which seem amazingly accessible to the advertising camera) swung round them in dizzying vertigo. There in photographic facsimile the great ladies of the land came demurely to the rescue of fainting Trade. Mrs. Bogardus told why her bath always leaves her body velvety soft and smooth. Mrs. Trafalgar's finger nails shone like jewels. Mrs. Regent's teeth were proof against film; Mrs. Beekman's pores were never clogged; Mrs. Ashland's perfume made the British ambassador inhale with ecstasy. Mrs. Morningside Peachbottom slept soft on a Myrmidon Mattress. Mrs. Schuyler kept fit for the hard grind of the season with a quart of aperient water a day. But presently even such receptive readers as Lucille and Gladys began to wonder. Perhaps it was hardly necessary to know these maharanees of merchandise socially since they admitted the masses with such gracious candor to the functions of the boudoir. Not less than any marquise of the eighteenth century they performed their toilet in public. Lucille and Gladys came near crying Boloney. So does the over-zealous merchant addle the golden egg.

If Richard could sort out the Financial Sections from that sargasso of print in which his women wallowed, he also rested in passive infinitive. Print, the strong narcotic, pours into the eyes, fills the system with its pacifying drug. The faith which his females gave to cigarette and toothpaste bravuras he reserved for the mahatmas of the Statistical Bureaus and Economic Services. "Technical studies indicate selective liquidation continues." . . . "Deflation is now an accomplished fact." . . . "The price the public is paying for goods is nearing the level where increased buying will be stimulated." . . . "There are no prospects of substantial change pending consummation of various readjustments." . . . "The current outlook for securities seems to be clouded by a number of conflicting factors." These naïvely cautious or Laodicean oracles were sedative, but he still had a residual shrewdness. He read war news, reports of sermons, real estate forecasts, but he was never completely hypnotized. Even when his glands reacted strongly to some injection of patriotic adrenalin by cartoon or editorial, he was not entirely swamped. Dumbly, dimly, he felt there was something wrong somewhere. It isn't all as simple as that.

Suppose the Unknown Citizen were to broadcast. Unidentified, with no danger of being held to account for his precious and secret thoughts, just step up to the mike and soliloquize. Suppose he were to say what he speculates about the Church, submarines, Russia, or the bringing up of children? How appalled the Authorities would be. How appalled he would be himself. For the most astounding achievement of society has been to train millions of people to think they believe certain ideas which they often don't believe at all. The Unknown Citizen would be quite staggered at the notions he himself was uttering. He had been silent so long about his innermost decencies he had almost forgotten they were there. The war of the future, the most terrible and rending convulsion of all, will be within the mind: the civil war between what you think and what you suppose you think. Great sedentary areas of intellect will be ravaged by bomb and gas. Many minds will perish.

Perhaps it was the neighborhood of the Museum of Natural History that gave Richard his painful little twinges of detachment. They bothered him now and then like a troublesome tooth. Was some nerve of credulity decaying in his mind? He did not enter the Museum very often, for usually he had Peke with him on his walks. He could take Peke to Woolworth's (a place almost equally instructive) buttoned inside his overcoat, with only that small grotesque Chinese mask looking out between his lapels. Peke enjoyed Woolworth's which is our nearest approach to an Oriental bazaar. Like a mandarin in a palanquin he looked down from the fork of Richard's overcoat, surveying the crowded counters with alert curiosity. Also with something of disdain: the Pekinese has been taught through a million generations to think himself either a lion or a dragon, and no one has ever told him the truth. But sometimes Richard carried inside his bosom still another small and sharptoothed creature with a goblin temper. Shall we call it Doubt? Perhaps many carry this dangerous pet carefully buttoned up.

He felt more religious when he visited the Museum than ever in any church. The section of the giant sequoia, 1400 years old, with its concentric patterns of growth, was more awful than a cathedral altar. He could almost pray to that huge slab of smooth brown timber: it was a symbol of purity and patience. He tried in impotent imagination to conceive it as it had been in the living tree, scalloped with deep corrugated bark. He heard the wind of dead centuries in its lofty boughs. He could hardly have endured to visit it with any companion, which would have embarrassed him. You must go lonely to your God. "You noble, noble thing," he whispered to it, and was ashamed, hurrying off to look at the wax enlargement of the house-fly for relief. The fossil tree-trunk estimated to be fifteen million years old did not affect him so. His mind had no grasp for such distances. But 1400 years is within reasonable reach.

There was another exhibit which he sometimes pondered. It was growing a bit shabby, but he loved it. "The Struggle for Existence Illustrated by the Meadow Mouse." In a glass case of earth and rocks and stumps a colony of stuffed mice lived in fatal proximity to all their enemies. A cat, a skunk, a weasel, an owl, a snake, threatened them from all sides. Above, poising deadly in air, a hawk suspended. The imperilled mice continued their innocent affairs regardless. The legend on the case was gruesomely impartial. "Every living thing is engaged in an unconscious struggle for existence, which ranges from a somewhat impassive test of endurance to active warfare." It never occurred to him that the name Meadow Mouse had exactly the same cadence as Richard Roe.

So in those crowded halls of wonder he sometimes strolled on rainy Sundays, perfectly at worship. Here was man at his best: groping for law and meaning. The lectures and pamphlets and other activities of the great society he did not pursue, but he wanted to help. He thought of leaving the Museum a modest bequest in his will, but he rather feared this might cause his heirs to try to break the testament on the ground of eccentricity. So in a period of good business he sent the Director a check for a thousand dollars, asking him not to make it public. No one, not even Minnie, knew about this until she and Hubbard went through his personal files. Richard did not have very many secrets, but those he had he kept.

The Museum gave him an unusual sense of simple reality; so much so that once, thinking a shrub in the park looked undernourished, he bought some ten-cent cartons of "fertilized earth" at Woolworth's and spread the soil round the roots. This, he admitted, was a good joke on him, for apparently it killed the bush— or perhaps it was the fault of all those police dogs. But this was one of his few agrarian impulses, for he was essentially urban.

He loved at night, in the shine of shop-windows, to tour his uptown domain. No great land-owner takes more pleasure in his colored garden beds than Richard in the changing displays of mixed merchandise. Certain familiar features he knew by heart: the dusty 35-pound lobster, "caught in the waters of Maine," in a chop-house window; the florist's sign, "We telegraph flowers." His observation had the unspoiled eye which can see a thing purely as object before deforming it by sophistry. Sometimes he caught himself wondering how flowers are telegraphed, or whether one tooth-paste is really any better than another? Many windows were constantly changing; he delighted in the pano-rama of electric clocks, sun-lamps, "hand-tailored neck-wear," California Sunkist Navels, cashew nuts—a name that made his nose tickle. He enjoyed a little late shopping in the savor of delicatessen stores, where he found always new varieties of whole-wheat crackers and strange jams to take home for his bedtime supper. All these goods suggested endless themes in mechanics, geography, commerce. He was grateful to be included in a world that offered so much material for thought and self-argument. He loitered to overhear what people said. "There's some Shalimar, only $1.35 a dram, I must get some," cried one girl to another at a display of perfumery. He wondered what young man's career might be effectually altered by that small vial of musky invitation.

It was an era of declining prices: he watched business grow more and more obeisant to the public. A modiste insisted that she was Exclusive but Not Expensive. Banks installed ingenious revolving slots for Night Deposit, urging him not to risk carrying large sums in the dangerous dark but to entrust cash to them at any hour. Drug stores offered him A Pot of Tea Free from 3 to 5. All this he studied with the alert mind of a trader, comparing prices, considering ideas for his own behoof. When a long rush of traffic was suddenly halted by a red light he sometimes smelt a fume of burning brakes. That was very like what was happening to business. The check had been jammed on so hard that everywhere was a whiff of hot bearings.

His mind was busy and happy as he admired this vivid show, yet he would have been rather speechless to any inquiry as to what he was thinking. "I can't make out what he sees in those walks of his," exclaimed Gladys after his attempt to expound the symbolism of the burning brakes. "He does notice the craziest things. It was probably only his old cigar he smelled." Gladys was very sensitive in the matter of masculine aromas. When Richard had had a cocktail he was careful to breathe through his nostrils at the dinner table in the hope of not offending her.

Going up and down that region of Broadway it occasionally struck him, when he needed to buy a collar or a shirt, that the milliners and modistes outnumbered men's outfitters about twenty to one. Sometimes he paused before an array of fragile pink gear or network hosiery, mildly speculating on the difficult comedy of sex. A window of those silken bifurcations can suggest as much as a tale by Flaubert. In an adjoining shop a coiffeur's wax bust with the gown cut very low was turning languorously on clockwork. As it revolved it met the corner of his eye and simpered at him. He turned away alarmed. No, there was no escape from women. Like the small efficient Japanese in the crumbling continent of China, women had invaded the old easy-going empire of man, burst open its flimsy pagodas and antique fortresses. Upper Broadway was a street in a conquered city. In almost every window were the emblems of the victors. Flowers, perfumes, ribboned steamer baskets of rich unwholesome nougats, aphrodisiac movies, trashy novels—all designed for women. Their most personal and physiological requisites flaunted everywhere in shameless display. Even the cigar store, the barber, the shoe-shine stand, old havens of masculine retreat, lay open to their triumph. Men were as helpless as the crabs packed in trays of ice and seaweed in the chop-house window, doomed and yet still bubbling a last heroic disdain.

Well, more power to them, he thought—meaning the women, not the crabs. Perhaps they'll make a better job of it than we have. But the thought of those network stockings and carmined finger-nails made him pause. Can we trust the future of the world to people who take that sort of thing seriously? Even white spats, even boiled shirts, are not quite as futile as that.

Very likely the future of the world will take care of itself, he thought later as he drank a bottle of ice-cold milk and got into bed. Even the giant sequoia had been through some bad times in its 1400 years: some of those circles in the trunk were very wrinkled.

In great social shifts such as these it is probably irrelevant either to applaud or protest. The deep tide of history moves too far down for casual control. Richard made his microscopic observations and at moments was filled to bursting with honorable ideas for which he knew no utterance. But he was too wise to be angry. Mostly he took things as he found them— or they took him—and assumed they were all part of the scheme. The Middle Class is run by its women: that is why it remains the Middle Class, unshaken by the exorbitant joys and horrors above and below. It is the gyroscope of society. People who are not in the middle it reasonably calls eccentric.

What a magnificent stride in civilization when even the Unknown Citizen grows anxious and uncertain, and feels the god-like pains of foreboding.

x

Streamline

IT WOULD be misleading to dwell too heavily on any elements of wisdom or anxiety in Richard Roe's thought. Hubbard warned himself against over-dramatizing him or lending him spurious sentimental appeal. Roe was no mystic. He was well aware of the world's enormous sinking fund of misery, yet even so it looked to him as though the status quo had high and humorous merits. He would never have presumed to formulate a code, but it might have been simply stated. To get discount for cash, not to argue with women when they tantivy, to wait for the traffic light, to hang up his clothes neatly when going to bed (because it is less trouble in the end). These are small-town virtues, but New York is a great city chiefly because there are so many small-town people in it. These middling qualities in him make the eventual riddle all the harder to understand, and suggest perhaps that life is a non-Euclidean affair. But we have a long way to travel before we approach that.

He was essentially a business man: he liked to see things orderly done. It pleased him to think that, though he had been going up and down his own narrow slot of Manhattan for a good many years, he had rarely witnessed any serious calamity. That is no bad record for a hive of several million promiscuous and mutually repugnant creatures. He had warm professional respect for anyone whose business seemed efficiently conducted. He liked the young night-man at Horn and Hardart's branch bakery because he was courteous and enthusiastic. He experimented with all sorts of bran muffins and loaves of cheese-bread because he liked new ideas. When Richard discovered the apple-square, a kind of gingerbread that had apple-sauce mixed in the dough, he was elated. He rejoiced in Horn and Hardart's triumphs as though they were his own, and gave some of the cakes to the elevator man who was going to have a baby.

He had no desire for motor cars, and never owned one, but he observed with interest the gradual improvement of their design. One night Lucille and Gladys and Peke took him for a walk. The ladies had been much excited about a raspberry-colored sport coupé slowly revolving on a black and silver turntable in a showroom. It was marked $1,373, and Gladys thought that at last her father was beginning to weaken. He admired its low cutaway shape, the little cabin rounded like an igloo. But all he said was, "Civilization is gradually developing streamlines, too. Little by little it's got to shed off unnecessary gadgets and windsurfaces. Anybody who loafs on his job is just a gadget; so is any job that isn't worth doing. Maybe it's going to shed off people like me." And then he added, "Maybe armies and navies and tariffs are only temporary gadgets." That was bad enough, but it was worse when he said he was relieved he hadn't got the order from the War Department for a huge consignment of fountain pens. He had put in a bid, for he needed the business, but someone else got the contract. "I almost think I'm glad," he remarked rashly. "I'd hate to think of a declaration of war being signed with a Roe pen."

When Peke was not with him, Richard's evening stroll sometimes took him farther afield—down Central Park West and across 59th Street to Fifth Avenue. In those last days there were frequent portents for a business man to ponder. To see a huge apartment-hotel, almost completed and then abandoned, standing dark and decadent, shocked him. That sort of thing sometimes gives ironic or malicious amusement to poets and radicals, but to a frugal trader like Roe it contradicts a fundamental piety. The rusting iron girders of the unfinished door-canopies projected over the pavement like gibbets; on the wooden fence in cracked and soiled glass frames were the floor-plans of luxurious apartments to rent. He examined these sadly: dressing rooms, bathrooms, living rooms "with a view of the Park," all empty, unfurnished, the glazier's X still on the dusty panes. A dangerous ghost lived in those dark rooms, the wraith of some economic law that men had transgressed. What was that grim veto: Not to Bite Off More than You Can Chew? It is even more vengeful than the imperatives of morals. Other great edifices, whose mortgagees might have been happier if these also had been barricaded empty, were shining with fallacious lights and militant with tall doormen uniformed like parrots.

Many lively officers spin the revolving entries of commerce and yet know no more of the meanings within
than those hotel militia.

Outside the Plaza still lingered one hansom cab, last
of a noble fleet, and Ceres, a country goddess, had
strayed into the paved square. Someone had taken
away her clothes, and her lovely back must have been
a little stiff from stooping forward over her corn-
basket. On each side of her terraced fountain were
two large stone Horns of Plenty. Richard always had
a simple curiosity about such public emblems, supposing that artists are wiser than most of us and must
mean something when they do these things. He even
climbed up to look into the big cornucopias: they were
empty, except for dust and soot. More surprising still,
the other end of each great funnel was carved in the
shape of a goat. Ignorant of the legend of Amalthea,
Richard could only conclude that this animal represented the public. And the whole affair was supported
by a patient tortoise, crushed very flat. These symbol-
isms were almost too painful for an average taxpayer.
Sadly he raised his eyes to a handsome office building
near by—as vacant as the horns of plenty.

Richard rarely saw that fashionable part of Fifth
Avenue except at night. Even in the dark it continued
to solicit: there were shops as lovely as jewel-cases or
tiny chapels, softly glimmering with subdued radiance.
In recessed niches, like blessed relics, stood single vials
of liquid rouge, skin tonic and freshener, foundation
cream or muscle oil. (The pathos of woman's incessant campaign!) There was a toy facsimile of
Madame Du Barry's boudoir. "Just look at that;
artistic!" he heard a lady exclaim to her mute escort
as they passed. There were furniture windows as

charming as stage-sets. There were furs and underwear; but unlike upper Broadway where each article
was labelled and price-ticketed, here it was tacitly assumed that you knew the names of such things and
that the price didn't matter. But even here the ghost
of outraged Economics was beginning to walk. He
saw a glittering cave of "semi-precious jewelry"
marked *Any article in this window now 39¢*. This
shook him badly, for he had trained himself to believe
that Fifth Avenue between 42nd and 59th was
exempt from the crude laws of Supply and Demand.
He never in the least resented Fifth Avenue's displays
of luxury. He found it highly amusing that people
should really covet such things. Most of what he privately esteemed as "culture" was derived from such
exhibitions. After seeing the facsimile of Du Barry's
boudoir he at once looked her up in the Erskine Encyclopædia. In a department store window on 42nd
Street he admired what they called "A Writing Nook
in the 19th Century American Spirit." As a manufacturer of writing materials this interested him: he
pressed close to the glass to see what were the books
above the desk. They were Johnson, Tennyson, Pope,
and Orlando Furioso. He looked up Furioso and could
not find that he had anything to do with the American
19th century. But this ranging curiosity made Richard
a good trader.

There were always surprises. At night the filigree
top of the R. C. A. building, behind St. Patrick's dark
spires, shines amber and blood-orange through stone
tracery, like the flower they call a redhot poker. While
Protestant churches are fast asleep, St. Patrick's
Cathedral is warmed and working. Little banks of
candles twinkle with sacred lights; sinners pass quietly

in and out of curtained confessionals. All this was mystery to him; the first time he entered he feared he might be put out for not knowing the proper motions. But he sat quietly in a pew, and by assuming the posture of supplication its reality visited him. From the raised terrace outside the church he looked across the glamour of that rugged excavation where men were founding Radio City. It was best seen from the L-platform at 50th Street, where he took train to return home.

Brilliant flood-lights whitened the zigzag trenches and rock-cuttings; it was like a moon-crater in that milky glow. Derricks leaned in black diagonals, little braziers sparkled in the cold pit, drills rang and chattered. It was so perfect as a spectacle, he wanted to cry, Hold it! Keep it like that!—As far as Roe was concerned it did remain so, for he never saw it finished.

By adroit questioning Hubbard managed now and then to elicit from Gladys other episodes which seemed to her characteristic of her father's foolishness.

"One of the first things I remember," she said. "I was just a small kid; we were all walking in the grounds outside the Museum, a windy day. I had a green toy balloon on a string, it slipped out of my hand and blew away. Of course I yelled and ran after it. Father and I both chased it. I remember dogs barking and people grabbing at the balloon as it bobbed along. It bounced on a tree and Father almost got it, but each time the wind puffed it out of reach. I simply howled. Father ran right across Central Park West among the traffic, trying to catch it—as a matter of fact I think maybe he was knocked down by a car, because I remember he looked awfully muddy afterward and Mother made him go home and change. But the wind took the balloon clean away over Central Park, it flew up and up and the last we saw of it was a little green bubble disappearing in the sky. I was terribly upset, but Father said, Think how pleased that balloon is. That's the very best thing that can happen to a balloon. . . . Don't you think that was an awfully heartless thing to say to a child?

"Another thing I remember: One day we saw a blind man who was singing as he went along tapping with his stick. Father got all excited about it. If a blind man can sing I don't see why we shouldn't, he said. He started singing, right there on the pavement. Of course I was dreadfully embarrassed, because he had no idea of music. His favorite tune was Dorothy, Old English Dance, that crazy thing they always give children to practise on the piano. I was learning it then, and he used to ask me to play it I don't know how many times. When he started to sing it on the street I was so ashamed of him I ran home."

Minnie Hutzler contributed a thought that stayed in Hubbard's mind. Minnie lived in a walk-up apartment where one ascended three flights of heavily carpeted stairs. The friction of feet on the carpet, especially in cold weather, generated a strong charge of electricity. When Minnie put her latch-key to the lock, in the dim hallway a beautiful spark leapt out to meet it. Minnie was so used to this that she had almost forgotten to notice it, but the first time Hubbard saw it he was delighted. "Richard liked that too," she said. It was the first time she had mentioned him except as "Mr. Roe." Hubbard had invited her to dine with him that evening to talk things over, but it was the spark on the latch-key that first penetrated her reserve.

XI

Tell Me Everything

WHAT, then, is a human being? Hubbard, looking over his notes, had to ask himself. How might one attempt to describe the incredible phenomenon? A creature alternating sixteen hours of mischief with eight hours of innocence; aware of death at every street-crossing, yet rarely scathed; a moving eddy of self-consciousness wasting most of its time in irrelevant necessities and seizing desperately upon casual laughter. A toy balloon blown into the Park—a blind man singing on the street—a spark when the key meets the lock it fits. Then, engrossed in this impossible inquiry, the biographer became more antic. It was not likely that the ultimate definition, having eluded Æsop, the Bible, Shakespeare, and all the French aphorists, would accidentally run down from the small black cistern of Lawrence Hubbard's Roe pen. But he was happy, very happy, in watching what came forth. A human being, he wrote, is a whispering in the steam pipes on a cold night; dust sifted through a locked window; one or other half of an unsolved equation: a

pun made by God; an ingenious assembly of portable
plumbing; a folder of Unfinished Business; a mob of
intuitions governed by foreigners; a parliamentary
body in which the minority is always right; a tropical
island with a high protective tariff; a temporary compromise between the impulses of self-preservation and
self-destruction; a diminishing variable of Certainty;
a superb actor in a hokum play; the chorus of a song
whose verse everyone has forgotten; a trained animal
who distrusts its trainer; the only animal concerned
to identify itself.

Words, he concluded, are a commodity in which
there is never any slump. Talk is the greatest industry,
and all human beings move in clouds of it—not merely
their own, but in the rumors and representations of
others, to which they are sometimes painfully sensitive. If so, they hurry back into the all-forgiving ego.
But how extraordinarily well-trained they are, on the
whole. He remembered with delight how he had seen
the sudden shift that takes place now and then at a
formal dinner party, when the hostess switches over
to talk to the man on the other side. With a soft
creaking of shirt bosoms and a turning of white necks
the pairs simultaneously rearrange themselves all
round the big table. Marvellous creatures! In just
a few million years an anthropoid of uncertain temper
had drilled itself to such genteel deportment.

But what are you going to do about people when
you're not with them? Into what far-away loneliness
do their minds travel? What uncanny thoughts do they
think? You can visualize them, see them walking,
laughing, sulking; see their amusing clothes (so re-
markably a part of themselves), the delicate way their

hair grows, their bright serious eyes; hear their unmistakable voices repeating favorite opinions. Does all that go on, just the same, and you not there? Yes, they are pursuing their own relentless privacies, but are they real? Even if they were dead, would they be any farther away? You grope clumsily toward them, but it is really they you seek or some new reassurance of yourself? Hubbard thought with amazement of Minnie Hutzler. How keen and cool her gaze: if you passed her on the street you would never guess about the electric spark. The phantoms of so many friends rise before you. What's happening to them? Tell me, tell me everything (you'd like to say); I'll never hold it against you. I'll match each grief that plagues you with grievance of my own. Ring, telephone; come, letter; I need you.

I don't like people who are Sure of Themselves, he said.

He tried earnestly to put himself in Roe's place. "I am Richard Roe, stationery novelties. I have a wife Lucille, a daughter Gladys, a dog Peke, an apartment on 81st Street, an office in the Flatiron Building. I have a secretary Miss Hutzler, I mean Minnie, with dark eyebrows; a brother Shad who owes me money and hopes to owe me more. I have a bunch of keys in the left trouser-leg of a gray suit, and in the right trouser some bills fastened together with a paper-clip. I have three cigars wrapped in cellophane in my vest. My overcoat is dark blue, and I am on my way to talk discounts with a jobber. What am I thinking about?"

It didn't seem to work. Apparently he wasn't thinking anything except that a cocktail would be in order. Was that what Richard would have had in mind? This sort of brooding is a bewildering affair, and he han-

kered for companionship. He remembered that on
Saturday afternoons the boys usually gathered at
Jules's place.

When there was time for a good long session they
sat not in the kitchen but in a tiny inside room that
opened off it. There, through the doorway, they could
see Jules and Madame side by side at the stove, tend-
ing various operations in perfect harmony. There was
something fundamental and close to reality about that
scene. Madame never guessed how these clients, not
inexperienced students of women, admired her. She
was too intent on the browning veal cutlet or the
colander of tender haricots. There was a natural be-
nignity about her. Presently she would come to the
doorway. Her face and voice were beautiful with
simple friendliness when she said, "What will the
gentlemen have?" It was a lesson in grace just to
watch her move about. Jules was more volatile: when
he had a specially fine ham or a haunch of venison he
carried it in to show them. When he shook up cocktails he usually found a small dividend for himself, so
that by midafternoon he was ripe to play the accordion. It was a noble instrument, inlaid with oyster-shell
and sparklers and an American flag outlined in colored
gems. The tunes Jules enjoyed had no terminus: they
went on and on, endless da capos with surprising blasts
of power and a secret humorous effect of which the
virtuoso himself was unaware. "Do you remember,"
said George Work, "how pleased Dick Roe was with
that line of Gene Vogelsang's? Gene said, life seems
so simple when you hear the accordion."

Life did seem simple in that unassuming place.
Here, Hubbard remembered, he had actually seen

Richard Roe, with these same men. Had Richard divined here some of that easy relish of being we all bitterly need? Don Quixotes of the revenue service go tilting at gin-mills, but at their best these places are true civilization and a lesson in economics. At Jules's, product and consumer were immediate, there was no waste, not even a waiter or a hat-check. Close behind his little back-yard towered an enormous new office building that had already gone through four bankruptcies. Beneath that monument of over-production Jules lived in plentiful content. His notice posted on the kitchen wall was an added touch of honest realism:

On account of the Management of this place having to get up early, In order to market and prepare for service. We regret to notify our customers we will close at 10 P. M.

With sinewy bare arms Jules stood over an omelet at the stove, intent as a painter at the canvas. When the crusted soot of the flue caught fire and roared, as it often did, he calmly threw a handful of salt up the chimney and continued his cooking. To see his family group around the kitchen table, sitting hours together in unappeasable talk after customers had gone, was to know the meaning of a home. The clients in the middle room could sometimes hear fragments of animated conversation about American institutions. Jules himself highly approved of America, and with reason; and you could see his boys, dark lads in their teens, growing by some magical chemistry more American every day.

To such hideaways come occasional fugitives from oppressive doctrine: fugitives from rectangular streets and rectangular ideas, from Noise and Nerves, from Efficiency and Haste. They meet clandestinely, like primitive Christians in the catacombs. They exchange grotesque confidences. Wine opens the heart; roof and fire, food and drink, a barred door and a wet winter afternoon outside, put almost any group of men in a candid mood, especially if they can sit and watch a woman doing the work. Few women have ever heard, or ever will hear, the naïve speculations their jaded hoplites venture in these hours of armistice. Though the wives of Messrs. Work, Vogelsang, Schaefer, Furness and Von Ulm perhaps imagined that their husbands were engaged in illicit gayety, the fact is that these plodding creatures were far happier in the exercise of argument almost as idealistic as Plato's. The Decline and Fall of the American Woman was one of their themes. Sitting very much at their ease, they suggested that she would really be much happier if she were in the kitchen all day like Madame. This led to Bill Schaefer's reminiscence of his friend who, at a charitable garden party, took up an impromptu collection from emotional patriots. When they asked for what he was collecting he murmured reverently, "For a Memorial to the Women who Fell in the War."

Gene Vogelsang remarked that women were insincere drinkers. "A fellow took me to lunch in one of those swell East Side speakeasies that are mostly frequented by dames," he said. "The place was packed with 'em, we were the only men in the room. Even the bar was full of women at tables, with just half a dozen goofs crowded down at one end of the counter. It was queer to hear that babble—a treble yell. If you stopped to listen, they sounded like a river going over a dam. Except for a couple of battleships with old-fashioneds, every one of those frails was drinking water. It didn't seem like fair play."

"Women don't enjoy drinks they have to pay for themselves," said Von Ulm. But Von Ulm was bitter in those days because he was out of a job and hunting for work. "Hard times are supposed to build character," he said. "But what are you going to do with all that character when you get it built?"

"The funny thing is," said George Work, "they let women into those places without a card, but a man has to be identified. Why is that?"

These eavesdroppings, if misunderstood, would be treason. But woman, the ruler of our scene, is an enlightened tyrant. She is wise enough to allow her subjects opportunity to blow off vapors, and pays no attention. Every government must learn when not to listen.

Hubbard, however, had no grievance against women except that the only one he had ever really wanted wouldn't have him. He waited for a chance to turn the talk in more profitable channels. Several of these men had worked for Erskine Brothers when Roe was there. "What was Roe's job at Erskine's?" he asked.

XII

Erskine Brothers

It was Herman Schmaltz who got Richard Roe a job in the publishing business. That was a long time ago—over twenty years. It was in the days when most publishing offices were within lunching distance of Mouquin's restaurant at Sixth Avenue and 28th Street. It was at one of Mouquin's marble-topped tables that Herman, good, steady traveller on the Erskine staff, introduced Richard to Sam Erskine, the sales manager. Richard needed a job badly. The theatre job had ended. There were a wife and baby in a tiny flat far uptown.

You can identify how long ago it was by this: the Singer Building was still the tallest in the world. In the Erskine Atlas, which had a big sale in those days, there was a profile drawing of relative elevations, and the Singer Building and the *Lusitania* (standing on her stern) were shown alongside Mount Everest and Kilimanjaro. The dear old Singer Building, with its matronly elevator ladies, many of whom must have been there from the beginning. When they celebrate its quarter-century in 1933, what a span of events might be remembered. Uptown makes a great fuss over Depressions, but they are nothing new in the financial district. Ask the pigeons; they began to observe hard times when horses became scarce. If you want to know how sharp-set those birds are, walk along Broad Street on Sunday, when all that region is deserted. Drop a few peanuts on the pavement and see how quickly the pigeons of the Stock Exchange cornice will swoop down. Perhaps there's a fable in it. Down Town is full of fables. Do women ever pay homage to that little tablet on Broad Street, "To Mark the Lost Thoroughfare called Petticoat Lane"? Is that not symbolic of their modern escapade? The great glacier of 1930–32 passed over Manhattan Island, freezing loans and depositing moraines of paper. Many a rugged boulder was polished pretty smooth. But men fighting for margin are tough mountaineers. With ice-pick and hob-nails, roped together in catenations of credit, they bridge many a crevasse. The southernmost deposit of the great glacial epoch is that mysterious little stone in the middle of Battery Park. It is encouraging, it says COAST AND GEODETIC SURVEY, BASIC BENCH MARK. Perhaps to many a poor devil, touching bottom on a park bench, it seems only tragic irony. But there is meaning in that lowest curve of the tall city. Standing there, you can feel energy growing and roaring behind you. The God's-eye view would be that even an Ice Age could not shatter these industrious bipeds. They used it for tobogganing.

Erskine Brothers is still going, after a reorganization (it is amazing how hard it is to kill a publishing business), but the house no longer plays quite the rôle it did twenty years ago. It served in a unique way as a kind of normal school in the publishing business. Many able men who afterward went on their own, or joined other firms, worked for the Erskines at one time or another. The high turnover of personnel in the staff was probably due to the fact that at the head of every main channel of the business there stood an Erskine, immovably intrenched. It was strictly a family affair. Whether your ambition were Editorial, Sales, Manufacturing or Mail Order, an active Erskine closed the prospect. Even the Publicity and Author-Chasing were commanded by the youngest Mrs. Erskine, one of the earliest of the new generation of college women to take up publishing as a form of conscientious frolic; and her father, an old gentleman of incomparable sagacity, acted as chancellor of the exchequer. It was Daisy Erskine, fresh from college and susceptible to the new currents of literature that began to flow about the year 1912, who inaugurated the custom of giving tea parties for poets. This was pleasant and harmless, but in the long run the mixing of social and business relations is dangerous. The three older Erskines never quite knew whether to feel aggrieved or grateful that their own wives did not take the same insistent interest in the business.

The three senior Erskines were remarkable in this, that they regarded publishing definitely as a business, not as a branch of culture. This was still something of a new idea in those days. They would have been extremely ill-at-ease if called upon to discuss literary values, and very shrewdly believed that if an author's books are really good reading he won't need to have tea parties given him. But with the exception of Sam, who presided over Sales, none of the Erskines moved very close to Richard Roe's humble orbit. It is worth dwelling on Sam Erskine a moment, for he taught Richard much.

The day Richard began work at Erskines' happened to be one of those occasions when Sam harangued the boys about their forthcoming tour on the road. He went over the list of new publications title by title, telling his salesmen a little about each book and what quantities he thought they ought to sell. Richard, to whom all this was complete mystery, felt very much out of it, but Sam, with admirable tact, asked him to take notes of the discussion. Richard did so, carefully recording all suggestions; afterwards he sat up late copying it all out, and had one transcript apiece typed for the salesmen. Sam thanked him politely for this zeal; it was not until some time later that Richard learned by accident that Sam had never given these notes to the men. He had shoved them away in a desk drawer. "Don't burden the boys with unnecessary memos," was his comment when he saw that Richard had discovered him. "I just wanted you to begin to get the line in your head."

Sam Erskine had that mysterious sixth sense, invaluable in the publishing business, of getting a notion of a book without the pain of reading it. Life was to him far too immediate and amusing to waste much time in enjoying it at second-hand. By a few words of hearsay, or reading what the advertising department had put on the jacket, or by some indescribable deduction from the shape, size, and typography of the book, he formed an intuition of its sales prospects. He would pick up a new volume fresh from the printer, by an unknown author; would give its pages a quick spin, and tell you with remarkable accuracy what it was likely to sell. One day he asked Richard to go with him to a big bookstore on Fifth Avenue, where he wanted to introduce him to the buyer. The argument turned on the relative sales of various titles —not Erskine books but those of other publishers. Sam was able to guess, almost exactly, how many copies of each book this store had sold, and in what quantities they had been ordered and reordered. *"The Age of Brass,"* Sam would say; "I guess you've sold close to four hundred. You've had two hundreds, a couple of fifties, and some small reorders since." The buyer would look it up on his card index. "Sam, you're good. We've had three hundred and seventy-five, and we're ordering more today." They would go round the counters together, Sam guessing quantities. He was proud of this gift, which was pure instinct, not based on any deliberate study. "It's not enough to know your own line," he told Richard. "You've got to know what the others are doing."

Sam was as quick and observant as a terrier. He had a profound distrust of the editorial department, but he wasted no energy in lamenting various plugs that were handed him to sell. Salesmanship to him was a delightful game, and even in the intervals of his leisure he would chuckle with joy when a possible new outlet occurred to him. His semiannual review of the troops, when he called the boys together to go over the spring or autumn list, was a brilliant *tour de force*. In the little smoke-blue Trade Room all the dummies were lined up for display. The boys knew, and he knew they knew, that he had not read these books, but they all enjoyed his innocent bravado. "Now here's this new novel of Hampton's, *Carbon Paper*. The private life of a young secretary in big business. Listen, there's

a love story in this that's really good. One of the most
appealing romances I ever read—Daisy showed me
the galleys. We ought to get seventy-five hundred advance. Gene, don't let the News Company off with
less'n a thousand."

"Listen, Sam," Gene Vogelsang would reply, "don't
forget we got stuck on Hampton's last one. The News
Company's got several hundred of 'em yet."

"Well, if they take a thousand of this we'll make
them an allowance on the old one. I'll take 'em back
for J'n'R's."

J'n'R's were Jobs and Remainders, in which
Richard Roe had his first experience of the publishing
business.

At the time of these semiannual conferences, which
lasted for several days of impassioned argument and
usually ended with a genial dinner at Mouquin's, Daisy
Erskine always hung hopefully in the offing. Her
theory was that she was better equipped than anyone
else to tell the boys what the new books were like.
She had actually read them, and she knew the authors.
She suspected that the dope Sam was giving the boys
was crude and inaccurate. He had small respect for
authorship as a high profession, and she thought it
deplorable that men representing the Erskine imprint
were going out to push those books on such crass principles. She did once succeed in arranging a joint meeting of the Sales and Literary departments, at which
several authors of the new books described their own
works. But the selection of authors whom she brought
in was unfortunate, and the salesmen were bored. A
well-meaning dominie who lectured them for forty
minutes on Economic Idealism might otherwise have
sold fairly well, but the boys decided they were damned

if they'd push that book. Sam never allowed Daisy to rope in authors thereafter until he had personally inspected them.

Sam's brilliance as a Sales Manager lay in his intimate understanding of salesman morale. "They're all prima donnas," he used to say; "if they don't feel pleased with themselves they're no good." An episode with Gene Vogelsang was a pleasant illustration. Gene, then taking care of the New York City Trade, was always temperamental. When he felt discouraged —for whatever reason, which may have had little to do with actual figures—he was convinced that he himself, the book business, and life in general were all gloomy error. On such days he would come in with his face carved in deep lines, fling down his heavy bag, and emit disconnected obscenities.

One day on his way to the office Sam happened to stop in at the office of a bookshop chain where for some unknown reason one of the Erskine books was in sudden demand. The buyer asked him to have a couple of hundred delivered at once. "I won't take the order," said Sam; "I'll have Gene come around, you give it to him. But don't just *give* it to him: make him work for it."

At the office Sam found Gene in one of his moods of discouragement. "Gene," he said, "I had a queer dream last night; I dreamed that Anderson's wanted a couple of hundred *Love Birds*."

"You're crazy," said Gene. "I was in there Tuesday, and they wouldn't touch it."

"Well, you know dreams are queer things," said Sam. "Play this hunch for me, won't you? See if they'll take fifty."

Gene took his feet off the desk and went out. In two

hours' time he was back with a different face. "Well, Sam, it's a good thing you hire some honest-to-God salesmen. I went round to Anderson, he gave me a terrible battle, but I planted two hundred and fifty on him. What do you think of that?"

"Great stuff, Gene," said Sam.

"It made me feel so good, I went to Schultz, and Barton, and Ryberg, and got some nice little pick-ups all down the line. Say, have some more of those dreams, will you?"

XIII

The Atlas

RICHARD'S earliest days at Erskines' were puzzled by his natural superstition that books were intended to be read. He took home Trade Order Lists and catalogues and wondered desperately how he would ever catch up with this enormous glut of literature which had been accumulating without his knowing anything about it. When he was given a list of remainders to be offered in bulk to various jobbers, he made a pathetic attempt to study the volumes themselves. But the mystic art of reading, a much rarer gift than might be supposed, was not natural to him. He could never accomplish it except when free from all distraction. He was instinctively alert in all personal relationships, but print was a foreign unreal medium in which he proceeded with difficulty. He was embarrassed by a native respectfulness toward books, a feeling that they are to be taken seriously. With growing perplexity he struggled through two or three mediocre novels, trying to justify to himself the adjectives printed on the jackets. Then he compromised by memorizing verbatim the descriptions given in the Erskine catalogue.

He would hand the pamphlet to Lucille and ask her to "hear" him. When she read out some title, such as *Dinner at Seven,* he would reply "Sparkling comedy of bourgeois life." "What is burjoyce life?" was her natural inquiry. "It's some kind of print," he said. "I heard them talk about it in the manufacturing department. It's a small sort of type, I guess it means a story that tells about small-time people." Lucille was not satisfied with this explanation, but she went on to another item. *"Acreage?"* she asked. "This novel of broad vision," he replied, "completes the author's triology of the Canadian granaries. It's a triple triology, that means a story in three volumes." Daisy Erskine, who wrote most of these catalogue notes, would have been pleased if she knew how attentively Richard studied them—and how he wondered where she had learned so many difficult words. But it was the buyer for Remainder Outlets, Inc., who discouraged this habit. Richard had waited nervously a long while for an interview. When he took in his bag full of books he spread them out as alluringly as possible and began his carefully memorized descriptions.

"Listen, drummer," said the buyer, "you're wasting your time. There's only two things that interests me: Is it a good-looking package, and can you make me a price? If you can, I'm wide open to be sold."

From that moment Richard began to be a valuable salesman. Though shy he soon learned to relish the hilarity of the office. Is it because the book business is one of small profits that it compensates itself in a large turnover of human comedy? The big main room was full of skirmishing typewriters, the incessant rattle of hammering keys and the zip of paper sheets pulled off the rollers, but those cheerful young women never

seemed too busy for some floating jest. As you went
down the middle aisle through the clatter of correspondence, there was always some elusive fragment
of chaff passing to and fro. When Gene Vogelsang, a
general favorite, passed through the office, there would
be half a dozen oblique flashes of the eye here and
there, half a dozen of those subtle instantaneous
recognitions by which people convey to each other
their mutual appreciation of some universal absurdity.
Richard was at first somewhat startled by the offhand
irreverent flavor of the Sales Department. Then he
realized that in any business the salesmen have the
privilege of the king's jester at court. They played
endless practical jokes on one another. When Herman
Schmaltz came in from his trip through the Middle
West he left his portmanteau unlocked in the office
for several hours before going home. At lunch time
Gene Vogelsang and George Work happened to see a
group of girls in the Mail Order department admiring
some delicate peach-colored lingerie one of them had
bought. They insisted on borrowing the garment and
putting it in Herman's bag, where it was duly discovered when Herman got home and opened his
portmanteau in triumph to show Hazel some trophy
of his journey. Even Sam Erskine, a member of the
firm, was not exempt from these simple japes. One
night there was a dinner of the salesmen at Mouquin's.
Sam, who lived out of town, laid his watch on the
table before him to be sure of catching the last train
for Long Island. But as the wine circulated Sam's
vigilance relaxed, and Richard was horrified to see
that Vogelsang and Work, sitting on either side of the
boss, were altering the timepiece. While Gene engaged Sam in talk, George would set the hands back.

Presently Sam consulted his watch. "Only 10:30," he exclaimed, "fine! Let's have another bottle." Later on Gene winked to George, and this time the watch was put several hours ahead. "Gosh," Sam cried when he noticed it, "one o'clock! Well, the train's gone now, may as well make a night of it." The evening ended about two, with Sam running furiously toward Penn Station believing he was about to catch the 12:50.

When they first took the trouble to gull Richard he was wise enough to realize that it was really a social compliment and implied that he was accepted as one of the gang. Like all the most successful jokes it was completely idiotic and unexpected. He was checking up a count of some books in one of the stockroom bins when he heard a voice round the corner of the next aisle. It said: "What's the name of that queer-looking old coon in the shipping department?" To which another voice replied: "His name's Roe. Extraordinary old specimen, and all his family are just like him." Richard was caught off guard and looked round the corner, where he saw Gene and George grinning at him.

The pivot on whom the Sales Department really revolved was Miss McCoy, Sam Erskine's solid, middle-aged, and competent secretary. She was always known as Miss Mac, for her given name, Birdie, was too grotesquely inappropriate to be employed face to face. In her was incarnate the traditional and proper attitude of satire which a Sales Department feels for the literary staff. Even Daisy Erskine hesitated to venture into the Trade Room when Miss Mac was present, for Miss Mac's comments though not very audible were annihilating. Gray-haired and with an appear-

ance of great firmness round the bust, she sat very
erect at her typewriter desk and answered two telephones in a calm competent voice. She wasted few
words, and what she first approved in Richard was
that she saw he also was a sparse talker. The boys
had learned that any remark she meditated was usually
withheld until she had finished the page she was typing. Her gray eyes, very large and clear behind glasses,
shifted impassively between her notebook and the
machine, with brief flashes toward anyone who was
speaking. One had to wait until the page was complete. The boys always tilted their heads a little, for
she spoke low. Then there was the rip of the paper
pulled crisply from the carrier, and her comment followed immediately, dramatized and pointed by this
sharp sound. Gene Vogelsang was particularly good at
eliciting her best sayings. "I see Daisy has some fresh
flowers on her desk this morning," he might say. Miss
Mac, apparently paying no attention, would go on with
her typing or telephone, quite unmoved. But as the
pattering ceased Gene would cock his ear carefully.
Zip! out came the sheet of paper, and as she methodically removed the carbon she would say, "Johnny Jonquil must be in town. You better go out and sell some
books." This was her name for a sentimental poet who
had once brought Daisy an armful of flowers and had
announced in tones of innocent simplicity, "Jonquils
for your equinox."

Miss Mac observed that any call paid by authors
upon Mrs. Erskine was usually followed almost at
once by an inquiry to the Trade Room as to how
many copies had been sold. In the case of Daisy's
favorite poets this was often embarrassing. So Miss
Mac had devised the stratagem of asking the poet to

sign a copy of his book for each of the salesmen. This
distracted him from morbid inquiries, and the autographed copies were tossed into a bin underneath the
display rack. Miss Mac was herself a great reader,
but (as Gene said) she didn't suffer over it the way
Daisy did. Daisy's office was lined almost to the ceiling with inscribed photos of authors; Miss Mac preferred as decoration a good lithographed advertising
cut-out. But she always carried a book home with her
at night in the subway, conscientiously turning the
jacket inside out, for she disliked to have other people
know what she was reading. "I give Erskines' all my
time in the office," she said. "I don't have to advertise
their stuff for 'em in the subway." Richard soon
learned that tips from Miss Mac were worth consideration.

It was a casual remark of Miss Mac's that first
interested Richard in the only Erskine book he ever
really studied with care. A new edition of the Erskine
Atlas was in preparation, but before it came out it was
desired to dispose of some lingering stock of the early
issue. Richard, coming in to his desk in a corner of
the Trade Room, found a memorandum from Sam
instructing him to offer 1,500 copies of the old edition
to a specialist in remainders. He hunted up a sample
copy of the book and was examining it.

"That's the best book we ever published," said Miss
Mac. "What you find in that book you can believe."

It was true. The Atlas had been the rock on which
the business was really founded. Much money had
been spent on it, the maps were accurate and well
printed. As Richard turned the pages Miss Mac left
her typewriter and came to look over his shoulder.

"I never look at it without a thrill," she said calmly. Richard was astonished at the thought of the austere Miss Mac being thrilled by anything. She pointed to a chart of winds and ocean currents. "Just look at those names," she said. "Doesn't it make your blood move faster? Look at them! South-east Monsoon, Roaring Forties, Equatorial Current, Great Australian Bight! That's what I call poetry, not the stuff Johnny Jonquil writes. I can sit here in a corner of this dingy office and see green water and black weather go roaring across the world. That isn't just paper and blue ink, it's an ocean. Look at those lines of railroad running through the United States. Here's Cincinnati—I can see Herman Schmaltz arriving at the station and going out to call on the trade. Those boys take it all for granted. When I ask Schmaltz whether the Middle West looks like other places he can't even answer me. My, what an education a travelling man could get if he kept his eyes open. Remember that, young fellow, when they send *you* on the road."

XIV

The Railway Guide

Another book which he used to see lying in the office also caught Richard's fancy. It was a thick-bound volume always carefully consulted by the sales boys before going off on their travels. Richard found it more to his taste than most fiction. It was called *The Official Guide of the Railways and Steam Navigation Lines of the United States, Canada, Mexico and Cuba*. It was filled with time-tables and the rather violently simplified maps of railroad companies, in which the route of the company under consideration is shown as strong and direct as possible while all the others are very spider-web. In odd moments Richard would pore over this massive concordance and gathered much miscellaneous information. The names of the famous limited trains sounded to him like bugle calls in the distance.

What a fascinating book it is. The old copy that first enthralled Roe is long since vanished, but Hubbard stopped in at Brentano's to buy a new one—over 1,600 pages of strong American romance for $2.00. His patriotism was a little startled to find advertisements of English railways in the forefront of the work, calmly announcing themselves as *The Fastest Train Service in the World*.

It was the smaller railroads of the Middle West or South that seemed like fairy tales to Richard. The Detroit, Toledo & Ironton: you leave Detroit at 8:15 a.m and arrive in Ironton 7:05 p.m. (just in time for dinner, he reflected)—no passenger trains on Sundays. Or the Green Bay & Western: you would rise very early, in that bright Wisconsin air, and have coffee and fried ham. The train leaves at 6:50: how clear the birch trees would stand round Lake Winnebago. And after passing through Scandinavia, Plover, Independence, Arcadia, you would be in Winona (213.9 miles) at 2:50 p.m. or maybe take the branch line up to Sturgeon Bay; even more thrilling, see the dotted line across Lake Michigan, the "car ferry" (magic sound) to Ludington. That would lead on toward White Cloud, Owosso, Saginaw, Ann Arbor. Names read in newspapers or seen in the office files or overheard in salesmen's talk suddenly became real.

The Railway Guide became Richard's Outline of History, his Story of Philosophy. There was the Toledo, Peoria & Western ("The Peoria Road") which doesn't seem to go near Toledo at all on its own rails, but begins at Effner, Indiana. He found himself in imagination on a Mixed Train ("passenger service connections uncertain") passing a long night on the way to Keokuk. Number 3 leaves Effner at 8:30 p.m. It arrives Peoria Yard at 5:20 a.m. There must be a chance for coffee and sinkers at Peoria Yard? And he would go out on Number 103 (good old Number 103!) at 7:45, arrive at Keokuk 2:30 p.m.—"Is there a bookstore in Keokuk?" he asked Miss Mac.

There were greater names too. Denver & Rio Grande; the Monon Route, more formally listed as the Chicago, Indianapolis & Louisville. That would take you through French Lick, on the *Tippecanoe* or the *Hoosier* or the *Daylight Limited* ("observation library car"). The Norfolk & Western offers the *Pocahontas* and the *Cavalier.—Pocahontas* leaves Norfolk at 1:20 p.m. and gets you to Cincinnati at 7:55 the next morning—and from the window you see Roanoke, Blue Ridge, Lynchburg, Appomattox, Disputanta. Perhaps you're on the Pocahontas, Goodwill & Wenonah branch: if so, "stops to take revenue passengers, and to leave passengers from Hagerstown and Shenandoah Junction." Surely you are a better American for brooding on these names.

The Nickel Plate was a road he often heard Herman Schmaltz mention with casual familiarity. Herman, he figured out, would be leaving Fostoria at 11:35 a.m. (Eastern time) and proceeding via Arcadia (you'd be surprised how many Arcadias there are), Findley, Lima (Central time here), Coldwater, Fort Recovery, Muncie. Probably he would stop over at Muncie, before going on to Montmorenci, Otterbein, Oxford, Boswell, East Lynn, Arrowsmith, Bloomington.

The Pere Marquette, another name to start one reading history. Again an early start: leave Port Huron 6 a.m., and through Teddo, Palms, Harbor Beach, Tyre, Bad Axe, to Pointe aux Barques. Does the name Bad Axe give a vivid picture of some old lumberman's disgust, now memorized forever?

The Southern time-tables were rich in suggestion: he saved up many questions to ask George Work when the latter returned from his "territory." Consider the minor twigs of the Chesapeake & Ohio company: the Hawk's Nest branch, Horse Creek branch, Loup Creek and White Oak branch, Piney River and Paint Creek branch. Or, on the luxurious side, here is *The Sportsman* to Old Point Comfort ("observation lounge, radio equipped"—that, of course, is of later era) and *The F.F.V.* to White Sulphur Springs ("imperial salon cars"). The subsidiaries of the Southern Railway: the Asheville & Craggy Mountain, the State University Railroad. The *Crescent Limited* to New Orleans ("women's lounge, shower bath, maid and manicure service, movable chairs, magazines, writing desk"); the *Ponce de Leon* to Florida. Names on the map—Manassas, Brandy, Culpeper, Rapidan, Charlottesville, Sweetbriar, Winesap, Alta Vista.—The steamers on the Chesapeake—"leave Baltimore on Tuesday, Thursday and Saturday for York River Landings. The Old Bay Line: Table d'hote dinner $1.25—dining room in gallery, upper deck forward." The Mobile & Ohio, Seaboard Air Line (the *Orange Blossom Special*). The little Maryland & Pennsylvania Railroad, loved as "The Ma and Pa," from Baltimore to York, Pa., 77 miles in 4½ hours. The Aberdeen & Rockfish in North Ca'lina—leave Aberdeen 8:35 a.m., arrive Fayetteville (45 miles) 10:50. The Mauch Chunk Switchback Railway, "cable and gravity road to Mount Pisgah: distance of circuit 18 miles. The oldest railroad in the U.S."—The Cairo, Truman & Southern, "in operation for Freight and Passenger Service from Weona Junction, Ark., to Weona, Ark. (3.83 miles)." This good little outfit was evidently a family affair. President, J. H. Tschudy. First Vice-President, Jay Tschudy. Second

Vice-President, E. W. Tschudy. Third Vice-President, Philip Tschudy. Treasurer and General Manager, R. H. Tschudy. Secretary and Traffic Manager, Fred Tschudy.

Bigger game by contrast: The Atlantic Coast Line with its *Florida Special, Palmetto Limited,* the *Tar Heel* (New York to Wilmington, N.C.), the *Flamingo,* the *Dixie Flyer* (to Jacksonville). Illinois Central: the *Creole* and the *Chickasaw.* The M.K.T., always known as The Katy, proud of the *Blue Bonnet,* the *Texas Special,* the *Katy Limited.* "There is no pleasanter courtesy," said The Katy, "than to be invited into the diner for afternoon tea and to have the steward suggest and provide chess, checkers or dominoes for games."—Richard thought with renewed admiration of these giants of the travelling leagues who had shared such transcontinental amenities.

There is no end to the lure of these names. You see the little flags fluttering, smoke pouring from squat racing funnels, the flicker of roaring wheels, tail-lights on a midnight curve. The *Sooner,* the *Alamo Special,* the *Lone Star.* St. Louis Southwestern proclaims the *Blue Streak,* "America's Fastest Freight Train." Chicago & Northwestern is perhaps as poetic as any in its christenings: The *Corn King Limited* (with "Solarium Sleeping Car"), the *Mountain Bluebird,* the *Columbine,* the *Gold Coast Limited,* the *Portland Rose,* the *Nightingale,* the *Viking,* the *Badger State Express.* From the "Solarium Sleeping Car" greet Pocatello, Minidoka, Boise, Pendleton, Spokane, Tacoma, Seattle. Or the Union Pacific: the *Oregon Trail Express,* the *Yellowstone Express,* the *Pony Express,* the *Owl* ("sleepers parked in Seattle for occupancy until 8 a.m."). The Southern Pacific and its proud *Sunset Limited* and *Argonaut,* on which "charity, D.V.S., employe, live stock contract, banana messenger and circus scrip tickets will be honored in coaches only." The *Sunbeam,* the *Lark,* the *Apache.* And here he imagined ventures into Mexico. Leave El Paso 11:15 a.m., and by way of Ciudad Juarez, Montezuma, Chihuahua, Jimenez, Torreon, Aguascalientes, Queretaro, reach Mexico City 10 a.m., two days later.

The Santa Fe, with its Fred Harvey Dining Car Service—how Sam Erskine, who used to "make the Coast," spoke of those royal meals. The *Chief,* the *Navajo,* the *Missionary.* "Because of late hour of arrival at the Petrified Forest Detour, trains 23 and 24 temporarily discontinued." "Frequently the Grand Canyon Limiteds are stopped at dining stations for the evening meal, offering patrons choice of dining aboard the train or at one of our artistic station-hotels." "Hollywood Stars and the Stars in every Profession and Business go Santa Fe and ride the *Chief.*"

Alternative temptation, to go Chicago, Milwaukee & St. Paul—America's Longest Electrified Railroad. The *Olympian,* "the first transcontinental roller-bearing train." The *Pioneer* (Chicago to Minneapolis). The *Sioux.* The *Tomahawk.* Or the C.B. & Q. The *Aristocrat,* the *American Royal,* the *Overland Express.* The Great Northern: The *Empire Builder* "saves a Business Day between Chicago and Puget Sound." The Canadian Pacific: the *Dominion,* the *Kootenay Express, Soo Express,* the *Red Wing,* the *Alouette,* the *Royal York.*

Wasn't there once something in Homer known as the Catalogue of Ships? Was it any more thrilling than this muster of trains and stations? Sometimes, studying the Railway Guide, you find yourself a long way from Fifth Avenue. Perhaps aboard the Alaska Railroad (run by the Department of the Interior) whose little chart marks coal and gold fields and Big Game District. Or it may be the Norfolk & Mobjack Bay Steamboat Company; or the Pensacola, St. Andrews, and Gulf steamers, where the *Tarpon,* 450 tons, "connects with all steamers on the Choctawhatchee and Blackwater Rivers." Or, if you're shipping freight, what about "The Poker Fleet, steamers *Ace, King, Queen, Jack,* and *Ten,*" freight service between Buffalo, Detroit, and Duluth? There's the Passamaquoddy Ferry & Navigation Co., of Lubec, Maine; and the Grace Line to Valparaiso, Antofagasta, Tocopilla, Iquique, Cerro Azul, Callao, Guayaquil, Esmeraldas, Buenaventura, Balboa. Queer we make so much of the romance of Europe and forget there's plenty in the Two Americas. What of the Compañia Ferrocarril Mexicano del Norte, the Ferrocarriles Unidos de Yucatan (see the ruins at Uxmal), the Toluca & San Juan Railroad (narrow gauge), the map and time-tables of the Ferrocarriles Nacionales de Mexico: standard gauge, 6,860 miles; narrow gauge, 1,512 miles? (Traffic suspended between Cadena and Dinamita, also between Guadalupe and Ojo Caliente. Wish we knew why.)

The Railway Guide, perhaps even more than the Erskine Atlas, made the curved and steel-netted surface of the earth actual to Richard. When Miss Mac saw him poring over these time-tables she knew he was a Born Salesman.

XV

"Like a Lover"

Sitting in the little inside room at Jules's, Hubbard could overhear jets of conversation from the group round the big table in the kitchen. He was alone, waiting for George Work to join him. The kitchen was packed with strong noisy life: it seemed to flow like a current through the openings, along the dingy passage where the coats hung; pressed against the barred basement door. There was the sharp crackle and hiss of cooking, the soft slam of the ice-box door as Jules drew out meats, the comfortable grumble of men's voices thinking while they ate. Through the basic savors of lamb, garlic, gravy, cauliflower, vinegar, and tobacco smoke came a cool whiff of vermouth. Jules was incessantly busy, both hands and face. His swarthy complexion glistened with warmth and pleasure. Compounding a human mixture is not less artful than shaking a cocktail. Jules moved round and round that table like a spoon in a saucepan. He gurgled and cackled with laughter, he added some mysterious spice of bonhomie which gave the gathering its good human tang. Unknown to himself and them, he raised his clients to great heights. They took their ease. The plotting mind, enemy of poetry, was off duty. Analogy and anecdote ran like perfume in men's brains. Meanings that never occurred before suddenly spread over common things. They grinned at each other, appraised and admired the comedy of one another's faces. The warm fluid air was crowded with talk. Unexpected cargo of words appeared from nowhere: words explored, radiated, ran along nerves of new excitement. They did not know they had so many words in their lungs.

There was a subtle rhythm in that rumbling smoky sound. Hubbard, waiting alone and deciding on a rye highball, listened sensitively—not to catch meanings but to identify the measure. First a passage of low leisurely undertone; then a cackle from Jules; a brief pause; perhaps Madame's interpolated murmur. Then an upward slope of timbre, a quickening tempo. The acute listener perceives a little increase in potential: half a dozen instinctive virtuosos, without knowing it, are approaching an artistic climax. The voices, all different, overlap in sudden dissonance; seem to withdraw politely from each other—then a glorious fraction of suspense: joy such as the maestro must feel in that fifth of a second while the baton holds in lifted premonition. Perfect creative expectancy . . . and then one other voice comes in, just on the needed slant of time and tone and accent. The clear bubble of human intercourse is exploded in sudden crash of uncalculated laughter. Will you orchestrate that for me, Respighi? *Moderato—animato—lento espressivo— molto vivace.* These performers are specially adept in the brass and wind instruments.

The theme resumes. Clink of cutlery, hiss of stove, rattle of ice, scrape of chairs, go cheerily on until the next crescendo. Madame, smiling and beautiful, says little but is madonna of the scene. She knows that men are children; like children they get severely punished. She does not grudge them their illusions of the moment.

Heavens, I did not mean to deal with the scene in detail. I only intended to say that, sitting there, Hubbard overheard one remark that stuck in his head. It was one of those chance epigrams that shoot out from a scrimmage of conversation like a puck from a mellay of hockey players: "A good salesman is like a lover."

George Work came in, apologetic for being late, handsome and charming as ever, adorably shy behind that easy chaff of his. Hubbard quoted the line to him. "George, did it ever occur to you, a good salesman is like a lover?"

There was an understanding evasive flash in George's clear hazel eyes. How does one ever guess, or record, the bland childlike wisdom—and mischief—in that impish person? Just a playboy, you thought perhaps? No, I see him carrying things even heavier than bags of books when no one is looking. He leaves them round street corners or in hotel bedrooms when he goes calling on a customer. You would seek in vain to guess his horrors—or any man's—by direct approach. Most elusive of Big Game, how does one trail the human animal? Be yourself, George, I am not watching! I'm looking the other way.

"Well," he said, "there's no harm in being attentive. What about a little drink?"

It was by George Work falling ill that Richard had his first chance to go on the road. George came down with flu the night before he was to leave for the

South. Sam Erskine was in a ferment, because he thought he'd have to make the trip himself. Sam had done a lot of travelling in his day, but he had grown stout and perhaps a little lazy; also he had a bad habit, for the sake of clinching a startling deal, of offering discounts that were much too lavish. Some of his orders sounded magnificent when they came snorting in by wire, but when the details were haggled out later by the accounting department there was bitterness in the private office. "My God, Sam," said his brother Joe (the president of the company, and parboiled by years of controversy with printers and binders: he had charge of the manufacturing department). "Who do you think you are when you visit the Trade? Ophelia? Don't you wear anything but a nightgown and flowers among all those tough booksellers?"—Sam's terms had to be backed up, as he was a member of the firm, but they caused much indignation among The Boys themselves who afterward had to cover the same territory and restrain the customers from delusions of a golden age.

Anyhow, in this emergency, Sam was ready to play ball. As usual he was rather enjoying the sensation of doing a lot of things at once: dictating memos and telegrams to Miss Mac, calling for a messenger to go and get his bag, belaboring the Accounting Department for a post-mortem on certain perished accounts. The classic description of this state of mind is Cæsar's note in the *Gallic War:* "Everything had to be done by Cæsar at one time." The Sales Room was in a turmoil when Richard returned from one of his humble embassies among the jobs and remainders. He happened to hear Sam exclaiming: "I'll stop off at Cincinnati on the way. I know damn well Herman isn't getting the quantities he ought to from John Kidd. What time does that afternoon train leave for Cincy?"

Richard had not brooded in vain over the Railway Guide.

"Four o'clock, Penn Station," he said. "The Cincinnati Limited."

"Fine," said Sam. "Miss Mac, phone for a reservation. Let's see, there must be a sleeper from Cincy to Nashville, ain't there?"

"Sure," said Richard. "Leave Cincinnati 11:05 p.m. on the Louisville & Nashville."

"Holy cat, Roe, do you know these time-tables by heart? Is there an owl from Nashville to Atlanta?"

"Yes, sir, you can leave Nashville 1:30 a.m., be in Atlanta for breakfast."

Sam leaned back in his swivel chair and took a long look at Richard. For an instant, in the creak of the thick spring under the seat there was the sound of another small destiny changing gears. Sam glanced at Miss Mac, and she gave an imperceptible nod. Like Cæsar he could make shrewd and sudden decisions when he had to. With comfortable relief, also, he reflected that he need not spend three weeks in the rolling jails of Pullman.

"Look here," he said to Richard, "*you* make this trip. Can you leave this afternoon? Go right home and get your bag. I'll switch Herman down to the South, just for this once, and you can make a try-out in the Middle West."

"A good salesman is like a lover." Certainly it was in the mood of high and tender romance that Richard approached his prentice wooing. The city of Harrisburg, capital of the great commonwealth of Pennsylvania, was the first rendezvous in his hastily planned itinerary. Like so many earnest lovers, he found the road strewn with unexpected boulders. He arrived late that evening, dreaming of generous orders. The legislature had just convened, the myriad schemers of that fecund state had gathered round the honeycomb, the hotel was full. The best they could offer him was a mattress spread on top of the grand piano in the hotel ballroom. He lay awake listening to the snores of political lobbyists disposed in cots along the wall. When finally he slept he was startled by some gerrymandering tippler who celebrated the resumption of specie payments by playing the piano at midnight. He consoled himself by imagining that this influx of politics should mean a demand for literature. But the next day he found Harrisburg disappointing. "My boy," said a grizzled bookseller, "politics and literature sleep in separate beds."

But the true lover is not easily dismayed. Richard never forgot Harrisburg; even years afterward he kept in touch, by occasional letter, with his first out-of-town customer. The orders were small, but the friendship was large. It was on that trip, after a week of weariness and discouragement, that he suddenly found himself whistling. He realized, with a shock of real embarrassment, that people liked him.

He began to learn the elements of the familiar routine. Lunchroom counters and the ketchup bottle. (When a travelling man dies he is crystalline with benzoate of soda.) Interurban trolleys. The definite equator across the middle of a lower berth. The fact that news means almost nothing when read in a strange newspaper. The peculiar freemasonry of understanding between travelling men and Pullman porters. And—most important of all—the philosophy of the Swindle Sheet. Like all beginners he wasted infinite time in itemizing every smallest expense. Each newspaper, shoe-shine, tip and taxi went carefully into his notes. He almost swooned with shame when he found that there was $1.35 he could not account for and which he must enter as *Incidentals*. As a result the bookkeeping department held up the account for weeks, and Sam had to expound the world-wide doctrine.

"Look at here, Roe," he said, "don't put all these picayune items down on your expense account. There's only supposed to be three kinds of amusements in the world, Wine, Women, and Song. Same way, there's only three kinds of expenses the accounting department can bear to listen to—Carfare, Hotels and Meals. Don't use that word *Incidentals,* it always makes trouble. If you've got anything you can't remember, or you don't want to remember, write it down *Entertaining Buyers.* A good manager doesn't waste time worrying about salesmen cheating on expenses. I never took a trip yet I wasn't out of pocket. When a man stacks up against the Road he deserves the best he can get. An accounting department will pass 'most anything as long as they don't have to ask questions about it. Sure, get your hair cut; I can't afford to have you running around like a damned lyric poet; but don't write it down."

In the discussion of that perennial topic, Ethics of the Road, Sam struck just the right note of easy chaff. George Work came in from a long trip and the Trade Department gang sat down to lunch at Mouquin's.

George unguardedly remarked that he didn't want much, he had indigestion.

"Sometimes they don't eat for three days after they get in from the road," said Sam. "Too much rich food on the Swindle Sheet. George, you shouldn't always pick out the most expensive stuff on the menu. Don't you ever notice the specials? They usually print them in blackface type."

George, who did not always recognize a joke quite fast enough, replied indignantly that he had positively stinted himself to keep down expense.

"On those Southern roads," Sam continued, "try drinking lots of water. It mixes with the soot and forms clinkers inside you. Then you don't need to eat so much."

About this time someone would remember the old story of George overtaken by conviviality at a convention in St. Louis. When the time came for itemizing his expenses, there was fifty dollars that he couldn't account for. It did not seem to have flowed through any of the recognized sluices. George pondered the matter; he did not dare increase any of the existing items; finally he put it down thus: *To upholding the honor of Erskine Brothers, $50.* He waited anxiously while Sam examined this entry. Finally Sam said something that endeared him to The Boys forever. "Well, George, if you really upheld the honor of Erskine Brothers for fifty bucks, it was a bargain."

And watch out for practical jokes, was another advice of Sam's. Old Herman Schmaltz, who was timid about women, got well hooked one time. He was in his room at the hotel, there was a political convention on and lots of trollops floating about. The boys saw that Herman had his door open on account of hot weather;

they persuaded one of the broads to go up to his room. As soon as she got inside she was to lock the door, throw the key through the transom, and yell. She thought it was a grand steer and went one better: she took off her dress and put on a theatre cloak. Then she followed instructions. The boys were waiting down the hall—when they heard the screech they tiptoed along the corridor and listened. Herman was nervously ejaculating, "Keep away from me, keep away; I don't want to have anything to do with you." After tormenting him awhile by telephone from another room, they unlocked the door and pretended to be very much shocked.

"Like a lover" was the phrase that started George Work on various lines of exposition, which would take long to cover. But I am thinking, more sentimentally, of the tomb of Andrew Jackson which George once described in recalling his visits to Nashville. In the garden of the lovely old Hermitage, Andrew Jackson is buried under a graceful marble canopy, and near by is the humble grave of his old colored body-servant. A small stone says simply: *Uncle Alfred, aged 98 years. Faithful servant of Andrew Jackson.* Perhaps some day when literature retires to rest in a lofty stone mausoleum there will be room alongside it for an unpretentious burial—that of its faithful and humorous servant, the publisher's salesman.

XVI

Morningside Park

THE Sixth Avenue L runs like a spinal thread through the story of Richard Roe. Sometimes, as I climb its tremulous old stilts or look off at its varied glimpses of surprise, I think what a book it would make. Who could write the History of the Sixth Avenue L? *Harlem train, Harlem train,* I hear those grizzled little men saying as they swing the iron gates open in the late afternoon traffic. Where do they find, for their conductors and platform guards, so many cheerful little grandfathers, all of the honest sexton type? I suppose that somewhere, lurking behind old mahogany roll-top desks or shopping demurely at Best's and Altman's, there are stockholders of the Sixth Avenue Road. I suppose it is not just a phenomenon of Nature that goes instinctively on: there must be power-plants, blue-prints, diagrams, inventories, all the appalling detail of any large human scheme. But I accept it as Richard did, one of the miracles. Its gruesome lavatories, its wooden counters eroded by the slide of coins, its schedules of lectures on Botany (which I never see anywhere else), the

chant of wheels grinding round curves, the breath of
pure air and sunlight on its morning platforms, all
these are part of my picture. The subway is all very
well for poets: There the busy mind is involved upon
itself, you speed through roaring darkness with flashes
of inward light. But the L is for historians, who cannot help gazing outward upon chaos disposed in rec-
tangles. Architects and Regional Planners deplore the
old L, as well they may. Yet I have seen beauty and
amazement from its palpitating trestles. Remember,
O proud posterity, that it once ran like a winding nerve
of feeling through our middle-class romance.

When Richard began work for Erskine Brothers,
he and Lucille were living somewhere off Manhattan
Avenue, below Morningside Park. It was a dark little
cell-block in one of the crosstown streets, but within
easy reach of the broad walks and rocky terraces of
Morningside Park where Baby Gladys had her earliest
impressions of life. Gladys was born, I gather, about
1911—a Taurus child; these are always difficult in
temperament, an astrologer assured Lucille. Gladys's
earliest memories were associated with roller-skating,
which perhaps accounted for her subconscious idea that
life was intended to move smoothly on wheels. But also
there were severe bumps on the many flights of stone
steps that scale the Morningside ramp. The greatest
joy of her early childhood was when the delightful
bronze of *Bear and Faun* was put there. Under an
overhanging ledge sits a goat-boy, listening with
startled air; above, a big brown bear has crawled up
the rock, flattened on his belly, and leans over with
scooping paw hoping to surprise the young Pan. Gladys
was then about three years old, and was one of the

first of the children whose clambering admiration has
brightened the bear's heels and polished his inquisitive
nose. Richard had to reassure her many times that the
bear didn't get the boy. Pan's goat-legs always puzzled her, and it was characteristic of her to remark, a
few years later, "My legs are prettier than that."

Morningside Park is one of New York's pleasantest places—not often visited from above, for the climb
back is severe for the very young. Consequently there
is an imaginary social division: Manhattan Avenue
lifts its eyes aspiringly toward Morningside Drive and
the half-built cathedral; at night it sees the lighted
windows of bishops and university officers and con-
ceives the Upper West Side as a high social plateau.
Of this Lucille was very conscious; she was secretly
indignant that Herman and Hazel lived above that
Tarpeian Rock among the glamours of Broadway and
subway, while she, now submerged in domestic pressures, inhabited a push-button apartment. For her, to
live in an apartment without an elevator was a painful grievance. Even when mild sunshine lay peaceful
upon the park and Gladys was absorbed in play so that
Lucille could really settle down in the sedentary comfort for which women are so charmingly cushioned,
she was aware of that steep rampart behind her. She
detested Hazel's innocent remark, "I'm coming *down*
to see you."

The incredibly high curve of the L bounds the park
on the south, and seems its only obvious exit toward
the more dazzling world which Lucille coveted. But
the L seemed to her a plebeian, even a rustic sort of
carriage. Her theatrical instinct leaned always toward
artificial lights; show people are more at home in the
subway.

Such thoughts did not visit Richard. The L was there, and he used it. Even in after years he remembered that there were ninety-five steps up to the station platform at 110th Street, and he knew them all. Hurrying toward the office in the morning he usually did not wait for the ancient and crowded elevators. It is a good sign when a young father, in a new job, prefers to run up ninety-five steps. One of the things I like about Richard is that it did not often occur to him to feel sorry for himself. After all he did not ask very much of life (few men do until too late). To have a job that offered reasonable possibility of advance, to have a home to return to at night, this was plenty. As the train swung off round that huge dangerous curve every morning he looked off at the little park as proudly as though it were his own private estate. All through the day, Lucille and the baby were in the background of his mind. Even the drudgeries of his work were irradiated by this new sense of security. Daisy Erskine, seeing in him a willing horse, kept loading him with sets of galley proofs of the new novels. She had abandoned hope of getting the senior salesmen to read books in galley form. But Richard was still young enough to regard it as a compliment. Galleys are an infernal nuisance to read, but to Richard they seemed the symbol of being an insider in a lofty affair. He would rummage out a long scroll of them from his pocket and study them on the L, rather proud to see other passengers wondering.

Miss Mac remembers a queer little incident. There was a manuscript, much talked about in the office, which seemed to be a special favorite of Daisy's. Some of the others had doubts about it: it was the kind of thing considered risky in those simple days. But

Daisy's emancipation from shock was complete. There was a curious air of purpose in her request to Richard when she asked him to read the script and tell her what he thought about it. Whatever may have been in her mind, apparently Richard missed it. Extremely busy just then with Sam's J'n'R's, he reported simply that "Lucy didn't like it," as if that ended the matter. —Daisy was furious.

Knowing now, as we do in this inverted perspective, that things later worked out more prosperously, there is an almost unhandsome satisfaction in contemplating the grievances of that era. The apartment was small and inconvenient, and in a neighborhood where there were many Spanish-Americans whom Lucille generalized as dagoes. She herself, born Lucille Geschwindt, had the Teutonic blonde's suspicion of any tint of amber in the skin. Money was scarce, and they had no regular maid. Although they became later the most inseparable cronies, she resented her daughter in those early years. She had imagined a stage career for herself, or at least years of delightful excitement in the box-office, and the unexpected arrival of Gladys seemed to her a bit of carelessness on Richard's part. But she was a creature of surprising energy and did not spare herself in the household tasks. She was not content unless Gladys outshone all the other children of Morningside Park, in smart bonnets or corkscrew ringlets or embroidered breeks. If the child looked pale she would even make her up with a touch of rouge to harrow the nursemaids of more sallow races. As a result of these endless ardors, when Richard came home at evening he often found her exhausted. Then his guileless anecdotes of what had happened at the office were, to his amazement, cause for indignation. Little could he guess that he was innocently operating on the oldest and most dangerous human fallacy. He had given a woman a home and a child, and in his simplicity he supposed that was enough. But what women require is endless diversion, as imperative in their being as the changes of the moon. And Lucille, convinced by experience that the life of offices is highly entertaining and that men's complaints of incessant toil are just a cunning stratagem, was increasingly annoyed by Richard's stories of publishing humors. They reminded her too sharply of the days when she also had a part in the great mellay of affairs.

No one will ever be able to pay sufficiently exquisite tribute to the nice oddity of chance which halts our human roulette on such and such a color. I know of one who became a person of large doings because on a day he wore, by accident, the wrong pair of trousers. They sorted very ill with his upper gear; consequently, that day, instead of trotting all about the office as usual, he remained assiduous at his desk with the incongruent pantaloons well hidden. He summoned to him all those from whom he required information, even asking the head of the firm, by telephone, to step in when he next went by. He discovered, by the end of the day, that he had dispatched more business than he usually did in a week; he wasted no time in genial to-and-fro; he strongly impressed valuable customers by not rising from his chair. He remained bashfully until all his colleagues had gone home, and so happened to catch an important long-distance call. He specialized in staying at his desk thereafter. By sitting still he rose to the top of the tree. It was the sheer hazard of a wrong pair of trousers.

It was no less a matter of chance that set off long
series of events for Lucille and Richard. Lucille had
noticed, with increasing annoyance, that the name of
Daisy Erskine occurred frequently in Richard's talk
of the office. Not that Lucille was silly enough to be
jealous of Daisy in any technical sense; she shrewdly
divined that Daisy was a good deal of a pseudo-
literary freak, and that the men in the office considered
her a bore. But she frankly envied Daisy (whom she
had never seen) for her amusing occupation, and when
Richard kept bringing home bundles of galley proof
with the remark that Daisy had asked him to read
them, she grew impatient.

"You're at the office all day, aren't you?" she cried.
"When you get back here you can think about giving
me a good time."

Richard protested naïvely that to be given these advance proofs was a mark of confidence, that Mrs.
Erskine was the wife of a member of the firm, that he
couldn't very well refuse; that he had promised
Daisy——

He was sitting by an open window with the long
strips of proof in his lap. At that moment a gust of
wind blew up one of the sheets into Lucille's face.

"The hell with Daisy!" she exclaimed. "She gives
me hay fever." Seizing the mass of proofs she threw
them out of the window. The street was an eddy of
flying leaves, like a snow flurry.

Richard was profoundly shocked. He took business
matters very seriously, and to destroy a set of galley
proofs seemed to him a deplorable impiety. He trudged
downstairs and collected as many of the sheets as possible, but some had vanished beyond retrieve or fluttered on trees and window-ledges. As a matter of fact,

the results of the incident were not regrettable, for Richard determined to sell as many of this book as possible, to atone for the mischance. The author of the work has never guessed why it sold specially well in the Middle West. But this started a dispute which, for the first time, sent Richard off on the road with a feeling of loneliness and grievance. Travellers going through the Panama Canal from Atlantic to Pacific have frequently remarked their astonishment at finding that in this transit they pass from West toward East. (Examination of the Erskine Atlas will confirm this.) Similarly, reflected the philosophic Hubbard, voyagers in the important canal of matrimony are sometimes startled to find themselves navigating by paradox. It is not always by obvious courses that one reaches the ocean of Peace.

XVII

Mrs. Geschwindt

Lucille would never mention the exact address of their Morningside Park era, but Hubbard learned from old Mrs. Geschwindt, the mother of Lucille and Hazel, that it was in the 300 block on West 114th Street, notable still for its wonderful façade of fire-escapes. These fire-escapes were a sore point with poor Lucille, who regarded them as infra dig., a suggestion of East Side tenements. It was on those iron projections that so many of the galley proofs caught and fluttered. But Mrs. Geschwindt had no patience with social pretenses. She was a remarkable old lady, over eighty when Hubbard met her. She was still living with Herman and Hazel, but mostly confined to her room. Her daughters, keenly aware of her freedom of speech, did not afford Hubbard much opportunity to interview her. The hullabaloo of the war years had given them a regrettable sensitiveness about their German inheritance. One of the great triumphs of Mrs. Geschwindt's decline was the last time they took her to the movies. A news-reel picture of the old warrior Von Hindenburg was shown on the screen, and some-

thing of unconquerable human fibre in the aged
shadow brought the audience into unexpected applause.
Mrs. Geschwindt broke into tears and had to be
helped home. Her wrinkled old face, which had no
eyebrows, trembled convulsively. She was too staunch
to say it, but her feeling was that having actually heard
Hindenburg applauded by an American audience she
could die content. And so she did not long afterward.
Hazel had a twinge of honorable pity when she found,
hidden away among the old lady's treasures, a secret
scrapbook where she had pasted the picture of the
Kaiser which they made her abandon during the war.

I wish there were room to dwell upon Mrs. Geschwindt. It would be significant of the endless radiations
that proceed from any nucleus of life. She was born as
long ago as 1850 and came to this country as a child,
just before the Civil War. She still remembered the
ball given in her honor at Meyer's Hotel in Hoboken
when she accepted Mr. Geschwindt. Her daughters
thought her tedious, but she was heartily fond of Richard because he listened with every sign of interest to
her reminiscences. One of the happiest afternoons of
her life was when Richard smuggled her out and took
her to a matinée of the *Black Crook* revival in Hoboken. *The Black Crook* had been the scandal of her
youth—and to see it again in the mellow Teuton air
of Hoboken was paradise regained. They had a glass
of beer afterward at Meyer's, and she described how
the hotel furniture had been arranged fifty years before. Her keen little eyes had observed that some of
the modern *Black Crook* amazons had needed padding
to represent the traditional hour-glass contour; she la-
mented this and embarked upon genial memories of
the age of flesh. She talked German with the waiters,

and when Richard finally got her back to the Schmaltz
apartment she was prostrated with ecstasy and hic-
cups. Herman and Hazel were shocked, and called in
the doctor; but I think myself that the adventure prolonged her life by about two years. She outlived Richard.

How lovely they are, the Old, when the jealousies
and skirmishes have lost their importance. And
specially so, perhaps, old ladies. Woman's years of
maturity are bedevilled by so many imps: the moon,
the hormones, and the clownishness of man. No wonder, if they escape that maze of nerves, they show
themselves so wise and humorous, so tartly humane.
Illusions of grandeur fade away; so much they
anguished over proves of small account. They cherish
laughter—what else is there? Character and comedy
and the beauties of past grievance come out upon the
face. Hurry up and grow old, my dears (I sometimes
think), so I can love you with the detachment you deserve. Why are there not more Old People in novels?
Chaucer and Shakespeare understood about the old.
Mrs. Geschwindt and Cicero would have got along
splendidly. I see all the old people in the world smiling at us as we muddle and fume. They have absorbed
so much more sunlight.

I like them to have their pleasure thinking our antics
don't really matter. They may be wrong.

But this was long afterward; we are talking now of
the Morningside Park epoch—say about 1913–14.
Mrs. Geschwindt, then in the prime of her sixties, was
recently a widow and full of energy. The Schmaltzes,
whose apartment near Riverside Drive was so much
envied by Lucille, found it hard to keep track of her.

The old lady's genetic instincts had never been satisfied with Hazel and Lucille; she needed children to
look after, and horrified Hazel by taking a camp-stool
out to the sunny pavement of Broadway. On one of
those church corners where by Upper West Side tradition curators of children congregate, Mrs. Geschwindt would lie in wait for an interesting baby. Occasionally she could persuade some nursemaid or mother
to entrust the child to her. Her reliability was patent,
and while the grateful woman did her errands or telephoned her young man, Mrs. Geschwindt patrolled the
pavement with the infant. It was a matter of indignation to poor Lucille that her mother seemed more interested in random urchins of Broadway than in her
own granddaughter. Indeed, the old lady's blonde
heart was strangely fascinated by the luxuriant babes
of that region. In those large velveteen eyes, gilded
chubs of skin, and delicious nubbins of soft nose, she
could see in microscope the future lineaments of rabbi
and theatrical producer.

But again it was really the abrupt palisade below
Morningside Drive that caused trouble. Mrs. Geschwindt, though sturdy enough, was short of breath in
climbing stairs; Lucille, until Gladys grew a little older,
could not hoist the baby up those difficult terraces. So,
while Gladys was still in the perambulator era, Mrs.
Geschwindt would look off from the bastions on top
and wave to Lucille far below, with all the grimness
of a grandmother deprived of her rights. And Lucille,
equally wearied in mind and muscle, was the more indignant at this social abyss. It was at the Carl Schurz
statue that Mrs. Geschwindt most often gazed down
upon her sundered grand-offspring; her annoyance
vented itself upon the figure of Mr. Schurz who stands

in bronze holding his hat in hand. Mrs. Geschwindt thought him a German insufficiently imperial in sentiment, and had the good old-fashioned idea that a real German always keeps his hat on.

It was an excellent day when Gladys grew old enough to toddle at least part way up the ascent, and they agreed upon the comfort-station terrace as a convenient compromise meeting-place. Hubbard wondered, when old Mrs. Geschwindt told him all this in her racy way, whether it was that early exercise in climbing which had made Gladys so shapely. About the time the war began in Europe, Mrs. Geschwindt was able to exercise the child along the upper levels of the park, or sit with her in those pentagonal terraces along Morningside Drive, while Lucille did her marketing on 8th Avenue under the enormous L. It was still a very carefully rationed shopping, for Richard's salary was only $40 a week, though the January salesmen's bonus added substantially if the year had been a good one. The bonus of January, 1914, was over $900, and Lucille began to dream of getting away from the L and the fire-escapes.

Another reason for Lucille's resentment was that her brother-in-law Herman had now been shifted to sell Boston and Philadelphia (Boston was considered a big plum for a salesman in those days), and Richard was put on the Middle Western territory. This meant that Herman was at home a good part of the time, while Richard was away. In Hazel's most casual remarks, if one knew how to look, one might discover— even though unintended—allusions to this situation. Not wives of diplomats or cabinet members are more distraught by official precedence than the wives of

travelling men who cover rival routes. In the course
of several years' listening Hazel had learned the
names of many personalities in the Middle Western
trade; when now these names began to appear innocently in Lucille's quotations from Richard, Hazel had
a way of gently corrugating her forehead—or an even
more damning way of saying nothing. Also, Hazel
sometimes accompanied Herman on a business trip to
Boston, and was not loath to give the impression that
she had been brilliantly entertained by the gallant
bibliophiles of the Hub. Richard, immersed in the
ardors of salesmanship, did not suspect the innumerable ways in which affectionate women can make each
other miserable.

For now, travelling the Trade proper instead of the
old casualty list of Jobs and Remainders, he began to
be aware of the fascination of the work. This is something that a salesman rarely puts into expression, but
of which, as an artist, he is keenly conscious. How delightful it is to return to the high spots of his route,
famous bookstores where against that colored tapestry
of bindings he sees friends waiting to greet him. Even
when it is tradition, or good sagacity, for them to pretend that he arrives as a nuisance, both sides know
that is only part of the comedy of human intercourse.
If he is a man well liked, and representing a good line,
he comes not only as a friend and an assistant but
brings something of the aura of romance, adventure,
excitement, that the voyager always brings to the
sedentary. Richard learned the special characteristics
and crotchets of each shop he visited. There was Kitty
Chambers in Cleveland, who would usually be found
in her Poetry corner and always alluded to the time
Daisy Erskine high-hatted her in the New York office.

There was Bill Kromesky in Buffalo who kept a vast
pile of a certain biography stacked up where his eyes
often visited it. Richard offered to take them back, but
Bill wouldn't hear of it. "That's the most valuable
bunch of books in this shop," he said. "I keep 'em
there to remind me never to buy more than fifty copies
of anything."

Richard probably never attempted to analyze the
sensuous impressions of bookstores, but they were real
in his mind. The jumbled colors of the lively jackets,
the faintly sweet odor of print, the quick glance of the
eye by which a salesman can spot his own wares among
so many others, the intuition by which he knows
whether customers are actually buying or just looking,
the tact by which he effaces himself when the clerk is
approached by a customer and yet remains within ear-
shot to hear what is being asked for. Perhaps most
thrilling of all to a man with mercantile curiosity is the
book department in great department stores, where an
island of literature is approached through a surf of
feminine perfume and scuffle. Here there is a crisp
lineny smell, little cuckoo-bells keep absurdly sounding,
there is the distant clang of elevators, the bright eyes
of young nymphs in black muslin seem absurdly frolicsome to be recommending the sombre grievances of
some middle-aged novelist. In the department store,
which is a microcosm of life itself, books find their
relative level: they are on the ground floor, or sometimes on a balcony, but they have to be approached
through other competing delights. At the entrance of
Hack Brothers' store, on a windy day in Detroit, the
revolving doors must have set up a spinning eddy of
air, for as Richard entered he noticed a queer thing.
Some brightly colored little female handkerchiefs, on

the corner of a near showcase, jumped up from the counter, did a dancing twirl, and subsided. He could not believe it at first, and paused to watch. Presently the doors slewed round and it happened again: two scraps of colored tissue leaped upward and somersaulted. It seemed as preposterously magical as everything else in that great bazaar of feminine excitement. He was telling his buyer about it, and a dark girl from the stationery department overheard. "I'm glad we've got *some* merchandise that's active," she said.

XVIII

Hack Brothers

Hack brothers was a big department store. By a process of self-education it was gradually raising itself in the social scale. It is a dangerous transition: the humbler patrons are likely to be scared off more rapidly than the elegant are allured. But Jake and Ed Hack (especially Jake) were canny merchants; they did not hurry their improvement of tone. Like their own personal rise in cash and culture it was steady but almost imperceptible. Little by little window displays became less cluttered, allusions to Fifth Avenue crept into the advertising, even a few French words appeared on the display-cards, with the accents frequently wrong. That was before the time when humor dared to appear in department-store advertising (even now only the firms of absolute top rank venture to trifle with the gravity of the public). It was a serious epoch, the period officially known as Keeping Out of War. If any spot in the store looked a little bare, they solved the problem by planting the American flag there—those special versions of the Stars and Stripes

favored by parade-meisters, with heavy gold fringes.
What an essay could be written, if you found anyone
rash enough to write it, on The Patriotism of Department Stores.

Hack Brothers moved steadily on the up-grade of
refinement. Space was found in the lunch-room for
afternoon lectures on female calisthenics or decorating
the dinner table. Underwear became lingerie, stockings became hosiery, men's clothes became garb,
fashion became The Mode. Floorwalker burgeoned
into floor manager, buyer into merchandising coun-
sellor. Cash carriers that chirped on wires were replaced by concealed pneumatic tubes: people don't like
to see their money flying away from them so obviously.
Ed Hack (but not Jake) took to wearing white piqué
piping on his vest. When they put on a doorman with
huntsman breeches and a cockaded top-hat, Ed's
daughter Genevieve was listed as a possibility for the
Junior League.

The refinement of the department store has been a
subtle phenomenon to watch. Indeed it was effected so
delicately it scarcely occurred to anyone to watch it.
How far the store creates, how far only reflects, those
sudden contagions of behavior that dominate the tribe,
is too nice a question. Sensitive as a standing pool,
beautifully it mirrors its age and its own peculiar culture. Quick as the mind of the artist it catches a hint,
a gleam, a windy ripple of suggestion; then the whole
surface sparkles with glamour, seems to move and flow.
It has raised imitation and quantity to a showman's
art. For those naturally infirm in taste it is even an
æsthetic education. A store with imagination puts on,
every day, a new and astonishing performance, collaborated between itself and its public.

When Richard first knew it, Hack Brothers was in the early stages of this exciting development. Jake Hack had made his great discovery that a department store is not just an enormous push-cart but a kind of theatre. A furniture envoy from Grand Rapids had redecorated the firm's private office with what he called a Jacobean Executive Suite. Jake took the word Jacobean as a personal compliment but he allowed Ed to sit at an uncomfortable replica of a spinet; he himself would not abandon the old yellow rolltop which oozed cigar-smoke from every pigeonhole. From this reeking nerve-center he would make tours of scrutiny round the big building. His comments to the staff were few but pungent. Little Mrs. Beaton, the manager of the book department, was a person of permanent sprightliness; her hair was beautifully white but her eyebrows and disposition were a generation younger. "Selling any books?" asked Jake.

"Once in a while," she replied gaily.

He gazed appraisingly at the loaded counters, considering them as inventory. "Try *all* the while," he remarked.

Jake Hack was interested in the book department, believing that in some mysterious way it added grace and intellect to the store. In the old days, according to a theory of the time, books and stationery and art goods had been neighbored together at the rear of the main floor. The philosophy of this arrangement was rational enough. Silk stockings and gloves and other feminine trifles put the customer into a mood of sentiment. Sentiment suggests correspondence, and one was imperceptibly in the stationery department. Writing

paper led logically towards the idea of reading; reading dissolved into paint-boxes and the graphic arts,
which in turn developed into toys.

But in a hopeful mood the Hacks had been persuaded that their literary patrons would appreciate
more privacy. Books are not just ordinary merchandise, they were assured; they need to be examined in
leisure and along comfortable shelves. Calculations
were even advanced as to the likelihood of customers
getting backache from bending over tables to look at
the volumes. In a flush of idealism Hack Brothers installed the book department in a quadrangle of its
own. Here secluded alcoves were furnished with rugs
and armchairs and glass cases of fine bindings. Toys
and Art Materials were shifted up to the Sporting
Goods floor; only Literature's wistful consort, Stationery, still lingered near her cloistered partner.
Books, so to speak, had taken the veil, but just outside the shrine the worldly sister remained faithful,
consoling herself with samples of nuptial engraving
in which Mr. and Mrs. Gunsaulus Bendix announce the
marriage of their daughter Margaretta Beulah to Mr.
Einar Tastrom.

There were fallacies in this theory of segregating
the book department. In the first place it is dangerous,
in the shopping arena, to give women an opportunity
to sit down. Mr. Hack observed with pain that Milady
(that phantom of the millinery world) was using the
literary alcoves as a rest-room or rendezvous rather
than as a place of purchase. Over the archway that
led into the department a high-minded architect had
painted, in Gothic letters, the legend 𝔅𝔒𝔒𝔎𝔖 𝔄𝔕𝔈
𝔉𝔕𝔌𝔈𝔕𝔇𝔖 𝔗𝔋𝔄𝔗 𝔕𝔈𝔙𝔈𝔕 𝔄𝔊𝔈. This, after the

next ensuing Mark-Down Sale, was found so obviously
untrue that Mr. Hack replaced it by the sturdy and
prosaic statement, in electric bulbs, ENTRANCE TO
BOOK DEPARTMENT.

Another thought might have occurred to Hack
Brothers if they had known more about the matter. It
is over falbalas and fanfreluches, not books, that
women desire to linger and loiter and exercise the
spasms of choice. In regard to books they have usually
made up their minds beforehand; they know exactly
what they want. ("Don't miss it, my dear.") And they
enjoy the bustle and color of the open aisles; enjoy the
skirmish of their many rivals pressing forward with
eager toddle, alert faces turning this way and that like
foraging poultry. To their quick humor it is all the fun
of a social event without the strain of having to be
polite. The quiet backwater of the book department
frightens them just a little.—But the book department had one great advantage, daylight on street
frontage. Mrs. Beaton and her clerks were never so
indignant as when a customer from within the main
store would come pressing through, disregarding their
zealous display of Latest Fiction, merely to verify in
daylight the color of some gay foulard. It was hard
then for plump and mettlesome little Beaton not to be
able to say, with just the right sardonic tone, "And
may I interest you in a little Literature?" Oh, the sum
total of Things Not Said to customers, any day in any
big store.

So Literature sometimes pined a little in the demure
enclosure Hack Brothers had arranged for her. She is
often a bit of a slut, when you get to know her; she
has unduly been ascribed austere and priestess qualities by sentimental spellbinders. She doesn't always

hanker for privacy—not she! She also likes to mingle with the world, to feel the warm tide of grotesque merry living. So it was sporting of her old rival Stationery to stand faithfully by and forward what patronage she could. By arts of suggestion Stationery collaborated. The Shakespeare book-ends on the notepaper counter must have helped. Though Shakespeare's vogue as a book-end didn't really begin until 1916, the 300th anniversary. (Dante had to wait twice as long to become a book-end—until 1921, the 600th year. I think no American author has yet become one of those little bronze buffers. Walt Whitman will be best, his massive head and beard will give plenty of weight.)

All this is a long way of explaining that Stationery was just outside the book department, and it was one of the girls from Stationery who was talking to Mrs. Beaton when Richard came in that morning.

It was one of those days—travelling men know them—when everything seems clear and sensible. He had rested well in the sleeper, shaved with a new blade, reached the hotel in time for a comfortable breakfast. He had been rather precise with the waiter about the details, which is one of the travelling man's compensations. "Grapefruit, coffee with double cream, and a soft roll" was the way he put it. "Don't put any sugar on the grapefruit." And now he was all opened up, which means he had unpacked his sample trunk, built up an engaging little display of books and posters on the bureau in his bedroom, sorted over his stock of jackets and circulars, and was ready to receive the buyers. He put some catalogues in his pocket and set off down Woodward Avenue, the élite highway of that city. The pleasantest thoughts came into his mind. His shoes, newly glossed, were brilliant. His hair, newly trimmed, felt comfortably close to his head and exhaled the faint sweetness of Pinaud. Seeing himself reflected in a shop-window he had one of those rare and exquisite moments of triumph. He was not the plodding drudge, he was an ambassador.

One of those mornings! Everything seemed in just balance and proportion. The gay little handkerchiefs that twirled in air must have been symbolic. He found himself saying just the right things without searching for them. Perhaps because he was conscious of his own barbering he noticed that Mrs. Beaton's hair looked even lovelier than usual. He said so, and asked her what she washed it with. For an ambassador does not plunge into the crude matters of trade, he first establishes a mood of pleasant chat. This is not deliberate craft but only decent manners. The book business, more social than most, elicits a high degree of tact.

Mrs. Beaton (she was very tiny) looked up at him delightfully. She *had* washed her hair the night before and was happy about it. Under his innocent compliments she blossomed. Suddenly she realized that Erskine Brothers had a fine list that season. Richard had sense enough to ask, before mentioning any of his own wares, how a certain Michigan novel was doing, published by another house. It was a local item, and Hacks were plugging it. "Nicely," she said. "We've just ordered another hundred." This made her feel good; without conscious decision she agreed with herself not to make an issue of that Erskine book of which she still had a dozen dead copies. Herman Schmaltz, a year before, had insisted on her taking more than she wished. Oh well, she'd get rid of them at the next Mark-Down.

"Look here, Sam," once said old Joe Erskine (the big tycoon) to the Sales Manager. "I've had a letter from Mrs. Beaton complaining that Herman refused to fill an order for ten copies and made her take fifty. Do our boys *force* the booksellers to overbuy?"

"Well, Joe," retorted Sam, "you know I hire salesmen, not order-takers."

"I'm all opened up," Richard said. "What time do you want to come round and look over the line? Wait till you see the window-display I've got for you on the new Hampton novel. *Carbon Paper*—isn't that a corking title?"

"I lent *you* my advance copy," said Mrs. Beaton, turning to the girl from Stationery. "How did you like it?"

"Slick. It's a good story. If you're going to put in a display I can help out with some stuff. Why not dress the whole window with sheets of carbon paper: it'll look like black velvet if we get the lighting right."

"Fine," said Richard.

"Tell you what we'll do," said Mrs. Beaton. "I'll come round to the hotel late this afternoon and check up the list with you. And there's a dinner of the Book and Stationery Group tonight, just a nice little party, you come along. All the boys and girls in the trade will be there. But don't give away that carbon paper idea to anyone else."

"You've got a swell-looking stationery layout," Richard said to the other. "All that notepaper makes me want to sit down and write letters."

"Go to it," she replied. "Correct for all social usages."

"Who is that kid?" he asked afterward.

"That's Minnie Hutzler, the new buyer in Stationery," said Mrs. Beaton. "She's got a head on her."

XIX

Convention

AT ONE of the annual booksellers' conventions, held in New York many years later, Hubbard met Mrs. Beaton and drew her on to talk of the days when Richard sold Detroit. It was what the trade remembers as the Depression Convention: instead of the traditional four days of sightseeing, hullabaloo, and exhaustion, the program had been cut down to two days of serious argument and only one social event, the Banquet. The famous phrase of independence, "I can Take It, or I can Let It Alone," was originally said about Liquor, but the public had evidently learned that the doctrine can be applied to Literature also. Customers were showing a deplorable majority for the second choice.

"Some fiend in human form," remarked Sam Erskine, "has been spreading the idea that books don't have to be bought, they can also be borrowed." In other words, the overcrowded book business—though far less badly hurt than many others—was having a little painful sense hammered into it. What had been a wide and shallow stream, loitering gaily in the sun,

found itself pouring darkly through the granite canyon of Economic Law. Both booksellers and publishers
had the jitters, a form of neuralgia that all men feel
on first encountering a law that nothing can repeal.

Consequently the business meetings had been even
a little more acrimonious than usual. Each party engaged in the good old human search to find some way
of making the other one admit the guilt for their joint
errors. Things were said more vigorously than they
were meant. Publisher and bookseller, as inextric-
ably interwoven in their functions as husband and
wife, exercised the connubial privilege of endless retort. Then came the banquet, and both sides breathed
a sigh of relief, tacitly agreed to forget their grievances—the more so because at this festival they are
annually twitted by their mutual perplexity, the author.
It was a smaller gathering than usual, but a delightful one. The book trade is compensated for the excep-
tional homeliness of most authors by the high spirits
of its females. Lady booksellers, in their gayest tif-
fanies, were charmingly apparent. Little Bessie Beaton, swathed in black fluff, floated in the dance with
Hubbard. Her lovely white head was beneath the
biographer's chin; her eyebrows also were white now,
but no slippers ever slid the polished floors of Statler
more lightly. As they danced, and he spoke of Richard,
she remembered that old meeting of the Detroit Book
and Stationery Group, seventeen years before.

Hubbard enjoyed the evening; it was not so violently carnival as conventions in the flush decade.
(Grievous to think how soon even this troubled Now
will be idealized as the Good Old Times.) There was
an undercurrent of sobriety; some chance for real talk.

He sat at the Erskine table with several of his former associates. Sam Erskine remarked that in the prosperous times the sales department's appropriation for heyday t the convention had been a thousand dollars. "This year," he said, "it's a hundred."

Yes, they used to shoot the works while they had them. In whatever city the convention was held, the Erskine suite at the hotel was social headquarters. Delightful panorama, never to be forgotten by those who enjoyed it. Regardless of dour official agenda, the cheerier anarchs of the trade would gather at all hours in those plushy hotel chambers to enjoy publishers' cellarage, Room Service, parlor games, and argument on the niceties of commerce. In an adjoining apartment a brace of wives, exhausted by devotions to duty, slept the afternoon away. Wardrobe trunks and dressing tables were foamed and trinketed with the rich apparatus of publishers' womenfolks. On the sitting-room settee snored in peace a prostrate author who had rashly matched his staying power against the Erskineers. While Sam Erskine was out playing golf, his room was occupied by a Bible salesman leading a chorus of Middle Western booksellers in sea chanteys. The Dobson Company's representative was taking a bath in Sam Erskine's tub; he had wagered to provide beer for the syndicate, and his own bath was filled with bottles and ice. In the haze of tobacco and to the jingle of trays borne down the hall, the Erskine gang would sit to bridge or poker. Even the Southern trade, reared on soul-shattering philtres of corn whiskey, did not often ride down that hardy crew. I suppose it sounds unliterary, if you have rigid preconceptions; yet there was more than mere animal frolic in those old-time conventions. They sometimes gave the accounting department the horrors, but they cemented strong and humorous friendships in the trade and begot many a stroke of business. Old Joe Erskine, the boss, was shrewd enough to stay away, so as not to embarrass the boys. Daisy had less sense. Once when she returned from belaboring the College Bookstore meeting on the Potential Sales of Poetry she found a valuable reprint salesman swooned in her room. She complained to Sam, who retorted that their account with Godwin & Dawes was more valuable to them than her feelings. She said she was insulted. "If you don't like the publishing business," said her brother-in-law, "you've always got something nice to fall back on."—They were often rather Elizabethan, these bibliophiles.

Hubbard remembered hearsay of these doings; he also remembered—but did not remind Sam, since Daisy was at the table—the story of Sam's old habit, at conventions, of sleeping on the bathroom floor. Some excess of calories in Sam's physique caused a fierce rise in body temperature under stress. Always, after a few highballs and a few dances with important customers, he radiated a perceptible glow. The fiery particle of his salesmanship genius flickered in his warm arteries like the spark in a Burmese ruby; the stiffest bosom of starched shirt went limp and sodden by midnight. Positive waves of heat ejaculated from him: you could feel the simmer right through the cloth of his coat. Many a lady felt long imprinted, on the so-called small of her back, the scorching afterglow of his large palm. When this thermal phenomenon became unbearable, it was Sam's habit to tear off everything and sleep soundly on the chill white tiles of the hotel bathroom. George Work and Gene Vogelsang averred that once, after an exceptionally brisk evening on the dance floor, Sam couched upon tiles that were moist. There rose a hissing and light puffs of steam.

But that was an era now past. This particular convention was agreeably decorous. There were still the bottles of ginger ale and gas-water served up to the Erskine suite—those bottles with the hotel's demure tags on their necks: *The contents of this bottle is sold to you with the understanding that it will not be mixed or used with any alcoholic-content liquor.* And there was a bowl of cubed ice and plenty of tall tumblers; but to the dismay of salesmen from other houses who dropped in, Sam Erskine now seemed to take these tags seriously. "A convention," remarked a visiting Erskine author, "without benefit of orgy." He was quoting from one of his own books, which an author can usually do undetected by his publisher. Indeed, the Erskine troupe were so pious in demeanor that rivals were alarmed and suspected some list-raiding might be under way. (The abduction of a writer on the list of some other house.) When one of Dill's best novelists, a new find that season, innocently crossed the room to visit the Erskine table, a humorist near by called in mock warning to the Dill salesman, "Cheese it, there goes your fall list." Young Mr. Dill, looking quite wan, made haste to round up the straying maverick. It was really the presence of Daisy Erskine that frightened other publishers. Daisy's hair of brief rippled brass, her agate eyes, her large resources of white skin, were peculiarly impressive to those who knew her slightly. Like a good advertisement, she had plenty of white space; unfortunately this was both mental and physical. Her strong effusion of musk and Park Avenue patter lured many young authors to tea, and alarmed other publishers because (they said) first

she passed around caviar, then cocktails, and then contracts. But the Erskines themselves had most reason
to be alarmed. They avenged themselves on poor
T. Bannister Erskine (Daisy's husband, and the most
innocent of the family) by keeping him in the Mail
Order department.

So there was plenty of fun at the dinner: the customary japes about the gold watch always presented to
the retiring president; the jocose interruptions of the
president by those whose humor works best when someone else is talking. There was a charming gallantry in
seeing all these people dressed up, anxieties set aside for
the while. Hubbard watched groups coming in late,
looking for their tables in the large ballroom, the ladies
gay with color like new novels, the men as uniform as
subscription sets. It was pleasant to think of them taking their pretty things from fragrant cupboards or
drawers, the various travelling, bathing, shaving, cold-
creaming that must have preceded this cheerful scene.
He imagined the rustle of lingerie, the silken stretch of
stockings, the popping of studs in crisp shirt-fronts, the
many nimble torsions of black bow-ties. How many
times had Richard also gone through this genial vaudeville? Under this rolling sea of chaff and chatter there
must lie—corroded perhaps—unguessed and unattaina-
ble memories of the elusive personality Hubbard
sought. Richard, in his decent black and white, had sat
at similar tables, and like these others carrying what
unsolved questions in his head? What jokes or speeches
had rustled across those forgotten meetings, what
ludicrous glimpses, evasions, or flashes of desire?
These very people at his table could tell him much, but
he knew not how to ask. Contemplating the queer pur-

pose he had set himself, he realized why many modern writers had abandoned the old sequences of direct narrative; had abandoned logic, tinkered with prim typography, fractured even grammar and punctuation in their struggle to express the unresting mind. In the mind all times and moods are tangled up together. Was the crude succession of events really so important? This dinner, and the sight of gay little Bessie Beaton down a vista of bright shoulders, was begetting for him some vision of another evening many years before. How grandly homogeneous is the universe: while novelists were trying to suggest the freaks of consciousness, scientists in their vaster realm were guessing the same thing. Which more important, to split the Atom or to split the Idea? Why be so startled at the thought that Space is curved? Thought, too, is curved, returns upon itself, occupies many places at once. Is the Atom a little solar system? So is, each idea a microcosm of its thinker's own identity. The noble human mind, in whose sight eternity is but a day.

So he thought, and suddenly felt enormously tired. At that moment the nobility of the human mind was regaling itself with some excellent chaff at the expense of the booksellers, uttered by one of the authors who were guests of honor. The publishers were all cackling, unaware that the speaker was about to lance their swellings also. Sam Erskine, sitting next to Hubbard, whispered in his ear. "Is he Scotch?" Hubbard interpreted it, and supposed Sam was asking about the orator.

He came back from meditation with a jolt.

"I don't know—he might be—he's got a sense of humor," he replied.

"Scotch?" repeated Sam.

Hubbard, a little annoyed, again tried to whisper politely.

"He may have some Scotch blood in him, I don't know."

"Idiot, I'm asking if you want some Scotch," insisted Sam. Hubbard now saw that his host had produced a silver flask and was holding it under the table-cloth.

"Grand," he said, and held a glass. It was just what he needed. Scotch that had been riding on Sam's hip was really a form of hot toddy.

After dinner and a little dancing Sam suggested to Bessie that she come and join the others in the Erskine reservation upstairs. "Just a nice little crowd," he said: "we'll sit around and chew the fat."

"Sure," she said, smiling at him from the grasp of a rival publisher. "As soon as I dance a little more discount out of this big stiff."

"It'll be a marathon then," Sam retorted. "Well, see you at One Thirty."

"I hope that's time, not just room number." Forty years of bookselling had not dimmed Bessie's keen gusto for small comedy. There were many leaves in the book of life she had not cut, but she had an acute idea of the general drift of the story.

"Jake with me either way," said Sam.

130 was a room number, but Bessie didn't go. Not if Daisy's up there, she explained to Hubbard later. That was how she and Hubbard sat out a long talk together, and he learned several things we need to know.

XX

"Hullo, Handsome"

WE LEFT Richard at Hacks' department store in
Detroit. As he made his calls on the Trade that day he
was enlivened by unaccountable moods of lightness.
Turning a street corner in the brilliant noon he found
himself laughing he knew not why.

The pneumatic phenomenon we call laughter deserves examination. The dark theatre of the brain has
apparently been wired for sound. Suddenly, like letters of Neon tubing, those nerves are lit up with an exquisite pattern of light. There seems too much air
inside the body. The cheeks are tucked back, eyes narrow and widen, a gust of sound and breath is expelled.
The exact details of the process vary deliciously. There
are some lungs that squeak like atomizers, others ex-
hale a deep asinine bray.

Richard's mirth was quiet, but it looked genuine. An
old gentleman who saw him stopped and said, "Excuse
me, but I'd like to shake hands. You're the first person
I've seen smiling today." Richard was abashed and felt
solemn at this. But he tried politely to keep smiling.

"It just struck me that things are pretty good," he said shyly. The old man was well dressed in a neat gray overcoat, he had a gay red necktie, his soft white face was overgrown with a silver grizzle of beard. His eyes were clear, and he had one of those square-topped derbies that men do not wear until the routine problems of life have settled themselves. "What line of business are you in?" he asked. "Books," said Richard. "That's an idea," said the old gentleman; "I haven't read a good book in a long while; I'll go and buy one." Richard wanted to recommend one of his own titles, but it occurred to him that there really was nothing on the Erskine list quite good enough for so delightful a patriarch.

"The old men at the club won't talk about anything but the war," continued the stranger. "They're all very hot about it. It's nice to see somebody who can still smile."

The flags at Hack Brothers had made Richard feel patriotic. Was the old man being ironical? "I'd forgotten about the war just then," he said. "I guess we'll have to get into it, show those Germans where they get off at."

"Don't be too hard on the Germans," said the surprising ancient. "We all get off sooner or later."

He walked away, and Richard stood gazing after him. It must have been Santa Claus himself, he thought. He remembered the red tie. The word *cravat* came into his mind, but he could not remember whether a cravat is a collar or a necktie. The gallantry of human beings, he reflected; they go on tying neckties neatly right down to the edge of the grave. At his next call he surprised the first clerk he met by asking, "What is a cravat?"—They made sure of it in the Erskine

Pocket Dictionary, and Richard took an order for five more copies of same.

I hope someone—perhaps our friend Hubbard—will do justice to those seizures of felicity that are a part of living. Important books and histories of great affairs are so solemn. It has been agreed, apparently, that a great deal of life may not be recorded because it is too grotesquely funny. Here is this planet of comedians, with sleight of hand, sleight of foot, sleight of mind, but how often do you hear a ringing blast of laughter in a public library? The real gods of mirth, I suppose, don't write books. The very act of writing, a solitary and morbid task, induces peevishness. The laughers are too busy enjoying life's freaks to sit down with a pen.

I wonder what book it was that the good old chap with the red tie went and bought for himself? I hope it was Sterne's *Sentimental Journey*.

Let's be precise about these fits of joy. They come without reason, they don't last long, they are usually followed by depression. Like those financial graphs that business men love, the zigzag is sharp; sometimes there seems to be a lot of zag for very little zig. But while it lasts, the zig is gorgeous. The pavement swims away behind your quickened pace. Every street is lined with irony and surprise. A news-stand of bright magazines seems as pretty as a bed of tulips. A Beauty Shoppe has golden letters on its window: *Finger Waving,* and you hope to see a white hand beckon. A starting trolley-car screams like the cry of a bull-moose: I never noticed *that* before, you say. *Your Weight Free If You Guess It* offers the sporting slot-machine, and even prints it on a card for you with an oracle. "You

are not afraid of work, but you must persevere," says
the motto. Well, I guess I do, self insists. I bet nobody
perseveres more than I.—Life seems desperately
short for all you wish to communicate. You rush
eagerly upon the arriving moment—how can I wait
until the red turns green to get across the street? The
belly and the members are in harmony; lovely are the
faces of friends, each of their gestures richly suitable.
Those faces vary from day to day, even from hour to
hour, yet always somehow the right mask for that
particular episode. Women's ingenious garments
flutter in the fresh air of day and enclose miracles of
sculptural surmise. Firmly they clutch their little
pouches of miscellany as they do their lovely sense of
seriousness. Otherwise they might laugh. In this clear
air this morning they seem in the optative mood. I like
the way they tick their feet on the pavement. Could I
stay for one tableau the hurrying feet of all the world
to get the outline of their nervous or plodding grace?
And the bravado of their hats! When a woman re-
moves her hat, what a gesture of confidence it is! How
much more readily she does it for men than for other
women. "I like my women with their hats off," said the
old French connoisseur. "Take their hats off and send
'em in, one at a time—not too fast." But what a superb
sight, a woman of spirit careering along the street by
herself. How intricate a fabric of schemes in her head
for so plain a cycle of humors. Well, good luck to her.
How much irrelevant ink has speckled her dear and
frolicsome simplicity.

From these high pinnacles of the graph, the mind
sees far, leaps to conclusions, looks upon glamour and
finds a word for it. Let saints have their Eternity if we
can have our Moments. I wouldn't trade the calm wis-

dom of a whole squadron of angels for that riotous illusion of adequacy that sometimes comes to the poor farcical sinner. It's grand. "Hullo, handsome," he says to himself, and almost believes it.

So when Bessie Beaton came round to the hotel that afternoon to place her orders, Richard was feeling prime. He had expected a good quiet session, with a chance to go over the whole list and take a liberal stock-order. But something seemed to have happened to Mrs. Beaton since the morning. Even her lovely white hair no longer had its crisp radiance of vitality. "I feel terrible," she said when she got up to his room; she sank into an armchair and groaned. "Maybe it was that shrimp mayonnaise I had for lunch."

This was disappointing; all afternoon Richard had been perfecting in his mind the talk he was going to give her on some special items. But, as any good salesman would, he considered that if he could get her mind off the shrimps and onto the Erskine line, it would help her. "Wait till I tell you about this book *Carbon Paper*," he said. "Bessie, this is a real story and no kidding. I've got this window cut-out for you, and I'll give you imprinted circulars or post-cards, and I've got a personal copy for you autographed by the author. Just look at that four-color jacket. We paid the artist two hundred bucks for that jacket picture alone."

He waved the book before her, and she reached for it languidly. But he was too wise to let her look at it yet: he always found he could talk about a book better if he actually held it in his hand.

"I can let you have a lot of extra jackets for display purposes," he said, "and I'll give you exclusive on that window idea, about using the carbon paper. You can cut out the title of the book in letters of carbon paper and paste it on the glass. You'll scoop the town on that display."

"Well, I should hope so," said Mrs. Beaton, feebly fighting for her rights. "It's our own idea."

"You know Hampton's been a comer for quite a while," Richard proceeded, "but in this book he really crashes through. We sent out early copies to the leading critics, and look what they say. I've got their letters here in this folder. Here's proof of our advertising layout on this book. This is the copy we're going to use here in Detroit on publication date."

"Twenty-five," said Mrs. Beaton.

"Bessie," he said solemnly, "I wouldn't be fair to you if I accepted an order like that. You'd be out of the book day after publication, and your customers going to other stores to get their copies."

"Well, then give me twenty-five more on consignment," said Bessie. "You're trying to take advantage of these shrimps. Really, Richard, I feel sick, I think I'll have to lie down a spell."

A travelling man is ready for any emergency. Richard helped her onto the bed, put a blanket over her.

"I'm terribly sorry, Bessie. Shall I call a doctor?"

"No, no, I'll be all right," she said. "My own fault, I was up late last night, washing my hair—I wanted to look nice at the party this evening. I was late this morning, didn't have any breakfast, then I ate that junk for lunch. I think maybe if I could have a little brandy."

Richard sent down for a bottle. "Now listen," he said. "I've got some tablets here, something Herman Schmaltz gave me. It's just the thing to pull you together. He always uses them after a rough night; they're fine except for a bad heart. Is your heart all right?"

"It always has been," she said faintly. "People take advantage of it sometimes."

He gave her two of the tablets in a dose of brandy. "Now you take a nice little rest and you'll feel fine. I'll go out for a walk and come back later. No one will bother you here."

"No, I feel better," she insisted. "Go on, tell me some more about those damned books. It'll do me good just to contradict you in my mind."

She lay listening while Richard harangued her over the footboard of the bed. Occasionally she sighed deeply, but whether this was due to some ptomaine twinge or to his attempt to get quantities, he could not tell. Then he saw that she was asleep. He hung the sign PLEASE DO NOT DISTURB on the door-knob, tiptoed out, and went to a concealed corner of the lobby to write up his day's batch of orders for Miss Mac in the New York office.

So it happened that Daisy Erskine, arriving in Detroit that evening (to attend some congress of poets), learned from the register that Richard's room was on the same floor as her own. She telephoned his number, having business instructions for him from the office. After a long delay an answer came, unmistakably feminine and apparently weakened by debauch. The tremulous quality of the voice Daisy interpreted as furtive. "Who wants him?" said the voice. "This is Mrs. Erskine," cried Daisy angrily.

"My God," said the stricken Bessie and struggled to escape. Her heart was intrepid, but the tablets had been too strong for it. She was still sitting dizzily on the edge of the bed when Daisy appeared. The notice on the knob seemed to Daisy the final evidence of illicit impudence. Do Not Disturb, indeed!—what are salesmen for but to be disturbed? She flung open the unlocked door. An aroma of cognac, a dishevelled lady tottering from a tumbled bedside, made cynical contrast with poor Richard's conscientious display of books and posters on the dressing table. "So this is what we hire salesmen for," cried Daisy. "At least I should think they'd pick someone their own age." When Bessie collapsed on the floor it was evident that she was really ill. Richard was summoned from the desk, and took her home in a taxi. "I can't manage that dinner tonight," said poor Bessie. "You go in my place; you'll have to look after Miss Hutzler; I was taking her as my guest."

Richard's explanation to Mrs. Erskine was polite and reasonable, but Daisy was convinced—and hastened to inform the office—that their salesman must have given Mrs. Beaton knockout drops with sinister purpose. "Fine," said vulgar Sam; "if they'd do it to buyers more often we'd all cut a melon." But Bessie never forgave Daisy some of her remarks. It was not even the allusions to white hair that rankled most, but the suggestion of drugs. "If I really like a man," said Bessie, "he won't need to dope me."

XXI

Be On Your Guard

I F HUBBARD had assembled the available data about Minnie Hutzler in the form of a confidential Who's Who entry, her biography up to the time Richard met her might have been condensed thus:

HUTZLER, MINNA ELIZABETH, b. Detroit 1889. Unmarried. Graduated Commercial High School 1907. Diploma from Business College 1908. Considered somewhat cold and self-possessed. Height, medium; figure, slender; hair, black, abundant; eyes, brown; hands, long, capable; chin, pointed; complexion, pale; cosmetics, none. Considerable instinct for clothes and clever at dressmaking. 1909–1912 employed as typist in Commercial Art agency. About 1911 began to be source of perplexity to her family. Had to have room to herself in attic because kept her younger sister awake typewriting at night. Took correspondence course in Advertisement Writing. Parents who had thought Art was safeguarded by the qualification Commercial dismayed to learn that figure-posing took place in the advertising studio; horrified to find recognizable sketch of her in underwear advertisement. To keep peace, obtained employment in big store, stationery department. Promoted buyer at Hack Bros., 1915. Nickname at Art Agency, Mona Lisa. First cocktail given her by writing-paper salesman, 1914. Acute instinct for merchandising display. Accident of being next to book department made her great borrower of reading-matter from Bessie Beaton. If you saw her on street-car on her way to work you probably would not look at her twice. Loss, yours. She would not look at you at all; probably reading H. G. Wells. Voice: low, clear, often faintly satiric in tone. Profile, imperfect; thought homely by casual observer, but unexpectedly beautiful from some angles. Reticent except among trusted intimates (few); surprising pungency of speech on occasion. Too mature to interest the average male of her acquaintance. Admired for her figure by artists, for her conversation by newspaper reporters, but in one or two affairs with the latter found them tedious, sentimental, and intemperate. Decided to have nothing to do with anyone beneath the rank of managing editor.

When Richard called for Miss Hutzler, to take her to the dinner of the Book and Stationery Group, he was feeling very low—all the more so by contrast with earlier high spirits. Bessie Beaton's illness, and the embarrassing arrival of Daisy Erskine, naturally disturbed him. He had found himself lonely and homesick, as a travelling man often does at dusk. He decided to telephone to New York to see if Lucille and the baby were all right. He put through the call. But in the apartment on 114th Street the bell rang at a bad moment. Lucille, after a long day of that knock-down struggle called raising a child, was preparing supper. Gladys, aged nearly four, was howling over some crisis in her microcosm. Richard, sitting on the edge of the bed in Detroit, could overhear the yammer of the indignant baby as she clung to her mother. "I didn't mean to," wailed the child—good old phrase, accurate for so much in human grief. "Didn't mean to what?" asked Richard. "She's a naughty girl," said Lucille, "she upset the milk bottle." Richard, needing encouragement himself, was simple enough to think that a mention of his own troubles would divert Lucille's mind from the pressure of menage. He began to tell of Mrs. Erskine's unexpected appearance. The long threads of wire that connected them must have been aware of a sudden increase of tension. China and glass insulators from New York to Michigan felt the tingle of a sharper current—one of those atomic shocks that fatigue sensitive copper. "So Daisy's out there with you," cried poor Lucille. "I hope you'll sell her a lot of books." She slapped the receiver back on the hook. He was cut off.

Do telephoners know—presumably they do—the misery of those long-distance angers? The wretchedness of far-divided simpletons when the artery, suddenly cut, bleeds long and secretly. Worse than toothache is that continual dull pain of lonely fever. There are two pulsations in the twisted throb—self-pity, self-reproach. Do women know how man, the well-meaning child, is destroyed by these needless freaks? There was once a famous appeal for charity—"forgive them, for they know not what they do." But that's easy. Forgiveness is more needed, and really divine, when we knew exactly what we were doing.

Richard at first thought of repeating the call, then

considered the expense. He straightened the bed still disordered by Bessie's seizure. He looked grimly at his careful arrangement of books and display material, put away his collection of circulars and catalogues. At that moment he did not care whether Hack Brothers or anyone else should buy five copies of *Carbon Paper* or fifty. He took a deep hooker of the brandy ordered for Bessie. Then he said to himself one of the most beautiful and satisfying monosyllables in our English tongue. Honor to those various instinctive sounds, so much older than ourselves, that come to us down the ages, rich with the glow and burden of all mortal moods.

"Hell," he said.

Miss Hutzler was surprised when Mr. Roe called at her home to take her to the dinner of the Book and Stationery Group. Richard explained Bessie Beaton's malady, and was introduced to Mr. and Mrs. Hutzler who were already at table. Mr. Hutzler, one of Detroit's solid mechanics, was relieved to see so respectable an escort for his daughter, and indeed an air of shy melancholy sat upon Richard. This rather pleased Minnie, who was easily wearied by the excessive joviality of travelling men. The dinner was not a formal affair, but she had exchanged the black gown of the store for a bright red dress which was brilliantly becoming. The feeling of being colorfully clad, and Richard's sombre mien, put her in an unusually gay humor.

"Somebody's had a drink," she said as they rode in the taxi.

"I'm sorry," he apologized. "Would you like one, to make it even?"

"We'll get some beer at the dinner," she said. "That's plenty for me. But I knew you'd had something because you smell so nice and pepperminty. I suppose you've been chewing hard, not to shock me."

He explained that the episode of Mrs. Erskine had been rather a blow.

"Well now, don't you worry a bit," she said. "We'll just have a nice evening and you don't even have to talk if you don't feel like it. I don't usually talk much, but tonight I seem to be cheerful, I don't know why. Give me a cigarette."

They lit up and rode in silence. Excused from the necessity of chatter, Richard suddenly felt better. Oh, well, he thought, life is life, and here we are in the middle of it. I hope Gladys has gone to bed happy. Poor Lucy, I guess it *is* pretty tough for her sometimes. I'll send her a wire in the morning.

Minnie looked at him in good-natured quietness, and he began to suspect that she was an unusually understanding sort of person. He found himself talking.

"I can tell you how I feel," he said. "I saw a funny thing the other day in New York. There was a lady taking her dog out for a Sunday morning walk, he was one of those little bitty things, what do they call 'em —not much bigger than a rat—some Mexican name——"

"Chihuahua?" she suggested.

"That's it. The poor little mutt had on a pink wool jacket, and he was tottering up the steep hill on 79th Street while the lady waited for him at the top. He was so comic, feeling his way up the grade on those spider legs, I had to stop and look at him. As he went by he looked up at me, sort of shy, with his big eyes, and I could see he was ashamed of being so small in such a big world. I thought afterwards that maybe he thought I looked unsympathetic, staring at him. I didn't really have time to get the right kind of look in my eyes. I'd have liked him to know I wasn't sneering at him, because I know just how he felt. I felt a bit like that this evening. That's why I took a drink."

"I'm glad you took it," said Minnie. "Better now?"

"Coming on fine."

"I like that story," she said. "Maybe you're the kind of person that queer things happen to. I am. They don't to everyone though. The craziest things happen to me, it's a riot. I had a new Easter bonnet one time, made of straw; someone threw a cigarette out of a window as I was walking underneath; it landed right in a bunch of muslin flowers on the brim. I thought the sun was getting pretty hot, and then people started yelling at me. I was trapesing along with my hat on fire. I've got so much hair I didn't notice what was happening until the thing was actually in a blaze."

"That reminds me of one time on the train," said Richard. "I bought a cardboard cup of coffee. It was so hot, I had to wait a little before drinking it. The car was jolting too much to stand it on the window sill, so I wrapped my handkerchief around it and held it carefully in my hands. Then I got thinking about things, how many books I was going to sell or something like that, and I guess several minutes went by. Anyhow, the hot coffee softened the cardboard, the whole bottom of the cup fell out and all the coffee went over my trousers. That's the kind of fool thing that happens to me."

By the time the taxi reached their destination, they were excellent friends.

The dinner was held in a mellow old German raths-keller. In the large upper room long tables were set out; the same meal was served to all—pickles, steak sandwiches, beer, and ice cream. At each place was a long white apron which the diners tied over their garments to avert the spatter of suds and gravy. In those days pure beer was plentiful entertainment for an evening, without the necessity of stupefying cocktails. They sat with a group from Hack Brothers, and elsewhere along the tables Richard found many friends in the trade. In their aprons the gathering looked almost like a hospital scene, but it struck Richard that the costume was peculiarly effective for Minnie. Above the white apron a flash of her red frock and the intense black of her hair were vividly contrasted. There was singing, and the speaker of the occasion was a swami from the Chamber of Commerce who urged the necessity of Better Business Letters. But in between times they found plenty of chance to talk. Richard, who read no books outside his own list, was startled to find Minnie's range so wide, extending from classic curiosa of the trade to the best modern novels. She agreed with him that *Carbon Paper* would sell, but startled him by dismissing its literary merit as negligible.

"You ought to be in the book department," he said.

"Nothing doing," she said. "I'm all for stationery. Only intelligent people buy books, but everybody's got to have writing paper. Hack's were going to send me abroad to do some buying in France this spring, but the war prevented it. I don't want to be working for

someone else all my life; I'd like to be in business on
my own. I'm getting up a pamphlet of famous letters
of all sorts, I mean reprinting real letters from well-
known people, to give away in our department. With
each letter we suggest the kind of stationery it should
have been written on. I guess I might call it *The Hack
Writer*."

"Better not," said Richard solemnly. "They
wouldn't get it."

Minnie was somewhat scornful of the Chamber of
Commerce expert who exhibited, by stereopticon,
slides of approved business communications of all
sorts. And it is true that to one who had been rummag-
ing the files of literature for the letters of statesmen
and poets, the commercial expert's correspondence
seemed a little bald. But Richard insisted bravely that
flourishes of wit have no place in diurnal dictation. He
reminded her of the familiar doctrine that the two best
business letters are *Enclosed find check* and *Please re-
mit*. "I should be afraid ever to send you a letter," he
said, "if you're so particular."

"If you sell Detroit regularly, you won't need to
write."

After the speaking the tables were removed and
there was dancing. But though Richard was plainly
enjoying himself, he suggested they telephone Bessie
Beaton's landlady to see if the invalid was comfortable. They did so, and Bessie herself answered the
phone. She insisted that they come round and see her.

They did so, and found Mrs. Beaton sitting up in her
lodgings, wearing an attractive kimono, and reading
Carbon Paper. "I'll make it fifty copies," she said,
"and you can send me an extra fifty On Sale."

"You must have been sicker than we thought," said Minnie.

"No, I'm all right. I'll give you both a nightcap. Did you have a good time?"

"Grand," said Minnie. "Mr. Roe's the kind of person I can talk to. He makes me feel human."

"He's good that way," said Bessie.

"Well, I thought maybe it'd be an amusing day," said Minnie, "because I had such a crazy dream last night. I dreamed I was in a telephone booth with a glass door, and Mr. Ed Hack was outside watching me while I talked. As I telephoned, suddenly I felt my garters loosen and my stockings started to come down. I tried to keep them up, but they kept wrinkling lower and lower, and I couldn't do anything about it because he was watching me."

"A very reasonable dream," said Bessie. "Let it be a warning to you. I don't believe the *droit de seigneur* should extend to department stores."

"No, but this is the comedy," Minnie continued. "I looked up garters in that Dream Book you have in your department. This is what it said, I copied it down: *Garters—dream of being presented with a pair means love, respect, admiration, and pleasure; of being without them or having them slip indicates future embarrassment. Be on your guard.*"

XXII

Mouse-Heart

Dear Miss Mac," Richard wrote the next day. "Business is good here, as you will see by enclosed orders. Some of the boys haven't been so lucky. Pete Sampson of Dill was telling me his orders at Sheehan's were so light he asked if they wanted the goods shipped by carrier pigeon. Can't get away from it, our Fall list is O. K. I'm putting plenty of pressure on *Carbon Paper*. Bessie Beaton came through with fifty and fifty more On Sale. I feel pretty punk though, because Oxide Daisy blew in unexpectedly last night and gummed things a bit. Mrs. Beaton was taken sick in the room up at the hotel, I had her lay down a while and rest, Daisy butts in and finds her there and thinks it's an intreague. If she makes trouble on this I hope you'll back me up. Also I called up home to see if everything was all right and the wife cuts off on me. You know that makes a fellow feel rotten.

"Was glad to get your wire this morning. I had to stay over longer than I expected on account of Bessie Beaton, but checked everything with her this A. M. She is all set, it was only some shrimps that went the

wrong way, but it certainly knocked her for a while.
Even her hair looked sick. Am taking train for Chi
this afternoon. Be sure to send me that extra display
material to the Blackstone, I want to make a killing
with Marshall Field.

"Pete Sampson was telling me of a horse some of
the boys put over on him, or thought they did. It seems
he got a hunch he ought to visit Chatham's bookshop
up in Saginaw City, none of the trade had called on
that account in years and they told him Miss Ludlow
would like to see a salesman. They give him a song and
dance about her being a willowy blonde and wonderful
company. He packs his bag and beats it up there, in a
blizzard too. When he arrives and shakes the snow
off his hat he asks for Miss Ludlow. She turns out to
be a dark wizzened little old maid, homely as a monkey.
But the joke was on The Boys, for she was starving to
be sold—he came back with a stock order for $4,000.
I was just wondering whether I wouldn't better visit
that account next trip. Ask Sam what he thinks. Best
regards to all, I hope checks are going to Lucy O. K.

> "Sincerely
> "Richard Roe."

In one of Hubbard's conferences with Miss Mac she
showed him this letter. Hubbard had been feeling discouraged. Only a divine purview and charity, he
suspected, could put significance into his fragmentary
record of Roe. "I've been reading some books," he said,
"both novels and biographies, to see how it's done.
They all seem to have some form, arrangement or
plan; convey some moral. But this cyclorama of
Richard—Richard the Mouse-Heart—seems meaning-
less. Also I begin to fear it's immoral."

Miss Mac was a helpful person to lean on in mo‹ ments of doubt. Her gray eyes were so large and clear behind her polished glasses it was natural to suppose that she saw more than most people. Her voice was so quiet that it lent an air of oracle to casual utterance. Her gray hair and rich bulky bosom were sedative in an era when most women seemed unnecessarily puerile and chattery. She had the tranquil tolerance attained by elderly virgins.

"It's queer that men are so easily shocked," she said. "Even when they outgrow being scandalized by other people, they still get terribly shocked at themselves. Why can't you just put down what you learn without adopting an attitude about it? Just imagine you're translating from a foreign language—like Russian—and you're not responsible for the sentiments."

"I'm trying to," Hubbard said, "but I can't seem to find any pattern. I'd like to be able to sum things up into a conclusion. The kind of wise dope that a publisher puts on the jacket of a book—This means so-and-so."

"I guess that's because you used to be an accountant," she suggested. "You want to make a balance sheet out of everything. Maybe life doesn't balance like that. There's an unaccountable surplus. Looking for a pattern *is* adopting an attitude; a very intense kind of attitude." "That's true," he exclaimed. "Sometimes we're so close to the pattern we can't make it out—but if we sort of lay back and pretend not to be looking for it, it becomes plain."

What a singularly wise person Miss Mac is, he thought. Queer that she had saved those letters of Richard's—she must have taken pains to preserve them when the files were cleaned out every few years. Was that also part of the elusive pattern? How much of life she had seen, sitting behind a typewriter in the Erskine office for thirty years. She knew, without being told, so much that poets and novelists make a clamor about. Solid as a lighthouse on the end of a break-water she had watched the deep-sea traffic go by— proud vessels making steadily for port, others fog-bound outside, some piled up on reefs or unreported forever. Perhaps all novels should be written by people like Miss Mac, mellow and generous women with noth-ing to condemn—except other women. She preferred men; they were absurd but magnanimous. How many of them she must have seen, in the full comedy of their excited fancies, in the dexterity of business where they are most charming. Yes, what a book *she* could write! On that rubbery and resilient bosom, how she could console the fretful babe of human consciousness. . . .

"You *think* too much," she said. "Narrate!"

Hubbard looked so startled that Miss Mac realized it was not yet time to tell him one or two episodes he would have to consider. He wasn't ripe for them, he must grow up to them gradually.

He looked again at the old letter, written on hotel stationery in Richard's rather formless hand. "Did Daisy try to make trouble over the Bessie Beaton incident?"

"Sure she did. She had her own good reasons, the tart. She went out to that Poetry Convention in Detroit because her fancy man, Johnny Jonquil, was going to be there. So of course she was specially sore when she supposed anyone else was shunting cars up a side-track. She figured that picking on Richard would be a good smoke-screen. She made a noise about it to Sam, but I laid for her in the washroom. I told her if she didn't quit, I'd tip off poor old T. Bannister to some of her capers.—Just the same, she managed to make things uncomfortable for Richard in the long run. That was what really started him thinking about a business of his own."

But if the novels were written by Miss Mac they would be too simplified. Her unruffled acceptance of humanity's prime factors is a great gift, but not the complete one. Doubt, pain, and folly, all the trickeries of choice and chance, are part of the story. Hubbard, though slow and too painstaking, had valuable intuitions. I told him of the Parisian critic who said, when the lucidity of French literature was praised, "That is our trouble. We need more obscurity." Richard was flexible, an awkward freight to pack in the neat octavo of a book. Stuff him carefully in here, he slips out elsewhere. How little, for instance, that letter to Miss Mac said of what he was thinking.

On the afternoon train to Chicago, Richard experienced one of those intensities of quiet which are travellers' privilege. A small dose of Time, the fatal drug, is condensed in pellet form, enclosed in a transparent soluble capsule so it can be swallowed without pang. In the entrails the sour medicine works unnoticed; elsewhere heavy weights of destiny may be shifting, but in the mind, for a few hours, all seems poised in even balance. Thought actually feels itself consider.

He was aware, with quickened sense, of the reality of what he had just left. He could see all that area of life persisting its affairs; in the great murmur of Hack Brothers, Bessie Beaton's white head alert in the book department; Minnie Hutzler's black brows conning her crowded stationery aisle. The rumble of the train made him hum to himself the rather melancholy tune of *Tipperary*. Like most men he was proud of his humming (*The Spanish Cavalier* was his favorite) and found himself wishing there were someone to appreciate it. Since Bessie Beaton had recovered so quickly it was a pity he and Miss Hutzler had not had one or two more dances. She was easy to dance with; he had not even looked down at his feet as he usually did. But in spite of these consoling thoughts his mood was solemn. The broken phone call still ached; and he was both annoyed and alarmed by the silly dispute with Daisy. Certainly she'll try to tie a can to my tail, he thought. Even his attempts to cheer himself up reacted unfavorably: he said aloud, "When you find yourself saying maybe things aren't as bad as you think, they're usually a good deal worse." And then another typically masculine sophism occurred to him—that one might as well do some of the wrongs for which he will be held guilty anyway.

Certainly no one who saw him there, watching Michigan spin by, would have guessed that his mind was so crowded with question marks—he could almost feel them hovering over him, as cartoonists love to indicate the perplexity of their clowns. In a dull twinge of homesickness he carried Lucille and Gladys with him, the fire-escaped vista of 114th Street, the crags of Morningside Park. A score of bookstores, loaded with the heavy furniture of shelves and titles, moved flittingly beside him like the shadow of the train; and like any decent salesman he conceived himself envoy of the virtue of his firm. Far behind him bells were ringing in the office. Sam Erskine was chewing his cigar, Miss Mac ticking arpeggios of accuracy on the typewriter, the old darky out in the stockroom hammering cases of books, the girls in the mail-order department, recovered from their lunch-hour hysterias of giggle, were in the thick of the mid-afternoon pressure. He must not let them down. "Representing Erskine Brothers," he said to himself with satisfaction. He idealized the imprint of a quite commonplace enterprise into a badge of honor. The long howl of the engine, sound that always floods the valves of travelling men, was a renewed trumpet call to the endless bicker of Selling Goods. All this would never have come to him in definite words. Speech has to be used in the actual process of business, but the simple mind evades it when possible. It is good to relax into those warm vague feelings which are wiser than words. Presently, emerging from a pure vacancy, he realized he had crossed a subtle frontier. His mind had turned forward to Chicago, and he was already framing the exact line of argument that should appeal to each various buyer.

No one approaches Chicago without some rise of spirits. Whether, by day, it is the Indiana sand dunes that catch the eye, or, by night, the fiery torches of her outlying steel mills, there is always magic in her neighborhood. The legend is that her name is the Indian word for wild onion; like that virid sprout she grows both rank and beautiful. It is no mere accident that has given her notoriety oftener than fame, for her temperament is unique. Gigantic in humor and audacity, whatever she does is in superlative degree. Whether blizzards, heat waves, æsthetics or insolvencies, they all have the quality of completeness. Her fresh-water surf can look as angry as the Atlantic, and she has more authentic Old English chophouses than London itself. A peculiar twist of direction affects most visitors in Chicago. We usually imagine her as built at the foot of the Lake, whereas she is really on the western shore. As a result, the stranger supposes he is looking north from her noble Michigan Boulevard, when he is really looking east. Chicago looks east more than you suppose at first, or than she herself will admit. In her glorious assurance she sometimes feigns to look down on New York. Just the same, she looks. But surely she need not. One breath of her vital air and impossibilities of all sorts seem natural and plain. Leonardo da Vinci would have understood her. To make a river run backward, to put up a beacon as radiant as two square inches of the sun's surface, to call a garage a Greasing Palace, are triumphs Leonardo would have relished, or the old Greek who, when he said *Panta Rei,* meant Everything Goes. Do not say she has not tried to warn you: even her police whistles with their double birdlike note sound like the lovely omen of the cuckoo.

But that was after Richard's time. It was the Blackstone Hotel that gave him his first taste of the grandeur of being a Travelling Man. He never visited that luxurious place without a feeling of enhanced importance, which is good for morale. And perhaps it was typical of Chicago's glamorous air that on his way to the book department at Marshall Field's he noticed some exceptionally charming garters. He remembered the Dream Book, and had a pair sent to Miss Hutzler. In Chicago even the Mouse-Heart has moments of Leo.

XXIII

Decibels

A DECIBEL," Hubbard read in a newspaper, "is a measure of loudness equivalent to the sound made by the fall of a pin."

How many decibels do you hear when a sparrow falls—or a Stock Market? Or even, he thought to himself, a travelling salesman?

It was a brilliant cool noon in late spring, after one of New York's sudden hot spells. The kind of day, the elevator boy said taking him up to the penthouse, that makes your clothes feel good on you. Hubbard was in a roof-garden speakeasy near the Erskine office, a pleasant place to sit out on the terrace, twenty stories above the street, and enjoy sunshine and thought. Countryman by nature, he liked it because it was one of the few places in the publishing region of Murray Hill where he could smell manure. The proprietor took his little roof-garden seriously, and the boxes of privet and geranium were heavily fertilized. The savor of Eggs Benedict and the tang of angostura and vermouth were dominated by a sharp whiff of synthetic sheep. The proprietor's name was Hyacinthe, which

The Boys thought very amusing. The government had recently ejected him from long tenure in a dark basement, but now on this high summit he saw sunlight again. The good French instinct of the glebe reawoke; he set out a spring planting of parsley and mint. As Hubbard sat considering the first julep of the season, Hyacinthe dug busily in his green troughs with a Woolworth trowel. Other patrons kept indoors, finding the air cool, and Hubbard was alone on the terrace. After talking to Miss Mac and others he needed to meditate. Like the acid odor of manure he wanted a smell of reality in his biography of Richard.

Thinking so persistently about the life of another man oversensitizes the nerves. Retracing the streets of Richard's habit, gathering clues from people who had known him, Hubbard was likely to see exaggerated meaning in casual things. But perhaps this was wholesome. Mostly we underestimate those fugitive suggestions; like the Parthians they shoot their arrows at us as they flee.

"I don't agree with Miss Mac," he said to himself. "This job needs not only a Narrator but a Nerve Specialist. It ought to tremble like a taut string. It's drawn from the juices and pressures of every day" (changing his metaphor, as a solitary thinker is privileged to do). "If only one could get the natural taste of those juices before reminiscent chemistry does its work on them. If they stand any length of time, either they ferment and foam up with sentimental alcohol, or else you've got to taint them with satirical benzoate of soda to keep them flat. Too much benzoate of soda in most biographies." He was pleased with this idea, so pleased that he looked quite handsome, and Hyacinthe thought this a propitious moment to ask Mr.

Hubbard what he would like for lunch. Hubbard replied that he was not ready to order his meal; he was waiting for a guest. Hyacinthe, a person of much humor, took his customary attitude of quiz. His right palm under his left elbow, his left hand curled under cheek and chin, a downward sparkle in the gaze. "A lady?" he asked. "Because if it is, you prefer to sit inside? She might be cold here, they don't wear many clothes nowadays." "Is that so," said Hubbard. "How do you know that? No, as a matter of fact it isn't a lady, quite a sturdy gentleman; he won't be chilly." Hyacinthe was disappointed, he went back to train some ivy up the trellis. He had the French preference for seeing the sexes well mixed.

It wasn't a lady, it was only me. Hubbard had asked me not to join him until late: he wanted an hour alone with a drink to put his ideas in order. It was obvious that his researches in Roe were educating him rapidly. He had spoken, a little too jocularly I thought, of Richard the Mouse-Heart. That reminded me of an animal shop in Upper Broadway which Richard must have studied often. In the window was a cage of white mice that twirl crazily in circles. It always interested me to watch the faces of people watching these Rotary Club mice. Onlookers, after their first surprise, usually wore a faintly superior smile, affectionately derisive of these midgets that spin so fast without getting anywhere. But perhaps, I reflected, an Infinite Reason would contemplate *us* with the same sympathetic grin. I myself knew nothing of Richard Roe: Hubbard was his biographer and I only the biographer of the biography; but I didn't want Roe's chronicler to wear a superior smile. It was too magnificent a task: to catch a human being in the very act of being human—and to set it down without chemical preservatives. To arrest, for the while, life's extraordinary power of tidying things up, cicatrizing wounds, softening the retrospect, healing and forgetting and just going on. That cruel and blessed process of making everything seem as though it didn't matter, the blind onward optimism of the universe against which the artist must make his hopeless triumphant stand. Already, in the solemn phrase of the old doctor, Richard was content to be as if he had not been. Yet this tiny specimen that had crawled across the slide had in rudiment all the organs of the greatest. Plasm and psyche were there, and all the chills and fevers—not essentially different from Shakespeare's.

Shakespeare had been in Hubbard's mind, for he had been lately to see a revival of that most gorgeous failure, *Troilus and Cressida*. He had taken Gladys Roe who was frankly bored, but had made one superb comment—that Cressida would be a swell part for Greta Garbo. This was admirably shrewd, for the psychology of that piece is mostly Hollywood. Also there is no theatrical manager of insight who has not coveted all the Shakespearean rôles for the siren Swede. But that is irrelevant. Hubbard, in the great line, "There's language in her eye, her cheek, her lip," could think of no one but Minnie Hutzler. And then, at the final curtain, he realized that perhaps Shad Roe, in an oblique way, was the Pandarus of Richard's story. Yes, Shakespeare would have been the best biographer for Richard. He was never afraid to set off the colored flares on the smallest occasion—the Bad Boy of literature, nudging the world with his mischievous "You ain't seen nothing yet."

Then the amazing thing was that as they were having a soda after the show, Gladys remarked: "Maybe because he once worked in a theatre, Pop was crazy about the Shakespeare Garden in Central Park. I certainly got tired of that place, it was his favorite walk on fine Sundays. He used to take Grandma out there too. She didn't give a hoot about Shakespeare, but she liked to see those German signs in the park—you know, where they have notices in four languages so everybody in New York can read 'em, Yiddish, Italian, German, and English."

Hubbard had never even heard of the Shakespeare Garden. He went to have a look at it.

New York is never so lovely as in early summer. In Richard's familiar region of Central Park West awnings burst out on apartment windows; asphalt streets feel soft under the point of a walking stick. Drug stores are draughty with electric fans, which blow out the gasoline cigar-lighter every time you snap it into flame. In the inner airshaft of apartments housewives indignantly observe little flocks of fuzz that come drifting over the sill from dustpans higher up. In the evenings the broad pavements of the Little White Way are thronged with strollers. Vegetable stores arrange piles of beans, radishes, carrots, sloped in colored strata under brilliant light. Issuing from the movies about 10:30 p.m. the Upper West Side likes to read its morning paper before it goes to bed. Already it hears the familiar cry of Manhattan urging hopefully toward the morrow—"*American, News, a Mirror.*" Day or night, in that warm, breezy weather life comes outdoors and shows itself. Each part of the city has its own moods. At Fort George men pitch horseshoes. In the Comfort Triangle at Times Square they sit on the low curbing near the international newsstand and read the papers. The Cowley Fathers on 46th Street are hearing confessions of the spring crop of sins. It used to surprise me to find their church just there, in that raffish byway, so very different from their monastery at Cowley near Oxford; but there must be more need of shriving on 46th Street.

The Shakespeare Garden, Gladys told Hubbard, was best approached by the 81st Street entrance to the Park—the one nearest the Roe apartment. He soon discovered the German warning which had pleased old Mrs. Geschwindt: *Es ist strengstens verboten, Papier oder irgend anderen Unrath auf den Boden zu werfen.* Presently, on a rock hillside below the "belvedere," he reached the little enclosure. It has its pathos, for lean appropriation, hard winters, scorching summers, a dead tree and an electric wire crossing overhead make it difficult to suggest a Warwickshire setting. Also the ragged mineral outcrop of Manhattan is scarcely the humus for cottage flowers. But as Hubbard explained, it was just that touch of unconscious pathos that endeared the place to him, and perhaps to Richard also. The old Irish gardener wrestles single-handed with his task. Hubbard, admiring the masses of eglantine roses, got into conversation with him. He had been there since the beginning of the garden. There were 125 varieties of flowers, all mentioned by Shakespeare.

"How did you pick them out?" Hubbard asked. "Did they give you a list?"

"No, sir," said the gardener. "A lady gave me three little books by Shakespeare, plays he wrote about flowers, and I read them. One of the books was called *Antony and Cleopatra;* I didn't find so many flowers

in that one. That Cleopatra was a very plain-spoken
lady.—Twenty-one years ago, when we started this
garden, it was all poison ivy. It would scare you—one
man I had working here, his head swelled up like a pot.
It's kind of hard on this hillside, we lose so much soil
in the rainstorms. After that storm the other day I
wheeled up twenty barrows of earth. Yes, I had to take
the labels off the plants because when people knew
what they were they stole 'em. Look there, you see
that place?"

He pointed sadly to an empty hollow in the earth.

"Yes, sir," he said, "that's what they do when you're
not looking. I had twenty-four wild thymes in that
bed."

Some other visitors, passing behind them just at this
moment, overheard the remark and looked startled.

Hubbard asked if he had known Mr. Roe. Not by
name at any rate. "There's lots of regular visitors," he
said, "folks that are just crazy about this garden. They
bring cuttings of their own to see if they'll grow here—
that Cherokee rose is from an opera singer's farm
down in Maryland, and there's a rose a lady brought
from France, and here's some pinks from Staten Island.
But they got to satisfy me it's something Shakespeare
knew about."

They were interrupted by a small freckled boy who
rushed up in great agitation. "You better come," he
appealed to the old gardener. "We buried that dead
squirrel down there and now there's a lot of bad boys
digging it up again."

The old fellow hurried away to halt this sacrilege,
and Hubbard wandered for some time round the little
hillside, enjoying the secluded corner of rose bushes
and the tiny cascade. From the brow of the rocky knoll

was a skyline of towers such as Prospero might have
imagined. What did it mean that Richard had discovered for himself this queer corner of peace? Richard, of all people—so thoroughly Upper West Side
that if he had seen the young moon rising anywhere
except over the roof of an apartment (preferably the
Apthorp) he would have been scandalized. If he had
seen her gilded curve above trees or mountains she
would have seemed almost naked. (Indeed there are
many who would have legislated a petticoat for the
moon if that were possible.) In this he was unlike Hubbard, who, if kept too long in town, felt as a dog
must, tethered in a forest of stone without ever an
honest tree for his relief.

"I should have liked some more talk with the old
gardener," Hubbard continued. "He was telling me
that before he joined the Park Department he was a
machinist on lamps for Pullman cars—I think that's
grand, going from Pullman to Shakespeare, God bless
him—but I could see he was busy. I wondered if I also,
trying to recreate poor Richard, was like those mischievous boys exhuming the squirrel. I strolled off into
that lovely maze of rocky paths and glens above the
Boat Lake. A thunder shower came up, and ducking
under the trees for shelter, I came upon a secluded
little summer-house. I hate to have to rely on coincidence, but these things do happen. There, in that rustic
arbor, peacefully reading the *Billboard,* was Shad—not
a picture but in person. I hadn't known he was still in
town, and I needed him. You see, he was in Chicago
that time—when Richard bought the garters."

XXIV

The Brass Ring

IN THOSE days, and perhaps still, many of the publishers had their Chicago offices in the People's Gas Building, but any symbolism implied by this was unintentional. Richard, after a busy tour among bookstores, arrived at the People's Gas to meet Pete Sampson in the advertising bureau of Dill's Magazine. His and Pete's itineraries were similar, and both had to remain in Chi over the week-end. They were feeling lonely and glad of each other's company. Richard had just stopped in at the Blackstone in the hope of a letter from home, but found none. "Let's have dinner together," said Pete. "There's a place called Schlogl's, over in the newspaper district. They say lots of writers go there."

This was 1915, and I believe Schlogl's had not then become so famous. Probably its collection of authors' autographs had not been started; I think it was not until Mencken's manifesto about Chicago as the literary capital that the town became autograph-conscious. At any rate, when Hubbard looked through the signatures, years later, he found no trace of Richard Roe's unassuming passage. But whether obscure or fashionable, Schlogl's kitchen and cellar were always honest. Pete and Richard sat comfortably over thick chops and mugs of beer, exchanging confidences on their adventures with their customers. Then Pete happened to say, "I see your brother's in town." He had noticed Shad Roe's name on a vaudeville poster. "Fine," said Richard. "Let's call up the theatre and find out where he's staying. He'll get us a couple of Annie Oakleys and we'll catch the show."

Richard had not seen his volatile brother for some time. They reached him by telephone at a theatrical hotel on North Clark Street, and he insisted on their meeting him backstage after his act was over. They made their way to his dressing room through a leash of trained dogs who were just coming off and a troupe of midgets about to go on. Shad, in his undershirt, was wiping off cold cream and make-up with a grimy towel. Perspiration stood in large drops on his shiny forehead: his act ended with some very strenuous eccentric dancing. "Well, boys," he cried, "what about that routine? It's a wow, a sensation. It's got to be, in a spot like that—trained animals ahead of me, and a pack of midgets behind. Never mind, they're great little folks. They're coming up to the room for a party, and you guys must join us."

It was Saturday night, and evidently Shad intended to make the most of it. Also he enjoyed startling his older brother, whom he regarded as something of a prude. "The midgets'll be along presently," he said, turning in at a barroom near the theatre. "Let's have a cocktail first. I'll match you." They had Bronxes, which were still in fashion then. Good old Bronx, the favorite cocktail of a pre-war world—who ever hears of it now?

"Have to open champagne for the little people," he continued. (Part of Shad's act on the stage was quick-fire monologue, and he carried the habit into private life. Besides, if the ghost has duly walked, troupers are in high spirits after the Saturday-night show.) "Midgets always drink champagne, I don't know why. Makes them feel bigger, I guess. Well, Dick, old stick-in-the-mud, here's luck. How's the book business?"

For some reason the actor always seemed to find something comic in the idea of Richard in the book trade. You would have to read the classified advertising in the *Billboard*—which should be studied occasionally by anyone wishing to be reminded of the fantastic richness of life—to get any notion of the very different world in which Shad moved. In that temperamental realm of vaudeville, circuses, amusement parks, dance halls, medicine shows, it would be natural to consider rather dull anything as slow and methodical as selling books. Even long after he had left the show business, Richard himself used to buy a copy of the *Billboard* now and then. It's better reading than most novels. How many temptations and Business Opportunities; here is the Hotsie Totsie Sport Handkerchief—"Miniature Pair Ladies' Silk Panties, worn in breast pocket as a dress handkerchief. Pure silk. Attractive colors. 25¢ in stamps." Here is the fresh crop of Mexican Jumping Beans, $8.50 per pound. "Lots of pep; every bean guaranteed alive."—Or Auto Hot Shot Bombs: "A funny new Joke for cars. Attach to spark plug. When driver steps on starter, BANG goes the HOT SHOT. No harm to car or driver. $8.50 gross." Horoscopes and Gazing Crystals; Baby Elephants, Pythons, Monkeys, Kangaroos; Whoopee Seat Squealers, Frozen Kustard Machines, Ferris Wheels, Miniature Railways, Whales, Flea Circuses. Are any of these any use to you? Here is a man advertising a Flea Circus, Complete with Banners, for $25. What short story could be more prettily told than the India Incense Company's suggestion for selling perfumery. "Work the Filling Stations," they advise. "As a car pulls in for gas raise the hood and put one drop of VAPORINCENSE on the hot manifold. Instantly the fan will blow the odor into the car, and the occupants will be curious to know where this most exquisite fragrance is coming from. Then explain to them what it is and its various uses in the home. AND YOU'VE MADE A SALE." Do you want a Pitchmen's Spiel Book, 35 cents? Second-hand moving picture films, "Westerns, Comedies, Hygiene Specials." Tattooing outfits, illustrated folder of designs free. Do you require Merrygorounds, Freaks, Girl Trumpet Players, Formulas? "Formulas—Our Literature will surprise you," says one mage, tersely. Legpads, Rubber Busts, Wigs, Opera Hose, Lung-Testing Machines and Laughing Mirrors.—"Make Big Money Selling Hair Straightener to Colored People" suggests Richmond, Va. Rochester has a Three-Legged Pig and Three-Legged Chicken, both in perfect health. New Orleans offers Chameleons, only fresh-caught stock shipped. Seattle has a ten-foot Devilfish for $25. Jackson, Mich., reports that Rice's Five Comedy Pigs are At Liberty. "Positively no other pig act on earth like it. Laugh insurance for your crowds." Also at liberty,

"Astrologist and Mitt Reader, wishes position with medicine show. Would consider lecturing for freak." An orchestra wants engagements, has played three seasons at Russell's Point, Ohio, "the Atlantic City of the Middle West." A Stilt Walker, young, sober, experienced; for any occasion. Ten feet or higher. And any number of saxophonists, all doubling clarinet, all "hot and sweet." Half-Man-Half-Woman is "young, strong feature; A1 wardrobe and lecture." A Show Boat at Spottsville, Kentucky, wants "Versatile Teams, Gen. Bus. do char. and spec. Comedian and Ingenue Team with hot specs. Good habits essential."—Comment on human frailty is the advertisement of a slot machine "especially designed to reject everything except genuine U. S. coins. It cannot possibly be operated with matches, toothpicks, cardboard, metal shims, wire, iron slugs or by any other popular cheating method." The student of these matters gradually begins to observe also a geographical specialization. Why do the acrobats and contortionists come from New England; freaks, medicine men, and clowns from Chicago; musicians and balloonists from the Middle West? Then, among these lighter notes, enters the deep voice of tragedy—

> *To Jennie Bertot, Lawrence Peterson, Jack Hozie, Freda McPherson, Carl Sowitz, Mrs. Conk, Mannina, Sarah Mason, Mrs. Flo Jones, James Mathews, George Wolcott and Chas. R. O'Donnell.*
>
> Will the above circus employees injured in train wreck at Iron Mountain, Mich., communicate with me *at once?* I just recovered $20,000 from the railroad company and will assist you.
>
> STEVE SABOL
>
> *Iron Mountain General Hospital,*
> *Iron Mountain, Mich.*

This was the queer, gay, generous, and cruel world inhabited by Shad Roe, whose nickname, we shall have to learn, was a testimonial to slick and slippery qualities. A world too likely to be romanticized by outsiders: it involves as much drudgery and arduous patience as any other. But it lives on the instantaneous response of its audience. Shad's own brand of salesmanship, on the vaudeville stage, was immediate and instinctive. If (in his own phrase) he put something over and it lay there, he knew at once what was wrong and varied his routine. Anything as slow and indirect as selling books seemed to him a waste of life's exciting hours. There was only one thing worth selling—Himself. Sometimes when overstocked with this commodity, he had to job off large consignments of it below cost. At such times he resented the security of Richard's employment.

But on this occasion Shad seemed to be flush. Apparently Mr. Merton, the manager of Merton's Midgets, had some private engagement that evening, and Shad had volunteered to give the troupe a good time. "But don't say anything about the war," he warned Richard and Pete. "These little folks are all Germans, and if you pull any patriotism on them they'll get sore. They might even paste you one on the beezer. They're mighty sensitive."

It was a party that required considerable tact. A theatrical hotel, fortunately, is never surprised at anything. Shad ordered Wiener Schnitzel and sauerkraut served on bread and butter plates in his dingy sitting room. A bucket of champagne came up, and liqueur glasses for the guests. They waited for them with the door open; Shad explained, "They don't like to have to knock so near the bottom of the door, it sounds funny." High chairs were brought. Pete and Richard, fearing embarrassments, thought it best to have a good start. They had considerably punished one bottle by the time the four midgets arrived.

Pete Sampson confessed afterward that the occasion rather gave him the willies. "They were dressed fit to kill," he said, "evening gowns and tuxedos, but their fingernails were black, like children's. But you should have seen Richard, he got on with 'em like a house afire. You'd have thought he was a midget himself. Although Shad warned us, there was something disconcerting about their strong German accent. Goodness knows what their names really were: they were introduced as Jumbo, the General, Miss Elsa and Miss Lena. The General seemed the leading spirit. I asked him if he was related to the famous General Tom Thumb. 'I do not know who it iss,' he squeaked. 'I am Scheneral Dismay.' They brought their own small-sized knives and forks with them in a little jewel-case. While the table was being laid they sat on the sofa in a row, very erect, the ladies most careful about the arrangement of their skirts. They talked politely about the business the show was doing."

But the midgets were in gracious mood. To be relieved from the supervision of their manager was evidently a welcome escapade. The General would not hear of taking his champagne in a liqueur glass, and held the large goblet in both hands to drink the health of his host. "Und you are in de book business?" he said to Richard. "Dat is excellent, I too shall write a book, ven I retire from de staitch. It shall be given out in a very small edition so it will not be heavy to carry." Richard said that the Erskines would be glad to see the manuscript, and they were immediate friends. After a few circulations of wine the talk became lively. Miss

Elsa complained of the embarrassment caused by appearing on the same bill with trained animals. When she met the dogs in the dark backstage a big collie licked her face and spoiled her make-up.

"Yes, it was quite a party," said Shad reminiscently. "I guess I oughtn't have let those little folks scoop up the champagne the way they did. Merton was very peeved about it afterwards. After a few dippers of wine the General went German on us. He stood up in his high chair and made a speech justifying submarine warfare. He was pretty sore about England; it was kinda pathetic to see him standing up in that baby-chair and telling it. Also he had a grouch on one of the stage crew who walked on him accidentally. Then, when we got him calmed down, Miss Elsa or Miss Lena, I don't know which, picked up her skirts and did a cooch on the table. They had a great time till the General fell out of his chair, and then they kind of folded. They passed out, all four of 'em. I felt responsible, I'd promised Merton I'd see they got home all right. They were staying in the same hotel, so Dick and I picked 'em up, one under each arm, and carried 'em back to their rooms. I was afraid they'd be mad the next day, because those little folks are strong on dignity. But I don't think they ever knew how they got to bed. The General asked me about it, and I told him he went off down the corridor as steady as Hindenburg. He believed it.

"Dick sure loosened up that night. He made a great hit with the midgets. I guess he must have picked up some Dutch talk from old Mamma Geschwindt, because I remember him and the General chinning German together. That fellow Sampson went out like a

light, we left him laying on the sofa. But by the time
the midgets were put away I had sort of a yen for
some life-size company. I could see in Brother Richard's eye that he wasn't as pious as he used to be.
'Let's go out and begin the evening right,' I says. Dick
says something about going to bed. 'Oh, nonsense, you
can lay in bed all day tomorrow. You're on the merry-
goround already, might as well reach for the brass
ring.' "

XXV

Diagram

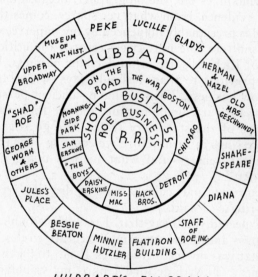

HUBBARD'S DIAGRAM

Y OU mustn't suppose," Hubbard said, "that I haven't
tried to approach this story in an orderly way. Here's a
diagram I made, but I haven't said much about it be-

cause when I showed it to Minnie Hutzler she seemed
to think it was rather cold-blooded. But I had to adopt
some device to visualize what was in my mind. Of
course this is crude and incomplete, but at least it
shows you the way I'm trying to work backward and
inward. We spoke of the biography as a kind of Round
Robin. Well, in that Round Robin there are concentric
rings. The outside one represents testimony available
Now, after Richard's death. The narrow ring inside
that symbolizes *me,* the biographer, because obviously
all the evidence, from whatever source, comes through
me and is presumably influenced by my imperfections as
a transmitter. The next circle records the critical episodes of Richard's life in the Erskine business. Within
that—previous to that, I should say—we go back to
the show business. Then we have sufficient perspective
to come forward again, in time, and see Richard in the
last days of the stationery traffic. We go round each
of these rings in turn before we come to Richard himself in the center—and what he was doing on that
ferryboat."

"You're not particularly good at drawing free-hand
piston-rings," I said.

"I expected you'd say that. I took the trouble to get
a compass and draw some nice accurate circles. Naturally that was my instinct as a C. P. A., to make everything neat. Then I decided I liked my wabbly sketch
better. More like real life. Perhaps they ought to be
polygons anyhow, instead of circles. Every time I get
a new slant on Richard it's like adding a new side to
the polygon—but no matter how many sides you add
to the circumscribed polygon you never quite reach the
perfect circle of Meaning. Geometry's pretty grand
when you stop and think about it.—I don't mind your

DIAGRAM   191

laughing at my silly little diagram: I know it's silly myself. There's no very satisfying way of making a map of human life on paper. At least I would need another dimension to suggest the to-and-fro of chronology."

"I'm not laughing," I said. "Only smiling. Lots of silly little things have been very helpful in great affairs. The philosopher Kant had an incredibly absurd con- traption of tapes and tackle for supporting his stock- ings from his shoulders; wearing garters, he believed, interfered with the circulation and molested the intellect."

I examined his synoptic diagram and could see that he had been following the rotations rather faithfully. "This reference to Diana," I said. "Who is she; I don't seem to remember your speaking about her?"

"That's Diana on the old Madison Square Garden —gone to Philadelphia now, they tell me. (What she's doing there I can't imagine. She and the statue of Wil- liam Penn won't get on so well together.) I told you that the Roe office in the Flatiron Building had a fine view of Diana. But I haven't dealt with that yet. I've got to soon, but I dread it. One of those little human foolishnesses that meant a good deal to the people concerned and probably seem trivial to anyone else."

It was thrilling to me to see Hubbard developing a sense of triviality. I thought, but did not dismay him by saying, that he had undertaken the hardest job in the world—mending roads or painting pictures is nothing to it. He gazed broodingly at the little circles in his drawing. I could imagine him almost hypnotizing himself with them. Evidently he had some inward vision of what the Life and Times of Richard Roe ought to mean: he was gradually getting it into his

head as a musician masters a symphony before a recital
—until he can feel it beforehand, finger by finger.
When he plays it he is also actually singing it inside his
mind.

"Well, anyhow," he said, "that's the target I'm
shooting at. There's a pretty good chance I'll never
get anywhere near the bull's-eye." He put the drawing
away in his pocket. "I'm having dinner with Lucille
tonight. She puzzles me. She seems to have forgotten
already that there ever was such a person as Richard."

"That also may have its significance," I suggested.

"But good heavens, he's only been dead six months.
She seems to have no conception of him whatever except as he was useful to her. When that stopped, he
stopped altogether. I'm getting some cold turkey on
the regardlessness of our scheme of things. You know
how hard Richard worked to sell those novels written
by Hampton. It was steady plugging like that that
made Hampton a valuable moving-picture property
and brought him a fortune. Well, just for fun I wrote
Hampton, asked if he knew anything about Roe. He
didn't remember even having heard of him."

It's queer to consider that the so-called Brass Ring
episode, which was for Shad just a casual and entertaining frolic (one of a hundred such), had profound
effects on Richard. The details of the incident are im-
pertinent here, but they struck him at a moment when
he was in a very unstable equilibrium. When he came
to, in the lonely mid-afternoon hours of a hotel Sunday, a great bubble of darkness and horror ballooned
up in his mind and burst in shuddering disgust. He sat
on the edge of his bed with stinging eyes and consid-

DIAGRAM   193

ered himself only worthy a goblet of iodine. The lively
Shad, to whom remorse was an unknown symptom,
called up presently—ostensibly to report on the bedfast
condition of the midgets, but really to discover how
badly Richard had been bruised by his fall from grace.
Richard, somewhat embarrassed, inquired what was
the name of the Brass Ring. "Her name?" cried the
comedian, "I haven't the slightest idea. It didn't seem
to be her name that you were interested in." The
queerest of poor Richard's horrors was that he felt
he had been false to Minnie rather than Lucille, for
all that day—the very day romanticized by the purchase of the garters—Minnie had been much in his
mind. But time went on and no fragments of outraged
sky dropped on him. He remembered a famous story
of the Erskine office, of the melodramatic punishment
of Gene Vogelsang on a transcontinental trip. In office
tradition it was always ascribed to the fact that Gene,
on his way to the Coast, had a berth in a car called
Nemesis, but was too unclassical to realize this might
be an omen. Briefly and crudely: in the diner he met
a lady; they approved of each other; she told him the
location of her couch. As the train rumbled through a
Rocky Mountain night he found his way to her car,
several removed from his own. Thus he missed the
information that at some junction point the caravan
divided. His own car, with his baggage, went on as
planned, to Denver; whereas Mr. Vogelsang found
himself presently, with no gear but slippers and dressing gown, on his way (appropriately) to Salt Lake.
But even this rather obvious form of rebuke seemed to
have passed Richard by. A new and strange thought
came to him: if he could have something he didn't

want, and the heavens not fall, why was it so impossible to have something he greatly desired?

The next time Shad was in New York he himself was At Liberty and low in funds whereas Richard had had a raise in salary. To Lucille's great delight they were moving to the coveted Upper West Side, and Shad was invited to dinner the last night in the little apartment near Morningside Park. Lucille's innocent gloating over their rise in fortune may have prompted some jealousy on Shad's part. Relating the evening on North Clark Street he remarked, "You should have seen Dick carrying an actress under each arm."

"You might add they were midgets," said Richard mildly; but Lucille was already on edge with packing and housework. The ground had been laid for a really lively argument, for at the annual picnic of the Erskine employees that summer Daisy had taken occasion to sow a little mustard seed in Lucille's ear. One of the few advantages of the European War was that it finally ended the Erskine picnics. Theoretically these affairs were to bring all the Erskine staff and their wives and children together in a genial expedition. A steamer was chartered to take them all for an outing up the Hudson. "The whole Erskine family," they liked to call themselves, and the family character of the outing was emphasized by the various quarrels that were started or aggravated. Somewhere near the storm center of these squalls you could expect to find Daisy. Sam Erskine found that it took at least two weeks to get his salesmen's morale back to normal after one of these picnics, because their wives were taking it out of them at home. At the famous picnic of 1916, the last that was held, Daisy had gone out of her way to give

DIAGRAM 195

Lucille an account of her visit to Detroit. "I don't think you should allow your husband to carry such strong medicine with him, Mrs. Roe," was her way of putting it. "It really isn't safe; that woman he had in his room at the hotel was made quite ill by it." This would have gone further, but about that time young Gladys, aged then about five, discovered a hornet's nest.

Memories of the picnic provided lively discussion. Late that evening, after Shad left, Richard went for a farewell stroll. He was sorry to leave Morningside Park and particularly the statue of Bear and Faun past which he and Gladys had walked so often. The move uphill and the quarrel precipitated by Shad seemed definitely the end of an era.

XXVI

Saying Good-bye

THE move beyond the Great Divide of the Morning-side cliff did change the view, in more ways than one. Richard, though not fanciful, now realized that there had been a sense of security on the lower level. To look up toward the Cathedral and the trumpeting angel gave a comfortable feeling that the world was a stable place, watched over by spiritual powers. But the region of Columbia seemed more naked to the winds of living. The great façade of the university library, and the sight of so many alert youths on that broad terrace of learning, are alarming to a humble man who thinks sadly how much more they know than he.

He noticed at once that on that hilltop they were much nearer the war. Battleships came up the Hudson, and the tomb of General Grant is more impressive than its neighbor, the grave of the Amiable Child. That autumn a German submarine visited Newport, and Herman Schmaltz, always cautious, gave up making business trips to Boston by the Fall River boat. Gladys's favorite excursion was now the ledge round

Grant's Tomb, where she scampered on plump legs and played hide and seek behind the corners. The new apartment was a great pride, a symbol of promotion; it gave Lucille intense pleasure to travel by subway or bus rather than the poor old L, and to mention her telephone number as *Riverside* so-and-so. But it was not a place to settle down for tranquillity, as they had hopefully imagined. There was little tranquillity that year.

The war had its effect on small affairs as well as great. It made changes in the Erskine itineraries. Herman Schmaltz, to everyone's surprise, went off to do Y. M. C. A. work at a training camp. He was childless, had saved money, and he had the restlessness of forty years. He had twinges of the intense Americanism of those conscious of German ancestry; also he was sagacious enough to consider that the wholesome life of Camp Dix would be an admirable holiday from the book business. He never came back to Erskines': one of his buddies in the Y. M. C. A. canteen later offered him a partnership in the paper-box business.

Herman's Y. M. C. A. uniform with its handsome red triangle gave Hazel an irritating advantage over Lucille, who sometimes imagined that all the convulsions of the universe were planned specially for her own annoyance. She thought she had caught up with her sister by the move to the Upper West Side, but now Hazel was continually alluding to "doing one's bit." Poor old Mrs. Geschwindt had her trials too. She had supposed that now Gladys was near by she would have consolation in her grandchild, but Gladys also was infected with patriotism. The old lady was unmistakably Teuton in garb and feature, so much so that when the pair walked together in Riverside Park, other urchins taunted. "Yay Gladys, your grannie's a Hun," screeched one young imp. Perhaps no history of the war has ever justly described how a composite nation was bedevilled by these intestine pangs. Gladys, with the cruelty of childhood, mocked the German nursery rhymes her grandmother tried to tell her. Mrs. Geschwindt sometimes groped her way along the paths of Riverside blinded with tears. Stony and angular were those tall streets, uncomfortable to one brought up in a softer, more genial earth. She felt sometimes as if she had no home anywhere: not a good way for an old lady to feel. Hazel, enjoying herself hugely at Red Cross bazaars and sewing circles, obviously regarded her mother as something to be apologized for. Lucille seemed to find her apartment and Gladys a full-time job. Only Richard, when he was at home, seemed aware of Mrs. Geschwindt's misery. Sometimes he was able to hunt out a movie that had nothing to do with Preparedness and take her to see it. Even there someone would usually come out on the stage and talk for a long two minutes about Liberty Bonds.

Herman's departure, and other shifts, meant changes at the office. Gene Vogelsang went back to cover the Coast. "Just my luck," he remarked to Richard. "You know I tried, two or three years ago, to get Sam to give me the Coast again. I had a lot of good friends out there—and say, a traveller has no idea what hospitality is until he hits that country. I don't know what it is, life feels different out there. More sense of fun. I tried to convince Sam that our connections in California really needed building up. No, he said he wanted me in the East. So I look through the little red notebook, all those nice names and numbers. No use any more, I say to myself, and throw it away.

Now I'm going out again—I wish I had it. It'd save
me a lot of time."

Richard said nothing of his own transfer. He was
to sell Boston now, which meant good-bye to Detroit.

There was a queer tension in the air as he came to
Detroit for that last visit. We have forgotten now that
dangerous terrifying energy with which a nation, after
long delay, groomed itself for war. The automotive
city, though the Chamber of Commerce had not yet
invented for itself the phrase Dynamic Detroit,
hummed in the ecstasies of production. In those days
even the book business was lively. Richard had grown
to know and love the city: when he registered at the
hotel and looked out over Grand Circus Park, he remembered the streets like old friends. There was
Cadillac Square and Woodward Avenue, Washington
Boulevard and the street mysteriously named John R.
—He was in that deliciously dangerous state of mind
when one says to himself: This is going to be good-
bye. This is the end.

He finished his work in the afternoon; he was to
take the midnight sleeper. He invited Bessie Beaton
and Minnie to dine with him at the hotel. It was a
warm evening. "Let's eat up in the room where we
can be comfortable," he said. "Is Daisy Erskine anywhere round?" asked Bessie ironically. "And I'm going
to ask Jock Edwards, the buyer at Griswold's, to come
too," said Richard.

"I've got a better idea," said Minnie. "You said
you've never taken the ferry over to Windsor. Let's
do that. You ought to set foot on Canadian soil while
you have a chance."

There had been a parade that afternoon, which they

watched from the windows of Hacks' store. Old Mr.
Hack was in a ferment of exaltation: he had declared
a half holiday in the store and turned his daily advertisement into a personally signed essay on Showing
Your Colors. (5,000 new flags had just arrived from
the bunting factory.) He was willing to allow any number of employees to enlist, and secretly determined that
he would not even grudge a bronze tablet for those
who might not come back. Bessie Beaton wept with excitement as the ranks marched by. Even the cool
Minnie showed curious tremors of emotion. Richard
was intoxicated by the repetition of martial tunes,
the slow swaying rhythm of feet. He felt a secret
envy of the marchers. To be one of that great brown
tide, flowing endlessly downward, all the pitiful decisions of every day swallowed up in one great unani-
mous obedience. He read Mr. Hack's announcement
to the staff, posted up in the store, encouraging them
for service. "Gee, that's pretty fine," he said. Then
Minnie startled him. "Bunk!" she said. "He's pretty
safe, isn't he? Not much chance of submarines getting
into the Detroit River."

They picked up Jock and crossed over to Windsor.
They wandered about that agreeable town and found
a pleasant café for dinner. "This is *your* evening," they
told Richard; "we'll do whatever you suggest." He was
deeply touched at their evident reluctance to have him
go. "I don't care who Sam sends, I shan't give him
any 50's," said Bessie. "Fifties!" cried Jock. "Dick
never got any orders like that out of me. It must be his
romantic eye, Bessie." "Never mind what it is," she
said.

"By the way," Richard remarked, "I've got a book
for you up at the hotel, Bessie. Stop there on the way

back, and I'll give it to you. Not business, this is a present."

"I was hoping it would be a pair of garters," she said.

"I'm glad you don't like leaving us," said Minnie. "But gosh, how I envy you. New York, Boston, Philly —that sounds to me like the real thing. I'm going to pull my freight out of here as soon as I get a chance." She was not very talkative that evening, but Richard thought he had never seen her so alluring. She wore a muslin dress with many tiers of flounces and a big straw hat. As the hour of departure came nearer, he grew depressed. How marvellous to be with people who understood him so well; why could not all life be like this?

"You know," he said, as they went back to the ferry, "this has been my first trip abroad."

On the ferry, Bessie decided she was tired. "Do you mind if I don't come back to the hotel?" she said. "Jock will see me home. I hate saying good-byes anyhow. Minnie, you go along and get the book for me."

Richard never knew exactly how it happened. She was upstairs in his room, where his bag was already packed for the train.

"How much time have you?" she asked. "You mustn't be late."

"Listen," he said abruptly. "Never mind about time, I'm something besides a bookseller. I'm also a man."

His arms were round her, as he had sometimes imagined them.

"Does that light turn out?" she said presently.

"Let's try it and see."

"My darling, I did want you, just for once, to have whatever you wished." This was whispered very low, but then followed by her characteristic laughter. "I thought you ought to have a souvenir of your trip abroad."

Minnie would not let him miss his train. She saw him safely to the station. Her last words were: "I hope you won't have as good a time in Boston as you did in Detroit."

Boston was indeed rather different. But in the ardors of a new itinerary he had little chance to meditate until an autumn day when he found himself at the old Parker House over Sunday. He went out for a stroll, occasionally murmuring the word Paakeh to himself, trying to pronounce it in its own way. He discovered the Public Gardens.

No social memorandum of Boston is complete without a note on the Public Gardens on a Sunday morning. The serenity of those clean lawns and fine old trees is perfect. Not there will you find notices in four languages. Observe the swan-boats gently pedalled by elderly men and bearing gravely elated passengers. Perhaps these craft are symbolic of the traditional New England literature? The great books of Massachusetts were swan-boats pedalled by elderly men.

Richard carefully read the General Rules of the City of Boston Park Department:

> *No person shall annoy another; or speak in a loud tone; or sing, or whistle; or utter any profane, threatening abusive, or indecent language, or loud outcry; or canvass; or solicit any subscription or contribution; or play any game of chance; or sit, stand, or lie on a balustrade, wall, or fence; or stand or lie on a seat; or sleep; or throw a*

stone or other thing; or drink, or be under the
influence of intoxicating liquor; or, except in
Franklin Field, preach, or pray aloud, or make
any oration or harangue.

He had no particular desire to do any of these
trespasses, though perhaps he was playing a game of
chance unawares. He sat very still under a tree, for
even the swan-boats were too distracting for what he
needed to consider. There was no real future for him
at Erskines'. That afternoon he wrote to Minnie.
"I've decided to start in business on my own, the first
of the year. Stationery novelties. Will begin with that
desk-set idea. Would you come on to New York and
help me with it?"

His mind went back to the last evening in Detroit.
"Gosh, and I thought I was saying good-bye," he said
to himself.

XXVII

Pathology

THE last selling trip Richard made for Erskine Brothers was shortly before Christmas, 1917, when he had to stay in Boston several days to take rush reorders during the gift season. Minnie had already given up her job at Hacks' and was in New York looking for an office suitable for the new enterprise. She and Mr. Gall, the red-headed accountant, were Richard's first—and for some while the only—employees. The model of the Roe pen-stand had been perfected, and Minnie had interested old Jake Hack to the extent of investing some capital. When Jake's check arrived, Minnie was exultant. This meant they could begin manufacture at once. She grabbed the next train at Grand Central and hurried to Boston to get Richard's signature on various papers and contracts.

Minnie knew nothing about Boston, but she happened to say to the taxi-man outside the South Station that she thought it was going to rain. He misunderstood and she found herself taken to the Hotel Touraine. There Richard found her, in a small genteel sitting room for ladies. They sat discussing business details. In the energy of argument (Richard was insisting that Jake must not have majority control of the company) he emphasized his ideas by tapping Minnie's knee. "Which," says Minnie, "all things considered, I think he had a perfect right to do." But a dour matron in black silk, apparently the official chaperon of the house, appeared beside them and said sternly: "You are not allowed to put your hand on a lady's knee in the Hotel Touraine." Richard flushed with painful embarrassment, but Minnie burst into delighted laughter.

Minnie remembers this because by coincidence it linked up with their choice of the Flatiron Building. Richard also had been having trouble with his knee: he had given it a bad wrench in a fall on the stairs of the Sixth Avenue L. Stiffness developed, and he was advised to go to a hospital to have the cartilage slit. He had recently done so. They gave him anæsthetic for the operation—first gas, then ether. The only previous time he had taken gas was in a dentist's office in the Flatiron Building. Whenever he visited that dentist he was always thrilled by the view from the chair, which included the ornate balconies of the old Madison Square Garden and the silhouette of Diana tiptoe in the sky. The goddess was far from his thoughts when he entered the operating room at the hospital, but at the first breath of gas she appeared vividly before him. Something in the outline of that slender shape made him think of Minnie—who also always seemed to have an arrow aimed and tightened against the string. For a few seconds of vivid sensibility, until the ether abolished all mind, he had this vision of the soaring figure. It came closer and closer, and the face seemed to

change into Minnie's. He had not written to her about
this, for it seemed difficult to put on paper, but after
the rebuke from the Touraine duenna he recalled it.
"I think it's a hunch," Minnie said. "I'll go to the
Flatiron and see if there's any space for rent."

In the uproar of great events then proceeding, so
small an affair as the founding of Richard Roe, Inc.,
was not noticeable. An entry in the routine list of business incorporations was the only time Richard ever
had a chance to appear in a newspaper until his obit—
with one sole exception. The exception was some years
later when the Inquiring Reporter for a tabloid newspaper was buttonholing people at random on the
streets and asking their opinions on current topics.
The reporter was flushing his covey in Madison
Square that day, and happened to pick on Richard.
He asked him some question about war debts and
reparations. "I don't know enough about it to even
give an opinion," said Richard honestly. The Inquiring Reporter was indignant: in his long experience of
touting for comments he was accustomed to receive
immediate and positive solutions for all the most
intricate issues of morals, politics, and finance.

"D'you mean to say you don't care whether those
foreigners pay their debts to Uncle Sam?" he cried.

Richard perceived that this was special pleading,
and begged to be excused.

"But all you've got to do is give me some sort of
reaction on the thing," said the inquisitor. "I want to
print it, with your name and address and your picture."

"I'm sorry," said Richard, "I don't know a damn

thing about it. I'm not going to fake up an opinion just to get my picture in the paper."

"Well, you're a hell of an American," said the disgusted interviewer.

But we need not suppose that Richard did not have a natural man's respect for the press; he saved with the greatest care clippings of a brief paragraph that appeared in the *Bookseller and Stationer* announcing the appearance of the Roe Pen-Holder.

There was plenty of talk in Richard's own little circle. At first Lucille was alarmed at the risk they were taking. But she soon reflected that to have Richard the head of his own business would put her one up on Hazel; particularly since Hazel had expected that Richard would apply to Herman for help in financing. Richard had not done so. "Never try to raise money from the family," he said. "I wish your brother had the same idea," remarked Lucille. "We're bound to be in wrong with Hazel anyhow," Richard said. "If the business makes money, she'll be just as sore we *didn't* ask them to come in as she would be now if we did." The capital necessary to start was not large, for Richard had excellent trade connections and credit was easy in that elastic age, but he had very little cash of his own, and the problem gave him much anxiety. He was greatly touched when Miss Mac took him aside, shortly before he left the Erskine office. "I've got some money saved up," she said, "and if you need any for this business of yours I can spare a thousand. I think you'll make a success, and I'd like to have a share in it." He accepted her offer, gratefully, but was disturbed when she said she had sold Liberty Bonds to raise the cash. "I'm afraid that wasn't very patriotic," he said. "What's patriotism between friends?" she replied. "Good luck, boy; I hope you make a killing, if it's only to get Daisy's goat."

Sam Erskine was sorry to have him go. "Especially just now," he said, "when our sales staff is all shot to pieces by the war. I don't suppose I'll ever get a team together like we've had the past five years. If you could just hang on here awhile, you'd pretty near have the pick of the work by the time it's over. It's a dangerous thing to have Herman Schmaltz and George Work and Bill Schaefer buddying up with all those men in the army. They'll learn that there's lots of jobs that pay better money than the book business. First thing you know, they'll be lost to Literature. Daisy says Literature won't even know they've gone. But you know how Daisy is."

Though too shy to say so, Richard did not want to improve his position simply by sitting pretty. When Lucille expressed anxiety for the future, Richard was reminded of a story he made up for Gladys after their earliest visits to the Museum of Natural History. Gladys was specially interested in the pigeons that flutter about the Museum. The lively curiosity of a child of six or seven had not yet been dulled by the shallow sophistication which is the doom of so many middling minds. She wanted to know what one of the pigeons would think if he got into the Museum among all the stuffed creatures. So Richard invented a story for her, of a pigeon of inquiring mind who saw all the children pouring into the Museum on Sundays. This pigeon, whom they named Mr. Koo, wanted to get inside and find out what happened there. One day

he waited by the revolving door until he saw a chance;
hovering politely over the shoulder of the person
entering, he flew in. He had a fascinating time, and
when evening came he slept in the Indian wigwam in
the West Wing, where an old squaw is represented
telling tales to the Indian children. On cold nights,
though, he was distressed to find that the fire in the
wigwam was only red glass with an electric bulb
under it. Pursued by the guards, who wanted to put
him out, Mr. Koo flew up to the bird rooms and sat
so still they thought he was a stuffed specimen.

Richard remarked to Lucille and Gladys that perhaps there was a fable in the idea. In any kind of job
—particularly a municipal job, perhaps—if you sit so
still they imagine you are only a stuffed image, there
is small danger of being detected and fired. "But I
don't want to hold a job by just sitting still," he said.
"I want a little show of my own." His mind felt comfortable with the inward glow and pleasure that ac-
company thought. But Lucille was prompt in retort.
"Schmoos!" she objected. "There didn't seem to be
much sitting still in the Erskine job. You always said
they had you on the run every minute." She was growing into that peculiar condition, characteristic of aggrieved females, of desiring to prove Richard wrong
as often as possible, and believing that everything that
gave him enjoyment was necessarily a deduction from
her own pleasure. Probably what she needed, Hubbard
believes, was a lot more maternity to occupy her mind.
But the doctor had advised against it, and she had
decided to go in for Pekinese instead.

(What biography can be justly written, Hubbard reflected, without intimate knowledge of the pathology
of the subjects? Why, furthermore, is an intelligible

biography of any woman so very rare outside of the field of medicine? Not because her system of causation is obscure, but rather because it is so horrifyingly direct.)

If it was desired to prove Richard wrong, there was always one to whom it could be done most easily— Gladys. Left to herself, the child would have been likely to conclude that her father was not difficult to get along with. But children, knowing themselves rather helpless, are enormously shrewd to adapt their conduct to whatever situation gives the greatest immediate comfort. Gladys had to live with her mother the greater part of the time; she was prompt to see that siding with her mother made things much easier for herself. To take a strong line against Richard was sure of maternal approval. What psychological effect this may have had on the girl herself would be too long an inquiry to pursue. It will work itself out in her own life, as these lesions must. At the time of her father's death, when she had to turn to and look for a job, she began to suspect that there was something both humorous and tragic in the misunderstanding. The notion that man is the workhorse, destined by divine allotment to toil for woman's luxury, received some drastic revision in her mind when she undertook earning for herself.

But proving anyone wrong is so tragically easy, Hubbard said to himself. With the calm detachment of a bachelor sage, he embarked upon further speculation. Sometimes I think Lucille and Gladys were each other's most dangerous enemies, he said.—Or perhaps there was something rather sacred in their relation: who knows? At any rate, if one of them was unhappy, she insisted on the other being miserable also. Isn't that a very perfect intimacy?

"Poor old Mother Hubbard," cackled Minnie as he laboriously tried to reconstruct the fragments of this broken mosaic. "It's tough for you, accustomed to dealing with nice obedient figures and making trial balances jump through hoops. Figures behave, but people don't."

And at the same time, with a twinge of admiration, she admitted to herself that the persevering student was beginning to see beneath surfaces. On his side, Hubbard was alarmed by Minnie's fascination. She has a sense of humor like a man's, he thought; but was prudent enough not to say so. He would not look at her, but slowly picked among the tangled threads of his argument.

"As long as there are men in the world——" he said.

"It's going to seem a long time," Minnie put in.

"—every woman is a potential threat to every other woman. Only by standing together can they keep man in his proper subjection. But they can't pool their resources——"

"Hurrah!" said Minnie.

"The Life Force has created them for very definite purposes—why, it sticks out all over them."

"Are you getting personal?" she asked.

But he kept stubbornly on: "And man, the powerful helot, trades on their inability to coöperate."

"He does, does he? Listen, you take women too seriously. They're only stewing in their own juice."

"Minnie," he said, "I'm glad nobody hears you but me. You do say the most deplorable things."

But to return to the year 1918—about the time the Great German Drive of that spring was getting ready, Richard Roe, Inc., started actual business in the Flat-iron Building. It was an anxious time for everybody. Richard had dug his own little line of trenches and for-tified them as best he could. But there was a continual popping of small nerve-bombs behind the lines.

XXVIII

The Office

W E CALL it the Roe business, but certainly Minnie
Hutzler's energy had much to do with its foundation
and success. However, she had no hankering for the
outward appearances of importance: she never gave
any impression of being more than a stenographer.
This caused many business acquaintances to unburden
themselves more frankly than they might otherwise
have done. Minnie was merry enough when you knew
her, but her mask of cool reserve was always within
easy reach.

At first the office was only a tiny suite of three
rooms. Richard thought they could have got along with
two, but Minnie insisted on their having a reception
room for the display of samples and to impress customers. She alarmed Richard by giving it almost a
domestic look, with easy chairs and some modernist
pictures she picked up in Greenwich Village. They were
not very good pictures: in the first flush of her emancipation from Detroit and in the joy of new independence she ran a bit hastily toward the Left Wing of
æsthetic taste. But she was also shrewd enough to off-

set these things by hanging an engraving of George Washington, whose portrait (she had observed) always gives the American business man a feeling of confidence, of solid ground underfoot. At least she was ahead of her time in thinking that a business office need not be ugly and bleak. She pleaded that the Roe pen-stand and other specialties should be colorful and attractive in design. In her brief lunch hour she hung about antique shops and art galleries alert for ideas which might be translated into desk fixtures. The Diana Ash Tray, with its moistened extinguisher pad, was her own idea, suggested by the acrid fume of crushed cigarette and cigar stubs left smouldering by callers. She kept a vase of flowers in the Reception Room. This did not make life easier for Richard, for when Lucille visited the place she was scandalized by its informal air; and one or two old-fashioned stationery buyers felt there was something vaguely libertine in having fresh flowers in a business office.

It was unfortunate that on Lucille's first visit to the Flatiron she was accompanied by Hazel. Lucille, innocently hoping for a good chance to impress her sister, contrived that during a joint shopping expedition they should run up to Richard's office, where he would give her a check. Sore was her indignation when Richard explained that his personal checkbook was at home, and a check on the company would not be valid without Miss Hutzler's signature also. Miss Hutzler at that moment was out for lunch—would they wait? They did so, rather to Richard's chagrin, for he was embarrassed at the idea of using a company check for private expenses, even if refunded the next day. But Lucille, seeing his uneasiness, was the more determined to have a glimpse of the Miss Hutzler of whom she

had heard much. Also an infuriating demureness in
Hazel's bearing seemed to imply that the double signature of checks was really a mysterious form of in-
trigue.

Minnie returned almost immediately. To Richard's
relief it was one of her sallow days; she looked grati-
fyingly homely. Lucille was delighted as soon as she
laid eyes on her; an excellent phrase, for the laying-on
of eyes is almost a physical impact in the case of high-
tension females. Minnie sized up the situation at once,
and seemed to grow visibly more plain. She was so
briskly matter-of-fact that the check-signing was accomplished without fracas. A smaller woman would
have made it an opportunity for picayune satisfactions.
But Minnie had found what she wanted, a full devotion. The whole force and tact of her strong will were
now in motion to help Richard, always and however.
In the essential Richard, when he was not being put
over the jumps by circumstances, she saw something
clear, unspoiled and childlike; unaware but quickly re-
sponsive; something to be enjoyed, not just owned.
With fine insight, on this trivial occasion she obliterated herself; became illegible. Lucille and Hazel went
off to Wanamaker's in good humor, and Richard
thought to himself, "I was never so pleased to see a
woman look terrible."

The entire staff of Richard Roe, Inc., numbered only
three at the beginning. Richard negotiated with the
factory and did all the selling. Minnie did the stenog-
raphy, telephoning, and office routine; and good old
Charlie Gall, the red-headed bookkeeper, cared for the
accounts. They thought of him as old, though he was
not much past fifty in 1918; his bald head ringed with

copper-colored hair and his earnestly solemn Irish face
gave him an air of goblin antiquity. Richard had met
him once at Erskines', when Mr. Gall had harangued
Sam Erskine on the idea of publishing a History of
Writing Ink. The chemistry of ink was Mr. Gall's
hobby: the fact that early writing fluids were made
from nut-galls pleased his fancy and perhaps had
started him on this research. After the day's figuring
was over, and he and Richard and Minnie sometimes
sat for a smoke together before closing the office, Mr.
Gall would enlarge upon the fortune awaiting whoever
would invent a formula for a perfect modern ink.
"These synthetic inks can't compare with the good old
medieval stuff," he often said. "The monks went out in
the woods collecting those big warts from trees; the
ink they made is still black and fresh on their manu-
scripts. Why, even the word *book* really means a beech
tree. The whole of literature stems out of growing
trees, natural things." One of his grievances was that
he had been moved on from lodging to lodging by reason of his furtive and smelly experiments. He was once
arrested for trying to chip off a specially fine oak-gall
from a tree in Central Park; occasionally he brought
flasks of his home-made ink for Richard to try. But
this hobby never interfered with office hours, and was
even valuable on one occasion. Minnie was feeling faint
one very hot day, and he brought her round by making
her inhale the neck of the office ink-bottle. "Better than
any smelling-salts," he insisted. "It's the ferrous salts
and indigo-sulphonic acid. Wonderful stuff!" And
Minnie had to admit, sniffing the odor of ink for the
first time, that it was very refreshing.

"And why shouldn't ink be perfumed for ladies?"
he would continue. "Think of its exhilarating or aphro-

disiac qualities. Makes correspondence an ecstasy; people would write more letters, use up more pens. The
perfect ink would be not only non-corrosive, non-
poisonous, and permanent; it would also be an æsthetic
drug."

"It's not always desirable to have it so permanent,"
Minnie objected. "Why don't you invent an ink which
would vanish completely after thirty days—very valuable for indiscreet lovers?"

"What does *aphrodasic* mean?" Richard asked Minnie afterward.

It is the little things that are remembered. All the
great drums and tramplings of the war went past beneath the windows of the Flatiron, but they seem to
have faded away into a dim echo, while the small human comedy of the office lives in memory. The Roe
pen-stand did well from the first; they soon needed
larger quarters. Minnie learned from the renting agent
that one of the big suites in the corner would be available; the layout seemed admirable, and though Richard
was alarmed at the cost, she was firm. She wanted him
to have one of those magnificent big chambers at the
forward tip of the building. "Buyers will come in just
to see your office," she said. And truly, every New
Yorker must have wondered about those corner rooms
in the Flatiron. It was a big triangle with a rounded
apex, two huge windows on each side and three in the
arc. In the wider stretch of the room was the sacred
Conference Table—what a thrill it gave Minnie when
she bid it in at the auction sale on 23rd Street! As business quickened, this table was usually spread with specifications and estimates to be gone over with Mr. Gettleman from the factory in New Jersey. Richard's own

desk was far in the corner, where he looked up the di-
verging channels of Fifth Avenue and Broadway. On
windy days, when great gusts boomed and sang round
that æolian angle, he was like the captain on the bridge
of his ship. The whole bulk of the narrow building
seemed to be steering steadily uptown. When you entered the room you saw Richard from behind, bent
over the desk or leaning backward in the spring-chair,
telephoning. He did not like turning his back on the
rest of the office, but it would be worse still to disre-
gard the outside view.

That room is important: for thirteen years it was as
solid a center of living as Richard ever knew. In the
apartment uptown he never had the same feeling of
permanence, for he knew that sooner or later Lucille
would express a desire to move toward bigger and better bathrooms. But here, in that great breezy triangle,
so open to daylight and the sight of New York's weird
vitality, he felt that his will was operative. Forces of
living seemed to flow through him outward. Has the
love of man for his office ever been celebrated? When
he arrived in the morning his desk was neat, the mail
already opened, letters neatly piled, sometimes with
Minnie's annotations pencilled on them in reference to
decisions. The nine o'clock chime tolled across the
Square. In the adjoining room, with her door closed,
he heard Minnie's typewriter going already. It was a
luxurious gesture to postpone saying good-morning to
her until he had had time to savor the new day, this
new helping of Time. Almost unconsciously he de-
ferred this rite until he was well balanced; feeling
good, as the noble phrase is. How important to watch
those habitual old sayings, see how they spy into mortal reality.

(Why did the word *phrasemonger* get its deroga-
tory meaning, Hubbard asked himself? Because the
monger uses phrases just as parcels of trade, without
considering their simple truthfulness? And how many
kinds of mongers are there? I can only think of six:
fish, iron, scandal, news, whore, and *phrase.* Is it a compliment to books that you never hear of a book-mon-
ger? But you might have a book-chandler, because
according to the Erskine Dictionary a chandler deals
in candles, things that burn and give light. I want to be
a chandler, not a monger.)

Yes, in that room Richard felt good; he felt virtue in
himself. The little unnoticed satisfactions of office life:
he dipped his pen to sign Minnie's beautifully typed letters with the little dictation symbol at the bottom, R.
R.—M. H. He dropped cigar ashes unreproved; went
over balances with Charlie Gall and was sometimes
diverted from the problem at issue by imagining the
dancing pattern of figures that must be shimmering to
and fro just under that warm pink scalp. In the afternoon, putting down the telephone with a click, he would
suddenly see that lights had come out in all the great
buildings; Madison Square was framed in tissues of
clear gold, and Diana a small negress on green sky.

They hired more help. At Miss Mac's suggestion
Richard engaged young Ed Furness to travel for him.
Ed had formerly been an office-boy at Erskines' and
had the mixed practical training of all Erskine alumni.
Richard now had opportunity to study the old problem of the Swindle Sheet from the other side. He remembered Sam Erskine's humorous talks on the subject, and passed on the traditional counsels of The

Road, specially mentioning certain hotels that have a reputation for overcharging travellers.

"And here's a tip, while I think of it," he told Ed. "If you ever need to cash a personal check, where you're not known, give it a good high serial number. All the Erskine gang were at a convention in Atlantic City one time, and we exceeded our expense allowance. The boys pooled their jack, we had about fifteen dollars cash. I was the only one who had a personal checkbook with me—I had just started my own account. They told me to go down to the hotel desk and get it cashed; I was wondering whether they'd take my check. 'Not like that,' said Gene Vogelsang; 'change that number 8 to something bigger. Make it 3806. If they think you've put through 3800 checks on that account they'll be sure it's o.k.' "

Ed Furness proved a good choice, but the first clerical employees were not so satisfactory. Minnie dismissed them without compunction; she remembers Armistice Day not so much for the end of the war as for the discovery of that unique pair Jenny Hoerl and Peggy Whaley. She had gone up to 42nd Street on an errand to an advertising agency; when she came out, Fifth Avenue was jammed with a jubilee throng. Walking was impossible, she managed to find a seat on top of a bus. In front of her were two gay little creatures remarking that they had lost their jobs by going out to celebrate without permission. One of them (this was Peggy) had bought herself some brilliant cerise material for a blouse; she opened the package to show it to her companion, but then, carried away by the mounting excitement of the hour, she flung it to the winds like a banner. Jenny helped spread it, they stood up on the seat, supported by Minnie and other

passengers. With that vivid silk streamer as a standard the bus rolled down the Avenue, Peggy and Jenny
hurraying a lively treble. Minnie was captivated by
the gusto of these young mænads, both under twenty.
She got into talk with them, found them alert and experienced, and gave them the card of Richard Roe,
Inc. To her surprise they both turned up at the office
the next morning, looking pleasantly shy. She put them
to work.

XXIX

Peggy and Jenny

PEGGY and Jenny at once became loyal and zealous members of what Richard now began to think of as his "organization." It was Minnie who caused him to think of the staff as such. A very un-selfconscious person, it was a long while before he realized that she was gradually creating for him a synthetic personality as The Boss. By erecting about him a scaffolding of imagined power she really made him more powerful. His decisions became more prompt, his confidence more solid. Her intuition about the triangular office was shrewd. In a room of that shape one seemed moving, going somewhere. Sometimes, when he had been away from the office and found the world dangerously big, Minnie saw to her dismay that the scaffolding had collapsed. She was clever at rebuilding it. This could be done best indirectly: letting the busy sounds of the office form a cushion about him, like a diver's pressure chamber. Only orders and encouragements were laid on his desk for first perusal. Complaints, disputes, disappointments, could wait half an hour or

so. Under the guise of stenographer she was Secretary
of State.

In the morale and good fun of the office Peggy and
Jenny had important part. It was their first steady
connection; previously they had been sent out on
emergency jobs by an employment bureau. Now, taking cue from Minnie, they began to develop a sense of
office patriotism. She bought a little toilet cabinet for
them; by the time they had filled it with cold cream
and curling tools they were perfectly at home. Jenny
sat by the toy telephone switchboard as gay as an old
lady by the fireside. There is a wonderful feeling of
vitality about those telephone boards: their continual
buzzing or purring, the winking of lights, plugging of
cords (like a furious game of cribbage), and voices
coming through from nowhere, keep the operator excited and young. In thirteen years at that board Jenny
has rubbed through I don't know how many of those
felt seat-pads, but Hubbard says she still looks a mere
child. She was a gipsy little creature when she first
came. Her waist was so tiny you could almost span it
with two big hands—at any rate, Ed Furness believed
so, but Jenny had no taste for being handled. She
had ripply caramel-colored hair and dark mischief
eyes; she wore skirts shorter than anyone else dreamed
of in those days; she jingled with earrings, bracelets,
and yards of beads. When she looked upward from her
low chair through a tilted fringe of charcoal lashes, the
caller on Richard Roe, Inc. felt he had acquired even
more Information than was warranted by the little
sign over her head. He had a strange suspicion that
he knew what life meant. There was Lou Kaskel, who
sold them the artificial onyx used for the pen-holders
—Mr. Onyx from the Bronnix he called himself. He

was an impudent fellow, accustomed to capitulation.
But the offensive and defensive alliance of Jenny and
Peggy, who stood together in all moments of stress,
was too strong for him. He gazed downward at
Jenny with admiration a little too frankly appraising.
"Eyebrows, eyes, eyelashes, lips," he said, and allowed
his gaze to travel a little farther. "It looks to me as
though all the nice things come in pairs." At least
two retorts devastating flashed in Jenny's mind, but
she was busy on the phone at that moment and could
not say them; fortunately, perhaps, for we do not need
to quote. But Peggy came to the rescue. "Yes," she
piped from her desk in the opposite corner, "and
there's feet. Better use 'em, Mr. Roe's waiting for
you."

"Tie the bull uptown," Jenny advised him. "There's
some things come in fours, like fourflushers."

"Jeeze," she said to Peggy, "it's a good thing we're
not womanly women, they'd trample all over us."

Minnie, sometimes overhearing dialogues like this
from the adjoining room, recognized the gallantry of
young kindred amazons playing a losing game with
excellent spirit. A losing game, because even winning
it is imperfect consolation. But how thrilling to see
these children meeting the old enemy with his own
weapons. Only those who have never needed it will
sneer at the sharp blade of ribaldry, which can sometimes defend a very tender heart.

Jenny was by instinct agile in self-defense; it took
more time for Peggy Whaley to fashion the armor of
proof. She was the clown of the office at first; her big
blue eyes were wide and troubled when Mr. Kaskel
and other humorists said things to scandalize her Flat-

bush simplicity. She would disappear to the washroom, down on the 10th floor, and weep with misery. Here Minnie would find her, sponge her face and persuade her it was all a joke. Peggy was terribly shocked when the rumor went round that girls from the Follies came to pose for corset ads in the Art Studio on the floor above and some of the models had been seen on the roof of the building. "They say those janes run around up there without a stitch on," she said. This was old stuff to Minnie. "Probably a publicity story got up by the renting agent," she suggested. "He wants to fill up his empty space." But occasionally Peggy, on her way to the washroom with towel and soap and powder-puff, would see some unusually comely creature in the elevator and be thrilled by a mysterious sense of melodrama.

When the weapon of comedy was put into her hand, Peggy's Irish inheritance came to her aid; she soon learned how to use it. But she had Irish melancholy too. She was unhappy at home, and the beginning of her better times was when Minnie invited her to share her own tiny two-room apartment in Greenwich Village. Here Peggy blossomed. Her naïveté was a continual joy to Minnie; although the girl was only ten years younger it was almost like having a child of her own. She taught Peggy to sew, to cook, to smoke, and (very important among women living together) not to rummage other people's underwear when short a chemise of her own. She gave her practice dictation at home and improved her spelling. Peggy developed a strong sense of domesticity: she was never so happy as when cleaning the little apartment to the neatness Minnie approved. Minnie came home one warm evening and found her stripped to the buff and on her knees scrubbing the floor. "I'm so happy," said Peggy. "I wish Flatbush could see you now," Minnie observed. In the old house where they lived they shared a joint bathroom with an actor in the next flat. They rarely saw him, for he was out at night and slept all morning, but he was a source of romantic indignation to Peggy because he always left a dark rim of sediment in the tub. "I suppose he can't help it, it's his make-up," she said. Minnie was more severe: "Nobody, unless he's playing Uncle Tom, needs as much make-up as that."

The two girls worshipped Minnie; Peggy imitated her so faithfully that Minnie had to be careful about uttering her comments on life too candidly for fear Peggy would put them into effect on insufficient provocation. Even Jenny, observing the effective simplicity of Minnie's clothes, reduced her cargo of beads and bangles by several ounces. But Jenny was butterfly, not moth; color and ornament were of the essence. The hopeless adoration of a long succession of office-boys was more difficult for her than the brash advances of the Kaskels. After a few months each office-boy in turn began to peak, and his usefulness was ended. Sometimes the malady took the form of verse. There was much gayety in the office over a Christmas present left on Jenny's switchboard by a languishing youth. It was accompanied by a poem:

> *You are my Oriental queen*
> *With midnight eyes and morning hair,*
> *No one that I have ever seen*
> *Is anywhere near so fair,*
> *When you look upward through your lashes*
> *Your lover feels imperative pashes.*

All other ladies who control
 Telephone boards and switches
Seem totally devoid of soul,
 And only bitches.
Your radiant beauty sweet
 This office hallows,
Since I can't kiss your hands and feet
 I give you these marshmallows.
In short, you certainly are the cats
 As sure as my name is

IRVING GRATZ.

The social consolidation of the office was hastened
by the episode of the Fire. It was on a Friday afternoon, just about closing time. Jenny Hoerl had what
the girls called a Heavy Date for dinner that night;
she had been for a long while in the washroom, cold-
creaming her face. She thought she heard muffled
noises but, absorbed in woman's closest concentration,
she paid no heed. Coming out into the hall she found
herself in a choking fog of smoke. The cigar-store on
the ground floor was on fire; the thick reek of innumerable stogies and perfectos poured up the stairway
and open elevator shaft. The office was three flights
above; if she tried to get back there she might be
overcome on the way. On the downward side of the
stairs the smoke was unbearably thick. Everyone on
that floor seemed to have got out already. She moistened her towel, wrapped it round her face, and then
tried to attract the attention of the elevators. But the
hall was dark with fumes, and the cars that went past
were crowded as full as they would hold. She shouted,
and banged on the grille-work doors, but car after car
slid by in the gloom. She was just getting panicky when

Minnie with a white towel turban on her head stumbled down the steps.

"Hurry," she said. "This car's coming up for us. I was afraid you might get caught on the stairway."

The fire itself was not serious; mostly smoke; but the appearance on the street of the Follies ladies in fur coats and corsets made it a news event. Jenny felt a little faint as they waited for the firemen to finish.

"That's what you get for being in the washroom all the time," said Minnie.

Jenny, who thought she had behaved rather well, was indignant. "Well, I guess you got a bit rattled yourself," she said. Minnie, through all the excitement, stood with her hands in her muff. "Were you afraid your hands would get cold?"

"Don't fool yourself," said Minnie. "I've got the payroll in there."

As human relations in the office became more intimate, old Mr. Gall grew to consider himself the special adviser of the girls. He was a lonely man, his wife had left him long ago for someone more exciting, his children had grown up. Even his researches in the chemistry of ink sometimes grew tiresome to him. He loved to linger in the office after closing time and talk. A neighboring bootblack came in every day at five o'clock to shine his shoes; that was the signal for Mr. Gall to clean his desk, put a little dust cover on the adding-machine, relight his pipe, and reminisce on the various offices he had known. Minnie learned that he still hankered for the cup of tea of his Dublin days. The girls delighted him by buying him a little spirit-lamp and kettle, and even if she stayed late afterward to clean up her desk, Minnie would contrive to take

half an hour off at five for tea and talk with Mr.
Gall. Richard also, when he was not in a hurry to get
uptown, greatly relished this interlude. Certainly it
was more wholesome than gin, which was Mr. Gall's
weakness.

Mr. Gall was greatly flattered, even rejuvenated, by
the mingled respect and banter with which the girls
treated him. In return he offered sound advice. Peggy
Whaley particularly he took under his wing, for he
saw that her combination of good nature and impulse
might make trouble for her. He was not in the least
offended by jokes that were played on him. For instance, he had sent out a suit to be cleaned; the salesmen persuaded Peggy to dress up in it while he was
out of the office. When he returned he found her giving an excellent representation of himself, leaning
back with a pipe in garrulous mood, while Jenny im-
personated Berto, the bootblack. This was the occasion when Peggy after many refusals had taken her
first drink. It was neat gin; and they told her to take
down a paper cupful at one swig. At first she coughed
in anguish. Then, as she tried afterward to describe
to Minnie, strange sensations followed. The coughing
turned miraculously to mirth which seemed to have no
end. Her cheekbones tingled, a faint flush appeared,
warmed and spread downward into the valley of her
blouse where it met an urgent glow moving outward
from her central areas. Her eyes looked circular and
surprised; a small pearly dew broke out on her soft
nose and in the roots of her hair. Her spine tickled as
though ants were crawling, her feet felt light as wings,
her knees deliciously flexible, her fingers moist. Suddenly she was marvellously aware how friendly and
comic a place the world is; everything anyone said was

deep with exquisite humor, her body was full of blissful harmony. The outlines of buildings grew extra
clear and sharp, the Metropolitan chime sounded on
her very ear-drum.

"It's six o'clock!" she exclaimed, and exploded with
laughter. The idea of it being supposed to be six
o'clock suddenly was plain to her, in all its Einsteinian
relativities, as the most profound and far-reaching jest
the world had ever known. Dressed in Mr. Gall's own
clothes, she tottered upon him and implored him to
keep it always six o'clock.

She was very penitent afterward and said she de-
served to lose her job. Mr. Gall however said it was
a valuable experience for her and took occasion to
warn her against Lou Kaskel. "If you ever go wrong,"
he said, "sell it; don't give it away. You won't get any
thanks for it anyhow."

XXX

Those Were the Days

Wहात a grand thing it is for anyone to have some particular epoch to look back on, believing that that was really high tide. Just one period, no matter how brief it actually was, of which he may say Those Were the Days. The poet Blunt has remarked, He who has once been happy is for aye Out of destruction's reach. It is well that poets are so little read, for it is always disconcerting to find that they have said everything already.

Minnie is no sentimental praiser of the past, but she quite honestly thinks that the first years of Richard Roe, Inc. justify her as a human being—and justify life as what happens to such. The year 1919 and thereabouts, for instance. Trying for Hubbard's benefit to recall the feeling of that time, Minnie says that with the whole subsequent perspective in view she would not change with any other person at any time or place. No, not with Queen Elizabeth or Anna Held—especially not with Queen Elizabeth, she added, for she had read Lytton Strachey. To Hubbard, who was timid and needed frequent reassurance, her supple and knowing vitality was beef, iron, and wine. She never worried, never pitied herself, or anyone else.

"It was a great time," she said. "Every few days Fifth Avenue won the war all over again with a parade. It got so that I had to keep the telephone directories hidden to prevent the girls tearing them up and throwing them out of the windows every time someone who had won the war went past the Flatiron. They built a Court of Victory in Madison Square, appropriately ornamented with gas-balloons. Old Mr. Gall used to get so excited by those parades that once he tore up all the papers on his desk, including a whole year's income-tax figures. When I heard a parade coming I used to rush round the office and put all the important papers in the safe. I kept old copies of the Sunday *American* in a cupboard so if the children had to tear up something they would be handy."

Hubbard distrusted historians' generalizations about the End of an Era and all attempts to put locks and dams across the swift stream of living. Wiseacres come to the end of a sheet of paper and call it the close of an epoch. But life never makes a final balance, and the ticker always lags behind the trading.

Yet in some ways 1919 really was the end, for a while, of a certain sort of Good Old Times. They will return; are returning already; humanity needs its Good Times so much that when they don't exist it invents them. Men of affairs now pursue the phantom of Better Business like the jolly horsemen of England chasing the fox across the shires and through other people's cabbages. They cry *Yoicks!* and *Gone Away!* (or whatever the catchwords are) and the whole hunt, led by some lively publicist in a red coat, goes careering over fences. You think the parallel too fanciful? I asked Hubbard. Why, only the other day I overheard a party of icebox salesmen singing one of their pep-tunes. It had the very accent of a foxhunting madrigal, each chorus ended "And merrily we'll whoop and we'll holloa!"

In 1919 there was a peculiarly subtle ratio between what was permitted and what was forbidden. This lent zest to the latter. Women did not smoke in restaurants, they still wore long hair, and stockings in bathing. A great deal of public attention was focussed on these minutiæ. It is desirable always to keep as large a proportion as possible of the public mind upon irrelevant trifles. It kicks up a dust, in which a few cheerful souls can go ahead, as they always have, and do what amuses them. Public smoking is relatively little fun for women now, but it was an adventure then. Minnie remembers the look of mischief she got from Jenny Hoerl one day in the Fifth Avenue Restaurant. Jenny was being taken to lunch by an important customer from up state. (This was good business for the firm; Peggy Whaley had to stand by the telephone on these occasions.) Jenny described him as an old fossil, and Minnie, just for mischief, came into the same restaurant for lunch to see how Jenny managed him. Minnie was enjoying a cigarette, but the buyer from Buffalo, who did not know Miss Hutzler by sight, was horrified. He called the maître d'hôtel. "Please tell that woman to stop smoking," he said. "Tell her I'm here with *a lady*."—When the girls took a tiny cottage at Long Beach for the summer Minnie was thought to be a Bad Woman because she bathed without stockings. She used to smile to herself to think how much worse than that she really was.

These were small matters: there were profounder reasons for the special ecstasy of that time. In the back of most people's minds was the delicious belief that the war had been Won. This was particularly comfortable and evident on Fifth Avenue, which had long been an almost continuous vista of flags and parades. It would be impossible not to feel an uplift of assurance along that great road of Display. It was to take a dozen years for people to learn that wars like that are not really won by anyone. "I saw a pamphlet not long ago," Hubbard remarks, "with a title that hit me hard. It was called *Who Won the San Francisco Earthquake?*"

But that satisfied feeling was very real at the time. Fifth Avenue was then still dominated architecturally by millionaires and churches, in both of whom We Trusted. Neither were as conspicuous twelve years later. In 1919 one could feel the first trembling thrill of that glorious decade of Going Up when vast buildings sprang in clear lattice against space. "How high your window-sills are," said Little Red Riding-Hood. "The better to jump from, my dear," said the Wolf. Little Red Riding-Hood laughed heartily and thought it a good joke.

"Would you have missed all that, just for the satisfaction of being wise and far-sighted?" Hubbard asks. "I wouldn't. It was wonderful. If anyone uttered words of warning they shouted him down. They were having a grand time. Do you remember that fine story in the Bible, when the business interests of Ephesus seemed to be threatened by St. Paul's preaching? He was telling them that Diana wasn't a real god, only an idol; but the silversmiths' Chamber of Commerce, who did a big traffic in images, were pretty sore about it. 'All with one voice about the space of two hours cried out Great is Diana of the Ephesians.' There's a lot of Ephesianism in the human animal. Why not?"

Diana brings us back to the Roe office. They weren't worrying themselves over the cosmic aspect of affairs; they had plenty of their own excitement to think about. If we could have eavesdropped from the Reception Room an average forenoon we would have heard a lively mixture of business and social communication, interspersed with the purr of the switchboard annunciators and fragments of voice breaking in from various quarters of the suite. Running through this medley of sounds would be Jenny's matter-of-fact reiteration *Richard Roe* in answer to each incoming call:—

"Hold the line, please . . . Mr. Kaskel for Miss Hutzler . . . Just a minute. Irving did you take that package up to Ovington's? . . . Richard Roe . . . For you, Peggy . . . I'm awfully sorry, Bill, I'm all balled up on my dates this week; I'll give you a call in the morning . . . Caledonia soandso? Mr. Furness calling Mr. Sonneborn . . . Richard Roe . . . He's busy talking, will you hold on? . . . Who put this thing on my desk from the First National Bank? . . . Sorry, the wire's still busy . . . He's not here right now, is there any message? . . . Yes Mr. Roe . . . Miss Whaley please get out the Joseph Horne file for Mr. Furness . . . Replying yours of 28th, goods were shipped direct from the factory as per instructions . . . Well you certainly got a nerve . . . pale green, it was a knockout . . . Richard Roe . . . Sure, the Brevoort at 12:45 . . ."

Mingle this with click of typewriters, murmur of dictation, rattle of papers, ringing bells, Mr. Gall's habit of sneezing, and the smell of Richard's cigar. The Metropolitan chime rolls across the Square, a deep confident voice; or perhaps the all-hearing ear would catch a fainter sound, the protest of Irving the pale office-boy. They could not understand why even the nearest errand took Irving so long. He was reproached, and promised to do better. But finally he came to Minnie. "Miss Hutzler, I think I'll have to give up this job," he said sadly. "Up and down fourteen flights of stairs is too much for me." "What on earth do you mean?" asked Minnie. He explained that his mother had made him promise not to ride in elevators, which she did not think were safe. "Well," said Minnie, "then you'd better get a job with the street-cleaning department."

Richard, bred in the free and easy ways of the theatre and the publishing business, did not insist on rigid office discipline. If they sometimes stayed out longer than the conventional hour at lunch, they more than made up for it by remaining late in the afternoon. Richard himself lunched most often at Mouquin's on Sixth Avenue, where he met old cronies of the book trade. The level-headed Miss Mac sometimes joined him there and listened attentively to his reports on the progress of the business. She never alluded to the fact that she was a stockholder, but it was always in the back of Richard's mind; he was enormously proud when he could celebrate the first anniversary of the company by handing her a small dividend check.

But it was Minnie who was in many ways the motive center of the enterprise. There is no human activity more satisfying than that of a small busy office, small

enough to preserve the humors of intimacy, busy
enough to give the sense of achievement. Happiness
depends on the delicate balance between forgetting
and remembering one's self. The best hours of the day
speed exquisitely fast in brisk companionship and continual absorption in detail which keeps the mind alert
without wearying it. Minnie, in the prime of her intuitions and with the intoxicating freedom of full independence, exulted in a refreshed sense of power. Perhaps she abused it a little, as woman usually does. She
had that rare virtuoso grasp of business as an intricate fascinating game in which the skilful player fore-
sees the moves a long way ahead. Once when old Jake
Hack was in town he invited her up to his room at
the Waldorf to discuss business plans. He was their
principal backer and had shown surprising confidence.
Minnie described the Roe campaign in detail and
showed him proofs of the advertising she had been
writing—*What the Well-Dressed Desk Will Wear.*
"Your stuff has made a real hit with us," he said. "I
don't know why we ever let you get away from Hack
Brothers. If I was twenty years younger I'd make
you an offer to go back into business with me. I mean
personally."

Minnie was both amused and touched: the over-
ture was so thoroughly in keeping with the plushy and
slightly faded furnishings of the Waldorf. "Never
mind about the twenty years," she said. "If I went
into business with you it would be just that, *business.*"

He recognized the skilful negative. A shrewd merchant knows well enough when the goods he offers are
not adequate for a deal. Jake continued to have for
her the affectionate respect one sharp bargainer has

for another; extended the notes of Richard Roe, Inc. without hesitation, and gave her good counsel about too hasty expansion. "There's talk nowadays about a freeze-up of credit," he said. "Don't let it scare you; it's nothing. This is only a sprinkle of frost. The momentum of the war will carry us on quite a ways yet. The real Cold Wave will come later. Look out for it."

He pondered in a deep armchair, pulling on his cigar, drawing downward his thick pads of grizzled eyebrow. He was in the mood of candor that comes upon a business man away from his own shop.

"I shouldn't wonder we'll feel it first of all in Detroit," he said. "If I hear any wolves howl I'll tip you off."

"We'll keep an eye on the stock market," Minnie ventured.

"Don't fool yourself. Wall Street ain't climate; it's only thermometer. You can set your thermostat at seventy, what good does that do you if there's not enough steam in the boiler?—You keep your eye on the cash department stores. They play mighty close to the customers."

They had a whiskey and soda together, and Jake reflected that it had been an ideal restful evening: intelligent talk about sensible matters. She gave him a friendly kiss when she left, for she saw it would be good for his morale. Indeed who can say that the gesture did not have its own bearing on increased carloadings in the Wolverine City the next few weeks? Even Minnie herself, riding back toward Washington Square on a bus, was not unaware of elation. "Little Minnie Hutzler," she said to herself, "been kissed by the biggest retail man in Detroit."

Minnie was a spirited taskmaster in the office; she did not even hesitate to ring up Richard at Mouquin's if she thought he was tarrying too long over lunch; she stood out for prices and contracts where he himself would have weakened. When the salesmen came to the office, looking forward to resting their feet and a little flirtation with Jenny and Peggy, she already had lists of new agenda for them. One of her tactical triumphs was hiring Lou Kaskel, which she did for its moral effect on Jenny. Jenny was always susceptible to what might roughly be described as glamour. While Mr. Kaskel appeared as a bold ravisher from outside, with dark hair slicked into a solid balsam paste, pointed cordovan shoes, and a dashing roadster available for week-ends, he was a possible menace to Jenny's peace of mind. Seen in the routine of every day, he lost much of his magic. But he was a good salesman. "Always have at least one kike on the sales force," said Minnie. "He sets a pace for the others. I ought to know."

The various complications of Jenny and Peggy provided Minnie with as much comedy relief as she could absorb. It's a pity, Hubbard reflected after some of her anecdotes, that the story can't be written only for women to read. What a literature could be created if one were quite sure that men, with their rigid preconceptions, would never read it.

Herman Schmaltz happened to go down to the Brevoort for lunch one day. He saw Minnie and the two girls sitting with a bottle of wine and great hilarity. As a matter of fact they were enjoying some harmless jape about sending a cold drumstick of chicken by mail to Mr. Gall's pet cat. But Herman's experience with the Y. M. C. A. and some phases of mortal frolic he had seen in France had made him dubious about mirth.

He did not think it altogether seemly that his brother-in-law's stenographers should be laughing so hard in business hours. He even said so to Hazel, who hastened to repeat the idea where it would do the most harm.

XXXI

Expectation of Life

MINNIE, who had learned some of the hard necessities of self-control, felt a particular tenderness for
Jenny Hoerl. There was evident in Jenny that highly
specialized surcharge of vitality which most women
are so clever to disguise. She had a brilliantly feminine
capacity for complicating almost any situation. To
some extent she was a conscious artist, but not entirely; she could throw a ripple of invitation into the
most casual telephone call without even being aware
of it. When she was in the room men's eyes followed
her. The advertising artists soon spotted her in the elevator and implored her to come upstairs and pose.
Poor Ed Furness, who worshipped her with spaniel
humility, became quite lean and sallow with hopeless
yearning. His wooing was so obviously futile that it
did not get much farther than sending her picture post
cards of the hotels he visited on the road. Beneath a
chromo of the Hotel Cleveland he would write *Registered here tonight wishing you were the same Respfly
yours Ed F*. He confided in Minnie and begged her advice. She told him candidly that he was lacking in

Allure, after which he spent much time in the barber shop on the 11th floor of the building.

A close intimacy grew between Minnie and Jenny. At first Minnie, to whom the other turned for counsel in various perplexities, tried conscientiously to avert disaster. She smiled a little sardonically at seeing herself in the rôle of the guardian of chastity. But she was never one to waste energy on a lost cause. Jenny glowed with radiation too vivid to be disregarded. When the girls had their cottage at the beach Jenny was a sun-bath devotee, long before the days when nudistry became popular. Indeed she was sun-burned all over before the drugstores sold remedies for it. They took snap-shots, and the photographer who developed the film took the trouble to deliver the prints to the office himself. "Lady," he said, "I hadn't ought to charge you for that work; it's a pleasure."

Gay, beautiful, and completely mad by any prudential calculus, Jenny was one of those premiums that life puts into the package every now and then, to vary the dull standard of factory product. Minnie, who had a high regard for occasional quiet evenings, was often relieved that she had chosen Peggy and not Jenny as apartment-mate. But she saw, what the say-so of print can never report, the lovely quality that lay beneath the gipsy recklessness. Do you call it faith in living? Dull words for a shining thing. Jenny was comedy, laughter, defiance. She was sweet, Minnie says. Now she has almost settled down (Hubbard had a twinge) and is very happy and domestic. And what does that prove, Hubbard wondered?

Minnie stood between Jenny and trouble, in large ways and small. For in her job Jenny was superb.

When she had been out all night at a dance she arrived at the office still in her ball-gown rather than be late. She ran all the way up the stairs to avoid the homage of the elevator man and burst in on Minnie flushed and panting. Hastily they found a sweater for her to wear over the low corsage; Minnie kept her sitting at the switchboard all day, and brought lunch to her there to prevent discovery. Old Mr. Gall would have been shocked, and even Richard might not quite have understood. (There were definite limits to Richard's understanding.) When Jenny fell into a doze during the afternoon Peggy took the board and Minnie smuggled her up to the advertising studio where there was a couch. The artists clustered about and sketched her as she lay asleep. But even in trance she was a proclamation of frailty. The silver spike of a slipper, the random fall of her dress, the golden crisp of hair softened on her warm neck, the appeal of her hanging hand, all seemed messages To Whom It May Concern. Among the draughtsmen was one cleverer than the rest, who called his drawing *R. S. V. P.*

Jenny was always innocently surprised to find herself once again short-circuited by an emotional storm. Her mind was well lit; humorous and quick; but when the biological fuse blew out, all her bulbs of caution went black. When there was a crisis of any sort she would come down to Minnie's tiny apartment and spend the night on the sofa. After Peggy had gone to bed the other two would get down to cases in arguing the uneven comedy of Man. It was not fair, they said, to destroy Peggy's delicious illusions; besides, she had to go to confession. "Peg's a romanticist," chaffed Minnie. "She's fallen in love with a line of scum in a bathtub." In fact Peggy had met the bathroom actor on the stairs and said he looked interesting. "His eyes are as blue as special delivery stamps," she said. "Return to sender, wrong address," suggested Minnie. "You've got blue eyes of your own."

Jenny was sitting draped in a big bath-towel with her feet in a pail. She told Peggy she had a chill, and the obliging child had arranged steaming mustard and water. A pink glow crept up her white shins, the light glimmered on her polished knees, her short hair was damp and crinkly as her childish head drooped between her hands. "The trouble with you, darling," said Minnie, "you're just an unconscious Valentine. You can't even eat a ham sandwich at a lunch counter without looking like Juliet on a balcony. When the good Lord made you He certainly went back to first principles."

First principles have their merits, but they often attract second-rate demonstrators. Shad Roe, coming down to the Flatiron to take a lunch off Richard, saw Jenny in the elevator. Shad was watching the progress of the stationery business with much interest, and though hampered by the difficulties Minnie put in his way felt that the time was approaching when something might be done about it. When he saw Jenny pass ahead of him into the Roe office he was surprised and pleased. While waiting to see Richard—which Minnie, as usual, contrived to delay for a few minutes; in this case it was an error—he managed a little banter with Jenny. He had just those glib and urbane manners that she enjoyed. His mind, with the instinct of a casting director, rapidly visualized her playing various useful rôles in his own private theatricals. It did not take long for him to convey colorful allusions to the stage; he gave her tickets for a show. Jenny can hardly be blamed for assuming that to be friendly with the Boss's amusing brother was a reasonable form of team-work. Yet by some queer instinct she did not mention it to Minnie when she first went out with Shad. The actor at that time was careful to suggest that secrecy was better; Miss Hutzler, he said, was strangely prejudiced against him; perhaps even jealous of his influence over Richard.

Shad was a spirited companion, and he had for Jenny the glamour of the Great White Way. He was by nature a fast worker, but he could also be a slow one when it suited his purpose. It tickled him to borrow money from Richard to entertain a girl from Richard's own office. Their relations, somewhat to Jenny's surprise, were merely humorous and sociable. Shad spoke vaguely of a confidential theatre enterprise in which Richard would also benefit largely; suggested that Jenny herself should consider a stage career; fascinated her by his familiarity with loud names on Broadway. In return for some amusing evenings Jenny prattled away merrily. Then, since concealment was not natural to Jenny's open heart, an accidental remark of hers informed Minnie of what was happening. "Lay off that bird," said Minnie. "He's no good." When Minnie really meant anything it was unmistakable. Jenny was disappointed, and even shed a few tears; but Minnie's word was law; she laid off.

Perhaps it was a pity that Richard himself was necessarily apart from much of the small vaudeville of the office. Minnie passed on to him occasional fragments of low comedy, and they laughed at them together; but she was careful not to break down any of the impalpable division which must subsist between employer and staff. She was discretion itself; when Richard heard her Mr. Roeing him round the office he could scarcely believe that they had been related in the most tender equation. So much of one's own experience is completely incredible to the backward gaze.

But partly by Minnie's management and partly by his own enthusiasm, he found for a while complete absorption in work. A young business is a jealous consort. Schemes for the Roe products were with him always, at the board and in bed. Lucille seemed to assume that the fact he was now head of his own concern implied immediate increase of revenue, which was not the case. But she had discovered one admirable anæsthetic in bridge; she was taking lessons in the game from a department-store expert, with whom she conducted an agreeable flirtation. This was also a method of stealing a march on Hazel; it was a rich moment when she was able to say casually to her sister that some ladies were coming in that afternoon for bridge. This put Hazel unmistakably behind until she and Herman had also taken a course of lessons. When mah jong arrived, some years later, Hazel took good care to be first: she almost went to meet it on the dock.

Bridge evenings became frequent, and involved some bickering as the two ladies had trained under different codes. Lucille had studied at Gimbel's, while Hazel was tutored in the Macy technique. But Lucille, whose hand had been kissed for luck by her maestro, was loyal to Gimbel rules. Hazel's retort was unromantic: that Lucille had her lessons charged while she herself paid cash. Richard, who was obdurate about learning the game, did not often sit in; sometimes Miss Mac or Sam Erskine was invited up to make a fourth; while they played, Richard helped

Gladys with her arithmetic or challenged old Mrs. Geschwindt to a game of checkers. But his mind made use of the suggestion: watching the family group prompted the Roe Bridge Pencil, with bidding figures engraved on a rotary gauge. Also it occurred to him to make up and give away to the railroad companies thick green boards which commuters in the smoking cars place across their knees as temporary card tables. These were printed with advertisements of the Roe novelties; conductors on the suburban trains know them well. You will have seen the homeward quartet, sitting in two facing seats, slapping down their cards on these boards with an air of deviltry. Why is it, Hubbard wondered, that they must raise their arms so high, smack the card down with such bravado? It is their brief pathetic interim of emancipation, perhaps; their only moment of pure choice, effective will. In that forty-minute card game they enjoy the bliss of decisive gesture. Elsewhere—both before and after —they consult the boss.

Certainly it never struck Richard, says Hubbard, that these game boards might serve as a profound psychic release. But if you can find an article that avails as such, and also use it as vehicle for publicity, you touch the nerve of profit. Richard put it better. "Try to get their attention while they're feeling good." He brooded much on what Mr. Gettleman, contact man from the factory in Newark, had told him. "Our electric sky-sign," he said, "uses more juice than all the rest of the plant." Richard was shocked by this paradox. "You pay more money to put up your name in lights than to run the machines?" But Mr. Gettleman insisted that the doctrine was sound.

Such problems as these were lively in his mind as

he smoked an evening cigar, or rode uptown on the car-platform of the L—almost his only meeting with a rush of open air. Especially on winter nights it was better than a cocktail to look down on the lighted pavements. What color, what appalling variety of suggestion. The whole gamut of romance was serialized in a succession of Sixth Avenue windows. The twirling tricolor pillars of barber shops; the pink flimsies of the undermilliner. Then on florists' panes the pretty rigmaroles of frost caused by the warm humidity within. And finally the drugstore with its depressing display of hot-water bags. More comforting to the mind were the honest cajoleries of food: beds of nuts in the grocer's window; red apples; a smell of bacon and Christmas evergreens. What is the magic of the Elevated railroad that preserves along its route the cheer of plain realities? When they put in bits of woodblock paving here and there on Sixth Avenue he could pause in mid-street (when the traffic light allowed) and see underfoot the grainy section of the growing tree. It's just as interesting as the redwood at the Museum, Richard said. But more dangerous, Lucille replied with truth. Then, as he came farther uptown big apartment houses blocked their patterns of light on the clear lazuli of winter air.

So it seems that those early years of the business were complete absorption. I guess you can't blame Lucille, Hubbard said, for concluding that as husband Richard was a poor-spirited fellow. Quit worrying about blaming anybody or anything, insisted Miss Mac. There'll be plenty of others to do that for you.

Hubbard and Miss Mac are a great pair when they get together. Old bachelor and old maid, no one has part ownership in their behavior and opinions. There has grown up between them that peculiarly pleasant friendship that often exists where the usual characteristics of gender are reversed. Miss Mac seems the more masculine of the pair; she enjoys the freedom suitable to those who have outlived the dangerous age. Hubbard however is beginning to suspect that in his case that age may last longer than he thought. Perhaps if it begins late it lasts late?

As an accountant Hubbard was interested in calculations. "By actuarial figures," he remarked, "I've pretty nearly reached my period of Expectation."

"Congratulations," she said. "What do you expect?"

"I mean my Expectation of Life. In the United States, for males it's 49.32—about 49 years 3 months and 26 days, reckoning a month at 30 days."

"As well as I remember, months are shorter than that."

He refused to be diverted and examined a clipping of print.

"For United States females, the expectation is three years longer—52.54 years."

"I haven't any kick coming," said Miss Mac. "I've exceeded expectations—I won't tell you how much. Every day I get is so much velvet."

"It's unfortunate," he continued, "that New York has the lowest expectation of any state in the Union. If you live in Kansas, Minnesota, or Wisconsin you have a right to expect about seven years longer."

"I'll stay right here, just the same."

"The biggest Expectation of all is in New Zealand. There a man can reckon on nearly 60 years. I was just thinking that if a woman wants to outlive her husband—and I suppose some of them do?—she'd better not marry a New Zealander."

"Don't be absurd. New Zealandesses live longer too, don't they? I expect it's all those hot springs and geysers they have down there. Or maybe the volcanoes." Miss Mac had not studied the Erskine Atlas for nothing.

"Yes, women and volcanoes have a lot in common," he said, getting a little peevish. "But say, I never thought of it before, I know why Macaulay wrote about the New Zealander studying the ruins of St. Paul's Cathedral. Of course, because the New Zealander will outlive everyone else."

This argument was suggested by Hubbard's remark that at any rate Richard had exceeded the table of Expectation. Born 1880—he must have been getting towards 52 when he died.

"I remember when he had his first gray hair," said Miss Mac. "It was about the time they moved to the apartment near the Museum. He was rather upset about it, thought it was pretty bad to be getting gray when he was only forty. They gave him a birthday party down at the office; I told him he ought to be mighty proud of a gray hair. To think of being in this incredible planet long enough to earn that, and still be out and around. Heavens, I told him, folks don't really begin to get interesting until God throws a little salt on their heads."

Hubbard approved this notion. "But I guess Lucille didn't like it," he suggested. "A husband's first gray hair is a kind of omen to his wife."

"He took out a big insurance policy about that time," said Miss Mac. "Bigger than I thought was necessary."

"Probably the influence of the Metropolitan chimes. They sort of get you after a while."

Miss Mac opened her mouth as though there was more to be said about the matter of life insurance, but checked herself. She had made a habit for many years of saying a little less than she knew. She changed the topic.

"Lucy shifted him to a bedroom of his own when they moved to the bigger apartment. He showed it to me once when they had me up there to play cards. I told him I see you're grown up now, they let you sleep by yourself. He gave me one of those queer little looks of his, the kind he saved for a few old pals. Yes, he says, I kind of miss falling over Lucy's slippers in the dark."

XXXII

St. Elmo's Fire

LUCILLE's new apartment, her Pekinese, her priority at bridge, even her charge account at Gimbel's, were subtly irritating to Hazel. Also it was annoying to see the Roe pen-holder, the Roe book-ends and blotters and ink-wells, the Diana ash-tray, displayed in all the department stores. She gave up shopping with Lucy, which had once been such a pleasure, because she grew weary of having these things pointed out. The improved egg-carton, with which Herman was doing well, was not equivalent as an emblem of social rise.

Retaliation was desirable. Hazel joined a literary club. Her allusions to "my husband who used to be in the publishing business" soon put her on the program committee. When it came her turn to entertain she planned a killing. Mr. Hampton, whom we remember as the author of *Carbon Paper,* was now the solidest property on the Erskine list. Hazel decided she would have him as the feature of her party. Good-natured old Sam Erskine, just to get her off the phone, said he would try to arrange it. Then, in the pressure of other matters, he forgot. At the last moment he referred the problem to Daisy, putting through a requisition to the Publicity Department for 1 Author, Set Up and Delivered (as per invoice). Daisy, taken short, knew that it was impossible to procure Hampton. She substituted her old favorite, the poet Johnny Jonquil. Johnny was a reliable man in these matters. His scalp had begun to glimmer through his hair, but this was not noticeable except from a balcony or unless you actually sat on his knee. His reception trousers, like his manners, were a little glossy after a decade of literary abrasion, but these also were not evident to his public. His long romantic poem about the Ice Man, representing that person as the hairy impulsive faun of the West Side, had been read a good deal south of 23rd Street and north of 72nd. (What happens to poetry in between these parallels is a mystery.) If what Johnny surmised about the Ice Man were really true, one could only be grateful for the spread of electric refrigeration. But the poem was always a thrill at afternoon clacks; Daisy had figured that either with a Pulitzer Prize or another fifty readings to women's clubs the book would actually pay out.

Hazel was disappointed not to get Hampton, but made the best of it. She hired a caterer, sent old Mrs. Geschwindt to the movies, and memorized a paragraph of tribute to the poet. But it was not in Daisy's technique to send Johnny out unescorted. It was unlikely, but still possible, that at a recital some macaroon in female form might make off with him, now broken to saddle and light harness. She insisted on introducing him herself. Thus the edge of the affair was blunted for poor Hazel. But in the secret intention of discomfiting Lucille it was an unexpected success. Lucy arrived, somewhat surprised at Hazel's sudden zeal for letters, but pleasantly prepared to tell Mr. Hampton how she had formerly encouraged her husband to sell thousands of his books. Instead she found herself encountering Daisy among the swarm of teacups and sandwiches. "Why, how do you do, Mrs. Roe. I didn't suppose you cared for this sort of thing."

Lucille, with all the resources of Gimbel's behind her, was not the woman to evade a challenge. Every follicle in her being (and women are honeycombed with them) was taut with anger. You could almost see the flurry of entrenching tools as she gallantly dug herself in.

"I had an engagement to play bridge this afternoon, but when Hazel told me I cancelled it. Of course, I'm glad to support anything that helps Erskines'. I remember Mr. Roe telling me that your tea-parties sold more poetry than all the salesmen put together."

"Quite possible," said Mrs. Erskine. "I'm so pleased to hear from Miss McCoy how well Richard is doing."

"Yes, we've been fortunate."

"Of course, in business so much depends on one's assistants. He's lucky to have a woman like Miss Hutzler to run things for him."

"Mr. Roe says she's a great help. She has a good head for business."

"A good figure too. When I heard that she posed for the Diana ash-tray I could understand its success."

There was the tinkling clatter of a spoon against a tea-cup. "Will the ladies please come to order," Hazel was saying. "We have the unusual privilege . . ."

When Lucille got home she looked sharply at the little bronze dish with its impudent goddess. There *was* a vague likeness. . . . The garbage man on 81st Street, often astounded at the things people throw away, was startled to find a perfectly good ash-tray imbedded in potato salad.

It's really surprising, Richard found himself thinking, how well a man doing a job can get on without —well, without (he was always rather delicate in his mind)—without women. He ventured this idea one day at lunch with the old Erskine gang. Sam Erskine, Gene Vogelsang, George Work, and Bill Schaefer used to eat together now and then, and occasionally Richard joined them. Mouquin's was gone, and this was before the era of Jules, but they discovered a French estaminet over in the Chelsea region. The sesame of the house was the word *lingerie;* it gave them a mild bohemian thrill to murmur this passport through the peephole. They mispronounced it, but evidently Madame knew what they meant.

Even under the most absolute despotism there is still freedom of thought. These men had been tamed and trimmed (perhaps to their advantage) until they saw life through a wire mesh of negatives which habit had made invisible. But, like any servile class, they had their pathetic little proverbs and aphorisms; homely lore and tradition passed on from mouth to ear, rarely confided to betraying print. It is unfair to quote these, Hubbard says, for they are the mere bravado of the moment. Men are by nature faithful and sentimental animals; when they turn to cynicism there is usually a heart-ache behind. But at lunchtime expansions, or on trains and ships (Truth is a great traveller) their grotesque or resentful maxims are likely to emerge. "When you see a car blocking up the road you can bet it's a woman driving."—"When a woman turns sour there's nothing you can do about it."—"If my wife would get good and pickled just once, she'd be more understanding. But she won't; she's too smart." —"Maybe I could do with a little less fidelity and a little more kindness."—They paused, embarrassed, on this dangerous sentiment, for T. Bannister Erskine happened to be present. Poor T. Bannister, who seemed so good-naturedly unaware of Daisy's extra-mural activities. The only memorandum Hubbard reports of him was relayed by George Work. Daisy and T. Bannister drove up to my place in the country in the middle of a thunderstorm, George said. Daisy was driving the runabout, with an enormous dog as big as Abe Lincoln on the seat beside her. T. Bannister was in the open rumble, soaking wet. I had them in, gave T. Bannister a hot Scotch, his teeth were rattling like dice. The drink must have warmed him up some, for he got quite masterful. "I didn't mind the rain," he said, "but when it began to hail as big as camphor-balls, I told Daisy we really must take shelter." "We're on our way to the dog-show at Huntington," Daisy said. "We didn't want the dog to get draggled." Too bad there isn't a Husband Show, I said.

So I don't make fun of those chance meetings when the gang blurted their crude notions, said Hubbard. They knew they were licked, but they still had a curiosity to examine why. They realized grimly that life is not always conducted on the comfortable codes of school and pulpit. How awful when no one, *no one,*

can decide for you. Each must hammer his own tools
from the heavy metal of doubt.

Sam Erskine and the others were surprised when
Richard said what he did. It was unusual for him to
make any remark that could be construed as autobiog-
raphy. It opens great gulfs when the usually silent find
a voice. Sam even commented on it to Miss Mac, who
scarcely rated as a woman to this group. In years of
bluff companionship with salesmen she herself had almost forgotten she had once been female. When she
appeared at the booksellers' conventions in a gown of
low ramp, her colleagues were always startled to be
reminded of the wealth and sculpture of her femi-
ninity. Having unconsciously assumed the masculine
point of view she underrated women's grievances. She
didn't see, she remarked to Hubbard, why people
should make so much fuss over a little bit of jealousy.
But Miss Mac had never had any opportunity to suffer—or inflict—that mortal pang.

A woman who thinks herself wronged, Hubbard
mused, suffers so damnably, that she sometimes man-
ages to make everyone within reach of her suffer almost as much. She has a thousand ingenious modes of
torture. Suspicion glows at her yard-arm like the green
St. Elmo's fire, runs in sultry shock through all her
rigging. By anguished alertness she creates the very
thing she fears. It's queer that women, knowing themselves inflammable, so lightly toss these fireballs
aboard each other's craft.

In the concentration of business, women—in any
specific appeal—seemed to have vanished from Rich-

ard's ken. He loved Lucy probably more than ever, but hard words are a meagre diet for the appetite. When he heard the Erskine gang talking about women it was like anecdotes of a foreign country—picturesque, perhaps amusing, but something he never expected to see. As usual, Lucy's indignations came at a time when they were quite unwarranted. Suspicion is an eccentric, mounted on a cam—revolves lopsidedly, behind the circle of the main wheel. Or, if the mechanic figure is ungraceful, like the light from a star, that reaches earth long after the meteor itself has burned out. In so far as he had thought about it at all, Richard had supposed that sentimental relations with Minnie were at an end. Under the stroke of Lucy's anger, loudly and uncomprehendingly echoed by Gladys, he made fantastic efforts to please. He watched their faces for signs of sudden annoyance as a countryman scans a hedge for the weatherwise cobweb. Looking forward, with imperishable optimism, to a sociable evening, he would find that Lucille and Gladys had suddenly disappeared from the apartment for a trip to the movies. Even the Pekinese seemed to sneer at him then. Lucy believed that these nightmares of celluloid were narcotic, but one may doubt it. Much attendance had made her a connoisseur in the ornate furnishings of illicit romance; she endured wistful torments of imagination while Gladys derived quite fatuous ideas of man's prowess. Richard, taking the dog for a walk, medicined himself with the familiar purge, in which a small grain of remorse is lost in a thick syrup of present virtue. Because he had once gone off the gold standard, must his coinage be permanently depreciated? He wondered at the apparent disappearance of all desires of flesh. He asked himself, in man's pathetic way, if he had become impotent?

Sometimes on these evening strolls he encountered old Mrs. Geschwindt, who escaped from Hazel's supervision to recruit herself by scanning the Broadway windows. The old lady always cheered him; he could talk to her. Long emancipated from vanity and social torsion, she was refreshingly human. She had a peppermint quality, both sharp and fragrant; and the immoral gusto of old people who have led virtuous lives and are not afraid to regret it. When she met Richard they always talked as long as Peke would allow; the dog's conventional mind disapproved her German habit of coming out on the street in elastic-sided house-shoes; he annoyed her by snuffing them with morbid persistence.

"Hazel and Lucy always hush me up when I ask about you," she said. "When they were young I tried to keep the facts of life away from them; now they try to do it to me. What's the matter, you got a girl somewhere? Lucy is angry? Well, don't take it too hard. Nix, nix! We all get over it."

It was no use, Richard thought, to insist that her idea was inexact. She was having the pleasure of relating it to her own memories.

"I remember I made old Papa Geschwindt's life a hell when that happened to me. *Schade, schade,* that don't get you nowhere. I learned how to manage him. When he'd been out I was extra nice to him and he got shamed. Besides, maybe a little competition is good for wives, *nit wahr?* Poor old Geschwindt, if he didn't die I wouldn't be living off these girls. They have a hard streak, there's a gristle in their hearts. Maybe they get it from me.

"Throw that dog in the river," she added, "and use the strap on Gladys when she needs it. Don't tell Lucy you saw me. She'll say you been setting her own mother against her."

She started away, but a window of negligee seemed to suggest an idea to her. She turned back and hailed him with an air of beldame mischief.

"Richard, business ain't everything. You tell that girl of yours I think she has good taste."

XXXIII

The Pain

Sometimes he had a pain in the upper left corner of his forehead. It was a queer little pain, as though a stitch had been taken through the skin of his brow; and some of the thoughts underneath had been puckered in by mistake. It came most often when he was tired; then it seemed to go a long way in, and shaped like a question-mark; or a fish-hook, for questions also have a barb on the point. Perhaps he was working too hard. There does not seem to be much testimony about his vacations. Miss Mac remembers that he went to Atlantic City one time, for she has a postal card he sent her: a picture of Clabby's Baths, "Salt as the Sea But Safer." On it he wrote: *Clabby is a fine word, sounds just like the feel of a wet bathing suit. It ought to be in the Erskine Dictionary. Regards to all, R. R.*

Does that mean, Hubbard asked, that he bathed in a pool instead of in the surf? Miss Mac had not thought about this. A biographer ought to ask all these questions before his subject puts on silence. She explored her memory. Richard spoke once of the Atlantic City smell, she recalled. A mixture of sea air and

molasses candy. If he did go into the surf I'm sure
he didn't go out of smell of the popcorn on the Board-
walk. Nature at large didn't interest him; I don't think
he really knew it was there.

On his desk at the office, Minnie said, was a little
tintype of Gladys, ten years old, taken on a pony on
the sand.

That curly stitch in Richard's forehead is a part of
the story, Hubbard thinks. Pain and uncertainty are
valuable. Lucille, with her own hungers to consider,
found nourishment in the child. Life must feed upon
something. With the cannibalism of mothers she de-
voured Gladys entire. Gladys was dressed and un-
dressed, dancing-schooled, churched and movied until
the whole sky dazzled through a prism of her own
activity. As she grew toward that age of assurance
when children realize how much more they know about
everything than their parents, Richard was aware of
her disdain. It was deliciously complete. In spite of
the fact that her mother always forbade reference to
any animals as female, under the doctrine that
maternity in beasts is disreputable, the Broadway pet-
shop caused Gladys to ponder. The sensible candor of
the public schools enlightened her further. "I'll bet you
don't know anything about sex-cells," she remarked
one day to her parents.

Richard, newly aware of loneliness (a queer feeling), became more observant of others. He had got
into the habit of watching people on the L and wondering what their problems were, their obscure conso-
lations. Somehow he identified the ache in his mind as
a detached and considering part of himself. I wonder what The Pain will think about that, he would

say. Silly, yes, but there's more talking to one's self than people realize. Who else is there to talk to, a good deal of the time?

In the office he forgot about The Pain. There was much to do, and everyone seemed cheerful. But they were all so respectful to him. In some mysterious way a fictitious screen shut him off from the others. It wasn't like the old Erskine days when he was one of the gang. He could hear bursts of laughter coming from the Sample Room where Lou Kaskel was perpetrating one of his freaks. Lou had begun his career as a train-boy on the New Haven line, and could still utter the vendor's cry with humorous variations of accent. "Hot coffee, ice cream!" he would call. "Have a fresh sandwich, folks; ham, chicken, and cheese!" Then, with an increasing timbre of appeal, "Cherce cake und rosy epples!" He could render these yells in half a dozen dialects, each perfect in character. But if Richard happened to enter the room, the performance ended. Or if he stopped at Mr. Gall's desk, old Charlie with antique politeness would rise from his chair to reply. Even the understanding Minnie seemed hidden behind a mask of efficiency. He heard squeaks of impromptu farce from the telephone room, but whenever he actually saw Jenny or Peggy, their smooth faces were as demure as oracles. Were the small gaieties of life something that other people lived and himself never?

It occurred to him, having lunch with Mr. Gettleman (who was on an aperient diet), that Minnie's eyes were exactly the color of prune juice. He looked forward to telling her this. But in the office she was so resolutely businesslike that he could not say it. He made a strong start. He pressed the buzzer. "See here, there's something I want to tell you," he said. "Yes, I know," she replied instantly. "Synthetic Bronze made a mistake in that estimate. I phoned Larus, he's sending corrected figures." She laid a pile of letters in front of him. "Here's that report on inventory. The drawings for the Patent Office will be in tomorrow morning." She stood at the end of the flat desk, he could even inhale the clean laundered freshness of her trim attire. But that radiation of cool competence was unassailable. Dark hair, white silk blouse, tweed skirt, were as remote as Diana herself.

There's only one way to get ahead of her, he thought. I'll give it to her in dictation. "Will you take a letter?" he said. She sat opposite him, all poised attention. He watched her lashes, bent downward over the notebook.

"Miss M. E. Hutzler, care Richard Roe Inc.—No, not Inc. Care Richard Roe personal. Dear Minnie . . ."

She looked up, a sudden flash. Was that fright in her bold brown eyes? Before he could know what it was, her pencil was going smoothly on.

"I used to be able to say silly things, but I haven't had a chance for a long time. Maybe I'm getting too grown up. I just wanted to tell you . . . I wanted to say . . ."

It wasn't going to sound nearly as nice as it had in his mind. Minnie's face was very still, her sharp pencil steadily waiting. This was queer stuff to be running out of that long clean-shaven point. Her lashes quivered a little.

"Don't build this damned business up between us. I can't live on synthetic bronze. I need *you*—"

The telephone, mounted on lazy-tongs close to his

ear, burst into a shrill peal of protest. Shocked and
frightened, he pulled it toward him. As he answered
he saw Minnie slip quietly out of the room. But when
he pushed the instrument aside he noticed she had
made her only breach in strict routine. She had left her
notebook and pencil on the desk. He glanced at the
sheets of symbols, each duly crossed through, except
the last, where a few lines of hieroglyphics broke off
in a smear. The page was wet.

When he looked for her to say good-night, she had
gone.

He cursed himself as cruel and clumsy fool. Of
course Minnie, in loyalty to the business (damn the
business), had known best. Probably she had a lover by
this time anyway. By her wise discretion all this long
while she had saved him from folly.

He was to go to Washington the next day, on business connected with registration of patents. He announced this fact at home; not with his usual air of
apology but quite calmly. "You won't be able to do
anything without Miss Hutzler," said Lucille tartly.
"Why doesn't she go with you?" The irony of this,
at the moment, was unbearable. "I daresay she would
if I asked her," he said angrily.

In the Pullman he and The Pain had a seat to themselves. It was long since he had had several hours of
travel; the dull roar of the car encouraged the small
voices of thought to palaver among themselves. He
looked with surprise at his own neat clothes, the familiar outline of socks and polished shoes, his hat
enclosed by the porter in a paper bag. How orderly
and formal those garments were to belong to one
whose mind was so shaken. In the same car he saw a

parson dressed in black and envied him, supposing (perhaps wrongly) at least *he* has no perplexities. He would have liked to consult the cleric, laying before him the riddle that seemed so stingingly new: how is it possible to love one and also desire another? But perhaps he knew only too well what answer the minister would give him.

Washington's air of spacious order and virtue is impressive: its heavy Roman façades impose upon the docile-minded twinges of obedience and the citizen conscience. His affairs attended, Richard had a chance for some sightseeing. He scanned for the first time the lengthy inscriptions on the Union Station which express approval of Fire, Electricity, Freedom, and The Farm, Best Home of the Family. (Nothing said about an Apartment.) The poem carved about Freedom might well have been written by Irving Gratz, but Richard thought it excellent:

> *Sweetener of Hut and of Hall*
> *Bringer of Life out of Naught*
> *Freedom O fairest of all*
> *The Daughters of Time and Thought.*

In some unexplained way this doggerel, the impact of Federal statuary, and the mighty dome of the Capitol made him wish to be good. He prayed a small, very confidential prayer about it, and in his quiet evening at the hotel he wrote a long and loving letter to Lucille. He apologized even for errors he had never committed and vowed endless devotion. He mailed it before he went to bed and slept well.

The following day he made some valuable calls on the stationery trade and got back to New York about

five o'clock. He telephoned the office to be sure everything was correct, and hurried to the apartment. Lucille
was out; "She's playing bridge," said Gladys. "Did
Mother get my letter?" he asked. "She didn't read it,"
chirped Gladys. "She says she's not interested in your
letters."

He found the letter, torn in half and unopened, in
Lucille's waste-basket. While he was emptying his bag
he heard the telephone ring. Gladys answered it. He
could tell by something transparently clandestine in the
child's reply that she was talking to her mother and
receiving some instruction. How saddening is an air of
discretion in a child. "Yes, he is," he heard her say. An
enormous pity for her moved him. He heard her determined little tread along the passage (how like Lucille's). "Mother be home soon?" he called. There
was no answer. If he could just meet Lucille at the
front door, put his arms about her, perhaps he could
tell her what was in the letter.

Then he heard the front door close softly. A horrid suspicion flashed on him. He hurried to the lobby.
Gladys had on her tiny coat and hat: how deliciously
composite she was; pathetic little woman to the knee,
comic schoolgirl from there down her wrinkly black
stockings and scuffed shoes. "You going to meet
Mother?" he asked anxiously. She would not answer
but kept pressing the elevator bell. "Don't you want
me to come with you? I'll buy you both a nice dinner."

She stuck out her tongue at him. The elevator was
coming and she felt safe. "We don't want you, you're
disgusting." The door of the car opened; with mimic
dignity she went out of sight.

A trembling sick anger possessed him. He tried

instinctively to allay it with some consoling thought.
"Perhaps my grandchildren will like me." But these
imaginary grandchildren seemed a long way off. The
bottle of whiskey in the sideboard was nearer.

What had he done to deserve the anguish of these
miseries? Lucille and Gladys would dine, chattering
gayly; they would go to a movie, come home and sleep
sound while he agonized in clownish humility. Inside
his forehead The Pain twirled in a spot of light, where
its dancing feet had rubbed thought smooth and hot.

He had no desire for dinner; he could not bear the
idea of a restaurant or even that uptown club of discarded husbands, blissful in the oblivions of billiards
and poker. The office was his only asylum. There, in
that big triangular room above the city's lights, he
would be alone, surrounded by heartening symbols of
his only efficiency. He would go over the arrears of
his two-days' absence and revise the specifications for
the new model pen.

Peke scowled at him, but he disregarded it. He
found himself hurrying for the L; about to run up the
stairs because a train was just coming in. Hold on, he
thought; no hurry; I'll take my time. It is *my* time,
isn't it? This was so new an idea, it quite absorbed
him. He stood on the open platform of the car in cool
night air, only half aware of the huge spectacle that
ought to make individual pains seem unimportant yet
does not quite do so. The long dark trestle carried
him over a sea of fire. Curling and blinking flames
reached up at him, flickered on the gantries of the L,
the grinding wheels ran in seethes of yellow light. The
train passed from dim channels into sudden blazes of
crude brilliance like open furnaces. He was unmoved.

Yet perhaps the glare of so much catering sharpened him unawares. How great a bonfire the savages of New York kindle for their evening meal!

He stopped at a lunch-room for a plate of soup. The counterman was in a talkative mood, but Richard found it difficult to reply. "Don't mind my spiel," said the white-coat; "I just feel gabby. Some folks don't like to chin while they eat. Even a dog drops his tail when he's feeding."

The office was dark. Before pressing the electric switch in his own room he stood in the forepeak of the building looking out. Evidently plenty of others were working late: the Metropolitan, the Brunswick, the Fifth Avenue Building, all were seamed with bright windows. The traffic of the great highways streamed past beneath him; lower still, underground, he could imagine the roaring subway trains flashing strings of light. Ferry boats blew hoarsely from the river. Telephone calls threaded their sweet nervous cry through every marrow of the fabric. He could see people loitering on the radial pathways round the fountain. They also were meshed in that huge net of human strain and crisscross. Along every streak of that burning web tightened obligation, ligature, responsibility. And in all that scene of color and curiosity his instinct yearned for only one small corner, which had turned to bitterness. So strangely domesticated is man, in the wilderness of the world.

The prow of the building seemed swimming uptown. In the delta of Fifth Avenue and Broadway a gulf stream of light broke in washes of phosphor along the ship's tall sides. How beggarly little he had ever known, or inquired to know, of this ocean of living. A small timid career of bargain and bicker, a drudge

of trivial goods. He looked up toward Diana, just
visible above pale gloom. One such, swift huntress in
the dark, had given herself, asking nothing; had
strengthened him when he was weak; had been, for a
moment, woman and sweet clown; then removed afar,
cool goddess of affairs.

He snapped a button; the city vanished. He went
from room to room through the office, touched by the
neatness of everything, the little traces of personal
habit showing through the careful order. Mr. Gall's
umbrella and his alpaca coat hung on a hat-stand; on
his desk were his curve-stem pipe and a can of tobacco. In the showcase in the Sample Room they had
laid out a trial display to advertise the new pen. On
Jenny's switchboard was a tiny mirror, dusty with
powder. Minnie's desk was swept clean. He sat down
at it, trying to imagine what it felt like to her. It feels
like a pair of bruised knees, he thought, crashing them
unawares against the underslung typewriter. He pulled
out the top drawer, guiltily. Stationery and envelopes
in ordered piles; pending correspondence in a manila
folder; sharpened pencils; a scrap of gauze which
smelled faintly of typewriter oil. A bottle of aspirin
tablets was the only admission of human weakness. At
this desk lived not Minnie but Miss Hutzler. Then, in
a rearward compartment, he saw the stenographic
notebook, rolled open to its current page by a rubber
band, a pencil tucked ready under the elastic. The last
page had been neatly torn out.

This, then, must be his life: estimates, orders, con-
firmations; telephone and telegraph; patent attorneys
and production schedules. It was a good life, too. Uptown, people might bury themselves in the movies,
caves of consoling shadow where they forgave, con-

demned, or lusted, by phantom proxy. He must con-
centrate on more tangible facts. Diana was only an
ash-tray. That page was torn out.

The light was bright on his desk. He was lost, hap-
pily, in checking the month's figures. He did not hear
the click of the latch, three rooms away.

"My God, you frightened me!"

He turned quickly; his weight swung back the swivel
chair on its hinge. Minnie stood in the doorway.

"I had a little budget-trouble," he said.

"I saw the lights through the door, I thought something was wrong. I pretty nearly called the elevator
man to come in with me."

"What are *you* doing here?"

"I wanted to work on that income-tax report. I don't
think Mr. Gall's got it straight.—I often come in here
at night."

"Haven't you anything better to do nights than
that?"

She came nearer, looking down at him. The reclin-
ing tilt of the chair gave him an air of ease he did not
feel. Her face was faintly flushed with outdoor air.
Business hung over them both like a cloud of shyness.
He felt he ought to struggle up to an erect posture,
but the effort was too great.

"How was Washington?" she asked. In that light
her eyes were not brown but black, and very large.
She was carrying a cardboard portfolio. Business,
always business!

"All right," he said slowly. "I'm not sure whether
we can get protection on that ink-syphon.—Damn this
chair!" He seized the edge of the desk and pulled himself upright.

She looked at him shrewdly. "What's been worrying you? You're tired. Why don't you go home and go to bed?"

Obvious replies to this occurred to him; he checked them; no, he would not appeal for pity.

"I'm sorry I was rude the other day; I mean the dictation. I just wanted to tell you——" He paused; stubbed out his cigar in the ash-tray.

She was taking off her gloves, standing at the corner of the desk. What grotesque children they are, she thought; how they boggle over things that are so simple.

"I nearly sent you a wire to Washington," she said. "Then I didn't think it was right to upset you while you were working. I was going to say *O. K., Minnie.*"

He tossed the portfolio of papers onto the conference table.

"A good business man *would* fall in love with a woman who could make out his income tax for him," he said.

"Richard, didn't you know I'm always here when you need me? I thought you didn't want me any more. Why don't you tell me things?" And then (the illusion of woman in her generous mood), "You can tell me anything."

"No, I can't. You don't give me a chance. I was trying to tell you, your eyes are just the color of prune juice.——Have you had dinner?"

"Long ago. It's way past dinner time."

"Is it bed-time?"

"It might be."

"I've almost forgotten what we do when we love each other."

"We go to a hotel. Can't go to the apartment, Peggy's there."

"Can't go to a hotel without a suitcase."

"Ed Furness's sample case is in the other room."

"You had this all thought out."

"I don't tell you all I think."

"We better put something in the suitcase to weight it. Don't want to shock the bell-hop."

"The telephone books."

And so ordered.

Later he said: "Tell me some comedy. I've needed it terribly."

"Is the pain gone?"

"Minnie, Minnie, how much time we've wasted."

XXXIV

Electrons

I wish I knew more about electricity, Hubbard said. Tension of some mysterious kind seems to encircle people: you can feel it accumulating, until it must discharge: some rending phone call, ripple of lightning farce or the crude slugs of human speech, burst through the fog of ease. Perhaps man is only a kind of condenser: a Leyden jar with a brass knob for a head. I must look up these things in the Erskine encyclopædia.

Hubbard had offered several previous metaphors, all perhaps too obviously suggested by his rambles round town. He had said that man's mind was a newsreel theatre, wired for sound; a sightseeing bus with a glass roof. But woman, he insisted, retained more of the privilege of Ancient Lights. I encouraged all these parables, for he was evidently groping for an idea.

My guess is that Richard became polarized, he said. When anything becomes polarized it aligns itself toward the supreme magnetic pole—Sex, I suppose? So it offers less annoyance—and less resistance—to any vagabond induction. Even electrons—is that what they call them nowadays?—obey traffic laws. Red and green, positive and negative, anode and cathode, male and female, whiskey and soda, there's no escape from duality.

Why try to escape it? I said. Jules refilled our glasses.

"At least Minnie might have thought that sur-rounded by porcelain she was well insulated."

"You couldn't insulate Minnie; even her latch-key had a spark on the end of it. But why surrounded with porcelain?"

"She was in the bathtub."

It was one of those peaceful Sundays that single women enjoy. Peggy was in Flatbush, and Minnie was revelling in the female Elysium. The weather was dark and wet, no temptation to go out. She spent the morning in bed; served herself one of those comic scrap-lunches (a remnant of creamed chipped beef, a fractured egg that had begun to ooze, half a glass of flat ginger-ale and three marshmallows) and read pages 316 and 1-85 of a novel. She went through the bureau drawers, did some sewing that Peggy should have done for herself, pressed a skirt, enjoying the warm smell of the ironing board. She smoked many cigarettes, hung up a festoon of long wet stockings on the curtain-rail over the bathtub. It looks like a centi-pede's Christmas Eve, she thought.

She determined to have a thorough house-cleaning in the bathroom; it was one of those old Greenwich Village wash-chambers which never quite satisfied her. But at least she had the feeling of complete privacy just now, for Mr. Valentine Bertie, the actor who shared it, was away on tour. The high-water mark had been effaced from the tub; the irrelevant shaving utensils were gone from the shelf reserved for him. Even his eye-cup was gone; it was blue; to match his handsome eyes, Peggy suggested. I suppose he has to bathe his eyes, it's the glare of the footlights that's hard on them. Listen, said Minnie, that ham never gets far enough down-stage to have the footlights bother him. He's just a walk-on. She attempted, by calling attention to beard-reapings in the basin and clots of dried lather on the mirror, to disillusion Peggy of romance. Even Mr. Bertie's bottle of scalp-elixir was material for Minnie's comment. He probably wears a toupee. This is a great opportunity for you, Peg; you can see what living with a man is like without even having to listen to him.

But Mr. Bertie was away; they had already almost forgotten he existed.

The climax of a happy female afternoon now approached; after busy and peaceful chores a hot bath. She lay in soak. Perhaps she too was polarized: the pleasantest rhythms passed through her. She studied her body with satisfaction, even the features of it she considered comic. It was a graceful body, slight yet moulded in full proportion; what might be the danger points of æsthetics—knees, hips, neck, elbows—merited approval. Even her toes pleased her; poor things, they lead a very restricted life, she thought. She tried whether a little soap would remove the faint pink torque of her garters. Perhaps even in the tub Minnie was a trifle businesslike: a woman of thirty (rather over that in fact) may well regard her own physical phenomena without surprise. They had been cordially admired; so much so that she felt a certain detachment. The body, she reflected, is a delightful utility; an instrument for the will. It blesses him who gives and him who takes. She rearranged these pronouns, and laughed. How fine it feels to be naked; why do people make such fuss about it?

Peggy, always forgetful, must have neglected to lock the door into Mr. Bertie's apartment. It opened, and Shad Roe was there.

There was nothing very extraordinary about it, Hubbard explained. Shad was in one of his periods of off-luck. He'd been put out of his room for non-payment of rent. Val Bertie was a friend of his and had left him the key of the apartment in case of emergency.

Shad was at least as much startled as she. His first assumption, not unnatural, was that Mr. Bertie must have given away more than one key.

"Excuse me, sister, didn't know you were there. This is fine: do you come with the apartment?" Then he recognized her. "If it isn't little Minnie, the watchdog of the Flatiron. Slick. Say, darling, I can use you."

He lowered the toilet lid, sat on it, and snapped open a cigarette case.

"You look cunning," he observed. "A nice Sunday afternoon scrub, hey? It's good for us all."

Minnie was amazed at the force of her instinctive recoil. Perhaps it's more natural than she had thought to make a fuss about it. But, after a first gasp of dismay, her chief annoyance was to be so bubbly with soap-lather. She stood up calmly, disregarding Shad's gaze of admiration, and pulled the shower-curtains together with a rattling click.

"Now you can just move your carcass out of here till I get dressed."

He lit his cigarette. "What d'you want to get dressed for? I like you fine the way you are."

"You're 'way ahead of your cue," she said. A white arm reached between the curtains and seized a towel from the rack. Draped in this she stepped out and faced him.

"There are two apartments here," she said, "and they both use the same bath, but not at the same time. If you want to talk, wait till I get some clothes on. You can stay right there if you like it so much."

She took her kimono from the hook and vanished damply into her sitting room. A bolt shot on the inner side, and he heard her voice through the door.

"I'll give you a highball if you like. You probably need it."

What a dame, he said to himself, and thought more respectfully of Richard.

The bathroom encounter was undoubtedly mere accident; but Minnie had anticipated a clash with Shad for some time. Now she was in no hurry; chose a dress she thought well of; lit the candles on the mantel, set out the card table with napkins, a bottle of whiskey, and was cutting some sandwiches when she heard Shad bang the bathroom door.

"Listen, sweetheart, did you forget that highball?" he was saying.

"Go round the other way," she replied. "Guests usually arrive by the front door."

She waited until he tapped at the brass knocker, and admitted him with polite formality.

"So this is the little hideaway," he said. "Very nice. What a piece of luck to run into you like this. It'll be nice to be neighbors—such intimate neighbors, too. What time do you take your bath in the morning?"

"Have a drink," she suggested. "It'll bring out some of your natural good manners."

He helped himself liberally.

"Thanks. I sure needed it. And a sandwich too. I hope you won't be so upstage with me after this."

Minnie was too shrewd to antagonize him unnecessarily. She and the distiller between them—a potent pair—could surely find out what was on his mind.

"Business is one thing, this is another," she said smoothly. It gave her a queer twinge to see him there, so almost like Richard, but with Richard's simple frankness sharpened to a hard foxlike grin.

"I like this better. As a matter of fact he owes it all to me. Did he ever tell you it was really me who started him on the downward path?"

She took a sip of whiskey to conceal the anger that was beginning to turn like nausea in her stomach.

"Are you speaking of your brother?" she said.

"Sure; who else? Richard Roe, Stationery Specialties. Does he come down here on a rainy Sunday afternoon?"

"He's never been here in his life."

"Now listen, darling, don't quibble with me. Here or elsewhere, what does it matter? I know the situation well enough. Why else did you think I spent my time buying drinks for your little chatterbox Hoyle?"

Minnie visualized him playing on Jenny's love of frolic, winding unnoticed suggestions into the talk, cunningly fishing in her naïve ripple of chatter.

"Well, Peeping Tom, what of it? Let's have another drink."

"I knew you'd be sensible. *I* don't care how he spends his spare time. Here's the point: he's making money and I'm on the beach. He does whatever you tell him. Make him shell out, or I'll start trouble for him at home."

There was a silence. Every electron urged her to say, Make trouble and be damned to you. Oh, if he only would! Richard might then be hers entirely; not by poor surreptitious evasion but in fulness and in fact. The Richard none knew as well as she, to fortify and cherish.

Shad misunderstood her pause.

"When I say trouble I mean real trouble, with lawyers 'n everything. It'll break him all up; he's soft; not the kind that can take it on the chin. He's not tough, like folks; like you and me."

"Nice brotherly disposition you have," she suggested. "Regular Cain and Abel stuff."

"I got my reasons. I'm good and tired seeing him strutting in to his damn pen-and-ink works while I'm panhandling White Rats for a lunch. He can come across; he can afford to."

"Well, I'll think it over," she said with apparent carelessness. "Here's to crime."

"Down the drain," he replied. "I give this Scotch a big hand. You act almost like a white woman when you come down off the high horse."

"I'm glad you tipped me off."

"It stands to reason, darling, you got your own pitch, you don't want it queered."

She found it difficult to keep her voice just on the casual note she wanted.

"I think I can make it worth your while to leave Richard alone," she said. "I'll have to figure what I can do. But I'll do one thing right away; buy Bertie's latch-key back from you."

"I call that unfriendly, just when we're getting on so nicely. I see it all: you just don't trust yourself with me around."

"I've got a kid living with me. She's different from me, she's romantic about actors."

"Fifty dollars will take me right back to Times Square, with a lovely memory."

"Make it twenty-five and forget the memory. I don't run a bank here."

"What's the matter with a check?"

"I never learned how to write my name."

"Darling, you're hard. All right, twenty-five and throw in another drink."

She handed him the money and took the key.

"I don't like this way of doing things," he said. "It seems a bit crude."

"Funny, we both had the same idea."

"I always knew you were smart, but honest I hadn't realized you were beautiful. I do hate to give up that bathroom."

"You're a great kidder."

"Now listen, honey, don't take it that way. What I'm getting at, if you ever have any time on your hands, well, why not keep it in the family, see?"

"Don't try to carry a woman right off her feet. Give me a chance to think about things."

"O. K., sister.—I'll get my hat and bag."

She leaned against the jamb while he went to the other apartment. Oh God, she asked, have I handled this right? To fortify and cherish Richard—to safeguard his peace—to be sure he was not harassed, tormented . . . She heard the gush of plumbing in the bathroom and felt a sickness of disgust.

She went to the head of the stairs to see him leave.

"You've got this straight, have you?" she said. "This is between ourselves."

"Sure enough; we made a good start anyway. Want to seal the contract?"

"Wait till we get the terms worked out." As he went down the stair she leaned over the rail and spoke close to his ear. "If a word of this ever gets to Richard, I'll kill you."

Shad halted and almost dropped his suitcase. He has not forgotten the picture in the dim hallway: her dark hair fluffed out from the shampoo, her dark eyes blazing.

Some dame, he repeated.

Minnie shut the door of her apartment gently. For a moment she thought she was going to be ill.

XXXV

Organization

LIFE, which had for some time seemed reassuringly stable, swung in dismaying uncertainty, but Minnie kept her head. She did not underrate Shad's power to cause nuisance for Richard, even tragedy; she admitted to herself that Richard was easy to hurt. He was too yielding, pliable—but perhaps that was why she loved him. A world peopled only by the strong, rigorous, discreet, would not have been to Minnie's taste.

She had no intention of surrendering to Shad's blackmail without a struggle. Like many women whom the dogmatic moralist appraises as uncertain in virtue, her personal scruples were delicate and clear. Her virtue was more consistent, perhaps more certain, than that of many circumspect sisters who would have buzzed her frailty. The gift of her favors (the words here are difficult to choose without clumsiness or hypocrisy) was a prerogative, not a perquisite. It was truly a gift; to be granted at her own pleasure, not by rule or rote; she was willing to assume the consequences. She had brooded without dismay on the paradoxes of ethics. Hubbard, after winning her confidence, was often obliged to retrace their conversations anxiously, picking up broken fragments of taboo. In gay moments she was the delightful heretic known as a traitor to her sex—a form of treason that apparently does not exist among males. In her talk Hubbard had glimpses of the forbidden country of what women really think about things. It alarmed him. In that rich jungle, Matto Grosso of the heart, colored birds cry harshly, strange faces peer.

After the first shock of distaste Minnie did not take seriously Shad's personal advances; she reckoned them a by-product of whiskey and Sunday afternoon. But she was able to consider them coolly as a possible solution. The thought was unpleasing, but she was equal to any sacrifice, any humiliation, to shield Richard. She did not idealize or overvalue the reciprocities of flesh, but she was not in the least casual about them. This particular concession did not look to her like successful strategy. She decided, though uneasily, to wait for Shad's next move.

Those days in the office she watched over Richard with special charity. She knew, with the pitying wisdom that only a woman of deep experience can have, that his pride and happiness were utterly bound up in his home; that his relations with herself even increased his real tenderness for Lucille. While he dictated, leaning back in his chair to grope for the word, she scanned his face warily. He seemed unscathed. She was alert to examine his mail, to identify all telephone calls, in hope to avert any malicious accident. With this anxiety hanging over, her senses were sharpened to recognize the familiar minutiæ of the place. They were doubly endeared because she was more aware of the secret bacteria of chance that circulate in the bloodstream of time. Ed Furness's solemn good humor, Lou Kaskel's ogling smirk, Mr. Gall's pink-white eyelashes, even the filing cases and radiators and life-insurance calendars, impressed her anew with their strong human reality. She saw a neatly typed little card on Jenny's desk, laid there by the office-boy—who took the switchboard while the girls were at lunch. *Please call Viaduct so and so and ask for "you know."* Even in the world of 9 to 5, stony limits cannot hold Love out; or ferro-concrete construction, Romeo would have said later. All he needs is a rubber mouthpiece and a copper thread. Did you ever try to find an empty phone booth about lunch time? Grizzled men and large contracts have suffered demurrage while Junior and Jocunda go through their litany and steam gathers on the glass door.

There was a note in her mail-box at the apartment, written from Shad's hotel in the Forties. *Sure am surprised to hear nothing from you. Shall I call again, or see our friend? Better keep the bathroom door locked, Val's tour has folded.*

While Peggy chirped innocently at her task of preparing supper, Minnie took a drink and considered this letter. Should she temporize with Shad further? Should she offer to pay him something every week out of her salary? Her personal expenses were small; she had been putting part of her money back into the business. She could afford to give Shad even as much as $20 a week to keep him from worrying Richard. Would that be enough? She doubted it. Hush-money never pays in the end. But was there any way to get this hybrid (not the word in her mind) by the short hairs?

"You seem to have something on your mind," said Peggy. "What is it, a love letter? Better have it analyzed."

Peggy had been greatly impressed by the campaign recently started by Mr. Balaban, their new advertising man. Samples of script, if sent in with a coupon from the advertisement and the name of the local stationer, were analyzed free by a specialist in graphology. This was intended to suggest how much one's handwriting was improved by using a Roe pen. Peggy herself had submitted specimens of autograph from various young men, and said that the professor's insight into their characters was remarkable. The response to this advertising had been enormous; so much so that they had hired a room down the hall for the expert to work in. There he sat all day over piles of letters, depressed by the fact that those whose writing and spelling were least commendable seemed to be most anxious to learn their latent qualities.

Well, it might be worth trying. Minnie was shrewd enough to know that handwriting betrays many secrets. But another thought was also in her mind. She evaded Peggy's questions, and managed that same evening to send off an ambiguous note to Shad, enclosing some money, which would stall him for a few days. Out on this errand, she telephoned Shad at his hotel. By some oddity of chance, he was in his room. She heard his voice reply, and replaced the receiver without speaking herself. Then she got Jenny on the phone.

"You're taking a holiday," she said. "Don't come to the office tomorrow; don't come at all till I tell you. I'll get a girl in to handle the board a few days."

Jenny protested she didn't wanted a holiday.

"Listen, darling," Minnie said, "you've got us into a kind of a jam, and you're the only one can get us out. I'll give you all the dope when I see you. Meanwhile, I want you to work fast. Call up Shad Roe at this number; he's there now, I just heard his voice. Tell him you've been heart-broken because you haven't seen him; and tell him you've been fired; yes, tell him I fired you. You're sore, see, and lonely, and you want a good time. Take that guy for a ride. Go the limit if you have to, but get something on him, I don't care what."

"I don't know what it's all about," said Jenny, "but O. K. You told me yourself to lay off that baby. I'll call him this minute and make a date for tomorrow."

"Meet me at the fountain in Madison Square at noon. I'll give you the inside stuff. You can sleep late in the morning; and fix up that silver dress. You've got to look lovely."

Jenny wept a little when they met; it was hard to be kept out of the office, which she loved. But her loyalty to Minnie, and to Richard, was complete. It was only right, she agreed, that she should undertake this embassy. When two like Minnie and Jenny put their heads together the opposite number needs all his guile.

"Here's this week's pay envelope, for your vacation," said Minnie. "I showed Grapho the Monk" (so the office called the eminent graphologist) "some of Shad's handwriting. He says the man's a crook; the way he makes his d's is a straight give-away. He doesn't dot his i's right either, and his f's and s's are weak. A man who writes like that has done something rotten somewhere. Get the goods on him no matter how."

"No matter how," repeated Jenny submissively.

"Take the line that you're sour on the whole Roe outfit. They've fired you; maybe you're looking for a stage job. And here; this'll help him to talk."

Minnie passed her a package tied with a bright red ribbon like a Christmas present. Jenny tilted it a little, listening.

"Scotch," said Minnie.

"Oh dear, I wish it was rye. Still, I suppose us tramps mustn't be choosy."

Minnie gave her a hug. "On your way, woman. You blessed little bum, I love you."

Jenny looked upward and pretended to spy something far above.

"What is that, way up there?" she said. "Is that the gutter?"

Like the Aztec nymph, arrayed in loveliness for ritual sacrifice, Jenny was driven by taxi to Times Square that evening. And after all, she said to herself mischievously . . .

Yes; vulgar, tragic, indefensible, grieves Hubbard. And by heaven, I think they're marvellous. What soldiers! Well might they think of themselves as an "organization."

XXXVI

Worse Than Death

Jenny's vacation in the world of Worse Than Death (she says the phrase is an exaggeration) lasted only three days. She begged to be allowed to come back to work. "The guy's money has run out," she reported by telephone, "but he says he's got a hunk of it coming in soon. He likes me. But I'm fed up: fun's fun, but I don't enjoy this drinking with a purpose. My mother says she'll put me on the street if I come home sozzled again. Not only that, you'll be losing a good switchboard lady. That man'll have me farmed out to a music show. Yesterday I had to put on rompers and line up with a crowd of janes doing chorus exercises for some director. I'm stiff as an old typewriter. On top of that he takes me to some joint to do tango. You know there's something amusing about that bird, otherwise I couldn't have stuck it."

"Did you get any dope?" insisted Minnie relentlessly.

"Not chapter and verse, but I think I got a slant. He's done R. R. dirt some time or other, no question about that. I kept saying I couldn't see how R. R.

could be so heartless, to throw me out on my ear and cetera. 'Don't mind that poor simp,' he says, 'we'll even him up. He's just a boob. I put it across him once and I can do it again.' It was something that happened when they were in the theatre together."

"Well, come on back to the job," said Minnie. "It'll give the Great Lover a fine twist if he drops in and sees you there."

"He wants to see you," said Jenny. "Say, a swell time was had tearing *you* to pieces. He's great on the subject. But he thinks you've got a grand figure. I was quite jealous. How did he get to know about that mole?"

"By accident," said Minnie sharply. "See you to-morrow. Try to look a little pale and ruined if you can, because you're supposed to have been sick. And for the love of mike keep your trap shut."

They decided to consult Mr. Gall. Fortunately Richard was downtown on a long conference that day; they were able to smuggle the accountant out of the office at lunch time without arousing comment. Mr. Gall's tiffin was usually limited to a sandwich and a pot of tea in the drugstore downstairs; he knew his weaknesses and did not trust himself in speakeasies. After his sandwich he would take a placid stroll round Madison Square, sometimes feeding the pigeons, sometimes chatting with idlers on the benches. It was really singular, he once remarked, how many Dublin men he had met there.

But this time he saw with apprehensive pleasure that he was being taken to what he called a dram-shop. "Now Mr. Gall," said Minnie when they were com-fortably in a quiet corner, "take something with plenty

of courage in it, because you're going to get some severe shocks."

He looked at them shyly, suspecting a joke. Minnie
was demure and official in a trim tailored suit; Jenny
had perhaps rather overdone the instruction of pallor.
She had chosen that day to go fluffy; she was a picture
of wistful innocence, her small bosom defended by a
frill of lace, her eyes like moist velvet.

"What is the nature of the shock?" he asked. "Is it
moral or fiscal?"

"Moral," said Jenny promptly.

"Possibly both," said Minnie.

"Straight gin, I think," he suggested.

They told him the story, abating nothing. Mr. Gall,
like most elderly hermits, rather fancied himself as a
referee of irregularity, but he was sincerely horrified.
He sneezed nervously, fidgeted with his pipe, and
called for more gin. He seemed disposed to linger unduly on phases of the problem which the girls deemed
irrelevant.

"Stop twittering," said Minnie. "Let's get on with
the argument. The thing that matters now is to slip a
banana peel under Shad's foot."

"You're quite right," he said. "Life's made a monkey out of me, I'd hate to see it happen to Richard."

"Do you know anyone who knows anything about
the time they were in show business together?"

Mr. Gall quit being flabbergasted philosopher and
put his shrewd mind on the problem.

"Don't think so. That was a long while ago; I don't
often hear him speak of it. Miss McCoy might suggest
someone; or how about the old German lady—what's
her name, Mrs. Geschwindt?"

"Good idea," said Minnie.

But Mr. Gall evidently had more on his mind. He coughed, mopped his forehead, and looked very unhappy.

"I didn't suppose I'd ever mention a thing of this sort," he said. "You know the cupboard in Mr. Roe's room, where he hangs his hat and coat. On the top shelf in there he has a big package of papers. One day he had a lot of them spread out on the table and I couldn't help seeing that there were box-office statements, old programs, and other theatrical papers. Of course I didn't make any comment, but he gave me a folder of auditors' figures and asked me to look over them. He said it was confidential, but he wanted my opinion. Theatrical book-keeping isn't my line, and the analysis was hard to follow, but I could tell from some of the entries that there had been trouble."

"What sort of trouble?" Minnie asked.

"I don't feel at liberty to say. This is very unprofessional anyway.—I asked Mr. Roe if he didn't think those papers should be put in the safe; he said no, they had nothing to do with the stationery business and ought to be kept separate."

"He always keeps that cupboard locked," said Minnie. "I used to wonder why he was so careful of his hat and coat, and then I supposed it was because he has a bottle of Scotch in there.—Well, you've got to say this much: was it the kind of trouble that would help the present situation, or hurt it, if I knew about it?"

Mr. Gall was reluctant to answer. "I've always got into hot water just by trying to be helpful," he mumbled. "I gave Mr. Roe my pledge of secrecy. The worst of it is, among those papers he gave me were some memoranda that I think he'd forgotten were there. I said nothing about them, he didn't even know I'd seen them."

"You're the damnedest old woman," Minnie said angrily. "Our only idea is to help Roe, isn't it? This bad smell in the papers, was it creditable to him or not?"

"Oh, most creditable, entirely creditable I should judge—to his heart anyway; maybe not to his judgment. Yes, if you were to see them it would ease your mind. It would be helpful."

"I'll see them, all right. I'll have a locksmith in there tonight and get that cupboard open—yes, even if I have to use Jenny as bait."

Mr. Gall was greatly disturbed. "Really—this is atrocious—I cannot make myself responsible for any more violations of ethics. If Roe sees that things have been tampered with he'll know I've broken my word. The only virtue of an accountant is his absolute discretion."

"You're not very tactful," said Jenny. "After what we've told you, to sit there and talk about virtue."

"Waiter, bring the check," said Minnie.

XXXVII

The Front of the House

I HAD a little glimpse once of Show Business from the inside, said Hubbard. Yes, I know it's a chancy affair; I remember that excellent line in the Bible about Saint Paul—when his friends "sent unto him desiring that he would not adventure himself in the theatre." But anyone who's ever been in it must get homesick for it sometimes. I hate to think that probably I'll never again hear the stage manager make his round of the dressing rooms before the performance. "Half an hour, folks; half an hour!" I was lucky; I had a small interest in a musical comedy that did well; I had the fun of watching and none of the responsibility. I had back-stage privileges and I never grew weary of dropping in to see things from behind. In an uncomprehending way I grew familiar with some of the moods and tricks of that difficult profession. I remember how puzzled I used to be by the stage manager's habit of shaking the edge of the curtain after it had come down, sending a ripple across the canvas. When it trembles like that the audience think it's going up again for another call: if it's done at exactly the right instant it revives the applause. I loved the little peep-hole,

stained by grease-paint rubbed from the brows of innumerable actors as they gazed out and estimated the
house. There was much I never did understand: the
complicated ropes and lashings, for instance, intricate
as the rigging of a sailing ship; once I was nearly hit
by a sand-bag that fell down accidentally from the
flies. I'd have been killed by it, likely, except that I had
in my pocket a rabbit's foot one of the company had
given me. I used to hear grand technical talk about
wood-wings and ground-rows, baby spots and effect
machines, tormentors and teasers. Do you know what
a tormentor is? It's a small wing at the side of the
stage directly behind the proscenium arch. In the old
days it was usually painted to represent a pillar or a
drapery—it "tormented" the audience by preventing
them from seeing what they shouldn't—which was very
often me. That was my chosen spot for watching the
show. Across on the other side I could see the stage
manager controlling everything—giving the electrician
his cues with one hand, looking at his watch with the
other to fill in the time-sheet. If I was sitting in one of
the dressing rooms I could tell—by a particular quality
of laugh from the house, or a strain of music—exactly what place we had reached in the script. I shall
never forget that racing patter of feet on the stairs as
the chorus came running off for a quick change, slip-
ping out of their dresses as they went.

And as I was an accountant I saw something of the
business side too. The other fellows in the syndicate
appointed me to check up with the management. I
mention all this only to explain that when Minnie finally let me look over that bundle of papers, relics of
Richard's connection with the theatre, I could visualize
some of the story. It's long ago—nearly twenty-five

years, I guess; even the theatre itself has disappeared.
But I was able to run down one or two people who
played there at that time. I saw in Richard's statements that Bruce Bealings was on their payroll for
juvenile parts at $25 a week. How he would hate to be
reminded of it now. But he was very decent, had me up
to his apartment on Park Avenue, and we went
through old playbills in his scrapbook. Why are fashionable actors so fond of suits of armor? He has one
on each side of his fireplace. I thought it was just
swank, but he showed me that they really are useful:
he likes to take a pose on the big raised hearth, and
flicks his cigar ashes into the visor. Actors are great
gossips and he gave me a lot of chat. Mrs. Geschwindt
helped to fill in the chinks.—Idyll in a Box Office, I
call it.

The Box Office is a little world of its own. It is close
to bohemia yet not itself bohemian. Exposed on one
side to the myriad humors and crotchets of the public,
on the other to the equally surprising vagaries of the
actors, there is every necessity for its instinct of wary
alertness. An old box-office man perhaps more than
anyone else is inured to humanity's endless ruses and
stratagems. He knows how many ingenious pleas there
are for crashing the gate; for complaining of injuries,
insults, draughts, disappointments; for desiring the
front seats—usually by pretense of deafness. He knows
how many excellent reasons an actor may have for
needing to draw salary in advance. To all these varied
problems he must return conciliation and tact. Surrounded nightly by laughter and applause, he rarely
has a chance to see the play himself. By the time the
count-up is verified and his statement prepared, he is

fit chiefly for bed. It is not surprising that in any experienced theatre treasurer you will note that subtle air
of cautious vigilance, ready for anything, as he leans
toward the wicket. But what a training for a salesman:
perhaps it was Richard Roe's experience at Humbert
Galloway's old theatre that equipped him to make good
in later affairs.

There was every reason why that box office needed
to be specially correct, for Galloway himself, a showman of the older school, was negligent about business
trifles. Moreover since he was manager, director, and
heavy lead, he did not have much time to spare for the
Front of the House, as the box office is always known.
Those were the palmy days of the stock companies.
Galloway ran a shrewd alternation of melodramas and
farces, with an occasional interlude of Shakespeare to
keep his larynx supple. When he came into the little
box office to look over the advance sales he loomed
enormous; it was an experience to hear him answer the
telephone. His resonant "This is Humbert Galloway
speaking" always gave Richard a tingle. There were
those who said that his first name was really Humbug,
but they enjoyed him no less. Once an irreverent musician playing drums in the orchestra could endure Galloway's mannerisms no longer. When the old trouper
had to do a dramatic death-scene on the stage, as he collapsed the drummer gave him a roll-and-cymbal crash;
one of those flourishes that go RRRRRRRRRRR—
ZING! as in burlesque. When Mr. Galloway looked
for him after the curtain that drummer was gone, and
never heard of again.

But the young house-manager had the greatest respect for his employer, in whom he saw incarnated the
dignity and glamour of the other-world of art. He was

secretly a little in awe of the actors, never ventured to mingle with them in their small greenroom, and almost felt he was taking a liberty when he went the rounds back-stage at Saturday matinées to pass out the pay-envelopes. More than once, in bad weeks or when the impresario himself had raided the till with his beaming air (those huge white manicured hands never looked so large as when they approached the cash drawer), Richard made up someone's envelope out of his own pocket. These were artists, he said to himself; it was a privilege for him to be working for so idealistic an enterprise. Besides, Mr. Galloway was the boss, and an imposing figure from his gray shaggy head to his enormous spats. He had a disconcerting habit of trying out his voice at unexpected moments. When the afternoon rehearsal broke he might be heard rumbling up the aisle toward the box office, experimenting a second-balcony barytone in Shakespearean tags: *"And when he falls*—hem, hem—*he falls like Lucifer*—hum, harrumph—Sorry, my boy, I shall have to have a little money—*Never to rise again.*—Yes, my I O U of course—a little short this week? Let me have a memorandum of exactly how we stand—No, no, not this moment; I'm just going out to dinner."—His benign method of disciplining his company for any tantrums at rehearsal was to use extraordinary words which he must have hunted out in a dictionary. "Come now, my dear," he would boom to a fractious ingénue, "give me an exhibition of resipiscence; in other words, a recognition of error, a return to good sense, Take that scene again."

Galloway thriftily kept his theatre under-staffed. Richard really combined two jobs: treasurer and house-manager. The care of a theatre is work that is never finished: it is housekeeping for a thousand people, and requires perpetual vigil. Perhaps that was why he was glad to spend his later years in an apartment, which so simplifies the detail of living. But to those who are sensitive to the mysterious charm of theatres there is a queer satisfaction even in the humble chores. Richard never forgot the pleasure of his morning inspections, when the house was cleaned for the day. The great dim auditorium, with white invasions of daylight where the fire-doors were open to the air, smelled faintly of disinfectant. From behind the balcony came a soft chatter of typewriter where Mr. Galloway's secretary, in a room panelled with photographs of the great man in his favorite rôles, attended to his correspondence. In the box office Lucy Geschwindt was at the morning routine—shifting the tickets from the advance rack to the daily rack; taking reservations over the phone; if business was slow, considering how to dress the house for tonight. This was Richard's time to see that everything was in order. How much there was to think of. Run a hand over the edge of every seat to make sure that no nails have worked loose to tear clothes. Examine the stair carpet to see there are no occasions of stumbling, no trodden gobs of chewing gum. From furnace to chandelier, from fire-escapes to lavatories, from front steps to dressing-room mirrors, is the house manager's care—save only the stage. There he has no concern.

Fascinating tasks! If the house is crowded, warn the janitor to cut down steam, for the audience will keep itself warm by its own radiation. If a bulb goes dead in the marquee, see that the door-man gets out his tall ladder and replaces it. (Richard was one of the first to

think of the long pole with a spring-clip to hold the
bulb, which saves the trouble of the ladder.) If one of
the ushers happens to be a heavy-footed wench, teach
her not to go pounding down the aisle, after the curtain has risen, with a tread that reverberates the floor.
Someone comes to the window just as the show begins;
his wife has a toothache and he won't use these four
seats tonight. May he have the money back?—Ice in
the water-coolers, candy in the slot machines, polish
for the brass orchestra-railing, first-aid packets for
accidents, soap in the washrooms, and be watchful to
erase any legend scribbled on the wall by the mohocks
of Fourteenth Street. These are lowly but necessary
parts of the illusion that begins when the foot of the
curtain brightens. It's not safe to neglect anything
There was the dreadful day when a skylight leaked,
and a steady drip came down on the dean of New York
critics.

While he supervised these matters, the blonde girl
in the box-office was a great help. She was pretty and
capable. Sometimes Richard thought she was a trifle
more stage-struck than is desirable in the box-office:
during the progress of the show, she would open the
door a crack and peep out to see what was happening
on the stage. She envied the players and naïvely
copied the jargon and clothes of the women. But she
was young and surrounded by a world of make-be-
lieve. It was a long time before he learned that she
came from Hoboken. One day she apologized for being
late, explaining that there was a fog on the river.
"What were you doing on the river?" he asked in surprise. Thus the innocent secret was out; but Lucy was

always sensitive to fancied social divisions. She begged him not to tell anyone else.

Yes, she was really beautiful, he thought, as she stood at the window, leaning forward to speak through the hole in the glass. The bright light overhead sparkled on her hair; as she reached up to take a pair of tickets from the slits in the seating-diagram (what a pleasant sound that was, the crisp click of the two thin cardboards snapping together when pulled out briskly) the strong mould of her figure was pleasant to admire. Sitting at the little rolltop desk he could even hear the faint creak of her corset as she stretched up to the top of the rack; catch a whiff of her perfume. He felt a delicate shyness at being shut in there with this mysterious feminine creature, for though he was twenty-eight he had never been the least bit interested in women. A girl in the box-office was more a novelty then than now, but Mr. Galloway believed it was good for business.

When she complained of being on her feet all day, Richard got the stage carpenter to build her a high stool; he bought her a tiny electric fan for hot weather. On rainy evenings he brought in a sandwich, coffee and cake to save her going out for dinner; he took the window while she ate at the desk and told him about her family and her ambition to escape from Hoboken. She was a brave little woman, he thought, to return across the ferry alone at night.

There was an almost domestic intimacy in the snug little room. The advance rack with its tickets of many colors, the telephone which did not ring but only purred so as not to disturb the audience, the shabby rolltop desk with a pile of play-scripts waiting for Mr.

Galloway to read, the little gimcrack safe which for
some unknown reason was painted with a picture of
a lake with mountains and two swans—all these, with
the procession of faces outside the glass window, the
feeling of Theatre behind them, the steadily mounting
pressure of subtle excitement that precedes every performance, gave a sense of romantic significance. When
the show was well under way, the window closed, the
door locked, the door-man brought in the box of stubs
and they counted up. Richard made out the statement
and they both signed it. It was then Lucy's privilege to
take it back to Mr. Galloway. She went down through
the dim little passage that led past the furnace-room
and right underneath the auditorium. Overhead was
the whole weight and glow of that mimic world: a
warm silence pressed upon her, in which she could hear
the tread of feet, clear distant voices, perhaps the
boom and rumor of applause. If Mr. Galloway was on
the scene she waited in the wings until he came off: he
always paused then, for his exits were important and
he liked to hear how the house took them. Then, waiting a moment longer, she followed him to his dressing
room. She would meet his gaze first in the mirror, and
never got over being startled by the glaring make-up.
He would turn and take the sheet with Olympian
casualness, the air of one who knew his own value even
if the public had, for that night, forgotten it.

There was a pretty touch of the German housewife
about Lucy. One week they ran short of programs, and
Richard collected as many as possible of the dropped
and crumpled pamphlets, to use them again. But he
was distressed by their slovenly appearance. "I'll take
them home and iron them," said Lucy. She did so, and

brought them back the next morning, cleverly restored. This enchanted Richard; that night when they counted up he could resist her thumb no longer. It was too tempting as it riffled a bunch of tickets, in the traditional manner, deftly snapping a pack of coupons in that rapid count that seems like magic. He kissed the thumb; that evening they had to do the count three times to make the unsold tickets verify the stubs. Lucy protested mildly, but it had already occurred to her that Roe was a prettier name than Geschwindt.

Richard had some secret pangs afterward; he felt it was perhaps a bit libertine to kiss a woman's thumb and not immediately follow it with a declaration. But presently he was invited over to Hoboken for Sunday dinner; in the afternoon they walked in the lofty grounds of Stevens Castle. He proposed to her by the old cannon on the brow of the cliff. The soft voices of river craft rose musically to them through a misty dusk; if there was a shriller hoot in any of those whistlings they did not notice it.

The older sister, Hazel Geschwindt, perhaps a little nettled by Lucy's satisfied mien, said the cannon was a bad omen. But privately she decided to give more positive encouragement to a young book salesman she had known for some time. His name was Schmaltz, and he also was soon taken up to see Stevens Castle.

XXXVIII

It Walks By Night

THEY kept the betrothal secret, for theatre managements are dubious of Cupid in the box-office. But Richard was saving for the future. About that time he obtained Mr. Galloway's assent to employing his young brother Morris—ten years younger—to help with odd jobs. Morris, who had already won the nickname Shad at amateur nights on the Bowery, showed a natural affinity for theatres. He had hung about stage doors from early boyhood; even before he was actually hired he knew most of Mr. Galloway's company by name, ran errands for them (often connected with a surreptitious shell of beer), and made himself a favorite by his gay obliging cheek. Richard was devoted to the youth, to whom he stood almost in a paternal relation.

Shad was useful in many ways. He delivered window cards and passes to the neighborhood tradesmen; carried huge bundles to and from the costumers; quickly picked up the technique of the box-office and helped sell tickets; ingratiated himself with the stage crew and joined them at cards in their exclusive den in the cellar. He learned to know the extraordinary hodgepodge of the prop room as well as the property man himself; when the door-man was ill he slicked up and took tickets at the entrance; when the boys in the gallery became noisy he was a genius at calming them. In a few months his glib attention had divined more of the inside workings of the place than Richard would ever dream. But his real bent was for the actual shine of the footlights. Put into one or two small parts unexpectedly, he seemed to know his lines without ever having studied them; he showed the unmistakable quality of projection that marks the natural performer. Richard was very proud. Mr. Galloway, before whom Shad kept his cocksure manners well concealed, admitted the youth had talent. He would have been still more sure of it, if he could have seen some humorous imitations done behind his back, which convulsed the stage-hands.

Mr. Galloway ran his enterprise on Personality. His image and superscription were everywhere. His likeness and facsimile autograph adorned the program every week; a huge painting of himself as Brutus hung in the lobby; tacked on the call-board there was always some admonition signed in his powerful scrawl; the mails were burdened with his photograph carefully safeguarded between two sheets of cardboard. Like many of the flamboyant old managers he was intensely conventional at heart, an odd mixture of Shakespearean ranter and Sunday School superintendent. He watched with aquiline eye over the morals of the cast, permitted no smoking in the greenroom, and was frequent in reminder of the dignity of the profession. The actors, sneaking a furtive cigarette or glass of beer in the back alley, attributed this severity to Mrs. Galloway, wife of his Later Period, who was supposed to have lifted him from abysses of bohemia. His young pupils relished the notion that Humbert had been a hellion in his day. At any rate he now drew his solid support from the established bourgeoisie of Chelsea and Washington Square; good old ladies who took season subscriptions because "Mr. Galloway, though an actor, is so innately refined." He insisted on his company taking the functions of popular melodrama with full seriousness. Some of his alumni believe there was a secret relish of humor behind this solemnity. At any rate it created humor in lighter members of the troupe. When the men were safely escaped from their somewhat dreary little greenroom, and gathered for late supper in a Sixth Avenue saloon, they sometimes sang an ironic ditty they had invented. It went to the hymn-tune of *Blest Be the Tie That Binds;* there were several verses, identifying traditional characters of a barnstorming company. Villain, Juvenile, Heavy Father, Character Man, Comedian, each had his individual stanza, caricaturing the business of his rôle. The Hero topped it with his genial bravura:

And I, I am the hero of the play:
I fill the Villain's bosom with dismay,
And before the final curtain
Virtue's triumph is quite certain—
Every night, and twice a week at matinée.

Whereupon the whole sextet would break into their joint chorus:

There isn't any bunkum we don't know,
We were born and raised on Dion Boucicault;
Any part from lead to super
Is all gravy to a trouper—
When you've got a cast like us, you've got a Show!

Bruce Bealings sang me as much of that canticle as he could remember, said Hubbard. I think myself that Galloway would have enjoyed it as well as any of them. Certainly he was a champion showman. Fourteenth Street long remembered his revival of *It Walks By Night,* and Richard preserved among his papers some of the old man's ballyhoo for this grisly piece. Galloway had a lush vein of proclamation not lacking in wit. His advance announcements for the play described it thus:

WORLD-FAMOUS VAMPIRE Horror, greatest of all dramas of the Spectral, Sinister, and Unspeakable. This play suggests the Ghastly Dominion of the spirits of Evil, returning from Corruption to trouble the souls of men.

IT WALKS BY NIGHT was the illicit stage terror of an earlier generation, the cause of the draperies always hung about the old-fashioned bedstead to prevent nervous inmates from seeing any spectre that might lurk beneath.

The scene represents a haunted castle in County Banshee, Ireland, traditionally the awful rendezvous of Werewolf and Ghoul.

This unequalled Classic of Shudders, revived by Mr. Humbert Galloway's company, also shows a vein of Irish comedy, which alone could make permissible the representation of such gruesome anxieties.

Mr. Galloway's attendants will be instructed to have spirits of ammonia, smelling salts and restoratives, ready for any patrons liable to swoon and hysteria.

Positively No One Seated during the Foreboding

Prologue, so that the spell of alarm excited on the audience may not be broken.

Reservations for IT WALKS BY NIGHT are already large. Those desiring Places of Vantage must apply AT ONCE.

The play—with Mr. Galloway as The Ghoul—walked a good many nights. It also dismayed many of his more timid patrons. But it would not need mention here except for one circumstance. In the course of the performance there were several interims of complete black-out, when absolute darkness was necessary back-stage. It was during the run of this piece that things began disappearing from the dressing rooms.

In such a congenial crowd there had never been much care about locking doors or secreting valuables. But now small sums of cash vanished from clothes. There was no possibility of attributing this to error, for underpaid actors know only too well, and to a penny, how much they have in pocket. Then the leading lady missed a bracelet; the juvenile (Bealings himself) a fine German razor; the comedian a corkscrew and a ham sandwich. There began to be gossip. Mr. Galloway still insisted there must be some mistake. The things had been mislaid, would turn up. Nothing of this sort had ever happened in his company; after all, my dear fellow, this is a company of ladies and gentlemen. "I suppose it's those Spirits of Evil, returning from Corruption," said the comedian as some of them talked it over at supper. At considerable inconvenience they took to locking their doors while they were on the stage. But when Mr. Galloway's gold watch disappeared—a gift from his wife—there was the devil of a row. Under cover of the roaring thunder-sheet and wind machine (*It Walks By Night* was the kind of play that has plenty of storm in it, and galloping hooves imitated with cocoanut shells) a window-pane of Mr. Galloway's dressing room, which opened onto the back alley, had been broken. Burglary, evidently? But Richard noticed that the fragments of glass had fallen on the outside.

A detective was brought in, and lingered for many evenings in the dressing-room corridors. The larcenies ceased, and the situation blew over, for the police found the watch in a pawn-shop. Everything went on peacefully. Richard and Lucy walked out together on Sundays; their favorite argument was whether she should keep her job when they were married.

In a book you enjoy, you can look forward (the greatest tribute ever paid to an author) to see how many pages still remain to be savored. But you can't do that in life; you may suppose the story is going to proceed indefinitely, and then suddenly it breaks off right across the page.

There was a discrepancy in the box-office figures. It was not discovered at once, for Mr. Galloway was lazy about checking up his personal account with Richard. But when they went over the I O U's, Richard happened to say something about an extra hundred the manager had taken out one week. "What extra hundred?" asked Mr. Galloway sharply. Richard showed him the slip. It was duly signed, but not dated. "That's very odd," said the manager, "certainly I always date my I O U's. Well, we all make mistakes, perhaps I had something on my mind. Queer, though, I don't remember."

It was equally queer that Richard didn't remember; yet he was not always in the box-office himself, and of course the manager's request would be honored by whoever was at the window. In the general informality of Galloway's régime there were several who helped in the box-office at busy moments. Richard questioned Lucille cautiously, she knew nothing of the item. By verifying bank deposits they spotted the date when Mr. Galloway must have drawn the cash. An appalling thought struck Richard; he could not verify it, because the I O U had been destroyed in the usual way when he had balanced accounts. Was it a forgery? Humbert Galloway's signature, used almost as a trade-mark for the theatre, was familiar to everyone; it would be easy to imitate.

A strange little notion had been lurking, almost unperceived, at the bottom of his mind. When he had gone with Mr. Galloway to the pawn-shop to identify the retrieved watch, he asked the broker if he could remember what the disposer looked like. The pawnbroker was vague. "As a matter of fact," he said, "he looked a bit like you." Mr. Galloway and Richard had laughed at this. Now he remembered it. And other coincidences, trivial and damning. About the time of the back-stage thieveries, Richard recalled, his brother had begun to shave. He remembered this particularly, for the boy had been chaffed because his beard was late in starting.

That evening Shad Roe was missing from the theatre and from the boarding house where he and Richard both lived. He walked by night, and left Richard to clean up the mess. One of the girls in the company was taken ill with hysterics.

Slippery Shad, like all his kind, had easily been able to convince himself it was everyone else's fault. The forgery was Mr. Galloway's fault for posting his signature all over the place. The girl's trouble was her own fault for tempting him, and she had to have money. The razor was the juvenile's fault for having an enviable beard so young. Most of all, everything was Richard's fault for having charge of so much cash and keeping his own brother on short commons. Shad had worked on Lucille's confidence until she did not scruple to leave him alone in the box-office occasionally; there was no reason why she shouldn't. And it was the fault of mere bad luck, he thought, that suspicion began to focus before he had had time to perfect his scheme of duplicate tickets. This required collusion with the door-man, which had not yet proved practicable; but if not pushed too far it would be difficult to discover, and leave no written record. He tried, that last afternoon, to remove from the box-office the parcel of carefully counterfeited tickets he had had printed and secreted there. He had no chance to do so. Fool, to leave them there with the printer's bill in the package. At that early age Shad's technique was crude in many respects; but he departed with the dangerous conviction that people are pretty easy if you're really determined to get the better of them.

To rectify the situation in mere cash was a simple matter—it only involved about two hundred dollars, including restitution to the actors on which Richard insisted. But even this was the larger proportion of his savings for marriage. The blow to his pride and affection was more bitter. Mr. Galloway, when the details became apparent, was generous: he was more shocked by the flavor of back-stage vice than by peculation. Or at any rate, under Mrs. Galloway's influence, that was the line he took. He agreed, since

Richard made full repayment, not to pursue the culprit by process of law. This would mean damaging publicity; and also, Richard pleaded, it would wreck the boy's whole career at the outset. (Shad was not yet twenty.) When the first scandal was past, Mr. Galloway was willing to have things proceed as before: he really enjoyed the confidential meeting of the company when he called them all on stage and with knitted eyebrows delivered a speech on the Recent Deplorable Episode. Mrs. Galloway sat in a box, rustling with outraged propriety. Galloway was at his very best on that occasion: the old trouper rose in flame and thunder to a thoroughly Shakespearean situation. The comedian remarked afterward that he had not known there were so many synonyms for strumpet.

But for Richard the whole position was altered. He felt shamed before the whole company, the whole profession. And he was shamed before Lucille. Lucy had put on perfectly natural and innocent airs of superiority toward Hazel: the glamour and romance of her job and her fiancé's position. Hazel was now not backward in subtle attitudes. Poor Lucy, her sympathy seemed to say, going to marry the brother of an embezzler. Dear, dear, how very unfortunate. The streak of gristle which their mother remarked upon long afterward now appeared in Lucy. She informed Richard that perhaps their engagement had better be cancelled. She left him only one loophole: he must get a full and signed confession from Shad. Otherwise, she shrewdly said, they would have no hold whatever on the young ruffian.

The boy had vanished, but he could not be far. Actors are the easiest to trace of all fugitives. Richard, with misery in his heart, trailed his brother through the Broadway casting agencies.

Shad, at first defiant, then tearful, was thoroughly frightened. There was a look in Richard's face he had not seen before: apparently in that gentle person there was a nucleus of something hard and solid. Shad gave an excellent performance in the rôle of penitent. He wept for Mr. Galloway, he wept for Lucille, he wrote out the desired confession and signed it under oath and witness. He vowed reformation, and hated Richard ever afterward. He borrowed money for a ticket to Chicago, where there was the chance of a job. Richard and Lucy saw him off. They were quietly married the same afternoon. Mrs. Geschwindt had stood up for Richard and advised Lucy not to be a fool. Richard was humbly grateful to his bride for forgiving him his connection with such infamy. The tender little thumb he had kissed was firmly upon him.

They were very happy, and with the confession in storage Lucille felt they might continue at the theatre. Indeed the repercussion of these events lent her, she felt, something of romantic appeal in the eyes of the troupe. But for Richard the job was finished. Obviously he should not quit at once, for that would give a false impression; but he could not continue permanently with the memory of this disgrace in mind. He imagined allusion to it long after it was forgotten. When Herman Schmaltz suggested a vacancy in the Erskine staff Richard was glad to accept. Lucy was not so keen: she saw in this another condescending kindness from Hazel. But there was a baby coming, she would have to leave the theatre job anyway.

I guess I've only touched the high spots, Hubbard

concluded. From what I gather, the Galloway period would make a book by itself. At least I have to make plain what lay behind Shad's malice. When Minnie Hutzler went through that parcel of old forgotten papers in Richard's cupboard she found Shad's confession. It was the weapon she needed.

XXXIX

Iron Ration

SHAD came to Minnie's apartment—to take up his option, as he expressed it—in good confidence. Whether she made settlement in cash or in kind, he would be satisfied either way. That's the kind of guy I am, he commended himself; generous. Therefore he was correspondingly enraged by her change of front. Her cold assurance was more convincing than any loud anger could have been. With relish she read him passages from a typescript which was evidently a copy of the ancient confession, memory of which still sometimes prickled him though he believed everyone else had forgotten it. She even made merry over the prose style of the abject document. "And your spelling wasn't any better than your honesty," she said. "Here's a funny word, *embesle;* I wonder what that means?"

To his savage retorts she replied calmly in the familiar phrase: "You can't insult me; I've been insulted by experts."

"So I guess you're out of luck," she concluded. "Better have a drink."

"The dirty hound; he swore he'd never show it to a soul."

"He hasn't. He doesn't know I've seen it. But *I'm* not bound by any promises."

"You can't prosecute for something that happened fifteen years ago. There's a statute of limitations."

"I dare say there's plenty more dirt I can dig up if I need to. If you did that sort of thing once you probably did it again. Would you like me to go asking at Actors' Equity?"

This was a random shaft but it seemed to sink in.

"If you make the slightest move to bother him in any way, or come near the office, or ever let out a peep about what's happened, I'll make things damned unpleasant for you around Times Square. There won't be a manager will touch you. Maybe Bruce Bealings might have some suggestions."

Minnie saw by his face that he was beaten. But she was aware that her own position was not beyond criticism. She was wise enough not to push too far.

"I tell you what I'll do," she said. "Richard told me once he saw an exhibit at the Museum showing that man, considered just as a package of chemical elements, has a market value of about $18. That's probably more than you're worth, because your chemicals are a bit sour. I'll pay you eighteen bucks a week, out of my own coin, until you get a job. Go and hootch yourself to death with it."

Shad was in control of himself by now. He said something that bit deep. "Good friend of his, aren't you? You don't want anybody to ruin him but yourself."

They parted amicably. "Well, I got some of the

breaks anyhow," he said. "Give my love to Jenny. She knows my address."

One thing puzzled Minnie. The night she got the cupboard open and went through the theatre records she noticed another soft package in a corner of the shelf, neatly tied in brown wrapping. She opened it, thinking it might be more box-office papers. It was apparently a forgotten parcel of laundry: a clean shirt and collars, pyjamas, underwear, a pair of socks. But there was also an open envelope containing five ten-dollar bills and a toothbrush. She wondered about this package. Richard had never mentioned it. Evidently he intended it to stay there, for occasionally, with the skeleton key the locksmith had given her, she opened the cupboard to see. It was always there.

Shad's intrusion left a bad taste in the Greenwich Village apartment. Also Peggy had suddenly become engaged to one of the young men whose handwriting was approved by the graphologist. She had checked up on him by all the soundest methods. His horoscope was auspicious; his palm had good lines, though rather warm and moist; his dancing was excellently rhythmic; he had a job in a bank which kept him in a cage at least eight hours a day, always desirable in husbands, and sent him out at dusk eager for amusement. Peggy was going to keep her job after marriage, but for a while her mind was full of trousseau. Minnie, the philosophical anti-maritalist, was amused to find herself spending evenings at her sewing machine doing ornamental appliqué, stitching galloons and lace lozenges for Peggy's nuptial filibegs. But she grew impatient of poor Peggy's praises of her swain. Even the office

was involved in the excitement. Jenny discovered Peg
sitting bare-legged at the typewriter while a pair of
new-washed stockings, dangling from the light-cord,
danced frolic in the breeze of the electric fan. She was
to dine with Padric and hadn't time to get a new
pair. Peg's eyes were pure blue as lakes in that sentimental time; they nicknamed her Filly of Soul. "Padric knows some fine speakeasies, but he never takes
more than one cocktail," she said approvingly. "And
he never drinks until evening; he says bankers
mustn't." She described to them the romantic suburban
roadhouse where the proposal took place. "You take
a key out of your pocket and lay it across the brass
numbers of the address on the door. That completes
the circuit and makes a bell ring inside. Only people
who know that can get in." Minnie remembered this
when she moved to an upstairs apartment in an old
house on Lexington Avenue and her latchkey sparkled
at the lock in cold weather. What a lot of electricity
there seems to be in keys.

From the window of her dark little sitting room she
could see the Metropolitan tower; it was good to
hear at night the same chimes that sounded through
the office by day. It gave a sort of continuity. It was
good, too, to be alone. She had much to think about.
Outside the office few people knew her number. AM-
bergris 5922, she had to keep it written on a card to
remember it herself. The only telephone that ever
called me a Bitch, she said affectionately to the little
black instrument. Jenny came up often and they sat
most of the night in humorous candors. Her greatest
joy was the rare occasions when Richard could take
dinner there. Then she marketed lavishly at the Italian
grocery across the street; cooked and served the meal

herself, with deep thrills of woman's oldest instinct. She always had a bottle of wine ready for him. "What a grand girl you are," he said once; "you always put all the grub on the table where one can see it and eat according. The first thing women do when they get high-toned and civilized is to move the food out of reach."

She loved him fiercely in his boyish moods, which called to some deep needful maternity in her. "As far as you're concerned," she said, "I guess I'm not civilized.—There'll always be such a lot of civilized people. Let me be Me, for a little while."

Sometimes he stretched on the couch, content to listen, while Minnie sat on a cushion on the floor or walked to and fro, smoking and talking. She poured herself out in anecdote, any grotesque thing that had happened since they confided last. What a comedian, when her wild sense of absurdity was roused. Other whiles they sat in peaceable silence, or lay linked in dreamy satisfaction. "It's nice not to have to carry a bagful of telephone books," she whispered. Often they discussed office problems. With the growth of the business they had taken over the whole output of Mr. Gettleman's small factory, and Richard was concerned to make some provision for his employees. With Miss Mac they worked out a scheme by which dividends over a certain percentage were to revert to the staff. Or Minnie told him about books she had found in the second-hand store down the street: she was becoming quite a collector. When he had to make a speech at a trade convention she put his notes into intelligible form and rehearsed him in it. She kept a pipe and tobacco ready for him in case he wanted a change of smoke. How queerly life gets twisted, Richard sometimes thought as he rang the bell and climbed the old banistered stair, that this should be considered wrong. Those who only knew Miss Hutzler of the office, Miss Hutzler of the cool head, the sharp judgment, the broad and buffoon tongue, would hardly have recognized the Minnie who waited at the open door, mistress of the dim and tender hours. Diana of Madison Square was gone now; he said to her pale body that she was the only Diana left.

"Richard, are you happy?" she asked him suddenly.

It was always difficult to get him to answer questions.

"I have The Pain sometimes," he said.

She never mentioned the secret search of the locked cupboard, but once, in one of their quiet hours, he spoke unexpectedly of the brown paper parcel. "That's my Iron Ration."

She did not understand the phrase. He explained.

"Isn't that what they called it in the war? Emergency victuals, hardtack and pressed beef or something of the sort, in case a fellow got cut off from his own lines, went down in No Man's Land. When things were very bad I put together just enough stuff to last me overnight, and some money. I thought that if I couldn't stand it any longer I'd just grab that package and pike off somewhere to think."

"Stand what any longer?"

"Oh, the things everybody does stand," he said vaguely. "Things in general.—That was before that evening you found me in the office."

"It's queer," he added later, "just having that package there, seeing it every time I hung up my hat, knowing I could use it if I needed to, has been a big help.—I guess you have to play some sort of game with yourself not to get lonely."

"You don't look at all lonely this minute," said Minnie. "Why not destroy that horrid little bundle and use *me* for Iron Ration?"

We need not suppose that because she spoke lightly she did not understand.

It's a strange thought, Hubbard reflected; perhaps more people than we ever dreamed are relying on some sort of Iron Ration. If we knew what it is, how much more we might understand. Lucille's Iron Ration is Gladys. Mrs. Geschwindt's is the memory of the old Germany of her childhood. Shad's is a long line of Mazda bulbs and an orchestra leader who'll feed him his gags properly. Jenny's is her new necklace of amber beads and an adorable green step-in. Miss Mac's is the Erskine List for next season. Mr. Gall's is his formula for non-corrosive ink. . . .

Sometimes it's the pretense of an escape they don't really desire. The idea of (just for a few hours) not being owned by anyone or anything, no matter how lovely. . . . And then how gratefully they hurry back where they belong.—They mustn't leave it too late to hurry back, Hubbard exclaimed. I know something about that. I've always been the cat that walks by himself. I know how it feels not to belong anywhere.— I think I'll call up Minnie and see if she'll dine with me.

XL

Accidents

So WE come down toward the later years, said Hubbard. I get flash pictures that I don't know exactly where to fit in. How does one suggest, in the poor brevities of print, the long slow rub of Time? Minnie says she could see that something was happening to Richard. He was more silent after the Accident, as they always called it. He was going past a garage where a truck was unloading gasoline into a vent in the pavement. The gas was in metal drums, which they rocked to and fro over the inlet to empty them. Somehow a spark must have been struck, there was an explosion. He was quite badly hurt by the blast, but able to get home in a taxi. Minnie, not knowing how serious the injuries might be, was terribly anxious, but Lucille would give her no satisfaction on the phone. Richard was kept in bed for a week, and Lucille nursed him with generous care, but when Minnie brought up some important business papers to be signed, she was not allowed to see him. She was kept standing in the lobby.

This reminded Minnie of her own grotesque mishap. It ought to cure me of the bad habit of going to the office in off hours, she said. It was a Washington's Birthday. The office was closed. But Minnie, who had no use for holidays, had gone there to see if some expected mail had arrived. A number of letters were sprinkled on the floor where the carrier had shot them through the slit of the door. Without bothering to go to the master light-switch, which was in the Reception Room, she sat down on the floor to examine the envelopes in the dim light. As usual on holidays, the office boy had left the transom open for the parcel-post-man to throw in packages. She heard footsteps in the hall outside but paid no attention. Suddenly she received a violent blow on the arm and shoulder. It was a heavy parcel sent over by mail from the factory —samples of the Diana ash-tray in new colors. She was lame for weeks. It would have been a good joke on me if I'd been killed by a bunch of my own ash-trays.

Sometimes, for a change, he went to the office by subway instead of on the L. Mostly, like any disciplined citizen, he took it for granted: stood cramped in the rush-hour throng, snatching what glimpses of his newspaper he could. Then there were moments of vision when he saw the experience in its contrasting aspects, both true. Which will be more accurate to say, Hubbard asks? Shall I say he went down through that hell of cruel pressures, into a world of senseless stone, a life of small chicane? Shall I say that exhilarated by the dark roar of haste, heartened by that mass of patient enduring purposes, he reached his downtown heaven of interest and curiosity? One small episode he mentioned. At 72nd Street, changing from the local, there was just a quick chance of catching the express across the platform. As the doors opened a dapper Chinaman—a prosperous looking fellow in a handsome soft hat and fur-collared overcoat—leapt out first, roughly elbowing his neighbors in his excitement. It was the only time I ever saw a Chinaman rude, said Richard.

But I think he was glad to have lived in the era of the subway, the airplane, the motor car, the radio, the electric ice-box. The radio, which had begun humbly by attaching one wire to the bedspring and another to the wash-stand to hear some cheerful concert from Newark, was now a serious affair. Eastern Standard Eternity was carefully parcelled out in fifteen-minute lots; the kilocycles, after so many ages of irresponsibility, suddenly found themselves burdened with heavy cargoes of toothpaste and ginger ale. At home the Roes kept the machine spieling as much as possible; it was an excellent preventive of thought. "What *is* a kilocycle?" Lucille asked once. "As I understand it," said Richard, "it's a unit of frequency making one thousand alternations a second." "Like Daddy trying to make up his mind over Christmas shopping," said Gladys. He lay abed, after the Accident, and heard space sounding its daily diapason, from the morning's kitchen counsel to the saxophone and saraband of bedtime. He had wondered whether he ought to buy a little slice of that airy nothing for the Roe pen. But after lying a whole day, helpless under the stroke of incessant petition and advice, he concluded that ether was overcrowded. There's not enough white space in it, he thought.—Suddenly, in the middle of a rather pretty song—something about *My Heart Stood Still*—there was a break. *Signing off for an S. O. S.*

call, said the announcer. A ship was in trouble at sea, appealing for help.

Yes, the web of life was being drawn very tight.

Johnny Jonquil reported an adventure of which Hubbard had not heard. Johnny had been to some literary picnic on Cape Cod, after which he found himself in Boston, without enough money for the train fare home. He saw a signboard of the Greyhound bus, advertising a special rate to New York. While he was considering whether to try the bus, or wire to Daisy for funds, he met Richard who had been on a business trip. He told him the problem. Evidently something in the idea of the bus—it was a brilliant spring morning—appealed to the old instinct of the travelling man. "Let's both go on the bus," Richard said. "I'll blow the meals."

It was very Chaucerian in flavor, Johnny says. There were full nine-and-twenty in the Tabard Inn crowd; the Greyhound carried thirty-three, a tight fit. Johnny's impressionable soul was much pleased by the all-day journey. How much more one sees than from the railroad. It's like reading a textbook of American history. "Dedham, Shire Town of Suffolk County." At Norwood, Mass., the monument to Captain Guild "who left his oxen standing and the plow in the furrow and departed for Lexington. He never returned."— At a crossroads near Wrentham there was a sudden wild swerve; the driver, by a prodigy of skill, just avoided another car that had suddenly broken line. When lungs, heart, and giblets calmed and reassorted themselves they saw the other vehicle below a grassy bank, unhurt but looking very pale.

"Roe had some chewing gum in his pocket," the

poet wrote Hubbard. "He gave me some, and for the first time I realized its spiritual value. Those busses move at terrific speed. Anxiously multiplying Mass by Velocity, the Pavid Soul finds chicle a consoling viaticum. Roe and I were both scared; we chewed and were tacit. But like Chaucer's pilgrims, Greyhound riders soon shake together for entertainment. The forward part of the bus was rather solemn, but toward the stern rode an Egyptian actor from Brooklyn. He and his little troupe were returning from a professional engagement in Boston. One of them was an Egyptian girl of great beauty. In the narrow aisle of the car they discovered folding seats, and by pulling these out they made room for music. A Syrian gentleman played the fiddle, and the leader got out a queer-shaped lute— he said it was an *oud,* an instrument of noble tradition, the same that King David played. It was plucked with an eagle's feather. With the Egyptian Cleopatra singing and doing sinuous pantomime, they improvised soft Lydian airs. It was what is called a macaronic ditty, of innumerable verses, with impromptu personal allusions to the stalwart chauffeur and other passengers. The language, they told me, was Arabic, with interpolations of Syrian and French.

"Roe and I sat on the last seat. By jingling keys, snapping fingers, drumming knuckles, we made a good accompaniment to the tune. When we got near New London, where the bus halted for lunch, the little concert had got so smooth we were all sorry to quit.

"If one Greyhound goes lame, all others pause to aid. We met one which had blown a tire or something of that sort. There were four of them gathered along the road near Saybrook while their four chauffeurs wrestled with a huge tire. We all scrambled out to uncramp our legs and enjoy the wayside turf. There was a wonderful cool grassy smell. I'd been in the city all winter and I'd really forgotten that grass is as sweet as that. It reminded me of something I hadn't thought of for years, the feel of a baseball glove on my hand when I was a kid.

"I kept the address of the Egyptian girl; I thought it would be amusing if Daisy Erskine would ask her up to tea some day, but Daisy didn't see it."

Hubbard thanked Johnny for this lively account. "You have a remarkable memory," he said. "Too bad you don't seem to recall much about Roe."

"Well, I fixed the more picturesque details in my head," said Johnny, "because I had a notion to make a long poem of my own about a bus-ride.—Wait a minute, though: I remember this. After that scare with the other car, he told me that he had taken out fifty cents' worth of insurance for us both."

Gladys had reached the age of twenty-one, and felt she was entitled to an occasional cocktail. Hubbard tried the experiment of providing one, in the hope of eliciting new testimonies. Biographers, it appears, have no scruples of conscience. He took her up to Hyacinthe's penthouse, where the vegetation was now so luxurious it almost threatened hay fever. They sat under an awning, a warm midsummer night. There had been an eclipse of the sun that afternoon; almost total in New York, and Gladys was much impressed.

"You know, it sort of gave me the heeby-jeebies," she said. "When I saw that spooky gray twilight, and realized we'd never see it again in our lifetime, and yet they know exactly when it will happen next—Oh, I don't know, it kind of made me want not to be such a sap about things."

"It makes even tougher people than you paw the air," Hubbard remarked. "A total eclipse of the sun is the one thing that always makes the New York *Times* sentimental on the front page. Did you see their article this morning?"

"I haven't seen the *Times* since the day of Daddy's funeral. That was his paper. After he died Mother switched over to the *American.*"

Gladys was really a pretty girl in her light evening frock, and on her narrow pencilled brows there was an unwonted apparition of thought. In a queer way Hubbard seemed to see the ghost of Richard shining through her, appealing for justification.

"Mother's really a scream about it all," she said. "She's gotten round now to talking about 'my dear husband' and 'when Richard was alive.' She's shocked when I tell her that's hooey. When he was alive she thought he was an absolute bum. Didn't I hear her say so often enough? I had that idea pretty well sold to me, but I've been thinking about it. The eclipse today, all that dope about shadows 238,000 miles long, gave me a Big-Time view of things all of a sudden. The last time there was an eclipse I remember Daddy wanted to take me to the Museum to see some model of how it all happens and I told him bushwa. Funny, today I was thinking I almost wish I could look at him again, just size him up for myself, see what he really was like.—I wouldn't be surprised we might have been fond of each other."

Hubbard's glass was empty; he would have been glad to have it filled, to help him digest these confidences. But he was afraid to move, lest he disturb the equilibrium. What far reaches of the universe impinged upon his theme: from solar eclipses to a stick of chewing gum in a Greyhound bus.

"I'm not saying Mother didn't get some bad breaks. For a long time I didn't know what it was all about, but she talked so much of course I got wise. If only Aunt Hay would have let her alone. Gosh, how I used to hate seeing her come round. It always meant trouble afterward. My God, if I didn't know more than that pair about how to handle a man. It was pathos!

"I guess maybe parents *are* a bit pathetic, if you sit down and think about them. Gosh, they can gum up anything! Look at Mother. What's she going to do with herself for the next quarter of a century? Poor soul, she's fed up already. It's terrible for a woman not to have anybody she can hang things on. I think she had an idea that bridge expert was going to proposition her, but she's kidding herself. I want her to start a dress shop; even if she loses money it'll give her something to think about. As long as she keeps her figure a woman can be happy with plenty of mirrors around.—I guess I'm talking too much. You're a nice patient sort of person, not mean and cussèd like me. What luck did *you* have in picking out parents?"

Hubbard was startled at this sudden pass. He dodged it by summoning the waiter. He was almost frightened by the poor child's candor. It came to him that it is not wise or safe to peer too far into the mystery of other lives.

"I was thinking of a silly little thing," she said. "Probably I oughtn't to mention it. It was when I was about fourteen; I was working hard at high school and I guess I was a bit jumpy anyhow. I didn't sleep very well, and if I heard anybody talking late at night it used to drive me crazy. I woke up and heard them talking. I rushed into Mother's room, Daddy was kneeling by the bed mumbling away. 'Damn you,' I said, 'get out and stop bothering Mother.' He got up and went back to his own room without a word. Poor fish, I think he was only trying to tell her he loved her.

"If I ever grow up, I'm going to see that I have some privacy."

"To the next eclipse, my dear," said Hubbard. "Even if we're not here to see it."

"Yes, hoping they'll all have better sense by then."

Gladys was thoughtful as they went uptown in a cab. "Some day I'd like to meet your friend Miss Hutzler," she said.

XLI

Head, Heart, and Hand

It was the day Richard had to leave to make his speech at the Stationers' Convention. The meeting was held in Detroit; perhaps this helped to give Minnie an intuition of a circle completed, a return of life upon itself. Richard was despondent about his address; she did her best to encourage him; gave him a carefully docketed folder of papers he was to check over with Jake Hack; messages for Bessie Beaton. But he remained strangely thoughtful, and looked rather gray. She telephoned for his reservation on the train, and then decided to go to the station with him. She was in a noticing mood: for the first time her eye was caught by the inscription at the 42nd Street entrance to the Grand Central—*To all those who with head, heart and hand toiled in the construction of this monument to the public service*. Something in the spirit of these words fitted her own secret intentions. "Head comes first," she thought.

She made him take a chocolate malted milk at the soda fountain, and had him cheerful by train-time. He

even recalled an anecdote of his own about Grand
Central. "I was going down the Vanderbilt Avenue
side of the station, one day about lunch time. Suddenly
I found myself with the greatest craving for corned
beef and cabbage; it seemed as though that was the
one thing I hankered for. I went into the good old
Murray Hill Hotel and had the biggest plate of it I
could find. I realized afterwards what had happened.
It was that big sign at the taxicab entrance to the
station, CAB BAGGAGE. I had seen that with one
corner of my eye, without consciously reading it. It
started me thinking about cabbage.—Just shows that
advertising sometimes pays even if people don't read
it.—Say, I think I can use that in my speech!"

"You're going to have a swell time," said Minnie as
he left. "Get a good rest on the train. Give my love to
Jake and Bessie. Be a good boy, and don't give Bessie
any knockout drops."

"Maybe they'll give me that same old room at the
hotel," he said, and departed feeling pleased with
himself.

Minnie walked once round the circular Information
Desk, nerving herself to her purpose. Ironically she
observed the intent petitioners at the oracle, soliciting
the definite judgments of time and place. "Trains to
Rochester," said one; at once received a printed folder
that solved everything. But where do you get the kind
of information you need most? What is right, what
is wrong, what is the just thing to do? She also had
toiled with head, heart, and hand for what she loved.
She did not dare delay any longer for fear her decision
would waver. She went to a telephone booth.

"May I speak to Mrs. Roe?"

"This is Mrs. Roe."

"This is Minnie Hutzler. Can I see you at once, on business?"

"Can't you see Mr. Roe? You usually do."

"He's gone. I just saw him off on the train."

"You would.—Why not wait till he gets back?"

"I'm sorry to bother you, but it's important."

She took a taxi, to have time for a cigarette. Instinctively she took out mirror and powder, then considered that this time the less grooming the better. She was looking satisfactorily plain, she thought. She had the driver set her down at the corner of Central Park West; in case Lucille happened to be watching out of the window she did not wish to be seen arriving by taxi. It would give an impression of luxury. I must try to be tactful, she thought. She felt ill with apprehension. She was pleased to see there was a doctor's office on the ground floor of the apartment house. I wonder if that's the doctor who takes care of Richard? If I'm taken sick I can go in there.

The entrance hall of Number 50 was rather like a Grand Central in miniature. Those who had toiled here with head, heart, and hand believed in marble and uniforms. The door-man hastily resumed his gloves before revolving the portal. The elevator boy seemed as bronze and impersonal as the car itself. Apparently the tenants were protected from reality by two ranks of petty officers.

Peke growled at her as soon as he saw her. As the maid ushered her down the passage she noticed the telephone. The other end of the famous epithet, she remembered. Then she forgot everything except to try to say what was in her mind. The only furniture she really saw was the scarlet smoking-stand; she kept her eyes on that, it was so unmistakably a part of Richard's life. Peke continued to curse. Then Lucille came in, dressed for the street. She looked very handsome in spring furs, very much in command of the situation.

"Well?" said Lucille. She made no offer of a chair. Seeing her so rigid, Minnie felt an unusual sense of pity—pity for them both. Lucy must have suffered much to be so bitter. Woman, woman, she wanted to cry, don't be a fool! But she feared already that her errand was futile. She might perhaps have attempted an impulsive human appeal, but Peke—after catching sight of Lucille's face—yapped louder than ever. The noise was painful to the nerves; also Minnie had not had much practice in humiliating herself.

"I wonder if we could be alone for a minute?" she said.

Lucille seized the animal and removed him to the kitchen, whence they could still faintly hear his reproaches. At least it'll keep the maid from listening in, Minnie thought.

"Was there anything special? Because I've got to go out," said Lucille.

"I never thought I'd be trying to say this," Minnie said. "I love Richard."

"That's interesting. Who is Richard? Do you mean Mr. Roe?"

(She scores, damn her, thought Minnie. I'm making a mess of this.)

"Maybe I haven't any right to; it just happened. I've been his mistress, and I've been selfish. Just now I'm not considering either you or me, I'm thinking about him. I thought perhaps I could tell you I was sorry, ask you——"

"It's a bit late to be sorry, isn't it?"

"I thought I was helping him, but he's not happy. He's not the type. I mean, he doesn't need a mistress, he needs a wife."

Lucille, in spite of considerable experience in getting angry, found new depths of emotion. She was amazed into silence.

"I can see in the office, he's not well. I wondered if you wouldn't take him back and forgive him. It was my fault, not his. I'll help all I can."

Lucille never took her eyes from the other's face. Her gloved hands were crisped a little as if for striking. God, she's really beautiful, Minnie thought. And indeed Lucille was drawing strength from inward instincts far behind the nerves of reason. Those angers of hers were the brightly uniformed door-men of her citadel, to seclude from visit her mysterious heart.

"I'll give him up," said Minnie, "but he's got to have *someone* to love him. We're grown-up people, can't we pull together somehow?"

"Was this all you had to come up here for? Well then, let me tell you something. I don't need *your* advice in my private affairs. I've been very noble: I've been a good woman, and now he can suffer for it. He deserves to suffer. Now I suppose he's tired of you too, he wants to crawl back to me, is that it?"

"Don't you think maybe he might be fond of both of us?"

"I knew you were a brazen piece, but I didn't think even you would come up here to my face and offer to divide my husband with me."

"That's not what I meant," said Minnie. (What a mess this is! What a lot I could teach this idiot if she'd let me! Speak softly, now, for Richard's sake. Don't try to tell the truth; tell what she needs to

hear.) "Of course he's fond of me. I've worked for
him for years. But he never would have looked at me
if you hadn't thrown him out."

"*You've* worked for him!" exclaimed Lucille. Her
elbow trembled so that her purse slid to the floor with
a heavy thump. The human and feminine quality of
this accident helped Minnie to keep her balance.

"What did *you* ever do for him?" Lucille continued.
"Did you stand by him when he didn't have fifty dollars in the world? Did you raise his child, keep his
home, cook his meals? No, you waited till he was
prosperous and then tried to sneak him away from me
when I wasn't in reach. And now he's not happy, poor
thing! When you're quite through with him you offer
to return him!—Let him find out for himself it's not so
easy to live without love."

"I'm sorry you take it like this, Mrs. Roe. I only
meant—I wanted—I didn't expect you to forgive *me*.
I'm trying to be honest. I'm worried about him. He
needs help. He loves you——"

"Thanks for telling me. I don't know what business
it is of yours. I think you'd better go, or I may begin
to say things."

Minnie wondered how she was going to get down
in the elevator and past the door-man without collapse.
Richard, my dear, I'm afraid I've only made things
worse.—God, I hope she won't tell him I've been there.
I'm glad I didn't ask her *not* to, anyhow. I was so
busy thinking things *not* to say, I hardly know what I
did say.

She reached the curb at last, a taxi, and a cigarette.
She opened her vanity-case to see if she still looked the
same. There were dark shadows under her eyes, and

her nose glistened. "She could hardly be jealous of that face."

The streets were busy with traffic, life was still going on. What a fool I must be, she thought; and what a state to get into, for a woman of nearly forty. She began to consider the relative age of Lucille. "I guess there's a time of life when all women go a little cuckoo. Anyway, she still loves him—as much as she ever did."

XLII

Dark River

MINNIE asked Jenny Hoerl to come and stay with her on Lexington Avenue; and though it may only have been due to the return of warm weather, she noticed at once that the spark seemed to have disappeared from the latch-key. Without anything being said, she quietly put her relation with Richard back on a business basis. Perhaps at first he was puzzled to miss the confidential glance of the eye, the touch of the hand, the hundred little graces by which a woman radiates her love.

But also there were matters more urgent than sentiment. The Detroit Convention of '29 was held at the very top of that roller-coaster graph which is now engraved in every business man's memory. Every week-end for three years the newspapers brought it down to date, and husbands spent Sunday mornings, while the family was at church, tobogganing those steep slopes of ink. They know by heart the various plunges of that line. The Wall Street Panic of '29, the Bank Failures of '30, the Gold Depletions of '31 and '32. The summer meeting in Detroit, held on the ap-

parently endless plateau of prosperity, was intoxicated
with a sort of laughing gas. But old Jake Hack grum-
bled certain warnings to Richard. He spoke mysteriously of freight-car loadings, motor-car production,
and gossip overheard at lunch tables in the Detroit
Athletic Club. Under the genial camouflage of Ath-
letics men speak their minds with unusual frankness.
"Things have been jacked up too high," he said. "If
I were you I'd pull in my horns a bit."

I'm not going to retell the story of the famous Depression, said Hubbard. It didn't hit Richard Roe,
Inc. as hard as some; partly thanks to Jake Hack's
warning, and his support at critical moments, they
were not too seriously extended. What hurt Richard
most was having to shut down the factory from time
to time, or to lay off some of the workers. Letters
of threat or of anguished appeal used to come to him
from the factory hands, but Minnie sidetracked them
ruthlessly. There was nothing he could do.

But the business crisis came upon him at a bad time.
He was tired, his energy was low. He was very silent
about his private affairs. Minnie says that in a foolish
way she almost welcomed the business trouble; it put
their backs against a wall and gave them something
to fight for. She tried to see to it that there was little
time for brooding. He remarked once that he wished
Lucy and Gladys had developed a little more Sales Resistance. He bought more chewing gum and fewer
cigars.

It had been the custom for many years for the
Erskine Sales Department to have a little celebration
on Christmas Eve. Miss Mac always rigged up a toy

Christmas tree on her desk; Sam Erskine provided materials for punch; the Boys, a few specially favored stenographers, and some alumni or old friends from the Trade, would gather in the Sample Room after most of the office had quit. They gave each other small humorous presents, sometimes of a rather scandalous nature. Christmas, the anthropologists tell us, was originally a festival of very pagan flavor; some of its primitive gusto reappeared in these little gatherings. That last year Gene Vogelsang discovered a peculiar book-and-curio shop on Sixth Avenue where he found astonishing oddities to startle his friends. Many of these were of pathological import: indelicatessen, he called them. It has always been noted that the book business, tilted just the least little bit on edge, slides into impudicity. Going over the presents with Gene, Miss Mac observed that he had allotted one to Richard which was rather too likely to hurt his feelings.

"I don't think I'd give him that," she said. "He's pretty sensitive."

"I guess you're right," Gene agreed. "Here, we'll give it to Sam. Let's give Dick the bottle of red ink instead; there's plenty of that going around this Christmas."

Richard turned up at the party. He was in good spirits; admitted that the red ink would be useful. He and Miss Mac drank a private health together.

"What would you like best to find in your stocking?" she asked.

"Fifty thousand dollars," he said. "That would keep the factory going until spring."

It was a clear January night with stinging northwest wind. No night indeed for middle-aged Peke to be abroad; the gusts were strong enough to swing him like a pendulum at the end of his leash, but Richard had taken him out by force of habit. He unharnessed him and tucked him inside his overcoat lapels. He walked swiftly, invigorated by the push of cold air. In the gutter outside an Amsterdam Avenue grocery lay a discarded Christmas tree with shreds of tinsel fluttering. Farther down the street he heard the crash of a shop window caved in by the gale. The corner of Broadway and 79th was deserted, where on milder nights he had listened to so much political harangue and al-fresco salesmanship. The wide pavements were clean and almost empty. He paused a moment to glance in at the window of the lunchroom where he had taken many evening cups of coffee. At once he was accosted—as always that winter outside lunchroom windows. "Buddy, will you help me to a plate of soup?" He gave the man a dollar. Anger at home always means kindness on the street.

Peke muttered with annoyance, he was not accustomed to the joggle of fast walking. But Richard had a craving for open space. He went down the steep hill on 79th Street—the hill where he had once seen the Chihuahua dog. All the way down, across Riverside, over the railroad tracks and out onto the pier. The black sparkle of the river was streaked with froth. Along the New Jersey shore the lights were brilliant. He stood there so long facing the wind that Peke began to whine and scratch inside the coat. So may the Spartan boy have stood with the fox in his bosom.

His old companion The Pain was there too. There's no future, no future at all, it was saying. Except your Triumph, the Triumph you've sometimes thought about. Didn't the Metropolitan chimes suggest any-

thing to you when you heard them this afternoon?
The business would get on just as well—as a matter
of fact, the factory could run until spring on that; and
things may be better by then? The annuity will take
care of Lucy and Gladys.

He remembered when Gladys was a child, practising
on the piano: the pause while he waited anxiously for
her to find the chord needed to resolve the harmony,
close the tune. Sometimes she fumbled on the wrong
notes by mistake, but at last came the comfortable
sound, closing that hole in the mind. Was this new
and friendly, almost peaceful despair, the chord his
tune required? For there was no other answer, no
success, no satisfaction. When had he ever done anything entirely on his own impulse? Always he had been
owned, mastered, cajoled or managed by someone.
He had loved Lucille, he had loved Minnie, now he
had neither of them.

"And I've had a swell time," he said to himself,
"A grand swell time." The lights across the river
reminded him of the old romantic visits to Hoboken;
the antique cannon on the bluff at Stevens Castle. "I
must go over and see if it's still there." He thought
of the Iron Ration in the office cupboard. "I've been
meaning to get rid of that stuff for a long time. It
would look idiotic to have it found there if anything
happened to me.—I'll take it over and leave it on the
cannon. Somebody will find it and get a great kick out
of it."

Peke's indignation could not be ignored any longer.
Richard turned from the dark river, the wind at his
back hurried him up the hill, toward those tall cliffs
of light, palisades of deficit. Out of breath, blood
pounding heavily, he felt better. "That's a lot of non-

sense you've been thinking," he said to himself. "You don't solve things by running away from them." There was a queer tightness in his head. It was late, he let himself into the apartment as softly as possible, and took a glass of milk. He was warming some for Peke in a saucepan when Lucille came in, wearing a blue kimono. "You oughtn't to take Peke out on a night like this. You know how sensitive he is to colds."

Richard did something very unusual. He stared at her a moment, and then laughed; really laughed, until something kinked in his ribs and he sat down on a kitchen chair with a catch of breath. Lucille and Peke were both offended and left the room. He sat some time in thought, then remembered that lights and laughter in the kitchen would annoy the Swede, whose bedroom was adjoining. He hung up the dog's jacket and leash.

Lucille was in bed as he went by her room. By the light outside he could see her head on the pillow. The window panes drummed faintly in the wind; even door-men in white gloves could not altogether keep out the great forces of the world. The pathos of her soft clothes, tossed over a chair, moved him. He leaned over and kissed her.

"Good-night, dear. I didn't mean to be rude."

He would have liked to kiss Gladys good-night also, just as he used to when she was small, but her door was shut. He remembered the marvellous softness of her cheek.

He left the office about dinner time the next evening; all the others had gone. His desk was clean. When he boarded the ferry the early rush was over; there were few passengers on the upper deck. He had

bought some chewing gum while waiting for the boat;
it might be helpful if he found himself thinking too
hard. But the marvellous River was too beautiful for
anxiety. All the blaze and argument of the town was
only a shimmer on the surface of the deep stream
which moved to its own laws of wind and tide. A
great liner came up, sliding softly as if in the very last
momentum of some enormous push from far away.
She was tall and proud, easy with accomplishment.
Her black side was perforated with lights, like dotted
lines waiting for signature. Once he had dreamed that
some day he and Lucy might see those distant coun-
tries. Was life there perplexing also? Standing beside
the rail he could see the square tower of the Castle
against clear darkness, and the name LACKA-
WANNA in red letters over the pier—a strange-
looking word when you looked at it intently. It would
be fun to leave the Iron Ration on the old cannon.
Perhaps better take a taxi up there, quite a walk from
the ferry, uphill; afterward he could go to Meyer's,
sit very quietly for a few minutes. He would telephone——

It was not unlike the sudden burst of a telephone
bell inside his head. The Pain, which had been waiting its moment, pierced in between two thoughts; found
them easy (thoughts are soft); hesitated half a
breath; decided that was the spot, went home in one
dazzling stroke. As he crumpled to the deck no one
noticed the brown paper parcel slip over the side.

XLIII

Rum Omelet

AND now Hubbard had collected as much material as anyone could ever gather about Richard Roe. Even some of that, he explained, is conjecture; biographic license. He had tried to do an Inside Job. He looked at his pigeonholes of papers, his pages of notes, the feeble diagram pinned on the wall. The little receptacle of the pencil sharpener was choked with cedar shavings. He was ready to begin to write the Life of Richard Roe. But in that also would the fine sifting of graphite be lost in a mass of curly insignificant shreds? He tried to put some ideas down on paper, the lead snapped.

You try to write with too fine a point, I suggested. Authors don't work like accountants; they use a blunter pencil.

"I guess it's all done with mirrors," he said angrily and pushed back his chair with a noisy scrape. He piled all his documents neatly in their classified compartments.

Jules's place is a lovely interior on a warm summer day. From the inside room you can see a green glimpse

of the little back garden. There is a blue shirt on the
line, the thick shade of the ailanthus tree hides the
huge towers above. You have to go down to the end
of the yard to get a clear view of those great verticals
and the steely gargoyles of Chrysler. There you can
see how two rows of small brick homes are honeycombed into the concrete eyries of the city. The coneys
are a feeble folk but they make their houses in the
rocks.

Jules was very happy in the kitchen, stuffing a
chicken he was to roast and deliver to a favorite client.
He appeared in the doorway every now and then to
show Hubbard and Minnie how the job was progress-
ing, and to remark how much Mr. Vogelsang was
going to enjoy it. It was mid-afternoon on Saturday,
they were alone in the place but had not yet decided
what they would eat. Jules suspected what Mr. Hubbard would choose: it had become a ritual among the
Erskine alumni. A rum omelette. When Jules had it
all ready they always turned off the light, then he
brought in the blazing dish, filling the little room with
pale blue flicker. This was always a sensation for guests
who had never seen it before, and Minnie had never
heard of a rum omelette.

But they were not ready to eat yet; they'd been
talking a long while over their wine and seltzer.

"You know, I can't write the book," he said. "It's
impossible. It would never make sense; it would only
hurt a lot of people. What's the use? I can't imagine
why I was such a fool as to even think of it. But I
don't regret the time and struggle I've put on it.
Maybe it's taught me a little more kindness. Kindness
is no mood for a modern biographer."

Minnie looked at him strangely. "I've got something

to show you," she said. "It's a note he left on my desk when he left the office, the night he died." From an envelope in her purse she took a slip of paper and handed it to him. On it was printed:—

OFFICE MEMORANDUM

To:
From:

The *To* and *From* were not filled in; beneath was written:—

> *Been cleaning up and thought of a good way to get rid of the Iron Ration. You'll be amused. I never told you Minnie, I learned what you tried to do for me. Didn't like to say anything about it. Too late I guess, I just wanted to let you know I understand O. K.*
>
> R.

"Miss Mac's the only one who ever saw that. She thought I ought to show it to you. She thinks—you see, she thinks—well, she's never forgotten his mentioning fifty thousand. That was the amount of his policy, payable to the company."

"She's crazy," he said. "There's nothing in that note to justify any such notion. He wouldn't have said 'you'll be amused'."

"It would be rather bitter if he meant that. He wasn't usually bitter. You can imagine how it hurt. If it was that, it can only have been my fault. Larry, do you think he thought I walked out on him when he needed me most? I tried so hard to help."

"You're all wrong. You knew him well enough to know that wasn't the way his mind worked."

"Does anybody know anybody?" she asked.

Hubbard was silent awhile. He lit a cigarette and pretended not to notice while she got out her vanity case.

"Jules!" he called. "Suppose you fix us up a rum omelette."

"I don't think I feel like eggs," Minnie said.

"These aren't just eggs; you wait and see. Don't be so masterful."

"There's another reason why I can't write this book," he said presently. "I know something about Richard by now, and I can guess what he'd say. He'd suggest I spend less time thinking about his life, and more about my own."

"My God," said Minnie, "you look so comic, I believe you're getting ready to ask me to marry you."

"I believe I am."

"You know I don't believe in marriage."

"You've never given it a chance."

"I couldn't love anyone else the way I did Richard. Don't you think he'd always be coming between us?"

"No. I think he'd be pleased."

"There's the business. That takes most of my time."

"Make Ed Furness sales manager. He's developing nicely. And say, it'd be nice to offer Gladys a job in the office. She's crazy to help, only she's ashamed to ask."

"You want to fix everything up in a nice Christian spirit, don't you?"

She took off her hat, as though it felt tight, and

shook her head to loosen her thick dark hair, now threaded with gray.

"Are you shaking your head at *me*, or just shaking your head?" he asked.

"A little bit of both, I guess. No, Larry, it wouldn't be fair to either of us. Richard was different. He needed me—anyhow I figured it that way. Besides, you don't want to marry a woman of forty-two."

"Heavens, girl, I'm forty-eight myself. Even at that I've still got one-point-thirty-two years of expectation. Or we could go to New Zealand; people live longer there."

"Well, I'll think it over. It's the first proposal of marriage I've ever had, naturally I'm flustered.—Do we eat or don't we?"

"Jules!" he shouted.

"Right away, Mr. Hubbard.—You can get ready for it."

Hubbard pulled off the light, to Minnie's surprise, and Jules brought in the burning platter.

"What on earth," she exclaimed. "What is it—hell fire? Why, you old sweetheart, did you think this up for me?"

"There was something else I thought up," he said. While Jules ladled spoonfuls of flaming spirit over the omelet, Hubbard whispered to her.

"And if it was a boy, we could call him Richard."

"No; no carbon copies, thank you."

"You're going to need someone you can make your terrible cracks to; someone who's learned not to be shocked."

"Larry, you've grown quite human, haven't you. I thought you were a sissy at first."

He turned on the light.

"Strike while the omelet's hot," he suggested. "The blue flame doesn't last long."

"Mmmm, but isn't it perfectly marvellous."

Perhaps she was thinking while they ate. "In the interests of public morals," she said, "I'm not going to put Jenny out on the street again."

And later still: "Anyhow I'm glad you're not going to write the book."

The thought of Richard Roe was in both their minds: not sad or bitter; a comfortable thought.

THE END

Modern Library of the World's Best Books

COMPLETE LIST OF TITLES IN

THE MODERN LIBRARY

For convenience in ordering
please use number at right of title